SKY'S THE LIMIT

SKY'S THE LIMIT

Janie Millman

THE
DOME
PRESS

Published by The Dome Press, 2018
Copyright © 2018 Janie Millman
The moral right of Janie Millman to be recognised as the author
of this work has been asserted in accordance with the
Copyright, Designs and Patents Act 1988.

This is a work of fiction. All characters, organisations and events
portrayed in this novel are either products of the author's imagination
or are used fictitiously.

A CIP catalogue record for this book is available from the British Library

ISBN 9781999855949

The Dome Press
23 Cecil Court
London WC2N 4EZ

www.thedomepress.com

Printed and bound in Great Britain by Clays, Elcograf S.p.A.

Typeset in Garamond by Elaine Sharples

For Mum and Dad

PART ONE

CHAPTER ONE

The earth wobbled a bit as I tried to take in the enormity of what my husband was saying. Everything seemed to tilt slightly on its axis and I grabbed the wine glass which seemed as if it might fall from the table. I opened my mouth to speak but no words came out. I stared at him. My heart was hammering and cold beads of sweat were trickling down my back.

'Sky?' His voice was wobbling as much as the earth. I held up my hand. There was no way I could take any more.

I gulped at my wine and concentrated on a fly making its way across the worktop. There was total silence in the room.

'Sky, for God's sake say something.' My husband had stood up and was gripping the back of the chair as if his life depended on it.

'We're going to Marrakech in two weeks' time.' My voice was barely above a whisper. 'It's all booked, we've paid for it, we're staying in a *riad* and we've got a room with a roof terrace.'

He stared at me.

'What the hell has Marrakech got to do with any of this?' He released his grip on the chair and started pacing the room. 'Jesus, Sky, have you been listening to a word I've said?'

I'd listened to every single word but I was still unable to take it in. I couldn't think of anything to say; my mind had gone completely blank.

'This isn't exactly the reaction I expected.' He shook his head.

The fly stopped in front me. I slammed my hand down savagely and flattened it. Hurling my wine glass across the room, I leapt up to face my husband, knocking the chair over.

'Not the reaction you expected?' I screamed. 'Not the fucking reaction you expected? What was it you thought I might say, Miles?' My face was inches away from his. 'Enlighten me because, I admit, I'm at a complete loss.' I grabbed him by the shoulders and shook him. I badly wanted to hurt him. '"I'm gay, darling. Our marriage is over. I'm in love with another man."' My voice had risen to a pitch I hadn't known existed. 'What's the correct response to that?'

'Sky…' He hesitated.

'Not that easy to respond to, is it?' I spat out the words with venom. 'A betrayal of unprecedented proportions, wouldn't you say? Given that the other man is my best friend. It's a bit of a double whammy.' I let go of his shoulders as the shock hit me once again. He staggered back and I turned to face the window, swallowing the bile that had risen in my throat.

'Sky, Jesus. Sky, we didn't mean for this to happen, that's what I've been trying to say, please believe me. I wouldn't hurt you for the world; neither of us would.'

'But you have, haven't you?' I leant my brow against the cool window pane, resisting the urge to push my head right through it. 'You have hurt me. Both of you have hurt me and, if you didn't mean for it to happen, then why the hell did you let it?'

'I love you, Sky. We both love you.'

'Just not as much as you love each other, apparently.' An emptiness replaced my fury, a cold, terrible emptiness.

'It's a different love, Sky.'

'Well, it's certainly not the love you promised me five years ago. It's not the love that we swore to each other standing at the altar.' I swung around to face him. 'Do you recall that day, Miles? The best day of our lives, or so I thought. Seems I was wrong. Perhaps you were already eyeing Nick up, wondering what sort of tackle he had underneath his kilt.'

'Oh, don't be stupid, Sky. Of course I bloody wasn't.'

'I am stupid, you're absolutely right. That's exactly how I feel, bloody stupid and totally humiliated.'

Miles moved towards me but I put my hand up to stop him.

'How long has it been going on?'

'Sky, does that really matter?'

'Yes, it really matters,' I said slowly. 'I think I have a right to know when you suddenly decided to let yourself out of the closet. Is Nick your first or have there been others?' I could hear my voice begin to rise again.

'No, there haven't been any –' But I cut him off as another thought came to me.

'Who else knows? Jesus, does anyone else know?' I was filled with horror. 'Has the whole damn world been laughing at me?'

'Sky, no one else knows.' He gripped my shoulders firmly, forcing me to look at him. 'No one is laughing at you and no one ever will. It started a few months ago.' He paused and took a deep breath. 'I don't know how to explain it, I really don't. It was like the final piece of a jigsaw falling into place.'

'I didn't know that a piece was missing.'

'Neither did I, Sky, trust me.' His handsome face was creased with pain but I didn't care. 'I love you very much and I always will, but, and I can't say this without hurting you even more, being with Nick simply makes me feel complete in a way I have never felt before.'

'But how could you never know you were gay?' I was genuinely struggling. 'I mean people are born homosexual, aren't they? They don't suddenly choose it? Well, obviously some do; you clearly have.'

'It's not really a question of being gay, Sky. It's about the person, the person you want to be with, the person you want to share your life with.'

'And the person who you choose to share your life with is Nick. Not me, but your wife's best friend.'

'It wasn't a choice, Sky. I didn't have a choice.'

'Didn't you?' I snarled. God, he was making me so angry. 'Didn't you really? I think you did. I think we all make choices. You had a choice, you just didn't choose me.'

'Sky, please, this isn't easy for me.'

'Oh shut up, Miles.' I slapped him then. I slapped him very hard across the face. I could see the imprint of my hand on his cheek. He gasped. There was a moment of silence. We were both shocked, neither of us liked violence, but I was certainly not repentant.

'You're going off with Nick, "*the person who makes you feel complete*". While I'm left with my world crumbling around me.' My breathing was ragged and I felt as if I was drowning. 'You know what really hurts the most? The fact that you didn't even talk to me about it.'

'I had no idea what the hell was happening to me! One moment I was a happily married man and the next moment I was having feelings for your closest friend, the nearest thing you have to a brother, what the hell could I have said?'

'I don't know, but you could have tried. We always said we would try to be honest with each other.'

'It wouldn't have made a difference.'

'You don't know that, do you?' I couldn't bear his calm certainty. 'You don't know that because you didn't try, you were too bloody scared. You didn't trust me. We could have tried to work things out.'

'You're right. I was scared.' He threw up his hands in defeat. His left cheek was still bright red. 'I was absolutely terrified and I still am.'

There was another silence. A deafening silence. We glared at each other, like boxers in a ring. I was waiting for the next punch.

'What hurts most, Sky?' he finally asked me. 'The fact that I am leaving you, or the fact that I am leaving you for another man?'

'I honestly don't know.' I really didn't know, my head was spinning. 'Maybe I should be grateful that you aren't leaving me for a young blonde with big tits, but then again maybe I should have cut my hair short, left off the facial waxing and grown a moustache.'

'Oh, Sky.' Miles grinned ruefully.

'What really hurts is that the two men I love most in the world have been suddenly taken away from me.'

'We are still here for you. We both love you so very much.'

'How can you be here for me?' I was incensed by his insensitivity. 'How can you possibly be here for me when you're there for each other?'

'Sky, please, we can work this out. Think of everything we've been through together, think of everything we've shared.'

'And now you're sharing each other.' I couldn't face hearing another word. 'I want you to go now.'

'But…' He reached out to touch me.

I couldn't bear to look at him. I turned around and stood still. 'Now, Miles.'

After the door had closed I sank to the ground. My legs simply couldn't support me anymore. I couldn't move a muscle. I stared at the floor tiles, willing the tears to come, but my eyes stayed resolutely dry. I have no idea how long I sat slumped and motionless on the floor. It could have been minutes, it could have been hours. I think I wanted to die then, I think if an angel had come offering me oblivion I would have accepted. But no angel appeared. Instead the telephone began to ring, bringing me slowly out of my trance. I heard the answering machine kick in. I knew exactly who it would be.

'Sky, it's me. I know you're there.' I heard the intake of breath as Nick inhaled his cigarette.

'Skylark, I love you.' I winced at the use of his pet name for me. 'Jesus, I don't know how the hell this happened, but it has and we've got to get through it. I'm not losing you, Sky. You mean too much to me.' He paused. 'We have to talk whether you want to or not…'

'No, we don't!' I yelled. I staggered to my feet and the room swayed dangerously. I grabbed the phone. 'I never ever want to speak to you ever again, never.' Flinging the phone to the floor I ground it beneath my feet. 'Never, never, ever again, never ever…'

I collapsed onto the floor as, from deep within, a keening noise erupted, a sound I didn't recognise as being my own. And then the tears started. Oh boy, did they start. They seemed to flood from every orifice: they poured from my eyes, my nose was streaming, and bubbles were coming out of my mouth. I wondered briefly if it were possible to drown in your own tears.

Nick stared helplessly at his phone. It was, of course, the reaction he had expected. He could hardly blame her. It was all his fault. Christ, what a mess. What a bloody awful mess. He stubbed out his cigarette and immediately lit another.

He could picture her now, her lovely face white and bloodless, the freckles standing out on the bridge of her nose and her dark blue eyes wide with shock. She would be hugging her arms to her chest with her face turned to the wall as if to shut out the world. He wanted nothing more than to rush over, pull her into his arms and comfort her as he had so many times before.

They had met on their first day at primary school and he could remember it as clearly as if it were yesterday, this tiny young creature standing alone, shy and uncertain. He had thought she looked like a fairy. He had walked towards her, held out his hand and said, 'Let's go in together.'

She had placed her small hand trustingly in his and smiled, her whole face lighting up with joy.

And now he had hurt her, his precious Sky, his soul mate, his fairy queen. He put his hands to his head and screamed.

CHAPTER TWO

Gail came back from the kitchen carrying the birthday cake. She paused at the lounge door just long enough to overhear her younger sister say, 'Gail would never come skiing. Gail doesn't do exciting, the only exciting thing she's ever done in her whole life is to have a bloody baby.'

Gail stood rooted to the spot on the threshold of the door.

'She might like to be asked.' Gail recognised the voice of Holly, her favourite out of her sister's friends.

'Gail works in a bank, Holly, has done for the last twenty years, enough said.' Dee sniggered and the others dutifully joined in.

The candles were dripping wax onto the cake but Gail was paralysed.

'Dee, why are you always so mean?' Holly sounded irritated. 'She's giving you this party today.'

'I'm doing her a favour,' Dee said dismissively. 'Let's face it, what else would she be doing on a Sunday afternoon?'

Gail thought of the precious Sunday afternoons spent with her son. The beautiful walks in Epping Forest, the cinema trips, the go-karting he adored and the lazy Sunday roasts or the occasional treat at Pizza Express. She thought of Sonny today, lying quietly and uncomplaining in front of endless DVDs while she entertained her sister's friends. Dee had hugged him briefly when she'd first arrived and then ignored him. Gail looked down at the birthday cake which she had baked last night at the end of a very long and very tiring day and felt a surge of pure white anger such as she had never felt before.

Vehemently kicking the door wide open, she marched into the

lounge tunelessly screeching 'Happy Birthday'. Startled, the girls leapt to their feet to sing with her.

'Blow the candles out quickly, Dawn.' Gail slammed the cake on the table. 'They're ruining the icing.'

'I never realised that Dee stood for Dawn,' Holly said.

Dee glared at her sister. Gail shrugged, the name had slipped out in the heat of the moment, it hadn't been intentional, but she'd always thought the nickname ridiculous, to her it sounded like a one-hit wonder pop star from the eighties.

'I think Dawn is a lovely name,' Holly said. 'The start of the day, the start of something new.'

'Just give it a bloody rest, Holly,' Dee snarled at her. Holly stared at her for a moment before deliberately turning to Gail. 'We're planning a skiing trip, Gail, do you fancy coming?'

'Sounds lovely,' Gail replied without a moment's hesitation. 'When are you going?' Holly glanced triumphantly at Dee who stared back in astonishment.

'End of March, beginning of April, there's been plenty of snow so we should be fine.'

'Damn,' Gail said, handing out the cake. 'In that case I'm afraid I'll have to take a rain check. I'm going to Morocco.'

'Morocco?' Dee choked on her cake. 'Morocco?' She screeched. 'Why the hell are you going to Morocco?'

'Well, it's somewhere I've always fancied and I think it's about time Sonny met his father.' Nothing in Gail's voice or face betrayed the fact that this was a spur of the moment decision. She didn't miss a beat.

'I didn't know Sonny's dad was Moroccan,' Holly said.

'Well, he certainly doesn't get that olive complexion from me,' Gail laughed, indicating her fair skin.

'When did you decide to go to Morocco?' Dee was stunned. 'Where in Morocco? You never told me. Why didn't you tell me?'

'Heavens, I didn't think I had to run it past you first, Dee.' Gail's smile didn't quite reach her eyes. 'I'm going to Marrakech, I'll show you all the arrangements if you're interested.'

Dee stared sullenly back at her.

'Well, folks, if you don't mind I'm going to love you and leave you.' Gail glanced around at the girls. 'I've promised Sonny some cake and then I have some bits and pieces I need to do before work tomorrow.'

Dee frowned and looked at her watch. She opened her mouth to speak but Gail turned to her first.

'Dee, could you make sure you lock the front door when you leave.' She walked to the door. 'It's been so lovely seeing you all, enjoy the rest of the evening, I imagine you're off clubbing or pubbing, the night is yet young, but sadly I'm not.' She laughed brightly. She knew that she was breaking up the party and she knew that Dawn had probably been planning on staying the night but she was certainly in no mood for that.

Dee was livid. What the hell did Gail think she was doing? First she dropped the Moroccan bombshell and now she was virtually showing them the door. She'd been planning on staying the night. She had been looking forward to drinking another bottle of wine, eating the leftovers and lazing in a bath scented with some very expensive bath oil, one of the few luxuries Gail allowed herself.

She had even brought over some washing for her sister to do. What the hell was she supposed to do with that now? Her tiny flat was cold and uninviting and the thought of going back there was not appealing.

Gail had ruined her whole birthday and she was furious.

'Gail?' Gail stopped at the bottom of the stairs and turned around.

'I just wanted to say thank you so much for a wonderful afternoon.' Holly had followed her out of the lounge.

'It was a pleasure, Holly. I hope you enjoyed yourself.'

'I did, I always have a lovely time here. You spoil us, Gail, and you certainly spoil Dee. She doesn't know how lucky she is to have an older sister like you.' Holly paused. 'I wish I did.' She sounded wistful.

'Oh, Holly, what a lovely thing to say.' Gail flushed with pleasure. 'Although I'm not sure Dee would agree, right now she has a face like thunder because I've pulled the plug on the party too early.'

'It's your house, you can do what you like, and besides we've been here for hours already.' Holly paused for a moment. 'I think it's amazing that you're going to Morocco. When did you decide? What does Sonny think?'

'Sonny doesn't know yet.' Gail hesitated, glanced towards the lounge and then leant forward conspiratorially. 'No one knows yet, I only decided five minutes ago.' She laughed at the astonishment on Holly's face. 'I overheard what Dee said before I came into the lounge.' Her voice wavered slightly. 'It shocked me and I guess I wanted to prove that I wasn't as dull as she made out. Bit daft really.'

'Oh, Gail, I'm so sorry you heard that, I'm sure Dee didn't really mean…' Holly trailed off at the look on Gail's face.

'I think we both know she did, Holly.' Gail ran her hands through her hair. 'But, you know, maybe it was no bad thing I overheard her, maybe I have become dull and unadventurous, my fortieth is fast approaching so maybe it's the kick up the arse I needed.' She grinned at Holly. 'I don't know what I've let myself in for and I don't mind telling you I'm shit scared.'

Holly began to laugh. 'Gail, you're mad.'

'Don't you dare breathe a word of this to Dee. I don't want her knowing what an idiot I am.'

Dee left the lounge fully intending to talk to Gail about staying the night. She would insist that they open a couple more bottles of wine and then the girls could go home. She really didn't want to go to a pub or a club, it would cost a fortune and what was the point when Gail had loads of booze left here.

She saw Holly and Gail giggling together and her mood darkened. She cleared her throat. Gail looked around.

'Hi, darling, Holly was just thanking me for a lovely party. I hope you enjoyed it too.' Gail moved towards her but Dee turned away.

'Well, yeah of course.' She shrugged. 'I just thought that…'

'I see you brought a bag of washing with you,' Gail interrupted. 'I'm sorry, I don't have time to do it now, sweetheart, but you can come back later in the week and pick it up.'

Dee felt rather than saw the look of amazement on Holly's face.

'Jesus, it doesn't really matter, don't make a big thing out of it,' she mumbled ungraciously even though this was exactly what she had wanted.

'Gail, thank you once again.' Holly was shocked by Dee's behaviour. They all knew that she liked to get her own way, but this was a side she had never really seen before. 'I'm off home now, Dee, I've an early start tomorrow. I'll um, well, I guess I'll see you around.' She blew Gail a kiss and headed back into the lounge.

'What a lovely girl.' Gail smiled brightly. 'Well, night, Dee. I'll give Sonny a goodnight cuddle from you, no need to come up.'

And as the two sisters looked at each other they realised that something had changed, the earth had tilted a fraction, something had shifted in their relationship, something infinitesimal had altered the dynamics and it would never be quite the same again.

CHAPTER THREE.

Philippe swore loudly. Roused from her slumber, Belle looked up and farted equally loudly. They regarded one another before Philippe wrinkled his nose in disgust.

Delighted that she seemed to have pleased her master, the old bitch settled back to sleep.

Philippe focused once more on the paperwork spread out on the desk. Nothing seemed to make sense; the figures danced before his eyes, taunting him. It simply didn't add up, in theory they should be doing OK, in fact they should be doing more than OK, but that was not what the accounts were saying.

Pushing his glasses back onto his head he stretched out his long frame, flinging his arms wide and knocking over his walking stick. Swearing loudly again he bent to pick it up and limped over to the open window.

The air was soft and fragrant but for once he failed to find any comfort in the view.

Instead of seeing the beauty of a courtyard bathed in the gentle morning light, he saw the weeds growing up between the old flagstones. A large crack ran up one side of the elegant stone fountain and moss had gathered around the base. The ancient barns for which he'd once had such grand plans stood derelict and abandoned, the beautiful sandstone gleaming in the sun. Even the regimented rows of vines normally guaranteed to set his pulse racing failed to lift his spirits. The early morning mist stopped him from glimpsing the River Dordogne in the distance but in his present state he very much doubted that would have helped either.

Turning away he hobbled back to the desk and glanced at the clock. It was eleven, perfect time for a pastis. In fact that was the beauty of pastis, there was never a time that wasn't perfect.

'Wine is for mealtimes, Philippe,' his father used to say. 'Pastis is for all the other times in between.'

He smiled, recalling his father's words. 'Roll it around your mouth, let it slide down your throat and stimulate your senses.'

Pouring a hefty measure into the glass, he topped it up with water and, swirling the liquid around, watched it turn cloudy. As a young lad he had thought it a miraculous sight and he still did.

The phone rang recalling him abruptly to the present day. He picked it up.

'Philippe.' The unmistakeable husky tones of his ex-wife.

'Beatrice.' He took a long swig of his drink. Philippe loved his ex-wife but he wasn't really in the mood right now.

'What is the matter, cheri?'

'Bea, I've only said your name.'

'I've know you for a long while. I know when something is wrong.'

'I'm in pain, Bea.' He sighed. 'I'm on heavy duty painkillers and I'm in a lot of pain.'

'Of course you're in pain. You have torn your cruciate ligament. You deserve to be in pain, you should act your age instead of tearing down the ski slopes like a ridiculous teenager.'

'Such words of comfort, Bea, you cheer me up no end.'

'And maybe you should think twice before mixing pastis with painkillers.'

He stared at the glass in front of him. Sometimes her ability to read him so well was unnerving.

'Philippe, what's really wrong? What is really worrying you?

He drained his drink and leant back in the chair. She wouldn't give up, he knew that.

'Money,' he said bluntly. 'I'm staring at rows of figures that make absolutely no sense to me.'

'I thought last year had been a good year?'

'So did I, but apparently not on paper. On paper it looks like last year was a catastrophe.'

'But that's crazy,' she argued. 'You spent money on the Chai, admittedly, but you also had new buyers for the wine, it doesn't add up.'

'No, cheri, it doesn't.'

'Where is cousin Claude? Why isn't he sitting beside you guiding you through all this? Isn't that his job?'

There was a slight pause before Philippe replied. 'Claude and Celine are on holiday.'

'Where?'

'St Lucia.'

'Mon Dieu.'

'Bea, they're entitled to a holiday.'

There was a silence. He could imagine her expression, her ice blue eyes darkening in anger, her finely drawn eyebrows closing together in a frown. To stall further discussion he spoke light-heartedly.

'Did you phone to berate me for skiing too fast and warn against the dangers of pastis?' he asked 'Or was there some other reason?'

She laughed. That husky, sexy laugh that he had first fallen in love with.

Their courtship had been passionate, wild and tumultuous. The love in their young hearts had made their eyes blind to the fact that they were totally incompatible. The marriage had been a complete disaster but the divorce amicable. That had been many years ago and they had remained best friends ever since.

'No, I want to talk to Stephanie,' she said, referring to his sister. 'I need to go to Paris and I thought we could have a few days together. Would she like that?'

'She would absolutely adore it, as you know, but at the moment she is out with Emmaline choosing hens.'

'Emmie?' Bea sounded puzzled.

'You know how much Emmie loves animals.'

'No, I mean why is Emmie with you?' Bea asked quietly. 'Why the hell isn't she with her parents in St Lucia?'

Philippe poured himself another drink. 'Well, I think they needed some time on their own,' he replied carefully. 'You know it's a very long flight for her.'

'Then they should have gone somewhere nearer,' Bea interrupted him sharply. 'I don't understand why you persist in making excuses for them, Philippe. They didn't take her because they are ashamed of her. They don't need time on their own, they're always on their own, they never take Emmie with them anywhere, they –'

'Bea, stop,' Philippe cut in quickly. 'I'm not in the mood for all this. Of course they aren't ashamed of her, that's a terrible thing to say. No one in their right mind could be ashamed of her.'

'But are they in their right minds, Philippe?' she replied coldly. 'They don't see Emmie as we see her. We see an angel with a soul full of love and happiness. Claude and Celine look at their daughter and they see a girl who is slow and they are embarrassed by her and it makes me furious.'

'Bea…' But she ignored him.

'I will never understand them, and I will never understand why you take their side.'

There was a pause. Philippe opened the desk drawer and reached for his cigarettes, then he remembered their bargain. 'Are you keeping to our pact?'

'Yes,' Beatrice lied, looking guiltily at the ashtray in front of her. 'And you?'

'Of course.'

He's lying, Beatrice thought. I bet he has a packet in the drawer. I have upset him, he hates anyone criticising his family, he will light up as soon as we are off the phone.

I don't believe her, Philippe grinned. She's angry, she hates what she perceives as injustice, she will light up as soon as we are off the phone.

He closed his eyes and pictured the scene. Her hands would be wrapped around a large cup of coffee, her sandals would be discarded, her pedicured feet with red toenails would be up on the table and her chair would be tilted back at an alarming angle, allowing her to glimpse the pool in the inner courtyard.

Beatrice was an only child and her parents had left her a small fortune when they died. She had converted the large family home in Paris into a stylish and unique hotel. People loved it: quirky, warm and welcoming, it had been an immediate success.

Constantly on the search for new projects, she had then bought a ramshackle riad in Marrakech. Leaving the Parisian hotel in the capable hands of a smart hotel manager, she had moved to Morocco a few years later and set about converting the old riad into one of the most magical and enchanting places that Philippe had ever been to. He loved staying there.

Once again, as if reading his mind, she broke into his thoughts. 'Cheri, you must come out here. You sound weary and worried. Your skiing holiday was, for obvious reasons, not a success.'

He laughed.

'I am serious, Philippe, come here, let Bushara cook for you, we can go through your figures and you can listen to my latest business plan.'

She paused but he didn't reply. He was conjuring up the scent of jasmine by the pool, the intoxicating smell of the spices in the souk, the taste of Bushara's succulent lamb tagine, the heat of the sun and the sound of the muezzin in the distance.

'Philippe, are you listening to me?' she said in exasperation. 'I'm not taking no for an answer. I'm going to book the damn flights today.'

Philippe was smiling to himself as he realised that this was exactly what he needed. 'Go ahead, Bea, book the bloody flights.'

Astonished at his easy capitulation she realised he really must be feeling rough. 'I haven't exactly helped you this morning, have I, cheri?'

'On the contrary, it's always a challenge talking to you, Bea, you make me think.' He heard a car pull into the driveway. 'Stephanie is back, do you want to speak to her now or call her later?'

'I'll call her later. Go and see the chickens and give Emmie a hug from me.'

He heard the car door slam and hobbled to the doorway. Emmie was coming slowly through the front door, nursing something in her arms. She looked at him and smiled and as always his heart turned over. Her chubby round face was alive with excitement and behind thick glasses her big blue eyes were sparkling. She knelt down and gently placed the bundle onto the floor at his feet. He gazed down in utter astonishment.

'Me's got a piglet,' she proudly announced, beaming up at him.

'Yes, Emmie, I can see that.' Philippe stared at the tiny pink squirming animal. 'The question is why?' He looked enquiringly over the top of Emmie's head at his sister.

'He was the runt of the litter,' Stephanie replied sheepishly.

'He was getting no milk,' Emmie added. 'He was going to die.' She paused for dramatic effect. 'Die badly.'

Philippe looked at each of them in amazement.

'Emmie fell in love with him,' Stephanie tried to explain further. 'She was desperate to look after him and Giles simply couldn't refuse her.'

Still Philippe remained silent.

'She's thought of such a clever name,' Stephanie persevered. 'Tell Uncle Philippe his name, cheri.'

'Sausage!' Emmie shouted with joy, throwing her arms around his knees. 'We've got us a sausage, Uncle Philly.'

CHAPTER FOUR

I had no idea what I was doing here. It had never occurred to me before to go to Marrakech on my own and yet here I was standing in the queue for check-in. How the hell had that happened? I glanced down at a case I couldn't even remember packing.

Everyone knew that I'd wanted to go Marrakech for as long as I could remember. They all knew how excited I was and I simply hadn't felt able to tell anyone why I now didn't want to go. I'd stayed holed up in the flat, alternating between surges of white-hot rage and utter wretchedness.

There were only two people in the world I'd ever felt happy confiding in: one was my sister, but she was touring Australia enjoying a belated honeymoon, there was no way I could suddenly drop this bombshell on her; and the other, of course, was Nick.

My heart somersaulted as once again I realised how much I had lost. I gasped out loud. The little boy in front of me in the queue turned around in surprise, his huge brown eyes gazing at me with curiosity. I quickly gave him a reassuring smile and he grinned back.

Out of the corner of my eye I sensed movement and wheeled around in time to see a figure running towards me. A very familiar figure, a figure with long loping strides. It was Nick, his face was flushed and his red hair was standing on end, he saw me and slid to an abrupt halt. He stood there uncertainly, as if unsure of the next move.

What on earth was he doing here? Despite his best efforts I hadn't spoken to him since the day my world had been turned upside down. Seeing him unexpectedly now, I realised how much I had missed him.

I felt a weight lift off my shoulders. Of course, he's coming to tell me that it's all been a mistake, he and Miles have made the most terrible mistake. It was a moment of madness, a rush of blood to the head, of course Miles doesn't want to leave me.

Where was Miles? I looked beyond Nick but couldn't see him. He was probably parking the car, he was slightly anal about parking the car and frankly it was something that had always annoyed me. That must be it, he had dropped Nick off and was parking the car.

Thank God I hadn't told anyone, no one else need ever know. I let out a long sigh of relief and the kid in front turned around again but I didn't care.

Of course it might not be easy at first, it would be slightly awkward, but surely we could put it all behind us, we could carry on as before. There may even come a time when we would look back and laugh about it, I thought.

Nick saw the smile, registered my relief and encouraged by it, walked slowly towards me.

'Sky.' He smiled uncertainly.

'Nick.' I felt very close to tears.

We looked at one another for a while and the silence grew uncomfortable.

'Where's Miles?' I finally asked.

Nick looked startled. 'He's not here, we kind of thought it would be better if I came alone.'

'Is he waiting for us at home?'

Still looking baffled, Nick replied carefully, 'Actually he's staying in a hotel at the moment, it um, well, it just didn't seem right him being with me.'

I remained silent, trying to take this in.

'We didn't really think you would want both of us coming with you.' He seemed unsure of how to proceed. 'Maybe we were wrong?'

'Coming where?' I was starting to feel distinctly uneasy.

'What do you mean?'

'You said I wouldn't want both of you coming with me, coming where exactly?'

'Coming to Marrakech, Sky.'

Suddenly cold realisation hit me. It wasn't a mistake, nothing had changed, nothing had changed at all.

'Oh, Sky.' Able to read me like a book, Nick realised immediately what I'd been thinking and the pity on his face was more than I could bear. Anger surged through me.

'And why the hell are you coming to Marrakech with me?' I hissed.

'We didn't think for a moment you'd go ahead with the trip. Sky, we're so worried about you, we couldn't let you go alone.'

'Couldn't let me go alone?' I couldn't believe my ears. 'I'm not a child Nick. I'm not exactly incapable.'

'No, I know, I just wanted to see you, to talk to you, to try and sort this out.' He took a deep breath. 'We can, Sky, we need to. I love you.'

I could only stare in utter disbelief.

'I rang the riad, they have another room for me, I, um, well I told them your husband was unwell.'

I rounded on him then, oblivious of the people around me. 'Get out of my sight, Nick, get out of my bloody sight now.' Never had I felt such hot rage, never had I felt so utterly humiliated.

'Sky.'

'NOW,' I screamed at him.

There was an exclamation from the man behind and the mother of the lad in front clamped her hand firmly to the back of his head, preventing him from twisting around once more.

'I'll go to the back of the queue.' Nick shuffled away, misery etched on his face.

'Would you like to come forward?' Mercifully, the check-in girl behind the desk was beckoning me.

I walked down the aisle of the plane, desperately praying that no one who had heard me at check-in would be near my seat. But, typically, the mother and young son who had stood in front of me in the queue were in the same row and my heart sank. Jesus, they must have overheard every word. Smiling uncertainly I slid into my seat and immediately took a book out of my bag; the last thing I wanted to do was engage them in conversation.

I had no idea where Nick was, but I'd seen him at the gate so I knew that he was on the plane. Mostly I felt furious with him but if I was being totally honest there was a very small part of me that felt almost relieved. What was that all about then? I was totally confused.

The last two weeks had passed in a blur. I had gone to work, operating on autopilot, and even managed a couple of meetings, so presumably I'd behaved as normal, but I had very little recollection of anything. I very much hoped so, I couldn't afford to lose my job.

Normally I adored flying but not today. Today there was none of the usual surge of adrenalin that I felt when the plane took off. The last time I had flown I'd been with Nick and Miles and we were going to Scotland. Miles had surprised us both with the tickets the night before and I remembered being blown away and thinking how very lucky I was. We had ordered champagne on the plane, it was early in the morning and it had felt wonderfully wicked, we'd all been in such high spirits.

Suddenly I sat bolt upright, my book falling to the floor with a clatter. Had anything been going on between them then?

My heart was racing. Had their relationship already started? Had the whole holiday been a complete charade for them? Were they already cheating on me?

I started to shake and my eyes filled with tears. I desperately searched for a tissue. I could feel the hysteria building in me. I became aware that the lady next to me was moving, no doubt trying to summon a stewardess, I'd be thrown off the plane, maybe that would be no bad thing but I started to panic nonetheless.

Then I felt an arm gently slide over my shoulder and heard a soft low voice in my ear.

'Take a deep breath now, in and out, in and out, that's it, just keep taking deep breaths, take it nice and easy, it's all going to be all right.'

The gentle voice was soothing and as I followed the instructions I gradually felt the panic subside.

'OK, that's better,' the soft voice continued. 'Here, I have a tissue here for you, well it's actually a wet wipe but it will do the same thing.'

I took the wet wipe and began to rub my face but my hand was shaking too much to be effectual.

'Have some chocolate,' she said, delving into her bag and producing a bar of fruit and nut. 'It will help.'

I smiled weakly. 'Chocolate always helps.' I accepted a slab. 'I'm so very sorry about all of that, I hope I've not upset your son.' I watched as the little boy tugged his mother's arm.

'Not in the least.' She smiled. 'He's been totally absorbed in his game and is now delighted that the chocolate has come out early.'

'Jesus, you must think I'm crazy.' I bit into the chocolate. It tasted like nectar. When was the last time I had actually eaten anything? 'I'm so sorry, I don't normally behave like this, I really don't but it's just that... well, the thing is...'

'It's OK, you don't have to explain.'

'No I do,' I replied. 'You've been so kind, you deserve an explanation, and besides I've got to practice saying it.' I bit hard on my lip and tasted blood. I wiped it away and took a deep breath. 'My husband has left me.' I paused before starting again. I knew I was talking faster and faster but couldn't seem to shut up. 'My husband has left me for a man, my husband doesn't care for the female form anymore…'

'Up to you,' she butted in very quickly, 'But maybe "due to irreconcilable differences my husband and I have split up".'

I turned to look at her for a moment. 'I'm so sorry, of course that's the one to go with. I think you've hit the nail on the head there, I think it's fair to say that the differences are pretty bloody irreconcilable.' I smiled at her. 'Do I look vaguely presentable? Have I managed to wipe the streaks of mascara away?'

'Not a trace left.' She smiled back.

'The trolley is on the way, can I buy you a large drink to say thank you?' I reached for my purse.

'Thank you very much, that's very kind. I'll say yes to a gin and tonic.' She held out her hand. 'I'm Gail, by the way, Gail Scott, and this is Sonny.'

'He's gorgeous,' I said, smiling at the young lad and noting his caramel complexion and huge brown eyes. 'I'm Sky, Sky Walker.'

'As in *Star Wars*?' Gail giggled.

'You're not the first to make that joke.' In fact everyone always made the same joke, even the vicar at the wedding, all very funny at first but now intensely irritating. 'Perhaps now is the time to revert back to my maiden name.'

'Which is?'

'Rossi, Sky Rossi.'

'Wow, how very glamorous, beats the hell out of Gail Scott.'

'I'm half Italian, half Scottish, with a father obsessed with the Highlands and Islands. My sister is called Iona. Unfortunately my father couldn't spell Skye.'

The trolley arrived and I bought two gins for us and a juice for Sonny.

'Cheers, Gail.' We clinked plastic glasses. 'I can't thank you enough for being so kind. I seriously don't know what I would have done without you.' I was sincere, I really didn't know what I would have done without her. I'd never experienced a panic attack before. 'Not exactly the ideal start to your trip, first the scene in the queue... you showed remarkable restraint, by the way, in not turning around.'

'Ah, but I was listening to every word.'

'Hard not to I imagine.' I grimaced. 'And then my hysteria. Certainly not the best way to begin a relaxing holiday.'

Gail turned to check that Sonny was occupied with his juice and Game Boy before replying.

'Well, if I'm truthful it was a most welcome distraction.'

I raised my eyebrows.

'It's my turn to be honest with you.' She gulped at her gin before continuing. 'This isn't exactly going to be what you'd call a relaxing holiday.' She leant towards me and spoke in a low voice. 'I'm actually going to Marrakech in order to find Sonny's father.'

'And does Sonny's father know this?' I was instantly intrigued.

'Sonny's father does not know of Sonny's existence.'

'Bloody hell.' It was my turn to gulp at the gin. 'We may need another one of these. And what has brought all this on?'

'I overheard my sister say I was dull and boring.'

'You seem anything but to me,' I replied with feeling.

A shadow loomed over me, and without looking up I knew it was Nick.

'Hi.'

He stood in front of me. He looked surprised to see me chatting. He'd clearly expected to find me slumped in my seat, tearful and morose, and I was pleased that I wasn't.

I looked up at him but didn't say a word.

'I, um, I just wanted to... oh, excuse me.' He broke off to talk to a passing air stewardess. 'Excuse me, would you be able to find me another seat, I'm currently crammed in like a louvred door in nineteen E. The couple next to me have embarked on a gargantuan picnic and egg sandwiches are on the menu.' He pulled a face. 'The smell is atrocious. I'll pay any money.'

She laughed. 'No worries, sir, we're not full.'

'I love you.'

She blushed. Nobody could resist Nick.

He turned back to me. 'I'm not sure if you know but the riad is sending a car.' I still said nothing. 'I just wanted to tell you. He's called Ibrahim, the driver that is not the car, and he'll be holding a sign saying Riad Fontaine.'

There was a gasp of surprise from Gail. 'Riad Fontaine, oh my God, that's where we're staying. How wonderful!'

'Really? You're staying there too?' I was over the moon.

Nick held out his hand to Gail. 'Well, it looks like we're going to be sharing the same quarters, I'm Nick.'

'Pleased to meet you.' She leant across me and took his hand. 'I'm Gail and this is Sonny.'

'Sonny, wow, what a cool name. What does it go with?'

'Scott,' Gail replied briefly. I could sense that she felt slightly awkward.

'Sonny Ray,' Sonny added, eager to establish his full credentials. 'Ray is after an uncle what's dead.'

'Sonny Ray Scott.' Nick said the names slowly, looking with admiration at Gail.

'I did think I had maybe gone too far with Ray.' Gail smiled.

'Not at all. It's wonderful.' He turned to the young boy. 'Sonny, you absolutely have to learn to play a musical instrument, I'm thinking the saxophone. With a name like that you are going to be a jazz musician, you can't possibly be anything else.' He bunched his fist into a pretend microphone.

'*Ladies and gentlemen, introducing the one and only Sonny Ray Scott on sax.*' He winked at Sonny who grinned, utterly captivated by this tall man with twinkly blue eyes and red hair.

'Sonny, Sky and Gail. You sound like a weather forecast.' Gail and Sonny both giggled. I didn't.

'OK, well I'll see you when we land I guess.' Suddenly the laughter had gone out of his voice. He looked down at me but I didn't look up.

'Bye, Nick, see you later.' Gail spoke quickly to cover the awkward pause. 'I hope you find a decent seat.'

'Nice man,' Sonny announced before turning back to his game.

'So everyone says,' I said flatly.

'He's very charming.' Gail shrugged apologetically.

'Yes, everyone loves Nick,' I said. 'Including, it would seem, my husband.'

CHAPTER FIVE

The heavy wooden door swung shut behind him and Philippe paused for a moment to savour the cool, quiet interior of the hallway of Riad Fontaine. It was a graceful hallway with a carved cedar wood ceiling and large wooden panels, a calm sanctuary away from the savage sun and bustling souk outside. Through the far archway Philippe could see the pool glinting in the inner courtyard.

Though he hated to admit it the trip had tired him out more than he'd imagined it would. His head was throbbing and his injured knee was agony.

He sank down onto the wooden bench and leant back against the soft cushions.

'Are you unwell, Monsieur Philippe?' Ibrahim gently enquired.

'Nothing that a mint tea and a thousand painkillers won't cure, Ibrahim.' Philippe smiled wearily up at the tall Moroccan. 'You go ahead, I'll follow you in a moment.'

Bending down he eased off his shoes, relishing the feel of the cool marble beneath his feet. He rolled up his jeans and massaged his knee. Then, closing his eyes, he stretched his arms above his head and gradually let the tranquility of the building begin to seep into his body, savouring the few moments of silence and breathing in the indefinable scent that belonged uniquely to Riad Fontaine.

Moments later he heard the clatter of heels, the murmur of voices and a low, smoky laugh. He reached for his walking stick and stood up slowly.

She stood silhouetted in the archway, her hair a shimmering halo, arms outstretched and the familiar Guerlain perfume emanating from her.

'Bea.' He smiled.

'Philippe, bare feet, how wonderfully bohemian.' She moved gracefully into his arms and kissed him full on the lips. Taken aback he looked at her in surprise.

She shrugged unapologetically. 'I have missed you.'

'And I you, cheri.'

They gazed at each other. He noted her luminous skin and clear blue eyes, she saw his pallor and the lines of pain etched on his forehead.

'You look amazing, Bea.'

'You don't,' she said with her usual honesty. 'Come, Bushara has mint tea ready for you.' She took his hand and led him through the archway to a small table shaded by a thick, gnarled olive tree.

The courtyard was as bright as the hallway was dim and the air was heavy with the fragrance of the flowers. As the cool interior of the hallway had calmed him so the brilliance of the colours of the courtyard began to energise him.

A grey cat was lying on a nearby chair. Philippe walked towards her but she arched her back and hissed.

'Why do your cats always hate me?'

'Because you hate them.'

'I don't hate them at all, I just prefer dogs.'

'And I prefer cats. We should have realised our marriage was doomed from the start.' She laughed but there was a slight hint of sadness in her eyes. 'And talking of animals, what is this I hear about a piglet?'

'Emmie rescued him, he was the runt of the litter, the tiniest thing you have ever seen.'

'Piglets grow into pigs, cheri, even tiny ones,' Beatrice said smiling.

'I know, I know,' he said, running his hands through his hair, then he looked at her and laughed.

'He is called Sausage and he's Emmie's new best friend.'

'And where does Sausage sleep?'

'I've built a small sty for him in the outbuildings.'

'And I ask again, where does he sleep?' She grinned at him mischievously, knowing full well what the answer would be.'

'In the kitchen.' He threw up his hands in surrender. 'It's ridiculous, isn't it? He's turned the whole household upside down, he's even given Belle a new lease of life, they chase each other around the pool.'

'That I have to see,' Beatrice said, trying to imagine the huge Bordeaux mastiff running around with a piglet. 'I despair of you all, what on earth does Rosa think of a piglet in her kitchen?' she asked, referring to his housekeeper.

'Rosa is the worst of them all, she's the one who bought him into the kitchen in the first place, said she couldn't bear the thought of the small baby alone and afraid.'

'Mon Dieu, you have all taken leave of your senses.' Beatrice shook her head in amazement.

'It's actually very good for Emmie, she has to measure how much milk to give him, she writes it down in a notebook and weighs him every day.' He sipped his mint tea. 'She's taking it all very seriously, she feeds him last thing at night, first thing in the morning and when she comes home from school. The animal never leaves her side. She really dotes on him.'

'And you on her.' Beatrice chuckled. 'Philippe, you know as well as I do that if Emmie had wanted a whole litter of piglets you would have said yes.' She paused for a moment. 'Should we have had children, Philippe?'

Philippe choked on his tea. 'Bea, we were little more than children ourselves when we married.'

'Any regrets?'

'About what? About marrying you?'

32

She nodded.

'No, Bea, no regrets, not then, not now, not ever.' He leant across the table and took her hand. 'Cheri, what is all this?' He grinned suddenly. 'Has your lover proposed?'

'No, they know better than that.'

'They?' His mouth dropped open. 'Are we talking in the plural?'

Beatrice smiled enigmatically.

'You never cease to amaze me.'

'Are you jealous?'

'Yes, I'm jealous, very jealous of the fact that you have a string of lovers while I have to make do with a flatulent old bitch and a piglet?'

She smiled. 'It's hardly a string, Philippe.'

'They're lucky men, Bea. I hope they know that they're very lucky men.'

'You should get married, Philippe.'

'I tried that once, remember?'

'You are the marrying type,' she continued, ignoring his last remark. 'I'm not, but you definitely are. You need a wife.'

'Who would have me? I live in a crumbling chateau with my sister and a business on the verge of bankruptcy. It's not exactly every woman's dream.'

'Are things really that bad?'

'They are certainly not that good,' he replied. 'But please let's not talk about that right now. Tell me about my fellow guests.'

'Not that many this week. We have a pair of ancient American sisters who want to see the world. This is their first trip abroad, they are delightfully eccentric and told me they had dreamt of visiting Europe all their lives.'

'Did you enlighten them or leave them in blissful ignorance.'

'I enlightened them of course and we now have a daily geography lesson over breakfast.' She swirled her tea in its glass. 'And from the

UK we have a Mr & Mrs Walker, well actually no, we now have only Mrs Walker, her husband is ill apparently, and in his place we have a Mr Nick McPherson.'

'And will Mr Nick McPherson be sharing Mrs Walker's room?' Philippe enquired with a saucy wink.

'No, Philippe, Mr. Nick McPherson has requested a separate room.' She shook her head at him. 'Then we have a mother and her young son.'

'No husband?'

'No husband.'

'So two husbands both conspicuous by their absence.' Philippe tapped the side of his nose theatrically. 'No doubt you will get to the bottom of this before the end of the day, cheri.'

'You are making a mystery out of nothing.' She laughed.

'Oh, I don't think so, there is always mystery and intrigue at Riad Fontaine. It has all the makings of a perfect Agatha Christie novel.'

'Well then, you can practice your rusty English and question everyone like Poirot.'

'My English is certainly not rusty and Poirot doesn't question until the end, he observes and that is what I shall do tonight. I will be a silent observer, lurking unseen, eating Bushara's tagine.' He smiled at the silly rhyme. 'Seriously, Bea, I don't feel like being sociable tonight. Tomorrow I will be the life and soul, I promise, but this evening let me be solitary.'

She frowned. 'You can be anything you like, Philippe, I don't need you to be the life and soul, you are here to get better.'

'I am not ill, Bea.'

She smiled gently and leant over to kiss him.

CHAPTER SIX

I lay back in my seat. I was very pleased that the car was air-conditioned. The gin and tonics on the plane had given me a nagging headache and dry throat. Why in God's name was I here? Why on earth had I gone ahead with the bloody holiday? I should have stayed at home and tried to sort things out.

My Italian grandmother had always told me to confront problems. '*You should never run away from anything, Sky, cara,*' she would say. '*Face things head on and do battle.*'

We had always done just that. Nonna, Nick, Iona and I sitting at the old kitchen table, talking through our various problems together, thrashing everything out. Now Nick *was* my problem.

God, what an unholy mess this all was. Tears threatened to overwhelm me once more and I gritted my teeth, willing them to stop. If the others hadn't been in the car I would have asked Ibrahim to take me directly back to the airport.

I stared out of the car window, not really seeing the camels grouped together on the street corner, the dark fronded palm trees, the men and women in their flowing robes and the hundreds of dusty mopeds weaving insanely in and out of the traffic. I closed my eyes and lay back even further in the seat. The beauty of Marrakech, the city I had dreamt about for so very long, flashed by me unseen.

Beside me Gail was silent while in contrast Sonny was chattering away non-stop. He was clearly in seventh heaven, exclaiming at everything he saw. I could sense that she was trying to be enthusiastic but she seemed tired and anxious. I opened my eyes and smiled at her.

'What am I doing here?' she leant over and whispered. 'I've come on a wild goose chase, I must be mad.' She lowered her voice even more. 'Sky, I'm going to ask Ibrahim to take me back to the airport.'

'I was thinking much the same thing,' I murmured.

'What about Nick? Will he mind?' She asked.

I wondered how Nick was feeling. Was he regretting coming? I imagined that it had taken some courage to follow me here. He at least was prepared to try and do battle, while I was running away. I had a horrid feeling that Nonna would be far from proud of me right now.

'Let's think about it when we get to the riad,' I said.

She nodded but didn't seem convinced.

Nick had a tic below his left eye that spasmed slightly whenever he was upset or angry and I could tell that it was twitching now. The heat had twisted his curls into tight ringlets. As he'd got older his hair had darkened and I knew that he didn't mind it now, but as a kid his bright copper curls had been the bane of his life. We used to joke about wanting to swap, I would be happy to have his auburn ringlets and he could have my straight, dark hair. We'd even bought wigs once to see what we would look like, we looked bloody awful but it didn't stop us from wishing.

He looked utterly wretched and I watched as he leant over to Ibrahim and asked in a low voice that I had to strain to hear. 'Are the flights frequent from Marrakech to London?'

I couldn't hear Ibrahim's reply but I had a sudden and overwhelming urge to laugh. Three people arriving in Marrakech and three people all desperate to leave, it was like a farce. What an eccentric group we were.

'Please to follow.' Ibrahim had parked the car and was opening the door.

I was puzzled, we appeared to be in a poky, dusty alleyway and there was no sign of the riad. A young Moroccan lad was busy loading our suitcases onto a small handcart.

'I don't understand?' I said hesitantly. 'Where is Riad Fontaine?'

'Through here if you please.' Ibrahim indicated an archway. 'No cars allowed in the medina.'

'Oh yes, I remember reading about that,' I said. 'I think the streets are too narrow for cars.'

'Too narrow for cars?' Gail sounded anxious. 'How do you get around then? What if you need to get away?'

I heard the wobble in her voice, saw the slight panic in her face and was quick to reassure her.

'I guess it's easy to organise a taxi from the riad to pick you up here?' I looked over to Ibrahim for confirmation and he nodded.

'I've made a big mistake, Sky,' Gail said. 'I think I should go.'

She looked for Sonny. He wasn't by her side.

'Sonny?'

'Here, Mummy.' We wheeled around and saw him crouched in the dirt, patting an old goat who was tethered to a spindly olive tree.

'Come here now, Sonny,' she cried sharply. He looked startled but scampered over to her. 'I'm going home, Sky. This is madness, it's total madness.'

'Let's go to the riad, Gail. We can't think straight right now,' I whispered.

'Mummy?' Sonny looked anxious.

I stared down at his little face and thought that he looked right at home there with his olive skin and dark eyes. I knew without doubt that she had to stay, she had to try and find his father. 'You have to see it through, Gail, we both do.' I gave her shoulders a reassuring squeeze. 'And besides, you can't possibly leave me here alone. I need you. You'll never forgive yourself if you leave.'

She looked at me for a moment before turning to her son.

'What an adventure, eh, darling?' We've certainly got some exploring to do.' She smiled brightly at Sonny but her voice was still far from steady.

'Can we start now?' Sonny's face was alive with excitement. 'Can we explore now?'

'Let's you and I be explorers, Sonny.' Nick held out his hand. 'Let's go and find the hotel, make sure that it's safe for Mummy and Sky to follow.'

Sonny looked at his mother who nodded gently and smiled her thanks at Nick. The two of them ran after the handcart. Ibrahim remained waiting patiently at the roadside.

'You're doing the right thing, Gail.'

'Oh, Sky, thank God we were on the same plane.'

'I couldn't agree more.'

She took a deep breath. 'Come on, poor Ibrahim is being so patient, he must think we're mad.'

'He wouldn't be far wrong.' I smiled as together the two of us crossed the alleyway and followed Ibrahim to Riad Fontaine.

I stood rooted to the spot in the archway which led to the inner courtyard of the riad. The others had gone in but I couldn't move. I was spellbound by the scene in front of me. I'd never seen anything so magical. I had never imagined colours so vibrant, their intensity was almost painful and I was overcome by their richness and depth.

My hands itched to get out my paints and as I slowly began to walk inside I started to imagine what my palette would look like. The crimson of the bougainvillea and the dark green ivy. The sharp white jasmine climbing the ochre walls. A shimmering turquoise pool surrounded by pale wooden sun loungers. Sparkling silver tray tables, deep amber and gold pottery and dark blue tubs housing exotic palm trees. The effect was breathtaking.

It felt to me as if the colours were palpable things, glinting in the air just beyond my reach. I stretched out my hands towards them like a child in a candy store.

'Sky,' Nick called softly.

I was in a world of my own. I turned towards him with a smile.

'Oh, Nicky, it's magical.'

His look of surprise brought me back to reality with a jolt and my joy vanished instantly.

I walked towards the table where a lady in an olive green headscarf and black robe was pouring mint tea.

'Hello, are you Beatrice?' I asked.

'No, Beatrice will be joining you in a moment.' She had a beautiful smile. 'I am Bushara, wife of Ibrahim who drove you here.' Her face was kind and serene as she handed out the tea and pastries and I had a bizarre urge to hug her.

I sipped at the tea, it was sweet and refreshing and the pastry was sublime. I watched Nick out of the corner of my eye. I could see him licking his lips, smelling his fingers, desperately trying to identify everything. I knew exactly what he was doing. He would automatically begin to analyse the taste.

I could detect almonds, cinnamon and honey but there was bound to be something I couldn't quite define. It was second nature to him to try and dissect the ingredients of anything new. It was an agonisingly familiar routine and one that I'd witnessed a thousand times.

A sudden exclamation from Sonny startled me.

'Look, a tortoss, mummy a tortoss.' His little face was a picture of happiness.

Beatrice was watching from the upstairs balcony. She always liked to observe her guests before meeting them.

She saw the two girls chatting as if they were old friends but she could see the tension in the knuckles of the beautiful dark-haired girl as she clutched her tea. She watched the way her eyes kept sliding to the tall man with auburn hair standing to one side. He was pretending to look around but Beatrice could see how taut he was, nervously chewing his bottom lip.

She watched the handsome young boy playing with the tortoise and had the strange feeling that she had seen him before. She heard his pretty, fair mother calling him back, holding out her arm protectively, but who was she protecting him from?

She saw Bushara look up and nod at her. It was time to go down.

CHAPTER SEVEN

I followed Beatrice up a flight of beautiful old wooden stairs that creaked with every step.

'It's simply impossible to creep around silently in this riad.' Beatrice grinned as she paused at the top. 'You cannot keep your movements secret here.'

I stopped to gaze at a group of photographs. 'Is this the riad before you restored it?'

'It certainly is.'

'My God, you've done an amazing job. What a huge project to take on.'

'Well, I had some help.' Beatrice retraced her steps to show me. 'This was my extremely talented architect.' She pointed to a young, good-looking man. He looked vaguely familiar to me although I couldn't imagine why. 'These were my team of builders and here in the background are Bushara and Ibrahim.'

'Gosh, so they were here right from the start.'

'Yes they were.' Beatrice nodded. 'My right-hand men, so to speak.'

'This is a beautiful photograph, who are you hugging?' I peered at a photo of Beatrice laughing up at a tall, dark-haired, handsome man.

'That's Philippe, my ex-husband. Actually he's here at the moment, you will meet him.'

'You're still on good terms then?'

'The best of friends.'

I thought of my best friend and turned abruptly away from the photograph.

Beatrice led the way across a small sun-dappled terrace and flung open a door at the far end.

'This is your room, Sky,' she said, ushering me in.

I went down a couple of steps and found myself in a small sitting room dominated by a large open fireplace. A beautiful wooden archway in one corner led to a bedroom and beyond that I could make out a white-tiled bathroom. The ceiling was the same dark cedar as the hallway, brightly coloured rugs adorned the floor and a small sofa was covered with sequinned cushions.

'Oh, Beatrice, it's stunning.' It had everything, it was comfortable and it was exotic and unique.

'It's one of my favourite rooms.' Beatrice smiled. 'If you want a fire then don't hesitate to ask Ibrahim, there's nothing he enjoys more than lighting fires. Frankly Bushara and I are convinced that one day the whole riad will go up in smoke.'

'It's an amazing place, Beatrice, it's everything I've ever imagined and much more.' I wandered around the room. 'I've been looking forward to coming to Marrakech for such a long time.'

'I'm sorry to hear about your husband.'

'So am I.'

'What is wrong with him?'

'He's gay.'

'I didn't think that was classed as an illness,' Beatrice said, completely taken aback.

'It isn't, I just don't think Nick knew what else to say to you.'

'And where does Nick fit?'

'At the moment neatly into my husband.' I quickly clapped my hand over my mouth. 'Jesus Christ, I'm so sorry, how crude.' I was horrified. I didn't normally behave like this. 'I can't believe I just said that, I'm so sorry. It's still all a bit of a shock.'

Beatrice shook her head. 'So, let me get this straight…'

'If only,' I replied. We looked at each other for a second and then both started to giggle.

'I don't know what's come over me,' I apologised.' No one knows back home and yet suddenly in one short day I've told both you and Gail.'

'Sometimes it is easier to talk to strangers.' Beatrice sat down. 'And anyway you cannot keep something like that locked up, you need to talk about it.' She smiled up at me encouragingly.

Taking a deep breath I sat down beside her. It seemed only fair to put her in the picture. 'Nick is, or rather was, my best friend. My absolute best friend.' I paused and Beatrice took my hand.

'He is the person who my husband is having an affair with.' I hesitated a moment before continuing. 'No it's much more than an affair, Nick is the one who apparently makes him feel complete, the "final piece of the jigsaw".'

'I see.'

'Do you? I don't.' I turned to face her. 'I thought we were complete. I thought we *were* the whole jigsaw.' The room suddenly felt stifling, I fanned inadequately at my face. 'I had no idea that Nick was coming here. I had absolutely no idea until I saw him at the airport. I don't know what his game is, or why he's here.'

'I doubt he is playing games, Sky,' Beatrice said softly, gently brushing my heavy fringe away from my hot forehead. Her hands were cool and soothing.

'I just don't know what to do.'

'Let's tackle the immediate future,' Beatrice said. 'First a shower to wash off the travel dust and then a long siesta. Bushara is preparing an evening meal so tonight you will stay at the riad, tomorrow is time enough to explore.'

'Sleep and I are rather fickle friends at the moment.'

'You will sleep here, everyone sleeps here.' She stood up and, leaning over, unexpectedly kissed the top of my head.

Beatrice smiled at the sight of Sonny stretched out on the ground face to face with the tortoise. They were in earnest conversation.

'I see he has a new friend.'

'He certainly has, I can't prise him away.' Gail laughed.

'Is your room alright?'

'Oh, Beatrice, it's more than alright, it's wonderful. As soon as Sonny has stopped talking to the tortoise we will go for a much-needed nap.'

'Do you have any pets at home?'

'I've managed to resist so far but I may have to surrender on my return. He was stroking an old goat outside, he loves your cat and now he's obsessed with the tortoise.'

Beatrice laughed and bent down to the little lad. 'Sonny, why don't you ask Monsieur Tortoise where his two friends are?'

'What friends?' Sonny was instantly alert and looked around expectantly.

'There are another two tortoises in the garden, maybe you will see them after your sleep.'

Sonny could not have been happier, his dark brown eyes sparkled, his smile was wide and again Beatrice couldn't shake off the feeling that he reminded her of someone. Without stopping to think she turned to Gail. 'Is his father Moroccan?'

Gail gasped and Beatrice watched the colour drain from her face. 'Yes he is,' she whispered. 'Sonny, get up, it's time to go.'

'I'm so sorry, Gail, I did not mean to pry, I've clearly upset you.' Beatrice was mortified. 'Please forgive me.'

'No not at all, it's just that, um…' Sonny was by her side. 'It's OK, really.' Gail smiled a bit too brightly. 'We'll see you later, thanks for everything.'

What can of worms had she opened there, Beatrice wondered. This was turning into a very interesting group. Philippe was right, there certainly seemed to be intrigue and mystery at Riad Fontaine this week.

Nick emerged from the shadows in his swimming shorts.

'I thought I might take a quick dip if that's OK?'

'Nick, of course it's OK, that is what the pool is here for.' She smiled. 'Is everything alright with your room?'

'It's perfect. Thank you so much for fitting me in.' He hesitated. 'It was a sort of last-minute decision.'

'So I gathered.'

He paused. 'Do I take it then that Sky has told you of our circumstances?'

'She has given me an idea,' Beatrice replied carefully.

'I can't imagine what you must think of me.'

'I think that you're brave to have come here.'

'Do you? I was thinking the opposite, I was thinking what a fool I was to have come charging in like the proverbial bull and that maybe I should go home tomorrow.'

'Don't make any rash decisions just now,' Beatrice advised. 'Don't do anything you will regret.'

'I already have.'

'Do you really regret it?' she asked, and then seeing the look of surprise on Nick's face began to apologise. 'That's the second time today I've probed too far. I'm not sure what has come over me. Forgive me, you don't have to answer, you are on holiday not in therapy.'

'I think that being on holiday is probably more beneficial than being in therapy, especially with you at the helm.' He smiled at her. 'It's OK, Beatrice, I'm happy to talk about it, frankly it's a relief to get it out in the open. Back home no one knows, we can't tell anyone of course before Sky is ready to talk.'

'That can't be easy.'

'Half of me wants to yell from the rooftops that I'm in love while the other half wants to hide in the corner in shame. I've no idea what to do. If I stay with Miles I will lose Sky, but if I hold on to Sky then I'll lose Miles, either way I'm buggered.' He grinned ruefully. 'No pun intended.'

'Even if you gave up Miles you couldn't go back to the way it was before. You cannot turn back time, the damage has been done.'

'I feel like we're all living in a terrible sort of limbo. I hate what I've done to Sky, if I could change things then I would, but it just crept up on us and we can't pretend otherwise.'

'You will move on eventually, you need Sky to forgive you and then you need to forgive yourselves.'

'I know. That's why I came, but we've committed such an unforgivable crime that I'm not sure she's going to be able to.'

'You haven't murdered anyone, Nick,' Beatrice observed drily. 'You have merely fallen in love.'

'It feels like I have murdered someone.' He ran his hands through his copper curls.

'Her world has been shattered. It will take time.'

Beatrice was used to people telling her things, she was a good listener and it came with the territory. Everyone was more relaxed on holiday, and they tended to let down their guard. But she made it a rule never to pry and never to offer unsolicited advice. She had broken both these rules with this group on their very first day and she didn't really know why.

She watched as Nick executed a perfect dive. His body was lean and toned and he sliced through the water with ease.

'Toy boy material?' Philippe appeared by her side.

'Oh most definitely.' She grinned. 'But for you rather than for me.'

Philippe raised his eyebrows. 'So not a replacement for the ill husband then?'

'No, quite the opposite in fact, he has replaced the wife.' She laughed at the expression on his face. 'All will be revealed over a glass of rosé.'

'Well, I was going to do my physio exercises in the pool, but rosé sounds infinitely more appealing.'

CHAPTER EIGHT

The muezzin began at around six o'clock the following morning. I lay in my bed entranced by the mystical sound of the call to prayer. Wrapping a blanket around myself I padded on to the little terrace and leant over the balcony, thrilled by the intensity of the deep sounds resonating across the city.

I'd been obsessed with Marrakech ever since I was a child. My parents had honeymooned here and I'd loved hearing their tales of the souks, the spices, the market acrobats, the magicians and storytellers who gathered in the large square every night. It had sounded so exotic and fascinating, a million miles away from the Scottish border town where I grew up. I had imagined being here a thousand times, I'd always secretly dreamed about coming here on my honeymoon but when the time came I hadn't been quick enough to tell Miles and he'd booked Paris. It hadn't really mattered, I knew I'd come here one day but never in a million years had I thought it would be under these circumstances.

I shook my head and, wrapping my blanket tighter, desperately tried to wrench my mind away from the current nightmare, focusing instead on watching this magical city come to life as the sun rose above it.

For a short while I succeeded. I was lost in the sights and sounds around me. Tomorrow, I promised myself, I would paint it but, for today, I was content to sit, breathe in the air and absorb everything.

I was exhausted, mentally and physically. I'd spent every waking hour, of which there had been many, with my mind in absolute turmoil. How on earth had this nightmare happened? How could I not have had an inkling? What had I done wrong?

The suddenness with which my world had started spinning out of control left me reeling. I'd spent the last two weeks examining every part of our marriage, going over every detail, wondering if I could have been a better wife, wracking my brains for any clues I might have missed, wondering if there was anything I could have done to prevent Miles from taking this step, but nothing came to mind.

I just couldn't see a way out and I didn't know which way to turn. I had no one to talk to, there was no way I wanted to spoil my sister's trip and I certainly wasn't yet ready to face my father and grandmother. So here I was in Marrakech, city of my dreams, trapped in this terrible three-way tangle from which there seemed to be no escape.

The tantalising aroma of fresh coffee permeated my thoughts. My mouth watered, I was a coffee addict. Glancing at my watch I saw that is was still very early, but someone else was obviously up and about. I'd have a quick shower and then follow my nose to the caffeine.

I stretched and took several deep breaths, letting the cool morning air fill my lungs. And slowly a small but steely determination took hold. To hell with it, I was going to try to enjoy my time here. I would try and keep the demons at bay for the next few days.

I was shattered and I needed to regroup. Nonna would say I was like a hot water bottle without the hot water. My grandmother was full of these odd phrases, inaccurately translated from Italian. They made us all roar with laughter but were always strangely appropriate.

As I went downstairs I heard the murmur of conversation and recognised Nick's low laugh. I wasn't surprised to hear him up. I knew he would be asking the way to the nearest food market, it was the first thing he would check out in any new city. Automatically I turned and was about to retrace my steps before I remembered my earlier resolve. Straightening my shoulders I resolutely marched forward. I had done nothing wrong, so why should I be the one skulking in my room? And besides which, I needed coffee. Much as I wanted to, I couldn't spend the rest of the week avoiding Nick, that was clear, and once again I was filled with fury that he had followed me. I paused on the step to let the anger and panic abate. I would try and be dignified, I would be cool, polite and distant.

The four of them, Ibrahim, Bushara, Beatrice and Nick, were in the courtyard drinking coffee.

Beatrice greeted me with a warm smile. 'Ah, we have another early bird.'

'She's probably been painting the sunrise,' Nick said, smiling uncertainly at me.

'Not painting, just observing,' I answered Nick but looked at Beatrice.

'Are you an artist, Sky?' she enquired.

'Well, I'm an illustrator, that's what pays the bills.' I smiled.

'She's a brilliant illustrator,' Nick butted in. 'But she's also an exceptionally talented artist.' I didn't respond and his bright smile faded.

'How interesting, I had a feeling you were creative. I would love to see some of your work.' Beatrice seemed genuinely interested.

'Oh, I've not really got anything with me, just my sketch pad.'

'But she has a website, a new one which showcases all her work.' Nick interrupted once again. 'Very innovative and it's, um, well it's very good, you should take a look.' I watched him struggle as he remembered that it had been Miles who designed my site. I remained silent. He paused and then said rather quietly, 'Bushara has trusted me with her shopping list. I'm off to do battle with the market.'

'Good for you,' I replied sharply before turning away.

That came out wrong. I was cross with myself. That didn't sound dignified and polite, it sounded petty and childish.

'Ibrahim must be checking everything you buy.' Bushara was handing several large baskets to Nick. 'Make sure they are knowing he is with you otherwise these thieves, they will be robbing you.'

'Don't you worry, I'm Scottish, haggling is our national pastime.' Nick grinned but then seeing her stern face added quickly, 'But obviously Ibrahim has the last word.' He hesitated for a moment before turning briefly to me. 'Do you want me to take photos for you?'

I was taken by surprise and simply shrugged my shoulders. I saw the flash of pain in his eyes but he was gone before I could reply properly.

He always took photos for me of the various markets he visited, or indeed of anywhere he thought may be useful to my work. He knew the things I liked, he knew that the vibrant colours of the food market in Marrakech would appeal to me. It wouldn't have hurt me to say yes, he was trying so desperately hard to reach me, but I felt incapable of responding. I was just hurting so much.

I felt a gentle tap on my shoulder and realised that Beatrice was speaking to me.

'Sky, would you like a coffee or a tea?'

'Very much indeed, I'd love a coffee, thank you.'

'How do you take it?'

'Black, no sugar and very strong.'

'A woman after my own heart.' Beatrice grinned at me and I tried to smile back.

'They are both in a terrible mess,' Beatrice said to Bushara in the kitchen a few moments later.

'She is fighting very hard to be staying angry with him,' Bushara replied.

'She's like that poor wounded bird in the garden last week, turning in circles, not knowing which way to go and who to trust.'

'I am hoping she meets a better fate.' Bushara grimaced.

'Well, the cat is hardly likely to eat *her*, is she?' Beatrice laughed.

CHAPTER NINE

'Mummy, hurry up.' Sonny was impatiently hopping up and down by the bedroom door.

'I'm just looking for my glasses, darling.'

'But you don't need glasses to eat breakfast.'

Gail looked at him with mock surprise. 'Of course I do, I need to see what I'm eating, otherwise how will I be able to tell the difference between cornflakes and camel tail?'

He threw himself onto the bed in a fit of giggles and Gail thought that she had rarely seen him so happy. He had snuck into her bed in the early hours, wrapping his arms around her, his little body like a hot water bottle.

'Mummy, I'm just so excited,' he had whispered in her ear. 'Can we get up now?'

She had persuaded him to stay in bed a while longer but now he was itching to go downstairs.

'It's still very early, poppet,' she said. 'It's not even eight o'clock, we may be too early for breakfast.'

'But what if Tortoss and Cat are hungry?' He stared up at her, his huge brown eyes full of concern. 'Buttress said that I could feed them, they might be waiting.'

'*Beatrice*, Sonny, not buttress,' Gail giggled.

'And we have to go exploring, you promised.' He jumped off the bed and ran to the door.

'OK, I'm coming.' She threw her hands up in surrender. 'But first help me find my glasses.'

She had decided that they would have a day exploring Marrakech, it was only fair on Sonny. He was so eager to see the city and surely another day wouldn't make any difference.

Tomorrow, she promised herself, tomorrow she would go and seek him out. Her heart sank at the thought. Perhaps she could ask Sky to come with her but Gail knew she was being cowardly. This was something that she had to do alone, it wouldn't be fair to drag someone else into it.

'Here they are, Mummy.' Sonny was triumphantly holding up her glasses. 'They were in the bathroom.' He was grinning from ear to ear, delighted to have helped her.

Gail gazed at him in horror. What was she going to do about Sonny? Why hadn't she thought of that before? She certainly couldn't take him with her. She could ask Sky to look after him but that seemed like a huge imposition.

She shivered in shock as the enormity of what she had done took hold of her once more. What had she done? She cursed herself at her stupidity in not thinking it through.

'Mummy?' He tugged at her hand. 'Mummy, are you alright?'

She gazed down into his earnest face, the joy of a moment ago replaced by anxiety. She bent down and scooped him into her arms, kissing and tickling him. He screeched with laughter and struggled to free himself.

I was delighted to see Gail come into the courtyard and waved her over. She smiled and made a beeline for me, while Sonny made a beeline towards the tortoise.

'I'm so relieved to see someone else up.' She sat down beside me. 'I thought I was too early but Sonny has been champing at the bit for the last hour.' We watched her son scampering around the pool desperately trying to locate the other two tortoises. 'Beatrice promised that he could help feed the animals and it has been like Christmas morning today.' She laughed. 'Have you been up for long?'

'Yes I was woken by the muezzin, weren't you?' I doubted it was possible for anyone to sleep through it.

'Yes, but I was trying to keep a restless Sonny in bed.'

'It's a rather wonderful way to wake up, better than any alarm clock.' I paused. 'In fact, I wonder if they sell alarm clocks that sound like the muezzin.'

'Did you sleep OK?'

'Surprisingly, the best night's sleep I've had since it all happened,' I replied. 'And you?'

'Like a baby. The Moroccan wine must be stronger than I thought, but I am feeling rather jittery this morning.'

'Are you going to try and find him today?' I was very intrigued. I couldn't wait to see how this story would pan out and I was in awe of Gail's courage.

'No, today I've promised Sonny that we would go exploring. Tomorrow is the big day.' She smiled uncertainly. 'Sky, I've been rather foolish and not thought this through, can I ask you a big favour, it's incredibly cheeky of me and feel free to say no, but...'

I reached over and took her hand. 'Gail, of course I'll look after Sonny for you, it will be a pleasure. I'd already thought about that.'

'Oh, that's so kind of you.' She looked relieved. 'I just go cold at the very thought of seeing him, I can't quite believe that I'm here in the same place as him.' I could see that she was actually trembling a little. I didn't blame her, I'd be bloody terrified too. 'It all feels rather surreal,' she continued. 'It's just so unlike me, usually everything is meticulously planned in advance.'

'Well, you didn't plan very meticulously five years ago.' I was deliberately teasing, wanting to ease her tension.

Gail looked at me for a second and then smiled. 'Oh, Sky, I can't tell you how glad I am that you're here, I feel like I've known you for ever.'

'The feeling is mutual.' I smiled back at her then hesitated for a minute before asking, 'Gail, why now? Why didn't you get in touch with him before now?'

She looked quickly away towards Sonny.

'I'm sorry,' I said, immediately concerned that I had gone too far. 'You don't have to answer that, I didn't mean to pry.'

'You're not prying, I imagine that he will ask the very same question.' She paused and took a deep breath. 'Tariq turned my life upside down, Sky. Before I met him I was nicely settled with a man called Simon, several years my senior, rich and reliable. I thought I was happy and we were planning on getting married. Then one day I walked into a room, I saw Tariq and nothing has ever been the same again.' She pushed her fair hair off her face and gazed into the distance for a minute before continuing. 'He quite simply took my breath away. The weeks I spent with him were the most amazing weeks of my life. I never wanted to leave his side and he never wanted to leave mine, he occupied my every waking hour, well, you know what it's like.'

I wasn't at all sure that I did, but said nothing.

'Then he went travelling, that was always the plan, that was the reason he had come to Europe in the first place, to study and to travel. He was training to be an architect. We kept in touch daily until I discovered I was pregnant.' She paused again but I remained silent. 'I was both terrified and overjoyed. I didn't tell Tariq, I thought that would be better face to face, but I did confide in a colleague. That was a mistake, a big mistake.' Gail's face darkened with the memory. 'She told me horror stories of Moroccan men kidnapping their children, she persuaded me that Tariq must have a marriage already arranged, that he would never marry a European girl, but that if he heard about my pregnancy he would find a way to take the child from me, especially if it was a boy.'

'Why on earth would she tell you all that?' I was shocked. 'And more to the point, why on earth did you believe her?'

'She was jealous, but I didn't know that at the time. I was hormonal, I was vulnerable, I wasn't thinking straight and I didn't know which way to turn. I didn't reply to Tariq's messages, I couldn't, I just didn't know what to say.' Gail sighed. 'Looking back now I realise how weak and pathetic I was.'

I leant over to hug her. 'Not weak and pathetic at all, just alone and afraid. Did you not have any family you could turn to?'

'I have a much younger sister who has been my responsibility since our mum died. She knew about Tariq, I told her how much I loved him but she didn't really understand. She was angry because she liked Simon, or rather she liked his lifestyle. She didn't know I was pregnant.'

'And so what happened?' I was mesmerised by the story. 'Did you get in touch?'

'No, stupidly I procrastinated a bit longer and then before I had a chance I received a letter.' Gail stopped suddenly, tears were welling up in her eyes and she brushed them away angrily. 'He said he hoped I had enjoyed our brief interlude and wished me luck with the rest of my life. I was heartbroken.'

'Oh, Gail.' I was nearly in tears too. 'And then what? What did you do then?'

'Well, I got on with the rest of my life. What else could I do? I knew I couldn't go back to Simon, not only was I pregnant but being with Tariq had made me realise that whatever I felt for Simon wasn't love. He's a wonderful man, even offered to take me and the baby, but he deserved better than me.'

'Gosh, that was brave, many would have been tempted.' But I was puzzled. Something didn't ring true. 'Tariq's behaviour doesn't make any bloody sense.' I shook my head. 'After what you said you had together, why would he write a letter like that? Even if you hadn't been very communicative surely he would have tried to find out why? Not just sent a strange letter.'

'With hindsight, you're right, but back then I was very angry, confused and hurt. I didn't analyse things. Maybe that's why I'm here now, to finally get to the bottom of it. My fortieth birthday is looming and I guess I'm taking stock of things.' She smiled ruefully at me. 'Oh, Sky, I'm so sorry, what a long answer to your question.' She shook her head. 'I can't really believe that I've unburdened all this, I don't normally behave like this and it's not yet nine o'clock.'

'Christ, don't be sorry, it's riveting, thank you for sharing it.' It was riveting, and it also gave me something other than my own worries to think about. 'However I do need more coffee and you haven't had anything at all yet.'

As if on cue Beatrice emerged from the shadows bearing a tray of coffee, water and mint tea.

'You're a bloody witch, Beatrice,' I exclaimed. 'How do you manage to do that? It's like magic.'

'I have eyes and ears everywhere, Sky. It's part of the job.' She grinned at me. 'Actually I came out earlier to see if you wanted anything and to get Sonny, but the two of you seemed so engrossed that I didn't want to interrupt.' She smiled gently at Gail. 'I've brought you some tea, cheri. I had you down as a tea drinker, am I right?'

'Sky is right, you are a witch.' Gail smiled. 'Tea is exactly what I want, I adore this mint tea.'

Sonny had leapt up at the sight of Beatrice and was hurtling towards her.

'Sonny, don't run by the pool,' Gail shouted sharply.

He skidded to an abrupt halt and walked with exaggerated care for the last few steps, grinning mischievously at his mother.

'God, he is so adorable, Gail.' I held out my arms. 'Come and give us a cuddle, Sonny, you haven't even said good morning to me.' He obediently obliged but as he clambered up onto my knee I felt the all too familiar tightening in my chest.

Would that particular pain ever ease? Would things have been different if I had managed to keep our baby? Would Miles still have left me? What the hell was going to happen now? Would I ever have another chance to try for a child? I was nearly thirty-five, not exactly old but nonetheless time would run out soon enough.

My mind was like a windmill and with each sail came a new thought. I wanted to stop it from turning but it rotated relentlessly. My arms must have tightened around Sonny. He squirmed out of my grip and slid down. I swallowed hard and looked up at the sky; this was not something I could cope with right now.

'Is it time to feed the cat, Buttress?' Sonny was tugging at Beatrice's sleeve.

'Buttress?' She grinned down at him. 'Well, I guess I have been called worse – or have I?'

Gail shook her head in despair and I gave a half-hearted smile.

'Would you girls like breakfast after Sonny and I have fed the animals or is it too early? Our American sisters won't emerge until mid-morning.' Beatrice asked us both but I felt her eyes boring into me.

'Oh, breakfast sounds perfect,' I said quickly, before she could ask if I was OK. I got the impression that Beatrice was fast to latch on to things and children was not a subject I wanted to discuss right now.

'Are we the only other guests staying here? I spotted an older gentleman sitting by the fire last night. Is he staying here?'

Beatrice gasped. 'That older gentleman is my ex-husband Philippe. The one you saw in the photo. Mon Dieu, he will be mortified to hear you call him old.'

'Oh my God, I'm so sorry.' I sat up. 'It was dark and he had a walking stick and I guess I just kind of assumed, please don't say a word.'

'And speak of the devil, here he is,' Beatrice said as a man entered the courtyard.

He certainly looked a million miles away from the impression I'd formed of him last night. He was tall and tanned, dark sunglasses held back thick curling hair and he was wearing a long flowing black and silver kaftan, flip flops and carrying an old wooden walking stick.

'Cheri, that really suits you, Bushara picked it out.' I watched Beatrice nod in appreciation. There was clearly still a spark there. I also noticed Gail looking on in admiration.

'Philippe, come and meet Gail and Sky.' Beatrice paused for a moment before winking at me. 'Actually, Sky did see you last night, sitting by the fire, she was under the impression that you were a geriatric.'

I was absolutely mortified. 'Beatrice, you promised.'

'I did no such thing, and besides he needs to be reminded that he is no longer twenty, he needs to remember that he can no longer race recklessly down the ski slopes or he will fall and injure himself badly, as indeed he has.'

'I was not reckless, Bea, I was merely unfortunate.' He gave his ex-wife a wounded look. 'I am in a great deal of pain and a little sympathy would not go amiss.' Turning to Gail he held out his hand. 'Delighted to meet you.'

'And I you,' she replied looking up into his hazel eyes.

Turning to me he said, 'I confess that I am perhaps less delighted to meet you having heard your description of me.'

I blushed furiously but was saved from replying by Sonny.

'Won't Cat be hungry now?' He tugged on the arm of Beatrice. 'She may have runned away because she's hungry.'

'Hello, what's your name?' Philippe smiled gently down at Sonny.

'Sonny,' Sonny replied. 'You've got a stick.' He reached out to touch it, fascinated by the old gnarled wood.

'Sonny, don't be so rude.' Gail frowned at him.

'It's OK, he's quite right, I have got a stick, but Sonny, this is no ordinary stick.' Philippe bent down to whisper in his ear. 'This is a magic stick.'

'Is it a wand?' Sonny's eyes were wide, the cat had been temporarily forgotten.

'No, not exactly a wand, but it performs magic tricks.' Philippe steadied himself on the back of a chair and theatrically twirled it around. I ducked instinctively. It was dangerously near my head. Perhaps this was his way of taking revenge.

'Philippe.' Beatrice grabbed the stick. 'Show Sonny the magic later, right now we need to go and feed Mimi and the girls want breakfast. Do you want some?'

'Well, if it won't disturb anyone, I was planning on a swim first. I didn't realise everyone would be such early risers.'

'Girls.' Beatrice smiled at us wickedly. 'Will you be disturbed by an ageing Adonis taking a dip?'

CHAPTER TEN

'May I introduce you to Radar.' Beatrice had her arm around a small, skinny lad of indeterminate age. He grinned at us, showing surprisingly bright white teeth overlapping each other in an overcrowded mouth. He was wearing dusty sandals, baggy jeans and a Liverpool football shirt. He held out a grubby hand to each of us in turn.

'When you said you had *a radar* to navigate us around the souks I assumed you meant some sort of sat nav.' I was amused.

'Trust me, Radar is better than any sat nav.' Beatrice smiled at Radar and I saw him glow with pride. 'He knows every square inch of Marrakech, isn't that right?' She turned to Philippe who had emerged dripping from the pool.

'You couldn't have a better guide,' he agreed, throwing his kaftan back on. 'There isn't an alleyway, archway or ancient goat track that Radar doesn't know about.' He winked at the young boy. 'You're growing out of your football strip but not into your jeans.'

'Radar, why don't you go into the kitchen and have some breakfast. Sky and Gail will come and get you when they are ready.' Beatrice gently pushed him.

He needed no second bidding and saluting her smartly ran across to where Bushara stood waiting.

'He's some character,' Gail chuckled as Sonny looked on open-mouthed.

'Where does he come from?' I asked.

'Well, he attached himself to Ibrahim and Bushara and then when they came here he sort of followed. He's a real street urchin, he stays here most nights but every so often he likes to rough it outside.' Beatrice silently handed Philippe a coffee. 'No one knows his background, we have no idea where he came from but we're very glad he did.' She looked at us. 'You will be absolutely safe with him. He will show you everywhere you want to go and maybe some places you don't. The souks are an absolute maze, this is the best way to see them for the first time.' She smiled at us. 'You're both very pretty, Radar will make sure you aren't bothered too much, everybody knows him.'

Gail coloured but I was still curious. 'Where were Bushara and Ibrahim before here, when Radar attached himself to them?'

'They worked in a tiny little café. I stumbled upon it completely by chance. The food was exquisite, the place was immaculate and the service was the best I have ever known. I offered them a job on the spot. They were being paid a pittance, the owner was a thieving bastard, it wasn't hard to entice them here. The best day's work I ever did.'

'I'll say.' Philippe grinned. 'Bea is the worst cook imaginable. No one in their right mind would stay here if it weren't for Bushara.'

'I'm sure people don't come for the cooking alone.' Gail laughed. 'I think Beatrice has created a magical place.'

'Not sure if it's magic or havoc she creates, she's a witch, aren't you, cheri?' He draped a wet arm around her shoulders and Mimi the cat hissed. 'And this damn cat is really her *familiar*.' He hissed back and the cat arched, ready to pounce.

'You'll get what you're asking for in a moment, Philippe, she'll scratch you.'

'You may be divorced but you behave like an old married couple.' I couldn't help but laugh at them.

'There she goes with the word *old* again.' Philippe frowned. 'I was reliably informed that these few silver streaks were distinguished.'

'I'm not too happy with that description either.' Beatrice shook her head.

'I didn't mean that you were old.' I seemed to be putting my foot in it left, right and centre. 'It's just an expression, of course you're not old, Beatrice, you're beautiful.' I meant it, I really did think she was beautiful. Her skin glowed and her blue eyes were bright and sparkling. I had no idea of how old she was, I guessed they both must be somewhere in their mid to late forties, but she certainly didn't look it. I really hoped I hadn't offended her. I opened my mouth to say something more but she patted me on the arm.

'It's OK, Sky, I am only kidding.' She smiled. 'So, is that all set then? Just come and find Radar when you are ready to go. Sonny, are you looking forward to exploring with Radar?'

'Is Nick coming?' Sonny asked. Nick had spent the previous evening teaching him card tricks and I could tell the boy was rather taken with him.

There was a short pause and then Beatrice replied, 'No, Sonny, Nick has gone to the food market with Ibrahim.'

'Why?' He demanded.

'Sonny, don't be so rude.' Gail scooped him onto her lap but I could tell she was curious.

'Nick is a chef.' I found myself suddenly saying. 'Actually...' I couldn't resist adding with a hint of pride, 'actually he's a very good chef, he's just been awarded his first Michelin star.' Now why had I said that, I wondered? After all that he had done to me, why was I keen to praise him.

'I'm impressed.' Philippe raised his eyebrows. 'Very impressed. Where does he work?'

'London,' I replied shortly and then quickly changed the subject. 'Are the Majorelle gardens near here?' I turned to Beatrice. 'They are an absolute must on my list.'

'Philippe is the Majorelle expert,' Beatrice said. 'He should take you this afternoon.'

I began to protest and Philippe looked none too happy but Beatrice continued regardless. 'Philippe adores the gardens, how many times have you been?' She gave him no time to respond. 'Sky is an artist, cheri.'

'Well, actually I'm more of an illustrator and honestly…'

'Bea, maybe Sky…' Philippe began at the same time as me.

'Just for a short time, she can get a feel for the place and then go back at her leisure later on in the week. Take it gently and it will be good exercise for your knee.' Beatrice smiled brightly at us before turning on her heel and heading towards the kitchen.

I was annoyed at the way Beatrice had suddenly taken over. I was delighted to have Radar guide me around the souks but frankly was not that keen on going to the gardens with Philippe. I had been looking forward to them and would much have preferred to discover them by myself.

I turned to Philippe at the same time as he turned to me. We both spoke at once.

'Philippe, please don't feel…'

'Sky you may prefer…'

He laughed. 'After you.'

'I was just going to say that you don't have to escort me this afternoon.' That sounded a little rude. 'I mean, if you have something else you would prefer to do…' I hadn't really made myself clear.

'Bea is right,' he said. 'I adore the gardens but obviously I don't want to impose upon you, you may prefer to be on your own.'

I could tell that he didn't want to go either, but it was all a bit awkward, neither of us could get out of it without sounding ungracious. I gave up. 'Well, if you're sure then it would be lovely.'

'Excellent.' Philippe smiled hesitantly. 'Well, I'll be here all afternoon so just come and find me when you are ready.'

I smiled back equally hesitantly

Beatrice didn't really know why she had done that. It was out of character. What demon had suddenly taken hold of her? She knew that Philippe was annoyed with her and she couldn't really blame him. It was true that he loved the gardens but part of their appeal was their solitude. He liked wandering alone. Sky hadn't looked best pleased either. She shrugged her shoulders, it was too late now.

CHAPTER ELEVEN

For the first time in weeks Nick forgot all about recent events. He was totally immersed in the moment, utterly captivated by the food market. He stood mesmerized, absorbing the colours, the fragrances and the sheer beauty and artistry of the displays. Closing his eyes he tried to distinguish the various fragrances. The air was heady with the scents of nutmeg, mint, cinnamon and saffron. The spices were piled high in exotic pyramids, their vibrant colours making his head spin.

The sharp smell of frying onions made his mouth water and turning around he spotted a wizened man perched on a low stool, deftly tossing onions and lamb in one pan while throwing a flatbread on top of another. He couldn't wait to taste them.

The air crackled with energy and vitality. There was constant noise, heated haggling, sudden bursts of laughter, music and the buzz of voices.

He edged closer to the stalls, watching the women test the fruit, observed them gently squeezing, shaking and smelling in order to secure the pick of the bunch. Deep red prickly pears lay alongside gleaming purple aubergines, vibrant green chillies, soft yellow bananas, ochre pineapples and shining lemons. Every colour under the sun lay spread out before him and he couldn't stop the smile of joy spreading across his face.

Delighted at his reaction, Ibrahim led him from stall to stall, handing him dates and figs, dried apricots and raisins, pistachios and pine nuts, grinning at his expression as he tasted everything. Ibrahim seemed to know everyone and they were all keen to share their produce with Nick. He loved it and completely understood their sense of pride in what they were selling. Everything was fresh, everything was bursting with flavour, and Nick was in paradise. His whole body felt alive and every one of his senses felt heightened. His mind was buzzing with new ideas and recipes and he longed to get into a kitchen. He would go on bended knee to Bushara and beg for the chance to try some of them out.

Finally the baskets were full and Ibrahim led Nick to a small local café, where the smell of cigarettes mingled with the sweet aroma of the hookah pipes. Coffee and honey-covered pastries were immediately brought to the table and Nick fell upon them greedily.

'You like to cook?' Ibrahim stated the obvious.

'With a passion.' Nick grinned.

'First time here?'

'I went to Tangier with a group of friends many years ago but that doesn't really count, we spent most of the week either drunk or asleep.' Nick looked around him. 'I can't believe that I've left it so long. I had no idea what I was missing. I've been here less than twenty-four hours and I'm already hooked.'

Ibrahim didn't comment but drew deeply on a cigarette.

'And you?' Nick asked. 'Have you always lived here?'

'I would never want to live anywhere else.'

'No, why would you?'

Nick arrived back at the riad just as we were leaving.

'Come with us.' Sonny looked overjoyed to see him. I was less so. 'We is exploring with...' He paused, not sure of the name.

'Radar,' Gail filled in the gap. 'Radar by name and Radar by nature apparently. He is our guide.'

'Pleased to meet you, Radar.' Nick smiled at the young lad. 'A Liverpool fan I see, I'm a Rangers man myself, have you heard of Rangers?'

The boy shook his head.

'No, well, they're not exactly top notch these days, you're better off sticking to Liverpool.'

'Come with us.' Sonny tugged at his sleeve.

Nick glanced over at me. I remained non-committal.

'Not this morning, Sonny, I need to sweet-talk Bushara into letting me cook.' Sonny's face fell. 'But you pay close attention to Radar and remember where he leads you and then maybe you and I can go another time.'

'How was the food market?' Gail asked.

'Sensuous, stimulating, exotic and exciting.'

'Heavens, sounds like you're describing something completely different.' Gail giggled. 'I must go.'

'I'll escort you.' Nick smiled, then hesitated for a moment before turning to me. 'I took photos, Sky,' he said quickly. 'I'll leave my camera in Beatrice's office.'

Once again I was caught off balance and merely mumbled an ungracious OK. I knew I should thank him properly but I was bloody angry with him for constantly putting me in these awkward positions. Why on earth couldn't he just leave me alone?

I stormed out of the riad wrapped up in my own world. I was so engrossed in my misery that I was totally unaware of my surroundings and marched quickly after Radar.

'Sky?' Gail's voice cut into my thoughts. 'Sky, slow down, we can't keep up the pace.'

'Oh, God, Gail, I'm so sorry.' I was immediately contrite. 'I'm being so selfish, you must think me incredibly rude.'

'I don't think anything of the sort, I just think you're walking too fast.'

'One moment I think I'm OK and then wham, suddenly it hits me all over again.'

'You're still in shock, it's still all very new and raw.'

'Do you think that I'm being terrible to Nick?'

'I think you're hurting, Sky,' Gail answered me carefully. 'And the people who have hurt you are the ones who love you, so it isn't easy to know how to behave.'

'I don't really want to punish him, and yet in a way I do because I want him to suffer as much as I am.'

'He is suffering, Sky, there is no doubt about that.'

'Only a few weeks ago I thought my life was pretty perfect, I thought I had it all worked out, how smug I must have seemed.' I raised my eyes to the heavens. 'How the hell could I have got it so wrong?'

But before Gail could respond to me Sonny called her.

'Mummy, look at the goat what's got babies.' Sonny had raced ahead with Radar and was now eyeing a goat with two kids. She was eyeing him back in a distinctly unfriendly fashion and pawing the ground. I could sense that he was about to go and stroke her.

'Sonny, stay away,' Gail called sharply as we both raced to stop him but Radar was one step ahead of us, he took hold of Sonny's hand and led him away.

'She bite,' he said, snapping his teeth dramatically at Sonny.

'Why?' Sonny asked. 'I'm not going to hurt her.'

'She has babies, Sonny,' Gail explained. 'She is protecting her babies.' She turned to Radar. 'Thank you.'

He grinned and pointing to a small, intricately decorated archway said. 'Souk begins.'

I had never seen anything like it. I was completely dazed by the tiny alleyways and the stalls spilling out onto the pavements. We were in the covered souk and the air was hot and intense. I wanted to touch everything. I wanted to go into every shop. I wanted to buy everything I saw.

'I'm going to need a new suitcase.' I turned to Gail. 'I want every single one of these in every single colour.' I was eyeing up a row of kaftans woven in a soft cheesecloth fabric and embroidered with intricate white stitching. They were beautiful. 'I am never going to wear anything else, I'll have a different colour for every day of the week.'

'They are gorgeous, but more you than me.' She smiled.

'Nonsense, they're for everyone, they would suit everyone, that is their beauty.'

'I can't quite see it catching on in Chigwell.' Gail laughed.

'Well, you can be the trail blazer,' I said. 'How long have you lived in Chigwell?'

'Pretty much all my life.' She paused. 'In fact pretty much in the same house, gosh, that really does make me sound dull and boring, maybe my sister was right.'

'Well, prove her wrong and buy one of these kaftans.' I laughed.

'Only to look now.' Radar stopped me as I grabbed one from the rail. 'Just to look now, buying later after you have seen all.'

'Well I guess that sort of makes sense.' I acknowledged, reluctantly leaving behind the brightly coloured garments.

We meandered slowly around the endless network of alleyways for the next couple of hours. I was utterly entranced. It was all I'd ever dreamed of and more. Every section had its own speciality, we wandered past vivid hand-woven baskets, mountains of coloured pottery, exotic perfume shops, leather stalls displaying slippers, belts and handbags, stunning hand-beaten silverware and of course the inevitable carpets and rugs. I honestly felt as if I had entered an enchanted kingdom and I never wanted to leave.

'This way to square.' Radar stood on the corner of a small street. We had come out from the covered market and the sun was blinding.

'Thirsty, Mummy.' Sonny tugged on Gail's sleeve.

'Me too,' I agreed. 'Is there a café nearby, Radar?'

'Come to square, plenty places.'

Radar led us to a small café on the edge of the huge Jemaa El-Fna Square. It was impressive, everywhere I looked there was drama going on. I felt as if I was seated in a giant theatre with a cast of thousands. It was hypnotic.

The eerie notes from the flutes of the snake charmers mingled with the cries of the water sellers. Hawkers spread their goods on coloured rugs and entertainers were everywhere, performing magic tricks or practising their somersaults. Mopeds and horse-drawn carriages weaved carelessly around each other. A young henna tattoo artist approached our table and I simply couldn't resist. I held out my left hand.

'Sky, you can't be serious?' Gail looked astonished.

'I most certainly am,' I replied. 'I've always wanted one.'

The young lass held out a sheet with various designs. I beckoned Sonny over. 'Which one do you think, sweetheart?' Without hesitation he pointed to a picture of a snake curling down around the fingers and twisting around the wrist. 'Good choice.' I smiled at the artist and she grinned back.

'Are you not tempted, Gail?' I asked.

'Go on, Mummy.' Sonny was fascinated by the artist, he was watching her every move.

'Not today, darling.' She laughed.

Fifteen minutes later the young girl was finished and I was overjoyed at the result.

'I love it, it's stunning.' I held it out for admiration. 'How long will it last?'

'Two, maybe three week,' she replied, holding out her hand for money. I reached into my purse and saw Radar frown at the amount I was giving her but I didn't care. She had made me happy for a while, made me forget my problems and right now that was worth any amount.

CHAPTER TWELVE

I stood on the pavement waiting while Philippe paid the taxi driver. I was hot and tired and wished I was back in the shade of the riad courtyard. I'd had a wonderful morning but I was still feeling off balance and fragile, almost as if I were waiting for the next blow to strike me.

I had brought my sketch pad and pastels but doubted that I would use them, especially if Philippe was looking over my shoulder. I loathed painting when people were watching and again I felt a surge of irritation towards Beatrice for suggesting that Philippe accompany me.

'Shall we go in?' Philippe smiled at me and I forced myself to respond with some enthusiasm, I knew that I was being unreasonably churlish, everyone was being kind and I was behaving like a spoilt brat.

We walked through the entrance into the inner courtyard and I literally squealed with delight. All irritability and tiredness vanished in a second. Turquoise and blue mosaics framed a square fountain surrounded by dark terracotta tiles. The water gleamed and the colours shimmered in the sun.

'Oh my God, it's beautiful.' I turned with a wide smile.

'Sky, this is just the start, you haven't seen anything yet.' But I could tell he was pleased. I must have been very offhand in the car and I vowed to try and behave better.

I'd heard so much about the Majorelle Gardens. I had spent hours poring over the old photographs that my parents had taken and had been enchanted. From the moment I stepped inside I knew I wasn't going to be disappointed.

We ambled slowly along shady paths overhung with plants and trees from exotic origins. Pools and streams were filled with water lilies and lotus flowers. The birds sang and the air was filled with a sweet fragrance. We passed unusual cacti and walked to the Yves St Laurent memorial.

I honestly felt that I had entered paradise, the weight had lifted from my shoulders and I was living solely for the moment. There was no room for the torment of the past weeks. I felt quite dizzy with the beauty of it.

We rounded a corner to find a Moorish building painted in such an intense blue that it almost hurt my eyes to look at it. I stopped in my tracks and stared open-mouthed.

'Philippe, I have to draw this. Can we stop for a short while?' Without waiting for his answer I made my way to a small bench, pulling my sketch pad from my shoulder bag.

'Of course. I need to take the weight off my leg for a while.'

'Oh God, I'm so sorry.' I was filled with remorse. I hadn't given his injury a single thought. 'I've been so inconsiderate wanting to see everything, I should have thought of your knee.'

'No worries, it's good to exercise it.' He headed off to another bench in the shade. 'You won't want me watching over your shoulder, I'll nod off here for a while.'

I smiled gratefully at him but he had his back to me. Christ, I've become a real misery, I thought to myself. I'm in danger of becoming a self-centred drama queen. I was aware that I was wallowing in a trough of self-pity but I couldn't seem to find a way to get out.

Pushing all this to one side I piled my hair on top of my head, securing it with a pencil, and determinedly turned to my sketch pad.

I had no idea how long I had been sketching. Time always became meaningless when I was painting. I was desperate to capture the magic

of the place, and was drawing quickly and confidently, blocking in the bright primary colours knowing that I could blend and shade it later on. I had to work fast, the light was intense, almost harsh, and I was desperate to capture it before it changed. Sometime later in the week I would come back and paint the same scene in the soft hues of the evening.

'Sky, the sun is very hot and your neck is getting burnt.'

I started at the sound of his voice but didn't look up. 'I'm OK,' I replied, not really paying him attention.

'You've been in the sun almost an hour. I fell asleep otherwise I would have warned you sooner. Combination of the heat and painkillers, I suppose.'

'I'm fine,' I muttered, desperate to finish my work. Why couldn't he bugger off?

'I know from bitter experience that the back of the neck is a painful place to be burnt.'

I grunted, I wasn't really keen to engage in conversation

'You need to be careful, you have very fair skin.'

'Yes, thank you, Philippe, but I think I probably know my skin better than you.' Shit, I'd meant that as a joke but it came out harsher than I'd intended.

'And I think I probably know the sun better than you,' he replied, turning away.

God, he's so arrogant I thought. How long had he been standing behind me? Had he been observing me for ages? I sincerely hoped not.

However, I knew he was right, I could feel the prickling on the back of my neck, but contrarily I continued painting for another ten minutes just to spite him.

We drove back to the riad in silence. I was extremely embarrassed at my behaviour. My neck was throbbing like hell and I knew I'd been stupid and childish. He'd only been trying to help me and I had reacted like a petulant kid. I shuddered to imagine what he must have thought of me.

Beatrice was in the courtyard when we arrived back. She looked at us enquiringly but I was in no mood to stay and chat. Not only was I furiously ashamed by my awful behaviour but the afternoon sun had made me feel a bit sick.

'Thank you very much.' I smiled awkwardly at Philippe.

He nodded, looking equally awkward, and as I scurried away to the sanctuary of my room I could feel their eyes on me. I dreaded to think of what he would tell her. I didn't know why but I hated to think of her disapproval. Somehow, it very much mattered what she thought of me.

CHAPTER THIRTEEN

I awoke once more to the magical sound of the muezzin the following morning. I could get used to this, I thought. It was a glorious way to wake up.

I got out of bed and, cursing myself again for being such a bloody idiot, plastered more lotion onto my burnt neck. The lotion that Beatrice had given me was soothing but sadly had not prevented small blisters from forming. It wasn't a great look. I'd also slept badly, it had been impossible to find a comfortable position.

Unable to bear the weight of my hair on the raw skin, I piled it into a bun and tied a loose, light scarf around my neck. Grabbing my paints and sketch pad I went out onto the small terrace. The morning air was fresh and invigorating. I leant on the parapet and drank in the beauty of the sunrise, letting the fresh morning air cool and soothe me.

The night before had been strained to say the least. Nick had disappeared to eat at a local restaurant but before going he'd asked if he could cook everyone a meal the following evening. He wanted to try out some new recipes and would be delighted if they could be his guinea pigs. Bushara was lending him the kitchen. It was to be his treat. As ever his enthusiasm was infectious and everyone was more than happy to agree to a meal cooked by a chef with a Michelin star.

Everyone except me, that was. I had been planning on going to the big square. I was keen to see it in the evening which, according to Radar, was when it really came alive. But I knew that it would sound churlish if I refused so I had kept quiet.

I'd guessed that Nick was going out mainly because of me and I'd felt guilty and then I'd felt angry that I should be made to feel guilty. I was the bloody victim here and yet somehow I felt that I was the one constantly being judged.

Of course Philippe must have told Beatrice about my sunburn, hence the ointment, and I was mortified at the memory of my pathetic behaviour. Philippe had avoided talking to me throughout the evening and I couldn't really blame him. He hadn't mentioned my painting even though I knew he had seen it over my shoulder and for some reason that really irked me. I'd no idea why I felt slighted by his silence, but I did.

I was at sixes and sevens with the world and I felt raw and edgy. It was as if a different Sky had emerged over the last two weeks, it was like living with a stranger. A stranger I was starting to hate.

I shook myself, mentally and physically, and breathing in the crisp air settled down to my painting, hoping it would calm me and bring a measure of peace however temporary.

Nick was back in the market with Ibrahim. He was planning a veritable feast for everyone tonight and was hugely excited. He had spent all yesterday in the kitchen with Bushara and had loved every minute.

He felt slightly guilty about having such a great time when he thought of the real reason he had come to Marrakech, but it seemed impossible to talk to Sky on her own. He had envisioned having a real heart to heart with her, drinking copious amounts of wine, just like the old days and naively he'd convinced himself that somehow they would be able to sort this mess out. He realised now there was no way that was going to happen. He knew of course that she was hurting but he had been unprepared for such undisguised animosity.

He had no idea how to get through to her. The old Sky he knew better than she knew herself, he knew what she was thinking at any given moment, he knew what made her tick, he knew her every nuance, every expression, every heartbeat.

But this new Sky, this cold and distant Sky who was cloaked in aggression, this Sky he had no idea how to deal with. He had never seen her like this and knew that he was responsible for her behaviour. He had lain awake most of the night trying and failing to find a solution.

Philippe wondered how Sky was feeling this morning. She had clearly been suffering last night. He was angry with himself; she was going through a huge personal crisis, she was bound to be emotional and unstable. She deserved sympathy and he was appalled at his lack of sensitivity. He should have been more tactful. He had angered Sky by barging in like that and telling her what to do. She was old enough to look after herself, he had patronised her and made her feel stupid.

He had loved her passion for the gardens, it mirrored his own and he'd loved her enthusiasm. Before falling asleep on the bench he'd watched her painting, he'd seen the intense concentration on her face, smiled at how she constantly bit her bottom lip and the way she occasionally held out her hands, reaching towards the scene she was painting. He had only glanced at her work over her shoulder but it had been enough to make him realise that she was very talented.

He would find the time to apologise to her today, try and patch things up.

Something else had been worrying him all night and that was his beloved Emmaline. He knew that Claude and Celine were due back from holiday today and that meant that Emmie would have to leave the chateau and go back to the ghastly monstrosity her parents had built a few years ago.

She loathed living there. Sausage would certainly never be allowed inside the hallowed gates and it would break her heart to leave the little piglet. He could hardly bear to picture her sweet sad face. He should be there to help her but on the other hand knew that would only make it twice as difficult for both of them.

After the death of his parents in a car accident, Philippe's younger cousin Claude had lived at the chateau with Philippe and Stephanie. He had grown up with them, he was treated like a son by their parents. It was as much his home as theirs and therefore it had seemed quite natural for Claude to remain living there following his surprise marriage to Celine. The chateau was large, there was plenty of room, in fact they had the whole east wing.

However, a few years ago Celine had suddenly insisted on building their own house. It had made no sense to Philippe, but Celine was adamant and the house had been built half a mile down the road in the grounds, but not in sight, of the chateau. It was big and soulless and nobody bar Celine and Claude liked it and Philippe even had his doubts about Claude.

Emmie in particular hated it. Philippe knew that she felt uneasy in the modern house. In the chateau the furniture was old wood with soft contours and the worn oak floorboards and tatty rugs were comforting underfoot, whereas in the new house the modern furniture was hard and unforgiving and the shiny new floor tiles were cold and treacherous. Emmie was clumsy, unable to see very well without her glasses and was constantly bumping into the sharp corners of the designer furniture Celine had bought. Her legs were always a mass of purple bruises.

He knew how much she disliked her bedroom. The walls were painted a glacial designer grey and she felt claustrophobic in the bunk beds Celine had bought. She had confessed to her uncle her terror that the bed above would give way and crush her but she was not allowed to sleep on the top.

To be fair Philippe knew that Celine and Claude had thought that

Emmie would love the little beds and consequently were all the more angry when he mentioned that she was scared. They had cost a small fortune, he was told, so Emmie would just have to learn to live with them. They were certainly not going back to the shop.

The little girl never complained, never moaned or whined. She accepted everything life threw at her with a courage and stoicism that made Philippe desperately proud and desperately protective. He suddenly missed her very much. He swung his legs out of bed, wincing at the pain in his knee. He would ring her now, before she went to school. He would reassure her that she could still see Sausage morning and night and that he would remain her special pet for ever. He would tell her how very much he loved her.

Gail had been awake for most of the night practising endless conversations in her head with Sonny's father but each one sounded worse than the one before. She couldn't envisage him being anything other than furious, and if she were honest, with very good reason.

She imagined that he would want to meet Sonny, but how would he react? Come to think of it, which she clearly hadn't, how would Sonny react?

Was Tariq married by now? Did he have other kids? All these questions went round and round in her head and by the time morning came Gail felt physically sick. Her stomach was churning, her head throbbed and she was short of breath.

She was tempted not to go through with it, indeed had almost convinced herself that it was best for all concerned to let sleeping dogs lie, when Sonny stirred in his sleep. She got up to check on him and gazing at his familiar face, a face so similar to that of his father, she knew that she had no right to deny them the chance to get to know each other.

Beatrice was also up and about very early. She had a meeting with her architect this morning to look at the feasibility of extending the riad. She also had details of another property in the coastal town of Essaouira that she wanted to discuss with him. She had a large mug of coffee in front of her and the plans spread out over the study table but she was unable to give them her full attention.

Philippe always joked about her witch-like qualities. She certainly wasn't a witch but she was highly intuitive and right now her intuition was in overdrive. She had lain awake for a long time trying to interpret her feelings and pull together the threads of the stories unfurling under the roof of the riad.

Despite laughing at Philippe's notion of her as some sort of sorceress, she knew that her brain worked slightly differently from others'. Her grandmother had been famed for her ability to see into the future and her mother, the wife of an ambassador, had been an ice-cold beauty with an unnerving talent for mind-reading.

She'd taught Beatrice well. 'Watch their faces, Beatrice,' she used to tell her daughter. 'You have to watch for any nuance, watch for the darkening of the eyes, the furrow in the brow, the nervous laugh, the fluttering hand. They give so much away and if you pay attention then you will learn to read them easier than any book.' And so the young Beatrice had watched, seated on the outskirts of the grand parties her parents were famed for, she had sat and she had watched.

Every so often her mother would flit over and whisper things in her ear. 'Monsieur Rousseau is having an affair, the lady is in the room, can you guess who it is, Beatrice?'

Her father may have held the title of ambassador but there was no doubt about where the real power lay. Like a lioness watching a herd of antelope, her mother stalked her prey, she found the weakness and she pounced.

And Beatrice had learnt from her, she had learnt to decipher the slight tightening of the jaw, the almost imperceptible twitch in the eye, the tension in the shoulders and the quick flare of the nostrils. Her mother had used her skills to expose people and capitalise on their frailty, and while admitting it must have had its uses in the world her parents inhabited, it wasn't a quality that Beatrice admired. She had no intention of reading people in order to ruin them.

Hearing a noise outside she tipped back her chair and saw Sky stroking the cat. Even at a distance she could see that her guest looked tired and pale. The sunburn had been bad and Bea doubted she had slept much.

I'd been engrossed in my painting for over two hours, I wasn't overly happy with it but it was early days and I would continue the following morning. Right now I craved coffee and, if at all possible, some more ointment for my neck. There was no one in the courtyard but as if on cue I heard Beatrice call me.

I walked across to her and hovered in the study doorway.

'How are you feeling, cheri?' Beatrice smiled at me gently. 'Are you still very sore?'

'I certainly am,' I admitted. 'But whatever you gave me helped. I wonder if I could have some more?'

'Aloe vera mixed with argan oil.' Beatrice smiled. 'Argan oil is used here for just about everything. It won't be long before the rest of the world discovers it, if they haven't already.'

'It was extremely stupid of me. You and Philippe must think I'm an idiot.'

'Philippe should have looked after you better,' Beatrice said drily.

'He did try but I ignored him.'

'That's probably because he was being high-handed.'

'You know him very well.' I laughed. 'But I can't let you blame him. It was my fault, I was being very silly.' I shook my head. 'I hate

83

having such fair skin and I hate having it pointed out. My sister has inherited my father's olive complexion but sadly I always burn. One of these days I'll learn, in fact I think that day may have just arrived,' I shrugged.

'You have incredible skin, like a porcelain doll. The envy of many, I'm sure.'

I blushed and to draw her attention away pointed at the plans on the desk. 'Are you having work done?'

'I want to put in a roof-top pool and bar area.' Beatrice stood up and stretched like a cat. 'I'm having a meeting with my architect today.' She glanced at her watch. 'Sky, would you like to come and have a look and I'll show you what we envisage? It would be good to hear your thoughts.'

'I'd love to, it sounds amazing, but I need a coffee before I can think coherently.'

'Of course, we'll both take one up.'

'Oh, Beatrice, this is going to be fantastic!'

I was standing on the spot where the proposed bar and terrace was going to be. 'This is breathtaking.' Spinning around I gazed at the panorama. The snow-capped Atlas Mountains provided the background and in the foreground were the imposing minarets of the mosques interspersed with palm trees and the crowded rooftops of the red city.

'The view from here is beautiful at any time but I imagine the night time must be very special.' I was lost in the wonder of it all.

'I want it to be everything to everyone.' Beatrice was pacing around pointing out different areas to me. 'I want seclusion, I want romance, I want warmth and friendliness, I want to create an ambience of peace and tranquility amidst the vibrancy of the city.' She smiled. 'Imagine candles and lanterns, soft plump cushions and low, inviting sofas. I want people to be transported to another world.'

'And they will be,' I said with absolute sincerity. 'Your riad is magical, you've already created something very special here.'

'Well, I have had help, I have one of the best architects in Morocco. He is a man with a vision and talent.'

Something was bothering me, I couldn't quite put my finger on it but there was definitely something tugging at the back of my mind. I thought for a moment but nothing came to me. Closing my eyes, I began to visualise the space Beatrice had just depicted.

'I'm going to paint your rooftop terrace,' I suddenly shouted. 'I feel inspired. I'm going to try to put onto paper exactly what you've described to me. Would that be OK?'

'Sky, that would be wonderful.' Beatrice looked startled but seemed genuinely pleased. 'But don't you want to go exploring again today?'

'No, I've promised Gail that I'll look after Sonny this morning while she searches for his father,' I said without thinking.

There was a short silence.

'Bugger, I shouldn't have said anything.' I was annoyed with myself. 'Please, please keep that to yourself.'

'Of course I will,' Beatrice replied. 'I guessed that might be why she was here. I wanted to offer to help but didn't want to interfere.' She paused for a moment. 'Does she know where he lives?'

'I imagine she has an address for him. His name is Tariq." I broke off suddenly as Beatrice gasped. 'What is it, Beatrice?'

'My architect is Tariq.'

'Bloody hell, it can't be, can it? That would be just too much of a coincidence.'

'Sonny did look vaguely familiar, and now I know why,' Beatrice said, looking equally astonished.

'And I thought your architect looked familiar in the photo.' I was shaking. 'Beatrice, we have to tell her, when is he coming here?'

Beatrice looked at her watch. 'He'll be here any minute.

CHAPTER FOURTEEN

At the bottom of the stairs, Gail bent down to do up her laces, which had a habit of coming undone, and Sonny scampered on ahead to the far corner of the courtyard where the tortoises could usually be found.

Busy searching in his bag for his phone, Tariq didn't notice the small boy running into the courtyard. He located his phone and made his way towards the archway that led to the stairs at exactly the same time that Gail emerged into the courtyard.

They stood looking at each other for what seemed like an eternity.

Gail could feel her heart hammering and the blood pounded in her ears. She was shaking like a leaf and was having difficulty breathing. She wanted to throw herself into his arms at the same time as wanting to turn and run away as fast as possible. However, she was rooted to the spot so neither was an option. Tariq broke the silence first.

'Gail.' He stood drinking her in. 'What are you doing here?'

Her mouth was dry, she licked her lips but no words came out. Out of the corner of her eye she could see Sonny looking around, she had to say something. She tried again. 'I came to find you.' The words emerged cracked and hoarse but they sounded beautiful to Tariq. He felt a warmth begin to flow through his veins. Could this really be happening? There had never been a single day in the last five years when he had not thought of her, his English rose, his princess, and now here she was standing right before him.

'Why?' he asked softly. 'Why did you want to find me?'

Beatrice and I burst into the courtyard at precisely the same time as Sonny ran over towards his mother.

I looked from Gail to Tariq. They were both pale. Gail looked as if she had been turned to stone.

'Mummy, I can't find them, they've disappeared.' Sonny's little face was creased in disappointment. Gail remained silent and I watched as Sonny suddenly became aware of the intense gaze of the man standing opposite him. 'The tortosses have gone,' he explained, looking up at him.

Tariq said nothing but he looked questioningly at Gail who nodded imperceptibly. His mouth fell open as he levelled his astonished gaze back down at Sonny, who began to squirm under his keen scrutiny.

'Sonny?' Beatrice stepped forward. Sonny looked up at Beatrice's voice. 'Sonny, shall we go and feed Mimi?' Beatrice held out her hand. 'And Bushara has made some special cakes for you.'

Sonny looked up at Gail. He was a perceptive little lad and I could sense that he knew something was wrong.

Gail smiled gently down at him. 'Go on, Sonny, go with Beatrice and Sky, I've got to talk to, to talk to…' Her voice quivered slightly and I leapt in quickly.

'After breakfast, Sonny, I'm going to paint on the rooftop, I've got paints and crayons and a huge piece of paper, shall we do something together?'

Next to animals, drawing was another one of Sonny's great passions but still he hesitated until, with a grateful look at both Beatrice and me, Gail gently pushed him towards us. I took his hand, stealing a sideways glance at Tariq. They were as alike as two peas in a pod.

'For five years I've had a son I didn't know about.' Tariq stared at Gail. His face was unfathomable but his eyes glinted.

She nodded mutely.

'Why, Gail?' His voice was a whiplash. 'Why did you never tell me before?'

Tears rained down her cheeks. 'I was afraid,' she mumbled.

'Afraid of what?' He came straight back at her.

'Afraid you wouldn't want him, afraid that you would want him, afraid that you might come and take him away.' She sounded pathetic even to her own ears.

'Take him away?' Tariq echoed her last sentence with incredulity. 'We're not heathens here, Gail, this is a civilised country, I'm a civilised man, I'm not in the habit of baby-snatching.'

'I'm so sorry.' She brushed away the tears.

'I'm the one who is sorry, Gail,' Tariq exploded. 'I'm sorry that I've been denied my son for five years.' He slammed his hand down on the table. 'Five years that I'll never be able to get back.' He glared at her, his face so full of hurt and anger that she could barely look at him.

During the silence that ensued, Nick, caught in the hallway with his arms full of flowers, wondered whether he should make his presence known. He hated eavesdropping but hadn't felt able to interrupt.

Philippe, caught at the opposite side of the courtyard by the bottom of the stairs, felt similarly trapped. Before either of them could move Tariq spoke once more.

'And why now, Gail?' He spat the words out. 'Why now, after five years, do you suddenly decide to find me.'

'I don't know,' Gail sobbed. 'I just suddenly thought, I just thought...' She shook her head, unable to explain the madness that had led her here.

'How do I even know that you did come to find me?' Tariq was on another train of thought. 'Maybe this is just all coincidence? Maybe if I hadn't happened to be working here I would never have seen you again?'

'Tariq, I did come here to find you, please believe me.'

'I find it hard to believe anything you say right now,' he snarled. 'How long have you been here?' He was pacing around her. 'You've kept me in ignorance for five years so why should I trust anything you say?'

'How could I trust you after your letter?' Gail was suddenly angry, Tariq had to take part of the blame. 'What was I supposed to feel after that? You *"hoped I had enjoyed our interlude and wished me a good life"*...' He started to speak but it was Gail's turn to vent her pent up hurt and anger. 'You tell me, Tariq, are those the words of a man in love? Are those the words of man you can trust?' She was shaking uncontrollably as the emotions she had bottled up for five years came pouring out. 'You hurt me beyond belief, I loved you, I loved you with all my heart and you broke it.'

Tariq stared uncomprehendingly at her. 'You left *me*, Gail. You never returned my letters and then I heard you'd gone back to Simon. It was *you* who broke *my* heart.'

Gail stared back equally uncomprehending but before she could say anything there came a sneeze from the passageway.

Nick appeared in the courtyard his arms full of flowers and his face red and embarrassed. 'I'm so sorry.' He looked from one to the other. 'It's the flowers, I'm slightly allergic, I really wasn't eavesdropping, I was just sort of trapped in the hallway, didn't want to intrude.' He smiled nervously and began to sidle past them.

Philippe used this opportunity to emerge from his hiding place and Gail and Tariq suddenly found themselves caught in a pincer movement. It had all the elements of a Feydeau farce and Philippe couldn't help smothering a grin at the thought.

Tariq turned on his heel. 'Please tell Beatrice that I will come back this afternoon,' he said to no one in particular.

'Tariq we need to talk,' Gail said urgently.

'Later,' he replied curtly. 'I can't take any more right now.'

Nick, watching him go, saw the look of heartbreak on his face and turning around saw it mirrored on Gail's.

He made a quick decision. 'Ask Bushara to put these in water,' he said, thrusting the enormous bouquet of flowers into the arms of a bewildered Philippe before running out of the riad.

He burst out into the little street and spotted Tariq immediately. He was sitting on a low wall by the fountain, drawing deeply on a cigarette.

Nick sat down beside him, reaching into his pocket for his packet of cigarettes. 'My name is Nick.'

'The eavesdropper.'

'Not intentionally, I was trapped in an awkward situation.'

Tariq didn't respond.

'Gail came to Marrakech to find you,' Nick said, lighting up.' I've only know her a few days but she strikes me as a very honest, loving person.'

'She kept a secret from me for five years, how honest is that?'

'She's come to find you now though and that takes some courage.' Nick ran his hands through his hair. 'Look, all I'm saying is that you obviously mean a lot to each other. It's worth trying to sort things out.'

'I thought we meant the world to each other but I was wrong.' Tariq ground his cigarette into the earth.

'Did you ever try and get in touch with her these last few years?' Nick questioned.

'No.'

'Why?' Nick persisted.

'She was with someone else.'

'Did she tell you that?'

'No, her sister did.'

'So you never actually heard that from Gail?'

'No, but why would her sister lie?'

'I'm not saying she did, pal, I'm just pointing out that maybe there is blame on both sides, not just hers.'

'What the hell is all this to you?' Tariq turned to the tall red-haired man beside him.

Nick paused before replying. 'I've just made the most monumental cock-up of my life, I guess I don't like to see someone else doing the same.' He stood up and looked squarely at Tariq. 'Think about it, don't let love escape.'

Tariq stared back.

'I'm cooking a feast tonight,' Nick said unexpectedly. 'I'm a chef, I'm trying new recipes, you're welcome to come.'

'Thank you,' Tariq said slowly and they both knew he wasn't talking about the feast.

CHAPTER FIFTEEN

Tariq's father and younger sister stared at him open-mouthed. Tariq hadn't meant to tell them. He had gone home for some quiet reflection but when he'd seen them sitting having breakfast it had suddenly all come flooding out.

'I have absolutely no idea what to say,' his sister exclaimed after a short pause. 'But I guess congratulations is the most appropriate thing.'

Tariq remained silent. His sister got up gracefully despite her advanced pregnancy and went to hug him. 'But you have certainly stolen my thunder.' She laughed softly. 'Here I am pregnant with the first grandchild and you suddenly march in and announce that you have a five-year-old son.' She shook her head. 'How am I supposed to follow that?' She was desperate to lighten the mood, Tariq was as white as a sheet and she could see the veins throbbing in his neck. It had the desired effect, the glimmer of a small smile reached his face.

'I apologise, Jasmina.'

'Why now?' His father, Amir, finally found his voice. 'Why now, after five years?'

'I'm not sure, she said she was scared, she was worried that I might steal him away.' His face darkened. 'Although why on earth would she think that? I mean, how could she possibly think I could do that?'

'When you are pregnant you're not thinking straight.' Jasmina stroked her stomach. 'All you want to do is protect your baby, nothing else matters.'

A look of terrible sadness came over Tariq's face. 'I've missed five years of my son's life, five precious years, how could she not have told me?'

'You should have gone after her, son, you should have chased her, I told you that at the time.' Tariq looked at him in amazement. What his father had actually said was, 'You are better off without her, I have any amount of women queuing up to marry you.'

'I thought she had gone back to her old boyfriend.' Tariq was desperately trying to understand what had happened. 'That's what her sister said, I can remember.'

But Jasmina interrupted his thoughts. 'What's he like, Tariq?' She was suddenly excited. 'What does Sonny look like?'

'Exactly like me.' Tariq grinned. 'He is just like me.' His face was shining with joy.

'You have to bring them here, they must come and live here,' Amir announced.

'Papa, for goodness' sake, she may not want to come and live here.' Tariq's brow darkened once again. 'It's not that straightforward. They have a life in England.'

'You are the boy's father, it is only natural that they come here to live. You have a duty towards him now.' His father looked him in the eye. 'You have to be firm, Tariq, you have to be the master and make the decisions.'

Said the man who had deferred to his wife from the moment they were married to the moment she had died. Tariq and Jasmina exchanged an amused glance.

'Something isn't right here.' Tariq was struggling to come to terms with everything. 'Gail never said anything about a boyfriend but that's definitely what her sister told me and if that wasn't true then why the hell didn't she try…'

He got no further. The earth suddenly felt as if it were trembling beneath his feet and grabbing the nearest chair he sat down abruptly. His carefully ordered world seemed to be spinning out of control.

'You have to go and speak to her, Tariq.' Jasmina laid a cool hand on his brow. 'There has obviously been some terrible misunderstanding and you must make sure that doesn't happen again.'

Back at the riad Nick was replaying the conversation with Tariq.

'He said my sister told him what?' Gail gawped at Nick. 'She told him I was with someone else? Is that what Tariq told you?'

'That's what he said,' Nick replied.

'But why would Dawn tell him that?' Gail continued. 'It just doesn't make sense.'

'I don't know, sweetheart, I'm just telling you what he said, but it seems clear that there has been some sort of misunderstanding.' He paused for a moment. 'I've invited him tonight. I hope that's OK.'

But I could tell that Gail wasn't really listening.

'I need to phone Dawn, I need to ring her now.' She was shaking like a leaf.

'Sit down for a moment, Gail, you're as white as a sheet. Drink some water.' I led her gently to a chair before turning slowly to Nick. 'That was a kind thing to do,' I said softly.

He opened his mouth to reply but before he got a chance Beatrice came out of the kitchen.

'Nick, a man has arrived at the back door with baskets of chickens, pigeons and half a lamb. Bushara is dumbfounded.' She turned to Gail. 'Cheri, are you alright? I feel somehow responsible, it was terrible that you had to meet Tariq like that.'

I nodded in agreement.

'I need to go and make a phone call.' Gail slowly stood up. 'Beatrice, Sky, can I ask you to look after Sonny a little while longer?'

'Use the phone in my study, Gail, if it is an important call,' Beatrice said immediately. 'The mobile signal is bad here and you need to talk and hear properly. I will bring in some mint tea.'

Gail looked around at us all. 'You are being so kind, I can't thank you enough.'

'Nick, have we got the King of Morocco and family coming for dinner tonight?' Philippe had wandered in from the kitchen.

'I may have got a touch carried away,' Nick admitted sheepishly.

'You'll need more help than Bushara to prepare all that,' Beatrice said. 'And I am a liability in the kitchen, I'm afraid.'

'I, on the other hand, am rather good. I mean obviously not up to your standards,' Philippe hastened to add. 'But my knife skills are OK, I'm more than happy to lend a hand.'

As Nick smiled at him gratefully I could see his eyes automatically search me out. I couldn't count the number of times I'd assisted him in the kitchen, the two of us chatting and chopping, a bottle of wine invariably open beside us.

I saw his plea and was about to turn away from him when suddenly I heard myself saying, 'I'll help.'

Nick looked surprised and so was I. Being stuck in the kitchen with Nick and Philippe was the last thing I felt like right now. What on earth had prompted me to volunteer?

CHAPTER SIXTEEN

Gail was trying to marshal her thoughts before phoning Dawn. She couldn't really believe that her sister would have misled Tariq and deliberately lied to her, but nonetheless a small, persistent worm of suspicion was gnawing away at her.

Vague memories came drifting back to her. She recalled her sister's fury when she had split up with Simon and her disbelief when despite her pleas she never returned to him. '*But I thought that if Tariq was no longer in the picture we'd go back to how life was before.*'

There had to be a rational explanation for this. Dawn would have an explanation, the alternative was too hideous to contemplate. She dialled Dawn's number.

The persistent ringing of the mobile gradually pierced Dawn's sleep. Her head was pounding and her mouth felt dry and raw, the hangover was kicking in quick. She rolled over, glancing briefly at the phone to make sure Gail's name was not flashing, and answered blearily.

'Yeah.'

'Dawn, it's me.'

Dawn sat bolt upright, shit, Gail must have been phoning from another number. 'Hi,' she mumbled. 'Listen I'm running a bit late, can I call you back?' She desperately tried to inject a sense of urgency into her tired voice.

'This will only take a few minutes.' Gail looked at her watch, there was no way her sister would be running late for anything at nine thirty on a Sunday morning. 'Just a quick question that I need clearing up.' She couldn't even be bothered with the usual pleasantries. 'Do you remember talking to Tariq about me, Dawn?' She paused a second. 'Specifically about me being with someone else?'

'Talking to who?' Dawn feigned confusion although her heart was hammering.

'Tariq,' Gail snapped. 'Sonny's father, Dawn. Don't pretend you don't know who I'm talking about.'

'Jesus, Gail, it was years ago, how the hell am I supposed to remember anything from back then?' Dawn lied, remembering exactly what she had said and why.

'It's very important, Dawn.' Gail's voice was like steel.

'So you've found him then, have you? What's he been saying about me then?' She was playing for time. This was exactly the scenario she had been dreading.

'He's not said anything directly to me yet.' Gail gratefully accepted the tea Beatrice handed her. 'I wanted to hear your side of the story.'

Dawn pulled on a gown and began to make her way downstairs to the kitchen. She needed tea and headache pills, she simply couldn't think straight. 'You're making a big thing over nothing as usual, Gail.' She tried to sound light-hearted.

Gail didn't say a word.

The silence became uncomfortable before Dawn stammered. 'I, er, honestly, well I can't really remember what I said, I mean maybe I mentioned something about Simon and you, just to make him jealous, you know, just to help you,' she blustered.

'When?' Gail asked quietly. 'When did you say this?'

'Jesus, I don't know, ages after he'd left here.'

'After he'd left the UK?' Beads of sweat were forming on Gail's brow.

'Enough of the bloody Spanish inquisition!' Dawn yelled, grabbing a packet of paracetamol. 'He didn't say where he was, how the hell was I supposed to know where he was?'

'So this was on the phone, Dawn? You were talking to Tariq on the phone?' The enormity of what Dawn had done was slowly beginning to sink in.

Too late Dawn realised her mistake. 'Yeah, maybe, I mean I guess it must have been, I'm sure I told you.'

'No, Dawn, you didn't, you certainly didn't tell me.' Gail spoke slowly. 'You know you didn't.'

'Well, I probably did you a huge favour.' Dawn was desperately fighting to regain control. 'I mean he never got in touch again so he couldn't have been that bloody keen, could he?' She was making a mess of this and she knew it. If only her head wasn't throbbing, if only she didn't feel quite so sick, if only she hadn't drunk quite so much last night.

Somewhere in the background a clock chimed. Gail heard it and caught her breath.

'Dawn, where are you?' she asked suddenly.

'In the kitchen,' Dawn said without thinking.

'In whose kitchen?'

There was a long silence before Dawn replied. 'I, um, well I came over last night to see if everything was OK.' Christ this was fast becoming a nightmare. 'You know you asked me to keep an eye on the place and it, well, it just seemed easier to um, well to stay the night.' A noise in the doorway made her turn around.

'Hi there.' Her mate stood yawning. 'Any chance…' But Dawn cut her off, quickly putting her finger to her lips.

'Who else is there?' Gail's voice was ice cold.

'Oh, just Mandy, she came over with me, so she um, well she stayed too.' Dawn was frantically signalling Mandy to shut the door before Gail could hear the others but it was too late, there came a loud yell from the lounge.

It was the final straw for Gail. A red mist descended over her.

'I want you and your friends out of the house within half an hour, Dawn. I want you to post the key into next door and I will ring them to make sure you do.'

'Bloody hell, Gail, I'm your sister, we're not burglars or anything.' She rolled her eyes at her mate who was looking startled, she had been under the impression that this had all been arranged beforehand.

'Half an hour, Dawn, or I will ask Margaret to call the police.' She put the phone down and before she could change her mind dialled another number.

'Margaret, hello, it's Gail here.'

'Hello, Gail, is everything OK?' Her next-door neighbour sounded alarmed.

'No not really, Margaret.' Gail took a deep breath. 'I need a favour. Will you ask Jeff to go next door in half an hour and make sure that my sister and her friends leave my house and please get my key.'

'He will do it with pleasure,' her neighbour replied with feeling, delighted that Gail was finally seeing sense.

'I've told Dawn that I've asked you to call the police if she doesn't leave.'

'They were making that much noise we nearly called them last night.'

'I'm so sorry, Margaret, so very sorry.'

'It's not your fault, sweetheart. Don't worry, I'll text you to say they've gone.' She hesitated before asking, 'Are you having a nice time?'

Gail smiled grimly. 'Nice is not exactly the word I would use right now, Margaret.'

She put the phone down and buried her head in her hands. She suddenly felt exhausted.

'Gail?' I stood in the doorway of the study. 'Are you OK?' She looked anything but and I felt desperately sorry for her.

'You think you know someone, you love them, you think they love you and then you find out they've deceived you. How could I have got it so wrong?' She looked up slowly.

'Tell me about it,' I replied with feeling.

Gail shot me a quick sympathetic smile. 'I threatened to call the police.'

'Because she betrayed you?' That seemed a bit over the top.

'No, because she is in my house without my permission.' Gail shook her head. 'It doesn't sound much but it was the final straw.'

'Beatrice has put breakfast out for us, come and tell me all about it.' I needed more coffee.

'It can't possibly still be that early, I feel like I've lived a whole year this morning.'

'So what did your sister say? Did you say her name was Dawn?' I asked as we made our way outside.

'Yes, her name is Dawn. She was born at six in the morning and I was born during a storm. I don't think my mother was blessed with too much imagination.' She gave a half-hearted grin. 'Technically speaking she's actually my half-sister.' Gail paused but I smiled encouragingly. I was keen to hear everything. 'My father walked out on Mum just after I was born and we never saw him again. She re-married some years later.' Again Gail hesitated. 'He walked out when Dawn was a year old.'

'Your mother knew how to pick them.' I raised my eyebrows.

'She certainly did,' Gail agreed. 'Several years later Mum died and I gave up university and came home to look after Dawn.'

'Oh, Gail, how incredible of you.'

'Not really, I didn't feel I had a choice and anyway I loved Dawn.'

'It sounds like she's chosen a funny way to repay you.'

'I can't believe what she's done, I simply don't understand it.'

'Maybe she was worried about losing you?'

'Maybe she was worried about me losing a very rich boyfriend.' Gail gulped the strong mint tea. 'I can't think about it anymore, my head is spinning.' She suddenly leapt up. 'Christ, where's Sonny?'

I grabbed her hand and pulled her back down. 'Calm down, Gail, Sonny is having the time of his life watching Nick butchering meat.' I smiled. 'He's got all the makings of a forensic pathologist.'

'Thank you, Sky, thank you so much. I'm sorry, I'm just all over the place.'

'You've had a shock Gail, a huge shock, it's not really surprising.'

'How are you?' Gail changed the subject.

'I have terrible sunburn on my neck which is totally my fault, I behaved rather stupidly and will have to eat humble pie with the arrogant Frenchman.'

'Do you think he's arrogant?' Gail looked surprised. 'I think he's gorgeous.'

'I guess he's sort of good-looking in a very arrogant French way,' I said, picturing Philippe's wavy hair pushed back with sun glasses, his Mediterranean complexion, his effortless elegance. Yes, he was good-looking, if you liked that sort of thing. Personally I didn't. I preferred blond hair and blue eyes. Dismissing him I turned back to Gail. 'I don't know why but I've offered to help Nick in the kitchen, which is the last thing I want to do.' I paused and shook my head.

'You are trying hard to hate him but you can't because you love him.' Gail's eyes filled with tears. 'I'm the opposite, I'm finding it hard to love and rather easy to hate at the moment.'

'Christ, we make a right pair, don't we?'

Gail was stopped from replying by the appearance of Beatrice.

'I wondered if you needed anything?' She looked from me to Gail.

'Our sanity, Beatrice.' I sighed. 'We both need our bloody sanity.'

'And so does Bushara. Nick has taken over the kitchen completely, he is singing at the top of his voice and Sonny is in seventh heaven.'

CHAPTER SEVENTEEN

'Tell Sonny the tale behind the ginger kitten,' Beatrice said to Philippe. Philippe had been telling us about the chateau and Sonny's eyes were like saucers at the thought of piglets, dogs and hens.

And, I have to admit, so were mine, it sounded like a magical place. I wasn't sure whether it was all true or whether he was making it up for Sonny's benefit. We were all gathered in the courtyard having pre-dinner drinks.

'A kitten?' Sonny asked. 'There's a kitten as well as all the other animals?' He shot a glance at his mother who rolled her eyes in despair.

'Home is going to seem like the most boring place on earth after this,' she whispered to me.

'Yes, Sonny, we're getting a new kitten.' Philippe smiled at the little lad.

Stephanie had told him about the new ginger kitten on the phone. Philippe suddenly frowned, his sister had been in a strange mood, talking non-stop without listening to his questions. He remembered that Bea's face had seemed rather grim when she handed him the phone after her conversation with Stephanie. There was something he wasn't being told and he needed to get to the bottom of it but right now Sonny was tugging at his sleeve.

'Tell me the story,' he demanded. 'Please,' he added quickly before his mother could prompt him.

'I want to hear it too.' Nick grinned and pulled the young lad onto his knee. 'Let's hear the story, Philippe, and then I'll fetch the canapés and you can pour your wine.'

'Once upon a time there lived a beautiful gypsy princess called Rosa. She had long black hair which fell to her waist, flashing dark eyes and a shapely figure. She was promised to be married to a gypsy prince from a powerful family. The young prince was as handsome as Rosa was beautiful but Rosa knew that beneath the good looks lay a cold heart. His only real love was power and wealth. She had no wish to be married to him but they had been betrothed since they were children and Rosa could see no way out of the marriage. As the wedding day drew nearer her heart became heavier.

One day while walking in the countryside she heard music, such sweet melodious music the like of which she had never heard before, and a beautiful voice that made her heart sing.

She rounded a corner and there sat upon a rock was a young man playing a guitar. He looked up and smiled at her with eyes that were as blue as the deep blue sea beyond. He continued to play and to sing and she sat down and listened.

He played until all her troubles had melted away and she was filled with happiness. The birds in the trees stayed silent to listen, a hedgehog rolled over on his bed of leaves and a small fieldmouse sighed contentedly. He wove a magic spell and when he had finished she knew that she was his for ever.

When she announced that she was not going to marry her intended there was confusion and wrath in her gypsy camp. Her father pleaded and begged her to reconsider but she remained resolute and her mother was secretly relieved.

Furious that they had been shamed, the family of the handsome gypsy prince cursed her.

The young gypsy princess knew the power of the spell and was frightened. But that night at the stroke of midnight her mother came to her rescue. She presented Henri, for that was the name of the young musician, with a ginger cat.

She told him that if he always kept a ginger cat by his side then no *harm would come to them. The ginger cat would ward off evil but without the ginger cat they would no longer be protected. Then the black magic would be able reach them and their lives would be doomed.*

Henri promised solemnly that he would heed her words and guard her precious daughter.

And from that day forward there has always been a ginger cat by his side and they have lived happily ever after.

The End.

Everyone applauded when he finished.

'It gets more dramatic every time you tell it, Philippe.' Beatrice smiled.

'It's beautiful.' I leapt up from the table. 'I want to paint the whole story.' I had been captivated by the tale and could already imagine translating it onto paper. I wanted to run away and start immediately.

'How much of it is true?' I turned to Philippe. He looked surprised at my enthusiasm.

'Pretty much all of it,' he replied. 'There are obvious embellishments but the facts are true.'

'And who are Henri and Rosa?'

'Henri is my right-hand man and Rosa runs the chateau.' Philippe smiled. 'Her flashing eyes remain the same although the dark hair is now dusted with silver but when Henri starts to sing the world still stops to listen. They remain blissfully in love and the ginger cat wards off the curse.'

'I want to be cussed.' Sonny slid down from Nick's lap.

'Cursed, Sonny, not cussed.' Nick grinned. 'Two very different things, and why would you want to be cursed?'

'Coz then I would always have a ginger cat,' he replied as if it were the most obvious thing in the world.

'Well then, I will have to think of a particularly good curse for you.' He smiled at the young lad. 'Who else lives at your chateau, Philippe?'

'My sister Stephanie. She sadly lost her husband not long after she was married, she sold their house, ploughed the money into our business and moved back in with her son Luc.' He ran his hand through his hair. 'She has been invaluable, she has the best palate of us all, and Luc is now travelling the world learning the wine trade, ready to take over when I am old and grey.' He glanced over at me. 'Which according to Sky is about now.' He grinned as he said it but I felt embarrassed.

Tonight he was simply dressed in jeans and a white linen shirt, his hair was curling onto his neck, his hazel eyes were teasing me and his face was alive with the passion of his story. It was hard to believe that I had thought him geriatric. I desperately wanted to respond in a light-hearted fashion but no words came. I just stood there rather awkwardly.

'Are your folks still around?' Nick filled in the gap.

'My father is sadly no longer with us but my mother certainly is, she's actually English and at the moment spends her time flitting between the two countries.'

'Ah, hence the reason for your excellent English,' Gail said.

'She was insistent that we all spoke both languages, including a reluctant Rosa and Henri.' Philippe chuckled at the memory. 'I'm trying to do the same with Emmie.'

'Is Emmie your daughter?' I asked.

'No, Emmie is Celine's child.'

'But he couldn't love her more if she was his own.' Beatrice grinned. 'He dotes on her, well, to be fair we all do.'

'How long have you known Celine?' I asked. For some reason it hadn't occurred to me that he would be in a relationship.

'How long?' Philippe was puzzled. 'I've no idea, I've known her for years.'

Beatrice smiled to herself. Sky had completely misread the

situation. She was about to put her right but was interrupted by Sonny.

'How old is she?'

'Emmie or Celine?' Philippe smiled. 'Emmie is nine years old, Sonny. But Emmie is a bit different from other children. You see, when she was born she didn't have enough oxygen.' He paused for a moment. 'That means she's a bit slower at learning things than you, but she's patient and she tries very hard.' His voice was so full of love and understanding that I was taken aback. I was seeing a new side to Philippe tonight.

'But she has lots of pets,' Sonny said in a voice that implied that more than made up for being a bit slow.

'You like animals, don't you, Sonny?' Tariq leant forward.

Sonny nodded.

'And which is your favourite?' Tariq asked him.

'I doesn't know every animal,' Sonny replied seriously. 'I like dogs, I like these tortosses and the goat what was outside.' He paused and then solemnly shook his head. 'I doesn't have a favourite.'

'You love the donkeys in the field near us,' Gail said.

'I know someone else who likes donkeys,' Nick said, standing up.

'Who?' Sonny demanded.

Nick looked towards me.

I frowned, it annoyed me when he tried to recapture our old relationship. Every time he brought up something from our shared past it only reminded me of how much I had lost.

Sonny was looking expectantly at me. 'Is donkeys your favourite, Sky?'

'Well, when my sister and I were little, about your age, Sonny, my father gave us both a donkey. They had been rescued from a very horrid person who hadn't looked after them very well. They were our Christmas present and we called them Mary and Joseph.'

'Well thank you very much,' Gail glared at me and groaned in despair. 'As if cats, tortoises and piglets were not sufficient you now have to introduce a donkey!'

'Do you still have them?' Sonny asked me.

'No, darling, they died a while ago, but we now have several others, we all became rather hooked on them, especially my father and grandmother.'

'And what about your mother?' Philippe smiled at me. 'Doesn't she have a say in it?'

'My mother died when I was little.' I paused. 'The donkeys were given to us the first Christmas we were without her.'

'Oh, Sky, I'm so sorry, how tactless of me.'

'Not at all, you weren't to know,' I said quickly. 'It was a long while ago.'

'Well, your chateau sounds enchanting, Philippe,' Gail said quickly to cover any awkwardness. 'Not too many families live all together like that in the UK.'

'It must sound a bit crazy to you but it works for us.'

'It sounds wonderful rather than crazy,' Gail said a touch wistfully. 'It must be lovely having your family around you.'

I looked over at her and felt a wave of pity. Hers can't have been an easy life. She was a brave lady and once again I felt in awe of her courage. Whatever my problems I'd always had my family whereas Gail appeared to have no one. Of course that may all be about to change, I thought, and I glanced over at Tariq who had remained fairly quiet but who had not once taken his eyes off Gail and Sonny. I prayed for her sake that despite the inauspicious start this morning things would work out second time around. She deserved it, they both did.

'Come and eat the canapés.' Nick motioned them to the large table. 'And we have Chateau Fontaine wine courtesy of Philippe.'

'Chateau Fontaine, as in Riad Fontaine.' Gail smiled. 'Who stole the name from whom?'

'It is Philippe's surname and even though I'm technically no longer entitled to it he allows me to use it here and for my hotel in Paris.' Beatrice smiled. 'My maiden name is Pignal, which is far less appealing. Pour some wine, Philippe, let them taste the nectar that is Chateau Fontaine.'

CHAPTER EIGHTEEN

Gail got up to go to the table but Tariq drew her to one side.

'I'd very much like Sonny to come and meet my family tomorrow. Would that be alright?' Tariq couldn't wait to show his boy off to his father and sister.

Gail felt a wave of panic engulf her. 'I'm not sure, he's um, well he's only just met you, isn't it too soon?' She stammered.

'No, Gail, it's too late,' Tariq replied curtly.

'But he doesn't even know who you are.' She felt dangerously close to tears.

'Well, we can tell him together tomorrow.'

'I don't know, Tariq, I'm not sure, I mean he's so young, he can't go without me.'

'Of course he can't go without you.' Tariq was angry. 'Credit me with some sense, Gail, of course I'm not suggesting that I take him on my own.' He glared at her. 'I assure you I'm not going to kidnap him, Gail, bring Sky if you're worried.' There was a steely look in his eyes that Gail recognised from their son.

The short time they had spent together that afternoon had been fraught. She had told him about Dawn and he had been horrified.

'Why on earth would she lie? Why would she do something like that?'

'I don't know, I don't really understand it either.' She paused. 'Well, actually, maybe I do but I'm trying very hard not to believe it.'

He looked puzzled.

'I think she preferred the lifestyle that she thought was on offer with Simon.'

'That can't be true?' Tariq was genuinely shocked. 'She can't be that selfish, surely?'

'I'm beginning to think that maybe she is.' Gail spoke very softly. 'In fact, I think deep down I've know that for some time. I've just been burying my head in the sand.' She ran her hands through her hair.

Suddenly another thought occurred to her, something that had been nagging at her since her conversation with Dawn. 'She did point out though that you'd made no effort to get in touch with me.' She looked accusingly at Tariq. 'Why did you never try and find out if that was the truth?'

'I never thought she was telling anything but the truth,' Tariq answered. 'No one in my family would ever lie like that, we weren't brought up that way.'

'And are you suggesting that is how I brought up Dawn?' Gail was furious.

'I'm not suggesting anything,' Tariq retorted, equally furious. 'I'm merely answering your question. It simply never occurred to me that your sister was lying.'

There was a long silence. Both of them were thinking of the consequences of Dawn's actions, and of what might have been had she not lied.

Then Tariq spoke. 'I'm sorry, Gail, I didn't mean to criticise you. I'm sure you did a wonderful job of bringing up Dawn.'

'I'm not,' she replied sadly.

'I could ask you the same question though,' Tariq said. 'Why did you never try and get in touch with me?'

'After reading your curt letter I assumed you wanted nothing more to do with me. I mean, what else was I supposed to think? I imagined that you had met someone else.'

'How could you have possibly thought that?'

'The same way that you thought I had gone back to Simon.'

'And has there been anyone else?' Tariq asked hesitantly.

'A full-time job and a child doesn't really leave that much time for anyone else,' Gail replied. She didn't add that no one could possibly have matched up to Tariq. The bar had been set very high.

Tariq let out the breath he hadn't realised he had been holding. 'And you?'

'My father tried very hard to marry me off but so far I have managed to resist.' He didn't add that not a day had gone by when he hadn't thought of Gail, his English princess.

'So is that OK, Gail?' Tariq repeated his request, breaking in on her reverie. 'Will you and Sonny come to the house tomorrow?' He was impatient. 'And Sky, if it will make you feel safer?' he added.

'Yes, I guess so,' she replied uncertainly. 'But I'm not sure about telling him. Meeting his father, grandfather and aunt all in one day may be too much even for someone with Sonny's sanguine disposition.'

'Well, you know our son better than me,' Tariq conceded. He paused for a moment before repeating the words softly to himself. 'Our son.'

'This looks amazing, Nick,' Beatrice said. 'You've worked so hard.'

'You ain't seen nothing yet.' Nick grinned. 'But I did have help. Philippe was my sous chef, Radar proved alarmingly deft with a knife and, of course, Bushara was overseeing everything. We lost Sky to her painting but we made do without her.' Nick smiled gently over at me. I could sense he was trying to be kind but it wasn't working.

I'd had every intention of helping in the kitchen. I had gone back to the rooftop just to put the finishing touches to my picture but as usual had lost track of time and suddenly it had been late afternoon.

I'd raced to the kitchen but had found that most of the work had been done. Philippe was sitting resting his leg with a glass of beer in his hand and Nick and Bushara were in earnest conversation over the lamb tagine. They all looked cosy and content. Nick of course had told me not to worry, that my painting was more important, and yet again I had immediately felt wrong-footed. I had let him down. Once more I felt that everyone was judging me and had found me wanting

I had determined to compensate by dressing up for the special dinner, but I'd fallen asleep and had woken with only fifteen minutes before kick-off. Desperate not to be late, I'd had a rushed shower, braided my wet hair into one long side plait and smeared on a quick coat of lipstick.

There had been no time to iron the beautiful long linen dress I'd planned on wearing, and I certainly couldn't have worn it as it was: linen may be fashionable slightly creased, but this garment had been rolled into a ball in the bottom of my suitcase and it showed. Packing had never been my strong point. So I had to make do with a simple T-shirt dress and flat espadrilles. I'd wound strings of beads around my neck and then immediately taken them off as they touched my sensitive skin. I'd tied them around my waist instead and draped floaty scarves over my shoulders. At the last minute I'd grabbed a flower from the vase and stuck it in my hair, but it was a far cry from the sophisticated look I'd been aiming for and I'd felt unattractive and childish.

However, I had managed to walk into the courtyard on the dot of seven o'clock.

'My God, Nick, these are incredible,' Gail said, reaching for a chargrilled red pepper stuffed with yogurt and pistachios.

'I'm impressed, Nick.' Philippe was licking his lips.

I watched Nick beam, nothing gave him more pleasure than seeing people enjoy his food. 'I will return the compliment, Philippe,' he said. 'This wine is bloody marvellous.' He swirled it around his glass once more and sipped appreciatively.

'I'll second that,' I said, helping myself to another glass. 'I find rosé dangerously easy to drink in the sun, not that I find it difficult in the rain either.'

Philippe smiled at me and said, 'Wait until you try the red.'

'You should use this in your restaurant, Nick,' Beatrice said.

'Maybe I should.' Nick nodded slowly. 'It's being redesigned at the moment so maybe a new opening and a new wine list.'

Beatrice was instantly alert. Ideas flew rapidly into her mind, she was itching to think about them but now was not the time so instead she let them gently settle, waiting to be sifted and analysed.

'Who taught you to cook?' Tariq asked. He was also clearly impressed.

'Well, I've been lucky, I've worked under some top chefs,' Nick replied. 'But I guess I really owe my love of cooking to Nonna, Sky's Italian grandmother.' He glanced quickly in my direction. 'I could cook fresh pasta before I could even spell my own name.' He smiled. 'She was an amazing cook and a huge inspiration.'

'And how about you, Sky?' Beatrice turned to me. 'Did Nonna also inspire you to cook?'

I opened my mouth but Nick got there before me.

'No, Sky was an artist even then.' He laughed. 'She was much more interested in what it looked like than what it tasted like. Actually, we…' He trailed off lamely but I knew exactly what he'd been going to say. He'd been going to say that we made a great team. He always said that. The despair I felt was like a physical pain.

'I'll just go and check on the rest of the meal.' Nick departed abruptly without glancing in my direction.

I stood up and walked towards the pool before anyone could see the tears in my eyes, but I should have known that nothing got past Beatrice. She followed me out and taking my hand said gently, 'It will be OK, Sky. Things will get better.'

I didn't trust myself to speak.

'You think you are broken-hearted but I don't think you are,' she suddenly said.

I stared at her. 'Really?' I was bloody livid. 'Well, thank you for pointing that out, makes me feel much better, can't think how I got that so wrong.'

Unfortunately she seemed undeterred by my sarcasm. 'To have your heart broken you have to give it in the first place.' She laid her hand on my shoulder. 'Something tells me that you never gave your heart to your husband.' She paused.

'Wow,' I said slowly. 'You've certainly got it all worked out.' I took a deep breath, trying to control myself. 'And there I was thinking I was devastated. I'll bow down to your superior judgment and stop being sad immediately.' I tried to sound light-hearted but inside I was seething. How dare Beatrice have the audacity to tell me what I was feeling?

I turned back to the table and grabbed the wine bottle. Why did no one seem to understand me? I poured myself a large glass of wine.

'Sky, I'm so sorry.' Beatrice was beside me. 'Trust me, I am only trying to help.'

'Well, it's not working.' I tried to smile to take the anger out of my words but failed so I gulped down my wine instead. I could sense Beatrice starting to say something, but thankfully she thought better of it and wisely left me alone. As if I wasn't going through enough without some meddling mind-reader telling me my heart wasn't broken.

I felt terribly alone. I wished I was anywhere but here. I had a desperate longing to be back in Scotland, back in the huge kitchen with the fire burning. I wanted to smell my father's pipe smoke and Nonna's cooking.

Out of the blue a thought came bursting into my mind. With sudden clarity I remembered Nonna saying, 'Sky, *cara*, Miles isn't the one for you, be sure of what you are doing.'

I had been furious at the time and things had been frosty for a while, but it was impossible to stay angry with my warm-hearted grandmother for long. She had never mentioned it again and those words had been forgotten – until now.

My thoughts were starting to spin out of control. I felt confused and disorientated and wasn't sure that I could face the meal. I really didn't think that I could keep it together for much longer but I had to, I had to get my act together. Christ, I couldn't break down now, they'd only think I was stealing the limelight from Nick's meal. Childishly, I didn't want to give Beatrice the satisfaction of seeing that she had upset me and I certainly wasn't going to admit to her or even to myself that maybe she had a point.

I heard Nick announce that the meal was ready and I stood, trapped, hysteria building. And then I felt Gail put her arm through mine.

'I'm here, Sky,' she said gently. 'Let's go in together.'

Philippe went towards the dining room but Beatrice laid a restraining arm on his shoulder.

'I've a feeling that I went too far.' She pulled a face. 'I told Sky that she had never given her heart to her husband.'

He shook his head. 'I'm used to you interfering with me, Bea, but it isn't like you to interfere with the guests.' He looked at her in amusement. 'What has got into you?'

'I've no idea, Philippe.' She was as bemused as him by her behaviour. 'I don't know why but I have a feeling about this group.

They are going to be important to us.' She smiled suddenly. 'It's just an impression I have.'

'Well, talking about feelings, I have a feeling that Stephanie was hiding something.' Philippe looked at her. 'Did she say anything to you? You were talking for a while.'

'Yes, she said that Emmie had been sick.'

'What's the matter with her?' Philippe said sharply.

'Something about a half-cooked pizza and too much ice cream.'

'Who gave her half-cooked pizza?'

'Well, it's hardly likely to be Rosa, is it?'

Philippe frowned and started to speak but Beatrice interrupted him. 'Emmie was also terrified that Sausage was going to be eaten.'

'Of course he's not going to be eaten.' Philippe was astonished. 'Where the hell did she get that idea from?'

'I can think of only one person.'

'Ah, Bea, stop it.' Philippe was exasperated. 'Celine wouldn't say something as cruel as that, or if she did then she obviously didn't realise the importance of Sausage.'

'Why you persist in defending her is a mystery, the woman is a monster and is capable of saying anything.' Beatrice glowered at him before heading back to the dining room.

The meal passed in a blur for me, I was aware of the conversation buzzing around me but I didn't take part. I couldn't stop thinking about what Nonna and Beatrice had said. What did they mean? I did love Miles, of course I did. They were both wrong. Everyone else had loved him. My father and sister's only concern had been that we were rushing things, we hadn't known each other that long. But then Iona and her Angus had been childhood sweethearts so no wonder she thought seven months too short a time.

I thought of his sweet proposal. He had woken me up very early one morning and driven me to Westminster Bridge. He knew that Wordsworth's poem 'Composed Upon Westminster Bridge' was one of my favourites and that dawn was my favourite time of day. He'd produced a bottle of rosé champagne and the stunning moonstone and diamond ring which had belonged to my mother. It had been one of the happiest days of my life. How dared bloody Beatrice suggest I hadn't given him my heart.

I knew the dishes were delicious, judging from the excited exclamations from everyone else, but I couldn't taste a thing. I pushed the food around my plate and continued to knock back the wine. I didn't mean to get drunk but my glass seemed permanently empty and Philippe was generous with the refills.

I could sense Nick and Beatrice watching me anxiously, well, let them bloody watch, they were responsible. I hoped they felt guilty. Everything was slightly fuzzy, slightly foggy, I was floating in a little bubble of my own. It wasn't an unpleasant feeling, in fact I welcomed it. It obliterated the sadness in my heart, the confusion and the terrible isolation I was feeling. I reached for my glass once more but as I did so I felt a tap on my shoulder.

'Maybe it's time for bed, Sky.'

I looked up and saw Gail's two pretty faces drift in and out of focus. I'm sure she wasn't but it felt like she was yelling in my ear. I smiled and tried to get to my feet. The room swayed dangerously, the world once more spinning too quickly on its axis.

I closed my eyes and tried to regain my balance. I felt strong arms around me and that is where my memory ended.

Nick had leapt up the instant Sky started to sway and Philippe hadn't been far behind. Together they supported her up the stairs. Once in her room they laid her gently on the bed, Nick easing her sandals off while Philippe covered her with a blanket. Placing a large glass of water by the bed Nick tenderly took the flower from her hair and stroked the dark heavy locks back from her face. He hesitated a moment before gently kissing her goodnight.

'I'm just going to have a quick cigarette on the terrace before joining the others,' Nick said, reaching for his packet.

'Mind if I join you?' Philippe asked. 'Only don't tell Beatrice.' Nick looked at him questioningly. 'We made a pact together to give up. As you can see, I haven't exactly kept my side of the bargain but neither, I suspect, has she.' He chuckled.

'Do you think you will ever get married again?' Nick asked suddenly.

'Beatrice and me?' Philippe was astonished. 'Why would you ask that?'

'Well, you seem so close, you still have so much in common.'

'Yes and one of the things we have in common is never to get married again.' Philippe laughed. 'I would lay down my life for Bea, we are the best of friends and that is how it will remain.'

'My best friend is lying in a drunken stupor hating me with every fibre of her body.' Nick ran his hands through his hair.

'She certainly seemed to enjoy my wine.'

'Trust me, she doesn't usually behave like that.' Nick suddenly felt it important that Philippe didn't get the wrong impression. 'She is normally sweet and loving. She is warm and compassionate, funny and fey, she was my little fairy queen.' He brushed away the tears that had started to flow. 'Sorry, this is a bit of a strange time for me, for all three of us.'

'It's a tricky situation.'

'That's one word for it,' Nick said grimly.

'Sorry.' Philippe grimaced. 'Sorry, Nick, that was inadequate. This is a bit out of my remit.'

'It's a bit out of mine too.' Nick drew deeply on his cigarette.

'How did it happen?' Philippe was curious.

'No idea really.' Nick was silent for a moment. 'It sort of crept up on us. Sky was, well, she was ill a while back and when she was in hospital Miles and I necessarily spent a lot of time with each other. I mean nothing happened then but I guess that was the catalyst.'

He could remember with clarity the exact moment when it had happened. Miles had popped into the restaurant one evening before service. They had been leaning on the bar chatting and laughing at some joke when one of the young waitresses had come up.

'I hate to disturb you handsome lovebirds but you're wanted in the kitchen, chef.'

Nick had been about to put her right when suddenly, like the proverbial bolt from the blue, it hit him that she was right. He was in love with Miles.

It felt like his heart stopped beating for a moment. He had looked at Miles and seen the exact same reaction mirrored in his eyes. They had stared at each for the longest time before Miles had whispered, 'I'll come back after you've finished, Nick.' And for the first time ever in a kitchen Nick had thought of something other than food.

A cough from Philippe brought him back to the present day. He glanced over. 'That sounds terrible, doesn't it?'

Philippe shrugged. 'These things happen.'

There was another pause and then, surprising himself and Philippe, Nick said, 'I've always got on really well with Miles, he's relaxed, easy-going and good-looking, but I never thought he was quite right for Sky.'

'Why?' Philippe was intrigued. 'Did you guess he was gay?'

'Christ no, otherwise I'd have told her.' He stubbed his cigarette out and immediately lit another. 'Sky is passionate, she's creative, she's emotional, she needs to be allowed to fly and she needs someone who stimulates her. Miles doesn't and before long she would have got bored.' He ran his fingers through his hair. 'I've never voiced that to anyone before but it's true.'

'You know her very well.'

'I know her inside out, or I used to.'

'It will get better, Nick,' Philippe said.

'Will it? How do you know?'

'I don't, but Beatrice says so and she has a sixth sense about these things.' Philippe smiled.

'Well, I don't need a sixth sense to tell me that Sky will be feeling like shit in the morning.'

'I take exception to that.' Philippe was indignant. 'My wine is organic, it is not stuffed with sulphites. Sky may feel a touch jaded but she certainly won't have a hangover.'

'Really?' Nick stared at him. 'Is that really true?'

Philippe nodded.

'Bloody brilliant, in that case I may risk another glass.' Nick grinned. 'Let's go and join the others.' He laughed suddenly. 'What a bizarre group we are. There's me and Sky, and then there's Gail and Tariq. It's like a movie plot.'

CHAPTER NINETEEN

Nick was lying in bed contemplating things. He was clearly getting nowhere with Sky. In fact he may well have made things worse. He should have let her come alone. She obviously didn't want him here. She'd wanted to escape and he had come barging in without thinking things through.

He could hear Nonna now with one of her favourite expressions for him. '*Don't jump into the river before first looking to see if there is a bridge, Nico.*' But Nick had never learnt to curb his impetuosity. He thought longingly now of Nonna and Sky's father, Carlo, in their big stone house with the roaring log fires burning all year round. Nonna had never got used to the Scottish climate. He wondered if he would ever be welcome there again. He decided it was time to go home. He was in limbo here.

He phoned Miles.

'Stay one more night, Nicky,' Miles advised. 'You've gone this far to talk to her so try one last time.'

'I miss you, Miles,' Nick said.

'And I you,' he replied 'And Sky.'

'What are you doing?'

'I'm watching tacky daytime television.'

'Where are you?

'In a tacky hotel in Bayswater.' Miles looked around the room. He had deliberately chosen a nondescript hotel. He could have afforded somewhere better but it had felt so wrong to stay somewhere luxurious. Bayswater was not an area that he and Sky frequented and therefore he would be unlikely to bump into any of their mutual friends. Luckily everyone thought they were in Marrakech together so the phone stayed reasonably silent.

'What a bloody mess.' Nick sounded incredibly despondent. 'The whole situation is hopeless.'

'Keep trying, Nick.' Miles was desperately sad. Nick had been so positive that he would be able to talk to Sky and make her understand. He himself had been less optimistic but had been buoyed up by Nick's confidence.

'Keep trying,' Miles repeated. 'You love each other so much, you can make it work.' He tried to inject some confidence into his voice.

Diving neatly into the pool Nick decided that Miles was right. He had come this far, he would stay another night and give it one last shot. If he got kicked in the teeth again then so be it, he would walk through hell for his fairy queen so it had to be worth another try.

Also, if he were absolutely honest with himself, he was reluctant to give up the market and the cooking sessions with Bushara. He loved learning new things and couldn't quite believe that he'd never delved into the delights of Moroccan cuisine before. He had already planned several new recipes for the re-opening of his restaurant and Bushara was taking him for a special lunch today.

Last night's meal had been an enormous success and Philippe's wine had been the icing on the cake, especially since it appeared that there were indeed no after-effects. At least, he didn't feel any and he very much hoped that Sky didn't either. That really would be some marketing ploy – a wine guaranteed not to give you a hangover. The punters would love that.

In her study Beatrice tipped back her chair and watched Nick slice through the water. He was a truly exquisite chef. His dishes were amongst the best she had ever tasted and she knew that great

Moroccan cuisine was hard to conquer. It was no wonder he had a Michelin star.

He was also a lovely guy, natural, wickedly funny and unpretentious. She could see why he and Sky made a good team, they were both creative, and his outgoing nature would complement her more natural reserve. She would be intrigued to meet Miles, she would very much like to see what he was like.

There must be a way forward for them and Beatrice determined that she would do everything she could for them, even if Philippe accused her of interfering. For some reason she felt close to both. No other guest had ever had the same effect on her and she couldn't quite fathom why.

She heard Philippe's voice calling a greeting to Nick. She just had time to cover the notes she had been making before he appeared in the doorway, resplendent in his flowing kaftan.

'You are looking furtive, Bea,' Philippe stated as he walked into her study and bent to kiss her. 'What are you hiding? Is it your cigarettes?'

'That's rich coming from you, you reeked of cigarettes when you came down last night after taking Sky to bed.'

'I'd been chatting with Nick on the terrace and he was smoking. Naturally it contaminated me.'

'You would have had to have kissed him for it to contaminate you that much,' she commented drily.

'Well, why not? He's a nice guy, a sublime cook and he enjoys my wine.' He grinned at her before gently removing her hand from the notebook. 'Come on, Bea, I know that look, what plans are you hatching?'

She glared at him before capitulating. 'I'm thinking about your wine.'

'Isn't it a little early, cheri, even for you?'

She tried to remain serious but ended up giggling. 'OK, I admit it, I've a few ideas.'

'You never stop, do you?'

'Do you want to hear them?'

'I doubt I have a choice.'

'Sit down then, you make the place look untidy.'

With a resigned smile he sank into the chair opposite. Beatrice continued, 'As you said, Nick enjoyed your wine.'

'And you think he should buy it for his restaurant and so do I.' He smiled smugly. 'I planned to talk to him today about sending him a sample case, so for once I'm ahead of you.' He sat back and folded his arms.

'Almost but not quite.' She smiled sweetly and reached for her coffee, taking her time. This was a game they had played many times. 'Not just Nick, but other restaurants. He must know many chefs that he can introduce you to. In fact, I was thinking that instead of sending one case, you should send several.'

'Nick has a Michelin star, Bea. If he finds a wine which he thinks is special, and mine obviously is, then he won't want to spread the word to anyone else. He will want to keep it to himself.'

She paused for a moment before replying, 'Well, maybe you could let him have first choice, he could have the best vintages, or the old vine wine.' She paused again. 'There must be a way of utilising his contacts. This is a God-given opportunity, we can't let it pass.'

'I'll have a word with him today, but don't hold your breath.' He smiled at her. 'He asked me yesterday whether you and I would get married again?'

Beatrice raised her eyebrows in astonishment. 'Whatever gave him that impression?'

'He said it was clear we loved each other.'

'We do, which is why we should never marry.'

'I adore your logic, cheri.' He laughed. 'Now, have you got any of my sweet wine left in your cellar, I have a feeling Nick would love that.'

'The pool is ready and waiting for you, Philippe,' Nick said, appearing in the doorway. 'I've finished thrashing about.'

'You're a powerful swimmer, Nick,' Philippe observed.

'I learnt to swim in a Scottish loch. Sky's dad didn't believe in going to public baths when you had a natural resource on your doorstep. You learn to swim bloody fast in a Scottish loch – it's the only way you can survive.' He grinned. 'You should see Sky in a pool, she's like a seal – or a selkie as they're sometimes known in Scotland.'

Philippe had a sudden vision of Sky sliding through the water, her long dark hair fanning sleekly out behind her.

'Philippe learnt to swim in the Med.' Beatrice was smiling. 'He barely moves a muscle.'

'Whereas Beatrice…?' Philippe looked at her.

'Sits on the edge dangling her toes in the water.' Beatrice laughed.

'Complete with sunglasses, hat and cigarette – in the old days anyway.' He winked at her.

'Not a swimmer, Beatrice?' Nick laughed.

'Not when anyone is looking.'

'Changing the subject completely, can we talk wines, Nick?' Philippe asked.

'Sure can, I was going to suggest it myself.'

'Maybe after breakfast.' Beatrice spotted Sky entering the courtyard. 'Nick is dripping everywhere and, cheri, you need to do your exercises. Go on, get out of here, this is supposed to be my private study!'

CHAPTER TWENTY

I woke once again to the sound of the muezzin and realised that I was still fully dressed. The events of the previous night were hazy to say the least, but I did have a vague recollection of someone bringing me to bed. I rolled over and saw the tumbler of water and my flower placed beside it. It had to have been Nick, no one else could have been that thoughtful.

But something was nagging at the back of my mind. I had a feeling there may have been two of them. Snippets of conversation came floating into my mind. Had Beatrice or Gail come with me, or, and my sprits plummeted at the thought, maybe it had been Philippe? He had a fairly low opinion of me as it was and last night would have done nothing to alter that. I don't know why that bothered me but it did.

Gingerly I sat on the side of the bed and waited for the hangover to kick in, but despite the amount of wine I'd consumed I felt remarkably OK. I had no doubt made a complete tit of myself but somehow I didn't really care all that much. In fact, I seemed to be drained of any emotion. I was becoming very tired of constantly feeling hurt and angry. I wished with all my heart that I could turn back the clock but I couldn't, nothing would ever be the same again and I needed to face up to that.

Maybe I should go home, I thought, being here was only making things worse. Everything had taken on a very surreal quality in the riad and I felt that I was living in a strange parallel universe.

I made up my mind. I would check the flights and take the first one home. There was no point in staying any longer. I was simply in the way, annoying everyone and behaving very badly, and Gail no longer needed me as she had found Tariq.

Well that was the solution, then, I would talk to Beatrice this morning and explain my change of plans. It was definitely the right thing to do, so why then did I feel quite so reluctant?

Shaking myself I got up and went to the computer, intending to search for flights, but the pictures I'd begun to paint of Beatrice's new roof terrace were resting against it. I hesitated for a second and then grabbed the canvases. Sod it, I decided, if I was going to jump ship today then I may as well make full use of the time left. I could check flights later. Pulling on a jumper and seizing my paints I went onto the terrace.

I painted as usual for a couple of hours before the coffee craving kicked in. I was pleased with my work. I felt I had captured the essence of what Beatrice wanted to create, but sadly doubted that I would ever see the finished rooftop bar.

I hesitated as I entered the courtyard. I could hear them all laughing and once again was overcome by a horrendous feeling of separation. I felt like an outcast and as vulnerable as a teenager. How the hell was Nick managing to have such a great time? Did he feel no remorse? I was angry.

Beatrice called to me from the window.

'I'll come back another time,' I replied tersely. 'I can see you're all busy.'

'Not at all, Sky, please come in, these two are on their way out.'

Reluctantly I made my way over to the study.

'Delighted that you enjoyed my wine so much last night, Sky.' Philippe was grinning at me. He clearly had no intention of brushing over my bad behaviour and I felt the blood rush to my face.

'I do apologise for being such a lush,' I said very quietly before turning to Nick and saying, 'Thanks for taking me to bed.'

'No worries, Philippe helped me.' Nick smiled gently.

I closed my eyes as my worst fear was realised.

Still grinning, Philippe added. 'I honestly don't think I've ever heard someone snore standing up.'

'God, how mortifying,' I replied. Christ, this man was insufferable. Would he never let up?

'Au contraire, it was rather sweet. It reminded me of our piglet.' He winked at me before leaving the study.

As they both left the office I heard peals of laughter. No doubt directed at me? My paranoia was working overtime. They seemed to have bonded so quickly, but then Nick always bonded with everyone quickly.

It certainly reinforced my decision to leave. I was like a fish out of water here. Philippe obviously disliked me and from Beatrice's comments last night it was clear that she also had little patience towards me. I'd never felt quite so solitary or ill at ease in my life.

'Sky?' Beatrice called gently. 'Sky, are you OK?'

'Sorry?' I turned around. 'Sorry, Beatrice, what were you saying?'

'Sit down and I'll fetch you a coffee.'

'One broken bird in my office,' Beatrice announced as she walked into the kitchen.

Bushara frowned and grabbed the long broom.

'No, I don't mean literally!' Beatrice laughed. 'I mean one of our guests.'

'Sky?'

'Indeed.'

'Nick is talking about her all the time,' Bushara said, preparing the coffee without having to be asked. 'Everything he has ever done seems to be connected with her.'

'We have to find a way to help them. She looks so sad and

vulnerable. I hate to see anyone looking like that,' Beatrice said, opening the drawer where she had kept her cigarettes hidden. Philippe would have found them in the office.

Bushara said nothing but gave a small cough.

'Just a few drags while you're making the coffee,' Beatrice pleaded. 'I need to have a sharp mind right now and nicotine helps.'

'Oh, Sky, these are incredible!'

Beatrice was staring at the two pictures I'd laid out on her desk. She handed me my coffee without taking her eyes off them. She seemed genuinely impressed and I couldn't help smiling.

They were my impressions of her new rooftop terrace. One was set just at the point when the sun dips below the horizon and the sky turns red and gold. I'd tried to capture the terrace as she had described, the pool a dusky shimmer with the dim glow of candles in colours that were muted and romantic.

The other was a complete contrast, set in bright sunlight. The sky was a cobalt blue, there was a sea of cream parasols, colourful cushions and comfy loungers, with vivid flowers spilling out of copper urns. It was bright and inviting.

Beatrice looked at me. 'You are an exceptionally talented young lady.'

I flushed. 'They're not really finished, there's much more that I could do.'

'They look pretty finished to me.' She smiled.

'Look, I wanted to give them to you because I think I might go back home today,' I said quickly.

'Cheri, no.'

She sounded shocked. Was she angry?

'Obviously I'll pay you for the full week, I realise that it's too late to get anyone else and I don't want you out of pocket, but I'm only in the way here and I'm so sorry I got so hideously drunk last night, I hope I didn't ruin the evening but I imagine that I did.' I knew I was gabbling. 'So I've checked online and there's a flight this afternoon, if I can get a seat then I'll grab that, so would it be possible for Ibrahim to take me to the airport? If not then I can easily get another taxi.' The words were spilling out of me as indeed were the tears. I couldn't seem to control either.

Beatrice walked over to me and gently folded me into her arms. Smoothing back my heavy fringe she dipped her fingers into the jug of iced water she kept on the desk and placed them on my hot forehead.

'Shush, cheri, shush, ma belle, shush, cheri.' Her voice was hypnotic and instantly calming. She somehow manoeuvred me into a chair and handed me a tissue. 'Blow,' she commanded. 'Now, drink some coffee and tell me what this is all about.'

I obeyed and felt the tension dissipate a little.

'Actually, Sky, I need to apologise to you,' Beatrice said. 'I spoke out of turn last night.' She smiled ruefully. 'I'm not saying I was necessarily wrong but it was the wrong moment to talk.'

'It's not because of what you said that I'm leaving, it's nothing to do with the riad or you,' I was quick to reassure her. 'Your riad is wonderful, it's magical and under any other circumstances I would want to stay for ever.' I paused and gulped at the scalding coffee as I tried to find the right words. 'I should have stayed at home to face the music, I should never have come here. I should never have run away.'

'Don't you think that leaving here is running away?' she asked me gently.

'I will be going home, how can that be running away?' I frowned at her. How come she always managed to twist things around?

'You will be running away from Nick.'

'I never asked him to come, he should never have followed me here!' I was furious that yet again everything seemed to revolve around bloody Nick. 'Anyway, I doubt he'll give a damn, he's fine, he and Philippe seem as thick as thieves and he loves cooking with Bushara.'

'He's far from fine, as you know.' She leant forward. 'You are stronger than you think, cheri no, let me finish.' She held up her hands as I tried to interrupt. 'Nick is part of your make-up, Sky, he is part of who you are and you are part of him. Deep down you know that. You are soul mates. He has followed you out here, that was a brave thing to do, now it is your turn to be brave and give him the chance to talk. You both deserve that.'

I couldn't trust myself to speak. I couldn't put into words the emptiness I felt at the thought of a life without Nick, but equally I couldn't contemplate a way forward. He had shattered my trust, nothing could ever be the same again.

As if reading my mind once again, Beatrice said, 'It won't be the same relationship as before, Sky. But strong relationships survive, cheri, they change and they evolve and that is part of life.' She grinned. 'No one believed that Philippe and I would survive after our marriage, but we did. We loved each other and we forged a new relationship which in many ways was much stronger.' She walked over to me and dropped a kiss on the top of my head. 'Things will work out, ma belle, but it will take time and it will take some work.'

I got up but still didn't trust myself to speak.

'Don't do anything hasty, Sky, there is another flight tomorrow. Promise me you'll think about it.

I merely nodded.

'Go and sit outside and Bushara will bring breakfast. You need to eat.'

As soon as she said that I realised that I was famished. I'd eaten virtually nothing last night. I cleared my throat. 'Thank you,' I managed to croak.

'And, Sky?' I paused at the doorway. 'Thank you so much for these.' She held up the pictures.

'Sky?' Gail waved at me from her seat in the courtyard. Sonny was, as usual, busy searching for tortoises.

'Just the person I was looking for,' she said as I sank exhausted into the chair beside her.

'Really?' I was anxious. 'I thought you might be disgusted at my behaviour last night.'

'Oh, Sky.' She chuckled. 'You were tired and emotional, you ate nothing and drank quite a lot, it's understandable, it's certainly not a crime.'

'Thank you, Gail,' I said with relief. 'It's all a bit of a blur to me, did I do or say anything outrageous? Did I tap dance naked on the table? Should I be ashamed?'

She laughed. 'You barely said a word, you were in a world of your own.'

'I was seeking oblivion.' I grinned weakly. 'Mission accomplished.'

'Sky, I have a huge favour to ask you.' She hesitated before rushing on. 'Tariq wants me and Sonny to go for lunch and meet his father and sister. I'm scared Sky, I'd feel so much happier with a friend by my side.' She grabbed my hand. 'I'll buy you dinner, I'll buy the kaftan you loved from the market, in fact I'll buy them all, but please say yes. It won't be for long, just an hour or so.'

I smiled but couldn't commit myself. 'Why are you so scared?'

'Well, what will they think of me? Will they hate me for keeping Sonny from them? Will they want to keep him?'

'Everyone who has met Sonny wants to keep him,' I laughed, watching the little figure scampering around the pool. There was a slight gasp from Gail and I realised that I'd said absolutely the wrong thing. 'I just meant that he's so gorgeous, but, Gail, of course they can't keep him. You're his mother.'

'And Tariq is his father.'

'What has Tariq said?'

'Nothing, really. I've no idea how he feels other than angry, and rightfully so.'

'It was a misunderstanding, Gail, a terrible misunderstanding, he can't blame you. It was nothing to do with you, it was your bloody awful sister.'

Gail was silent for a moment and I was horrified that yet again I had been so tactless.

'Jesus, Gail, I'm so sorry, please don't listen to me, I have size nine boots these days. I really didn't mean to offend you.'

She smiled. 'You haven't offended me, Sky. It's just that every time I think about Dawn another piece of the jigsaw slots into place and I feel so stupid for having been so blind for so long.'

'You're not stupid, you just love her and no one wants to see faults in the ones we love.' I paused for a moment. 'What about you, Gail? How do you feel towards Tariq?'

Gail stared into the distance with her eyes half closed. 'I feel the same way about him as I did when I first met him.' She smiled dreamily. 'He takes my breath away. He brings colour to my life. I love him more and more with every beat of my heart. He makes me glad to be alive.'

'Wow.' As I saw the love in her eyes and registered the naked longing on her face I suddenly realised something. I realised that whatever I had felt for Miles, it was nothing like this. It had nothing of this intensity or strength.

'Oh God, Sky, it's my turn to apologise. How incredibly insensitive of me. I just wasn't thinking.' Gail touched my arm.

'It must be amazing to feel like that about someone.' I was looking at her with more than a hint of envy.

'You must have felt like this, Sky?' She seemed surprised.

'Once, I was fourteen and he was seventeen,' I said, deliberately keeping it light. 'His name was Rob McNeil and I had a crush on him that lasted for six giddy weeks. I stalked him relentlessly. I couldn't eat, I couldn't sleep, I thought I would die if he didn't notice me.'

'And what happened?'

'I heard him fart and the magic was broken for ever.'

Gail burst into loud laughter and Sonny looked up from his search. 'Oh, Sky, that's priceless.'

I smiled too but the smile didn't quite reach my eyes. Why had I never experienced a feeling like Gail had described? What was wrong with me? Would I ever feel like that about someone? I wasn't stupid, I knew I'd been lucky with my looks. I'd never had a problem attracting men, but had never been sure if it was me they wanted or just my face. Of course I'd rather be pretty than plain and there was no point in pretending otherwise, but sometimes beauty came at a price. I had learnt to be wary when it came to men and I'd never really had that many close relationships. Desperate for one to work, I'd been delighted that Miles had seemed so genuine in his love for me. Perhaps I'd been too delighted, perhaps I'd mistaken relief for love, perhaps Dad and Nonna had been right and maybe I had rushed things. No, I quickly dismissed that thought. That wasn't possible, I'd been very sure, I'd never had a moment of doubt – well, up until now.

My thoughts were interrupted by Beatrice and Bushara arriving bearing plates of delicious honeyed pastries and bowls overflowing with fresh fruit and thick creamy yoghurt. I was pleased to see them, not only was I starving but I couldn't cope with much more introspection.

'Perfect after a night of indulgence.' Beatrice smiled. 'Although Philippe swears that nobody gets a hangover from drinking his wine.'

'It's actually true,' Gail said. 'I feel unbelievably OK this morning, but just as a precaution I will eat this amazing breakfast.' She smiled at Beatrice and said quietly, 'I've just asked Sky if she will come to Tariq's house with me. He's invited us for lunch to meet his father and sister and I don't mind admitting I'm nervous as hell.'

'Are you going to go, Sky?' Beatrice said it casually but I knew the hidden meaning.

'Gail has offered to buy me several kaftans from the market if I do and I can't let an opportunity like that slide by.' I looked up at Beatrice. 'Of course I'll go with her.'

Beatrice squeezed my shoulders gently in silent approval and I was pleased. I sensed that approbation from Beatrice was hard to come by.

'Bushara, do you think Ibrahim would take us in the car?' Gail was asking. 'And pick us up if I give him a time? I don't want to be stranded there.'

'Ibrahim or Radar will be walking with you.' Bushara replied.

Gail looked puzzled and Beatrice smiled at her. 'It's only a short stroll from here, Gail. If you suddenly feel overwhelmed then you and Sky can simply walk back. Does that make you feel better?'

'Yes it does,' Gail said honestly.

'Gail, I've known Tariq for a few years now.' Beatrice looked at her. 'He is a man I trust implicitly.' Bushara nodded in agreement and Beatrice continued. 'His family are very modern in their outlook, his father is intelligent and full of humour and his sister is the same.'

'Thank you, Beatrice,' Gail said. 'Philippe is right, you are a mind reader, that's just what I needed to hear.'

CHAPTER TWENTY-ONE

'Ready to talk wine?' Nick strolled up to where Philippe was sitting. 'I have about an hour before a hot lunch date with Bushara.'

Philippe raised his eyebrows.

'She's taking me to one of the oldest restaurants in Marrakech, we're leaving early to give me a chance to meet the chef and take a peek into the kitchen.'

'Mad.' Philippe grinned.

'I know, I'm totally obsessed, but this wonderful Moroccan cuisine has me all fired up.'

'No, I mean the chef's name is Maad.' Philippe laughed. 'I wasn't talking about you, I love your passion, I'm the same with wine. In fact I'm seeing someone this afternoon to talk about his vineyard, do you want to come?'

'I'd love to,' Nick said without hesitation. 'I want to cram in as much as possible.' He hesitated. 'I may be leaving tomorrow.'

'Why?' Philippe was surprised. He had grown fond of this young man and was enjoying his company.

'I'm not really getting anywhere with Sky. I was wrong to come. She needed time on her own and I came charging along thinking I could wave a magic wand and make it all better.' He grinned ruefully. 'All I've succeeded in doing is making things worse, which is quite an achievement considering they were pretty much rock bottom to start with.'

'You love her very much, don't you?'

Nick merely nodded, unable to put into words the incredible emptiness he felt at a life without Sky.

Philippe smiled. 'Don't make any decision without consulting the oracle.' He nodded towards Beatrice, who was heading towards them with a tray which she placed on the table.

On the tray was a slim frosted bottle of wine and three elegant, coloured glasses. 'This is Philippe's sweet wine which he thought you might like to try. It's a bit early, but I understand that you are going out with Bushara shortly.'

'I am indeed, she's whisking me away to meet... what did you say his name was?'

'Maad,' they said in unison.

'Did you meet him in the market?' Beatrice enquired.

'Not to my knowledge.'

'Trust me, you'd know if you had.' Philippe and Beatrice exchanged glances.

'What?' Nick looked from one to the other. 'What are you not telling me?'

'Nothing, he's a wonderful man, slightly... unusual, but a marvellous chef.' Philippe poured the wine and handed Nick a glass. 'Now see what you think. We're still experimenting with it, but I think we're on the right track.'

Nick sniffed it appreciatively and then took a sip. Closing his eyes he rolled it around his mouth. 'I'd say you were very much on the right track, this is ambrosia.'

Philippe smiled in delight. 'They will be very happy to know that a Michelin-starred chef had that reaction.'

'Who are they?' Nick asked.

'Well, as I said, Henri is my right-hand man, and I also have my sister Stephanie and my nephew Luc, our flying winemaker.'

'Bloody hell, what a glamorous title! Why didn't I think of becoming a flying winemaker?' Nick said.

'A friend of mine actually came up with the phrase, I don't think it's an official description but it's an apt one, he travels the world learning about different wines and experimenting with different methods.'

'Sounds like an amazing job, where is he right now?'

'California, I can't wait to hear all about it.' Philippe took another sip of wine. 'So, Nick, are you serious about wanting my wine for your restaurant?'

'I most certainly am. I'd love to sample a few more.'

Philippe winked at Beatrice. 'Then you shall, I'll send a couple of cases over as soon as I get back.'

'I have an idea.' Beatrice began but Philippe leapt in.

'And her idea is that you will be able to introduce my wine to other chefs. I've told her that a Michelin-starred chef may like to keep it exclusive but…'

He got no further before Beatrice tried again. 'Actually, my idea was…'

This time it was Nick's turn to barge in. 'I'm not that selfish, if the wine is good, and yours certainly is, then everyone is entitled to enjoy it.' Beatrice flashed Philippe a triumphant look and opened her mouth to speak again but Nick continued. 'I may keep one wine to myself, like this sweet one for example, or the old vine one you were telling me about last night, but…'

'Well, what I was thinking…' Beatrice cut in once more.

'Maybe you should come over to London, Philippe,' Nick butted in. 'Introduce the wines yourself, I could organise a meeting.'

'When will the refurbishments to your restaurant be finished?' Philippe asked.

'Not for a few months, but we could always find…'

'Enough!' Beatrice shouted, standing up and holding out her hands to silence the men. 'Mon Dieu, I've been trying to say something for ages, now please listen to what I have to say.'

They both sat up, startled.

'I have an idea.' She paused and glared at them. 'Now listen to me without interruption.'

They sat back and gave her their full attention.

'Rather than you go to London I think that they should come to France, to the chateau.' She announced. Neither said a word, they didn't dare, although there was a definite spark in Nick's bright blue eyes. 'We will organise a wine weekend, introduce them to the area and introduce them to your wine, Philippe.'

She paused and waited for their reaction. Philippe was hesitant, as Beatrice had known he would be. 'Where would they all stay?'

'Is there room at your chateau?' Nick asked.

'Not really,' Philippe replied. 'But they could stay at a hotel in Bordeaux or Saint-Émilion.'

'They will not stay in a hotel, Philippe,' Beatrice stated firmly. 'There are plenty of beautiful rooms at the chateau and if absolutely necessary there are a couple of very nice rooms in Veronique's auberge.'

'I think they would be more comfortable in a hotel,' Philippe insisted.

'No, Philippe.' Beatrice was adamant. 'They need to stay in the chateau. I want them to soak up the ambience and wake up to the view of the vineyards. I want them to understand the whole history of the chateau and hear the stories about your father and your grandfather. I want them to feel that they could share that history and become part of the family. If they feel that, cheri, if they feel that they will become part of something very special, then they will buy your wines.'

'She's good.' Nick gazed at her in admiration. 'She's very good. I like the sound of this.' He reached for his cigarettes, oblivious to the anguish he was causing the other two. 'Does the nearby auberge do good food?'

'It does,' Beatrice replied. 'But the other idea was that you should cook for them.' She turned to Philippe. 'We could put tables in the old chai and throw open the doors. We will seat them so that they face the vineyards sloping down to the river, they'll love it, everyone does.'

'You obviously have it all planned out.' Nick nodded at her appraisingly. 'Sounds bloody brilliant. Always slightly daunting cooking for fellow chefs but if I don't cock it up then it will do my reputation no harm.' He leapt up enthusiastically as thoughts raced through his head. 'I could cook Moroccan, your wine complimented it beautifully the other evening.'

'What do you think, cheri?' Beatrice turned to Philippe.

'I like the idea in theory but I'm worried about the practice.' He was cautious but he could certainly see the potential. 'How many are we talking?'

'Enough to make it worth your while but not too many, we want them to think they belong to an exclusive club,' Nick said.

'Philippe, there is more than enough room if we incorporate Veronique.'

'It's not the room I'm thinking about, Bea, it's the money.'

'Let's not worry about that right now.'

'When should we worry about it?'

'Later.'

'It will cost a bit,' Nick replied a little awkwardly. 'If we are inviting the crème de la crème of chefs and wine connoisseurs.'

'See.' Philippe looked across at Beatrice.

'There are ways and means,' she replied vaguely. 'The most important thing is that we think it's a good idea.'

'I do, I really do,' Nick responded eagerly.

'What ways and means?' Philippe was like a dog with a bone.

'We'll talk about it later, cheri.' She frowned at him. 'Nick doesn't want to hear us going on about money matters.'

'On the contrary,' Nick said. 'I could listen to you two all day, you make a brilliant double act, but I don't want to be late for my lunchtime date with Bushara.'

'Well, we have plenty of time to fine-tune things in the next few days,' Beatrice said.

'Actually we don't,' Philippe said. 'Nick thinks he may go home tomorrow.'

'No, not you too!' Beatrice cried. 'I'm clearly losing my touch. Normally people want to stay longer, not the other way around.'

'Who else wants to go?' Nick asked, although he felt pretty sure he knew the answer.

'Sky, of course,' Beatrice replied. 'She feels that she is in the way here. She thinks she ought to go home and face the music.'

'Well, one half of the music is here.'

'I said as much but she is pretty adamant.' Beatrice longed to grab one of Nick's cigarettes. 'She is scared and lonely and very vulnerable right now.'

'Oh, God, I know.' Nick looked wretched. 'I haven't helped, but I'm determined to give it one last shot.'

'You don't have much time,' Beatrice said.

'Why, when is she going?' Nick looked panicked. 'She's not going today, is she?'

'She wanted to, but Gail has asked her to go to Tariq's to lend moral support and she has agreed.'

'Of course she did, she is loving and selfless and would do anything for anyone.'

Beatrice nodded in agreement. Philippe kept quiet, he hadn't quite seen this side of Sky.

'OK, tonight it is then,' Nick said determinedly. 'Tonight I won't take no for an answer. Tonight we are going to sit down and talk, even if I have to tie her to the bloody chair myself.' He stood up. 'But first a lunch date with Bushara and the man you call crazy.'

'Maad, his name is Maad!' Beatrice laughed. 'Have fun.' And once again she and Philippe exchanged smiles.

'I'm not being given the full picture here,' Nick said, looking from one to the other, but they remained silent.

Half an hour later he realised why. He stood in the middle of a small courtyard garden with his jaw on the floor, staring with astonishment at the sight before him. Bushara was grinning; everyone had this reaction, it would have been impossible not to.

Maad was padding towards them. Dark brown eyes glinted beneath heavy brows and a huge bulging forehead. An enormous flat nose seemed to spread over most of his face. Thick black fuzzy hair covered all the parts of his body that were on display. Huge, powerful arms hung loosely by his side. His jaw protruded and his teeth were enormous. If Nick hadn't been rooted to the spot he may well have turned and fled. Anyone still questioning Darwin's theory of evolution would have had their doubts dispelled at the sight of this silverback gorilla wearing a chef's apron.

'Welcome.' Maad hugged Bushara and then held out his hand to Nick. 'And you are the chef?'

Nick merely nodded. Maad nodded back and led them both into the kitchen.

The couple of hours that Nick spent in Maad's kitchen were to have a profound influence on his life. In years to come Nick would be famous for the atmosphere that pervaded his kitchens and he would tell everyone the story behind it, the story of the Moroccan chef Maad who had cast a spell over him.

Maad moved around the kitchen with amazing agility and dexterity, his powerful arms lifting cast-iron pots as if they were made of plastic. His huge hands displayed a delicacy that defied belief. He was everywhere at once, guiding, steering and advising, and his team clearly adored him.

Remembering only too well the taunts and vicious comments that had come his way when he was starting out, Nick always tried hard to be kind and encouraging to his junior staff but was aware that sometimes he fell well short of the mark. He prided himself on remaining relatively calm and cool in the kitchen but compared to the serenity that ruled in Maad's kitchen, his was bedlam.

Here there was humour, not harsh words, when a young lad dropped a lamb tagine. There was a beautiful tenderness as Maad gently steadied the shaking hand of a young girl preparing the dainty desserts. There was an atmosphere of peace and tranquility that Nick had never witnessed in a kitchen before, and he understood with absolute certainty that this was something he should and would emulate.

He knew without having to taste anything that the food would be sublime and he was right. When Maad settled him and Bushara in the beautiful tiny courtyard and he took his first mouthful he was blown away.

They took their time savouring every last morsel, and for a few golden hours Nick forgot his troubles and concentrated on the moment. It was now and he was here, and as he polished off the delectable dessert of orange blossom pastries he thought that, frankly, life could not get much better.

CHAPTER TWENTY-TWO

Gail and I followed Radar through the narrow alleyways. Sonny skipped along by his side, keeping up a constant stream of chatter.

'I've never seen him quite so happy,' Gail said to me.

'He certainly seems very at home here,' I agreed, and then wondered if yet again I had perhaps said the wrong thing, but Gail didn't seem to notice.

'I'm not sure how he is ever going to return to normal.'

'Maybe he won't have to?' I ventured.

Gail shook her head, it was clear that she couldn't let herself even begin to contemplate that.

Radar stopped outside an old stone archway which led to a thick wooden door. Next to it there appeared to be some sort of pottery storage, glazed and unglazed tagines and pots of varying shapes and sizes tumbled down the steps and spilled out onto the pavement. They were piled precariously on top of each other, each one a slightly different shade of terracotta. The sun cast interesting shadows and I longed to paint them but contented myself with a photo instead. On the corner opposite a man was frying some sort of spicy kebab and my mouth watered. I had a weakness for kebabs.

I turned to ask Gail if she and Sonny would like some but Gail was standing stock still looking alarmingly pale. Abandoning all thoughts of kebabs I went up and gave my new friend a hug.

'I'm here with you. I won't leave your side.' I squeezed her shoulders tightly. 'Don't worry, Gail, it's going to be fine, and if you want to leave then just give me the nod and we'll walk straight back to the riad.'

Gail smiled gratefully. 'Thank God you're here, Sky, I can't thank you enough.'

Radar was banging on the large wooden door which opened immediately as if someone had been standing behind it, which indeed Tariq was.

If Gail was nervous then Tariq was doubly so. Before their arrival he'd been pacing around the courtyard all morning unable to settle.

'Tariq, sit down,' his sister Jasmina had said. 'You are making me nervous. You'll bring on the baby at this rate.' She patted her stomach.

'I just don't know what to expect.' Tariq came to a standstill in front of her.

'Of course you know what to expect.' Their father came into the courtyard. 'It's not like you don't know her. You have a son together.'

'I don't know what she might be thinking.'

'Then you will have to ask her,' his father said drily.

'It's not that simple!' Tariq exploded. 'I just don't know what is going to happen next. What's the next stage?'

'It seems fairly obvious to me.' His father ignored the warning glance that Jasmina shot him. 'You are in love with the girl, you have never looked at another woman for five years despite my best efforts, and now you find you have a son. I have no doubts about what the next stage is. It should have been the first stage.'

'Just take it easy, Tariq.' Jasmina stood up and laid a hand on his shoulder. 'Take one day at a time.' She smiled at him. She had never seen her brother in such a pent-up state. 'I imagine Gail will be very nervous too. We all are.'

'What is there to be nervous about?' Their father rolled his eyes and left the courtyard to check that Emil had bought the kebabs as instructed. Every boy liked kebabs. He himself had made the fresh lemonade that morning and had spent hours the day before dusting and polishing the old train set of Tariq's. He couldn't wait to meet his grandson and was as nervous as a kitten but was damned if he was going to show it.

'He's as nervous as hell.' Jasmina laughed. 'You should see what he has asked them to prepare in the kitchen. There is ice cream, there is honeyed rice pudding, there are endless pastries and just now he sent Emil out to buy kebabs. There is everything a young boy could possibly want.'

'I hope there are other things for Gail and Sky.' Tariq managed a small smile.

'There are plenty. That bit I oversaw myself.' Jasmina grinned at him, pleased to see him relaxing a bit. 'Who is Sky again?'

'Another girl who is staying at the riad.' Tariq shrugged. 'I think Gail felt happier having someone else here, no idea why, God knows what she thinks we are going to do?' He frowned. 'I honestly think she believes we may kidnap him.'

'Tariq, of course she wants moral support. I would feel the same. What does Sky do?'

'Can't really remember, she's some sort of designer or artist.' He looked at his watch for the hundredth time that morning. 'I'll just go and see if I can see them.' He hurried to the door just as Radar started banging on it.

Tariq ushered us into the courtyard where a young, heavily pregnant woman and a white-haired gentleman stood waiting for us.

'Gail, Sky, may I present my father Amir and my sister Jasmina,' Tariq said, a touch pompously.

I glanced over at Gail, who was standing stock still again. I was slightly uncertain what to do, did one shake hands in Morocco? Tariq's introduction had been so formal I felt as if something was expected of us.

Sensing my confusion, Jasmina stepped forward. 'Lovely to meet you, Gail. We have heard so much about you.' She smiled warmly at her and took her hands before turning to me. 'And Sky, welcome to our home.'

Sonny was hiding behind Gail. He had no idea how important this meeting was but he seemed to sense that his mother was nervous.

'And this must be Sonny.' Jasmina continued, laughing at the little boy peeping from behind his mum.

Gail finally found her voice. 'Yes, this is Sonny.' She drew the little boy from behind her and placed her hands reassuringly on his shoulders. I watched her take a deep breath and moved closer to her side. 'Sonny, sweetheart, say hello to everyone.'

Jasmina and Amir were staring open-mouthed. Sonny was a miniature Tariq.

'Welcome.' Amir held out his hands to Gail and I watched him scrutinise the face of the lady who had captured his son.

Gail was clearly nervous but greeted him with a steady smile. He nodded in approval before turning to me and then finally squatting down to the little lad.

He smiled gently but I could see that he was itching to hug him tightly. 'Sonny, I am Amir.' The little boy solemnly shook his hand. 'Sonny, is it true that you like animals?' Sonny's face lit up and he nodded enthusiastically, looking around for evidence of a tortoise or cat. There seemed to be animals everywhere in Marrakech. 'Well then,' Amir continued, 'I have a treat for you.'

Tariq and Jasmina exchanged a puzzled look. They had no animals in the house.

'Sonny, in my study I have a parrot. Would you like to see him?' Amir held out his hand.

Tariq looked astounded. 'A parrot?'

'Yes, a parrot, Fatima's parrot. I borrowed him for the day.' Amir winked at him and standing up turned to Gail and myself. 'Do please sit down and we will have some tea,' he said, ushering us towards a table.

I was utterly charmed by the old man. There was something delightfully old-fashioned about him, although he was childlike in his enthusiasm for Sonny. I had an immediate sense that here was someone who was trustworthy and honourable. I knew instinctively that Gail would have nothing to fear and I hoped she felt the same.

I gazed around me, their home was beautiful. A small fountain surrounded by dove grey and white tiles played in the middle of the courtyard. Ornate carved wooden pillars reached up to the balcony on the first level and burnished brass lanterns hung from the canopy. Exquisite white furnishing, gleaming cacti in large dark wooden boxes. It was understated in a very expensive way. There was an air of decadence and history and I began to realise that Tariq came from wealthy stock.

I wondered if Gail would live here, the choice between here or her house in Chigwell seemed a no-brainer to me but then I wasn't her. She could have been living here for the last five years if that damned sister of hers hadn't interfered. I was stunned that anyone could be that selfish. It was obvious that Gail had spoiled her rotten, understandably, but clearly it had done neither of them any favours.

'This is one of the oldest buildings in Marrakech.' Amir spoke proudly, confirming my suspicions.

'It is magnificent.' I turned to him. 'You have a very beautiful home indeed.'

'I will show you more later, but first, some refreshments.' He settled everyone down at the vast table. He was the perfect host, making sure we had everything we needed before turning to Gail.

'May I take Sonny to see the parrot and the train set?'

Sonny was hopping from one foot to the other in his eagerness. I smiled at Gail as she nodded her agreement but I could see how nervous she was. And so too was Amir. It was touching to see his face shining with excitement, and he was holding Sonny's hand as if he never wanted to let him go.

Sonny seemed equally hooked. He was intelligent beyond his five years and I think he realised that the white-haired man was somehow important to him. As he smiled up at him it was clear they were going to be the best of friends. They disappeared without a backward glance.

Tariq watched them and then rose and went over to Gail. 'Would you like to come and see the rest of the house?' He held out his hand.

Gail stood up uncertainly and glanced over to me. I immediately leapt up.

'Sky, she doesn't need a bodyguard, I'm not going to abduct her,' Tariq snapped at me.

'Tariq.' His sister spoke sharply.

There was a moment of silence. Tariq blushed and turned to me. 'Sky, that was unbelievably rude of me, I do apologise.' He shook his head. 'I know that you have come to support Gail and I am very grateful. Without you she may not have ventured here at all. Do please forgive me, and do accompany us.'

His formality made me smile.

'Don't worry, Tariq, I think everyone is a bit nervous, with the exception of Sonny.' I grinned as a burst of childish laughter came out of the study. 'Of course there's no need for me to come, I know you're not going to abduct her, but I did promise to keep close to her side.' I laughed but I nonetheless looked at Gail for confirmation that she was comfortable without me. She nodded imperceptibly.

'Go, Tariq, but don't be long, we will have lunch in about fifteen minutes.' Jasmina patted her stomach. 'I don't know about you but the baby and I are starving.'

'I was like that towards the end with Sonny.' Gail smiled sympathetically. 'I was constantly hungry but I was never sure what for.'

149

'I hope they can work things out.' Jasmina said candidly after they'd left, pouring me some iced water. 'Tariq was absolutely broken-hearted when Gail left him.'

'Gail felt pretty much the same,' I replied. 'You do know that she didn't really leave him?' I was anxious that she should be in no doubt as to what had actually happened.

'Yes, Tariq told us, a dreadful misunderstanding.'

It was more than a misunderstanding, I thought, more a wilful act of cruelty but I didn't say anything. 'I imagine this must be a bit of a shock for you all.'

'You can say that again.' Jasmina grinned. 'Papa will suddenly have two grandchildren in quick succession.'

'When are you due?'

'Supposedly not for another few weeks but I feel like I'm about to burst.' She patted her bump. 'My husband is away on business so the baby cannot possibly arrive until he returns.' Her stomach suddenly rippled beneath her loose top. 'But as you can see, he or she is very impatient.' She laughed. 'Do you have children Sky?'

I was caught unawares. 'No, not yet, well, nearly, but… it's sort of complicated,' I stammered.

Jasmina looked at me steadily and I could see the immediate understanding in her eyes. 'I had two miscarriages before this, Sky,' she said softly. 'The grief was almost too much to bear, especially after the second.' She paused a moment before adding, 'It doesn't matter how many weeks, months or even days pass before you lose the baby, it still feels like a piece of your heart has been ripped out.'

It was very still and quiet in the courtyard as she spoke. A gentle breeze cooled my face. Her words touched me in a way that none of the banal platitudes of the doctors and nurses at the hospital had. Their talk of it being Mother Nature's choice had driven me insane. In my drug-induced state Mother Nature took on the mantle of a starched sister marching down the wards choosing which baby would live or die. But Jasmina's words, coming straight from the heart, helped me.

'You will have a child, Sky, when the stars are right.'

And when I find a new husband, I mentally added.

Gail and Tariq came back into the courtyard about twenty minutes later. The tension between them was palpable but so was the electricity, the air practically crackled and fizzed. I looked at Jasmina and she raised her eyebrows. I got up and went over to Gail. She looked tense and nervous.

'Sonny is still playing with Amir,' I tried to put her at ease. 'We have heard him laughing non-stop.'

'I will go and fetch them for lunch,' Tariq said, a little stiffly.

'Are you OK?' I whispered as he left the courtyard. 'Did you manage to talk about anything?'

'Not really, Sky. I don't think either of us knew where to start.' She sighed. 'I have a thousand questions to ask him but all we talked about was the house.'

'It's early days still, Gail.' I gave her a quick hug. 'You're bound to be a bit tongue-tied with each other.'

The table was laid and Amir was bringing in drinks.

'Sonny is in the kitchen washing his hands,' he informed Gail before she had time to get worried. 'He has been stroking the parrot, who has behaved with remarkable patience.'

'Thank you so much,' Gail replied. 'I'm sure he has enjoyed himself.'

'You bet he has,' Jasmina said as she came to join them. 'I can tell that these two get on like a house on fire.' She smiled at her father. 'Will you be as besotted with this one?' She patted her stomach.

'Do you know if it's a boy or girl?' Gail asked.

'No idea,' Jasmina replied. 'I don't really mind.'

'I hope it's a beautiful baby girl like its beautiful mama,' Tariq said, coming into the courtyard in time to hear the last remark. 'That would make us all very happy.' He gave Jasmina a sudden hug.

'What a lovely thing to say.' Gail smiled at the brother and sister. Then I saw her face cloud over as she suddenly remembered what her own sister had done. I was about to say something but Amir beat me to it.

'Have you spoken to your sister?' he suddenly demanded, as if reading her mind. 'What did she have to say about her part in all this?'

'Father!' Tariq was shocked. 'It's none of your business.'

'Well, I think it is.' Amir was unrepentant. 'We have all lived in ignorance of Sonny for five years.' He turned to Gail. 'Why would she do such a thing? Why would she lie like that?'

This time Tariq did not interrupt. I guessed that he was interested in hearing the reply.

'I'm not sure,' Gail said slowly. 'I'm as shocked as you are.' She swallowed hard. I could see that she was trying to be as truthful as possible and I could imagine how hard it was for her.

'I'm afraid that she is rather spoilt and selfish, I'm only just beginning to wake up to that. She wants only what suits her.' She shook her head sadly. 'I clearly didn't do a very good job of bringing her up.'

'Well, you've done a marvellous job of bringing up Sonny.' I couldn't bear hearing Gail put herself down. 'He's adorable and you should be very proud of yourself.'

I could tell that Amir was not really satisfied with the reply but he didn't pursue it. He directed us all to the table. 'Tariq, you sit at one end, I'll sit at the other, Glee, you come beside me.'

'Gail, Papa, her name is Gail.' Tariq looked mortified but Gail merely laughed.

'Actually I rather like Glee.'

'Then Glee it is.' Amir held out the chair for her. 'And I hope someday I will hear you call me Father.'

There was a stunned silence. I could see Tariq glaring at his father and Jasmina was trying hard not to laugh. I caught her eye and winked.

'Please, Papa, it's a bit early to be talking like that,' Tariq growled.

'Bit too late in my opinion,' Amir retorted. 'No point in playing games, you two have wasted enough time already.' Gail was scarlet and Tariq was looking as if he would like to kill him on the spot but Amir didn't care. 'Tariq, there has never been any other woman in your life, and anyone can see from the way Glee looks at you that she is still in love.'

Gail gasped and I giggled.

'You are neither of you getting younger, you may want more children, I certainly hope so, and you need to get a move on.' Having delivered his piece, Amir contented himself with pouring the wine and Gail was spared any further comment by Sonny running from the kitchen.

'Mummy, the parrot was amazing, it could talk and everything and Pappy Amir has bought kebabs for lunch.'

'Pappy Amir?' Gail turned slowly to the man on her left. He had the grace to look slightly abashed.

'Amir just didn't sound right from a small boy.' He shrugged.

'You are going way too fast, Papa.' Tariq was seething.

'It is you who are going way too slow.' There was a pause and then the old man suddenly chuckled. 'Maybe I'm getting carried away, but someone needs to make you see sense.'

I smiled at him. He really was something else and I liked him enormously. He reminded me of Nonna. The same no-nonsense approach to life.

'You'll have to fight me for the kebabs, Sonny.' I tickled him under the chin. 'Kebabs are my all-time favourite food.'

'I think we have enough in the kitchen to satisfy everyone.' Jasmina raised her eyebrows at both her father and Tariq.' I think everyone has gone a bit over the top.'

I saw Gail peeking at Tariq. He was blushing. He saw her looking and gave her a gentle apologetic smile. The look she gave him back was so full of love I could hardly bear to watch. It didn't matter that they were tongue-tied, it was obvious what was going to happen.

'Would you like to go camel riding?' Tariq asked Sonny. 'I would like to take you tomorrow, with Mummy of course,' he added hastily. 'And Sky, if she would like to come.'

Sonny sat with his mouth wide open.

'Trust me, you don't want to miss out on this,' Jasmina said, smiling at us all. 'It's fun, we will pack a picnic. I'd come myself but it may not be the wisest decision given my condition.'

'Mummy, please,' Sonny begged.

Gail looked at me. 'It seems we have no choice.' She smiled at me but I didn't smile back. I hesitated before speaking.

'Um, you see, I think I may be going home tomorrow…'

'Sky, no!' I could see Gail was shocked.

'Why?' Tariq asked.

'Things aren't really working out too well here, it's a bit, um, well, it's a bit complicated.' I felt very ill at ease. 'I'm sorry. Can I let you know in the morning?'

'Of course you can.' He looked confused at this turn of events but remained polite. He suddenly turned to Gail. 'How long are you staying?'

She was caught off guard. 'I only booked a week.'

'A week?' He was incredulous. 'What are we supposed to achieve in a week?' he snapped at her. 'After five years you only book one week? It's not enough time to sort anything out.'

I could see Gail becoming angry but before I could intervene Jasmina stepped in quickly.

'Tariq, be reasonable, Gail had no idea what she would find when she came here.' She laid her hand on his arm. 'You could have been married, or anything, of course she only booked a week, I would do the same.' She smiled at Gail who smiled gratefully back, pleased that his sister was her ally.

Sonny was looking around bewildered. He could sense the tension. 'Mummy?' His little face started to crumple and Gail was swift to respond.

'All OK, darling, just a misunderstanding.' She swept him into her arms.

'Well maybe we can sort something out, maybe you can stay a bit longer,' Amir said, smiling at Sonny.

I watched Gail tighten her arms around him. Like a lioness guarding her young she glared around the room, ready to snarl at any given moment.

Amir looked taken aback by the ferocity of her stare but Tariq immediately understood her concern.

'I think all Papa meant was that we could perhaps try and change your flights.' He smiled gently at her.

'Well of course I meant that, what else would I mean?' Amir looked confused.

'I think Gail was worried that we might want Sonny to stay here. She's worried we're going to abduct him.' He was smiling but nonetheless I detected a slight edge to his voice.

Amir turned to Gail. 'Glee, is this true?' His eyes were full of concern.

Poor Gail looked trapped and again I opened my mouth to say something but this time it was Amir who beat me to it.

He gently placed his hand over hers. 'Glee, please relax. We're certainly not going to kidnap the boy.' He squeezed her hand and smiled at her then, unable to resist, he added, 'Well, at least not today, these things take planning and time.' He winked at her and I was pleased to see a ghost of a smile in return.

CHAPTER TWENTY-THREE

Bushara smiled at the young man by her side. Everyone responded to Maad in one way or another but Nick's reaction was almost evangelical. He was earnestly describing to her how he was going to try to emulate him in his kitchen, how he would try and capture the same sense of peace and harmony. He was going to have a staff meeting on his return home, the restaurant was closed for refurbishment so now was the perfect time to make changes. His passion was palpable.

It was at the corner of the small square with the fountain, where he had sat and smoked with Tariq on the first day, that it happened.

The moped was coming way too fast, the young Moroccan rider desperately fighting for control. Nick heard it before he saw it. Instinctively he threw Bushara into a small doorway, placing himself between her and the oncoming bike.

There was nowhere for him to hide, nothing he could do but watch in a sort of fascinated horror as the moped skidded around the corner, spilling its passenger and careering towards him.

Nick stood absolutely no chance. The bike slammed into him, catapulting him across the square. There was a sickening thud as he hit the ground followed by the sound of metal scraping against the stone. Then there was a moment of silence before all hell broke loose.

I was keeping Sonny occupied by playing *I Spy* while Tariq and Gail were deep in conversation behind me. It sounded as if the floodgates had finally opened and they were able to talk, and I was delighted. Lunch had been a gargantuan affair and we were meandering very slowly back to the riad. I rounded the corner and saw a crowd of people gathered around an upturned moped.

'There's been some sort of accident,' I called over my shoulder while pulling Sonny close to my side.

'Those damn bikes should never be allowed,' I heard Tariq say. 'The souks are not designed for them. We have campaigned…'

I heard no more. I came to an abrupt halt. The world spun around once more and black spots danced in front of my eyes. I gazed in horror at what lay before me. I opened my mouth to speak but instead emitted a kind of banshee-like wail. Tariq and Gail were beside me in an instant.

I pointed to a white baseball cap lying on the ground, saturated with dark red blood. The blood was already congealing in the hot afternoon sun and a swarm of flies were buzzing around.

'That's Nick's cap,' I croaked. 'Nicky's cap.' And then I fainted.

I came to in Tariq's arms as he carried me into the riad. At first I was disorientated. I'd never fainted before and had always imagined it might be romantic in an old-fashioned, feminine sort of way. It wasn't. I felt sick, dizzy and sweaty. Then rushing to the forefront of my mind came the image of Nick's bloodied cap. I struggled as Tariq placed me on a chair in the cool interior.

'Nick,' I whispered. 'Must get to Nick.'

Beatrice was instantly by my side with iced water and a cold towel. She laid it on my forehead and it felt good, but I had to get to Nick, I had to get there before…

I couldn't contemplate beyond before. Once again I struggled, but I was pushed back.

'I will take you shortly, Sky. Philippe is already at the hospital but first you must drink the water, sip don't gulp, otherwise you will faint again.'

I recognised the sense of Beatrice's words but now was not the time to be sensible. Now was the time to rush to Nick's side to tell him that I loved him. I loved him no matter what he did. He could commit murder and I'd still love him. He was my best friend, my soul mate and the person who knew more about me than anyone else.

I sipped the water and it revived me. I started to get up. Beatrice looked anxious but realised that this was one battle she wasn't going to win.

Beatrice drove at breakneck speed to the hospital. If I hadn't feared for Nick's life then I would have feared for mine. She skidded to a halt in the space reserved for ambulances and I was out of the car and running before she had switched off the engine.

I didn't see Philippe standing at the entrance. He caught me in his arms as I rushed past. I looked up at his sombre face.

'He's dead, isn't he?' I whispered. 'He's dead and I'm too late.' I started shaking uncontrollably. His arms tightened around me.

'He's OK, Sky,' Philippe said. 'He's not dead.'

I looked up at him. My breath was coming out in ragged gasps. 'Really?' I gripped his arms. 'Really?'

He nodded gently. 'He's very lucky. He's concussed and needs a fair bit of stitching up but otherwise he is fine.'

I burst into tears. 'I thought he was dead,' I sobbed. 'I thought he was dead and that I'd never see him again.' I could feel Philippe pulling me close to him. I could feel him stroking my hair, desperately trying to calm me down, murmuring soothing endearments in French. It didn't matter that I didn't understand them, I understood their essence. I leaned into his chest and stopped fighting for my breath. I heard Beatrice's high heels clattering up the steps.

'He's OK, cheri,' Philippe told her. 'Nick is OK.' Keeping one arm firmly around my shoulders he reached out for Beatrice with his other one. He held us both tight for a second before I suddenly broke away.

'I have to go and see him. Where is he?'

'I'll take you.'

Philippe guided us down a long corridor to the room where Nick lay. A young nurse was just walking out. She smiled when she saw us.

'He's all stitched up and as comfortable as can be, but he does have concussion so we're going to keep him in overnight.' She shook her head. 'He's a bit confused. He keeps talking about seeing the sky or not seeing the sky. I'm not sure he realises where he is.'

'That's me,' I said, looking past her towards Nick. 'I'm Sky, but he probably thought I didn't want to see him.'

'Oh, I see,' the nurse said, opening the door to let me past and clearly not seeing at all.

Philippe laid a hand on Beatrice's arm as she went to follow Sky.

'Let them have time alone, Bea,' he said softly. 'There are things she needs to say to him.'

Beatrice looked up at him and nodded in agreement. 'Yes, you are right.' She called quietly to Sky, 'We will wait outside, cheri.'

'Coffee?' Philippe asked, as they walked down the corridor. 'I saw a machine by the entrance.'

'It will be revolting but better than nothing.' She laughed.

'I'm not sure that it is better than nothing.' Philippe gazed into a plastic cup of frothy white liquid a moment later. 'I asked for black but this is what I got.' He sat on the chair beside her. 'It's turning out to be quite a week.'

'Mon Dieu, it certainly is,' she replied with feeling. She took a tentative sip of the coffee then stood up. 'Actually, Philippe, I think I need some fresh air.' Neatly depositing her coffee in the nearby bin she grabbed her handbag. 'I'll just go and have a wander outside for a while. I won't go far.'

Philippe got up to join her. 'I'll come with you, only I don't have a light.'

She swung around to face him. He grinned at her. 'I know you have a packet in your bag.'

'And where is your packet?'

'Jacket pocket,' he said, putting his arm over her shoulders as they wandered through the door. 'Did you even attempt to give up?'

'For about a day.' She chuckled. 'And you?'

'Very nearly a week,' he replied. 'Emmie said I was the horridest man in the world, Stephanie wouldn't come near me, even Belle kept her distance and finally Rosa placed a packet in front of me and begged me to light up.'

Beatrice laughed. 'I'm impressed, Philippe, you certainly tried harder than I did.' She reached up to give him a kiss.

'I thought you were dead.' I wept. 'I thought you were dead and that you had died thinking that I hated you.' I was holding Nick's hand in a vice-like grip.

'I thought I was a goner too,' he said sleepily.

'I saw your life flash past my eyes.'

'Isn't that supposed to be me?' His smile was lopsided.

'And did you?' I asked.

'No.'

'Well then, you didn't think you were dying, but I did and I hated myself for letting you think that I hated you.'

'Know you don't hate me, Skylark.' He was having difficulty talking. 'I'm a part of you, but I wounded you…' His eyes started closing as the medication took effect. 'Wounded you, but Miles not right… never right…' He tailed off. He had stitches running down the side of his face and his lips were cut but I was desperate to hear what he wanted to say.

'What do you mean, Nicky?' I leant in closer.

'You need shomeone different.' He was starting to slur. 'Shomeone like…' But it was no good, he was slowly sliding into oblivion. He needed to sleep, to rest.

I stood up and kissed the top of his head, gazing down at his familiar face, as familiar to me as my own, although the new scar would take some getting used to. I could imagine him telling the story of his bravery, each time with a tiny new embellishment, and I smiled to myself.

Just like the scar, our new relationship would take time to get used to. I wasn't at all sure what the future held but at least now I was fairly sure we had one.

'I love you, Nicky,' I whispered. I didn't know if he could hear me but I continued. 'I'll be here when you wake up.' I was sure I could see him try to smile.

PART TWO

CHAPTER TWENTY-FOUR

Celine stopped at the school gates and waited impatiently for Emmie to get out of the car. They usually drove in silence but Emmie was excited about Philippe coming home and could not stop chatting. Celine was excited about him coming home too but would never admit that to herself, let alone her daughter.

'And I has put Luc's name on the banner coz he's coming home today too,' Emmie was explaining. 'Rosa's made a cake and we got balloons what we is going to put everywhere.' She paused for a moment. 'Is Luc my cousin?'

'Something like that, Emmaline. Now time to get out of the car.' She leant over and opened the door. Emmie turned to kiss her but Celine was already looking in the rear view mirror.

Her daughter had barely got out of the car before Celine sped away. As she swerved at speed around the sharp bend something fell off the seat onto the floor. It was Emmie's lunch box. Celine swore. The girl was clueless. She glanced at her watch. She was cutting it fine for her appointment at the hair salon. Someone would make sure Emmie got something to eat. She could always come by after her appointment; it would probably be finished by the time the school stopped for lunch.

Two hours later Celine emerged from the salon. Her blonde bob had been cut shorter than normal, accentuating her sharp cheek bones. Usually a lady who favoured pale pinks, she had most unusually chosen a vibrant red for her nails. Adele had applied some dramatic make-up and the result was striking.

Dark eyeliner emphasised her pale blue eyes and the vibrant lipstick matched her nails. Celine felt good. She headed towards the little café, walking past the patisserie, deliberately oblivious to Madame Granet's desperate attempts to catch her attention. She stood at the corner for a moment deliberating whether to stop at the café or go further afield. A young man wolf-whistled from across the street and that decided her. Turning on her heel she headed towards her car.

Fifteen minutes later she was pulling into the driveway of the Hotel de Paris.

'Pretentious name for a hotel near Bordeaux,' Philippe had murmured when they had all been invited to the opening night a year ago.

'And pretentious prices,' his sister had murmured back.

Normally discreet, Celine rarely went into the foyer, opting instead for the side entrance, but today she was feeling cavalier and reckless.

A young man chatting to the receptionist did a double-take, it boosted her ego but she didn't condescend to turn in his direction. Lifting her head high she headed for the bar where, as she had suspected, Arnaud was chatting politely to the customers. As ever he was impeccably dressed in dark trousers, cashmere jumper and suede moccasins and Celine looked on appreciatively.

Arnaud walked towards her.

'Celine, how lovely to see you.' He went to kiss her on both cheeks, inhaling her seductive, musky perfume, whispering as he did so, 'Did we have a rendez-vous?'

'No, this is spontaneous,' she whispered back, and stepping away she said out loud, 'I wondered if I could steal some of your time, there are a few things I would like to discuss.'

One glass of champagne led to another, which inevitably led to other activities and suddenly she was running horribly late.

'*Merde*, I'll be late for Emmaline.' She leapt out of bed and headed for the bathroom.

'Phone Claude,' Arnaud replied lazily. 'Tell him you have been delayed, come back and let's try that last position one more time.'

'I'll text Claude,' she replied, dressing with care even in her haste.

'Then come back to bed.'

'I can't, we have a party tonight. Philippe is coming home, and Luc,' she added as an afterthought.

'Royalty returns.' Arnaud reached over for the last of the champagne. 'Do send the king my greetings.'

Emmie stood by the school gates, half hidden by the large, spreading plane tree. She was waiting for an opportunity to slip out unseen. The pupils were supposed to stay inside the gates until they were collected but Celine hated coming in and chatting to the teacher so Emmie had become adept at sneaking out. She knew it was wrong to disobey her teachers but she feared the wrath of Celine if she didn't. She called Celine 'Maman' to her face but never thought of her as anything but Celine in her head.

She peered around the tree. Madame Clement was occupied by a talkative parent; this was her chance. She darted quickly out of the gate and hugging the hedge turned left, scuttling around the corner where she could remain hidden until Celine picked her up. When her beloved form teacher Madame Martinez was on duty Emmie never stood a chance. Madame Martinez kept Emmie close to her side, but Madame Martinez was often involved in after-school classes so playground duty usually fell upon Madame Clement. She was scatty and much older than her sharp-eyed younger colleague, and therefore much easier to escape from.

Emmie sat down on the dusty pavement. She was used to waiting, Celine was often late and it normally never bothered her, but today she was desperate to get home to help Henri put up her banner. Her stomach rumbled, she hadn't wanted to tell anyone that she had forgotten her lunch box. She hated making a fuss so had instead filled up on water from the drinking fountain.

Half an hour later a car drove past, stopped and then reversed. A young man got out. He checked up and down the road before approaching Emmie.

'Hello, cheri.' He smiled.

'Hello.' She got up from the pavement. He saw that she had been crying.

'Are you on your own?' he asked very gently.

She nodded.

'Are you waiting for Maman?'

Once again she nodded and then her lip started to tremble. 'I got a banner what I wants to put up,' she whispered. 'For Uncle Philly and Luc, but now I is late.'

'Hop into my car, princess, and we'll get you home in no time.' He squatted down beside her. 'Do you remember me?'

Emmie looked uncertain.

'My name is Michel.' He held out his hands. 'I think, cherie, that maybe Maman has forgotten to come.' He smiled at her. 'I'll put the roof down, you'll like that won't you? I promise we'll be back in time for you to put up the banner for Uncle Philly.'

That sealed the deal.

Celine pulled into her driveway thirty minutes later, having broken every speed limit in sight during the journey. She had driven past the school but there had been no sign of Emmie so she assumed that Claude had received her text. Maybe they had stopped at the chateau, Emmie had been going on about some banner. She would give them a ring but first she would take a quick shower.

She was just getting dressed when she heard the car pull up. She smiled smugly to herself, what perfect timing, she was fresh and spotless, admittedly her head throbbed a little due to the champagne but no one would guess what a debauched afternoon she had spent. She would tell Claude that she had been spending time with Lysette, a friend of hers who was unwell.

'Salut, mon coeur.' Claude stood in the doorway. Celine hated that term of endearment. 'Stephanie just rang me.' He paused looking her up and down in admiration. 'She tried here but got no answer.'

'I was in the shower,' Celine replied. 'I didn't hear the phone.'

'Well she was wondering where Emmie was, she thought you were going to drop her straight off after school, she's supposed to be helping Henri put up a banner.' He smiled at her. 'You look absolutely stunning, by the way. Anyway I said I'd drop her down there. Where is she?'

Celine stared at him stupidly. 'What do you mean where is she? She's with you.'

It was Claude's turn to stare. 'Of course she's not with me, why would she be with me?'

'I sent you a text, I said I was delayed, I asked you to pick her up.' Celine was trying to quell the feeling of panic.

'I never got it. I've had my phone switched off all afternoon.'

'Why?' she yelled. 'Why have you had your bloody phone switched off?'

'I've been in the hospital all afternoon. You knew that.'

Celine reeled. How could she have forgotten his appointment? Of course he'd been in the hospital. How careless of her. So where the hell was Emmaline? Mon Dieu, this was turning into a nightmare. She started to shake.

'Where the hell is Emmie?' Claude echoed her thoughts. They stared at each other.

CHAPTER TWENTY-FIVE

Stephanie put the phone back on the receiver. She looked puzzled. Claude had sounded panicked. Surely if no one had collected Emmie then her teacher would still be waiting with her? But why hadn't they phoned the house? Maybe they had, after all she had tried and got no answer. Trying to remain calm, she went in search of Rosa.

Claude sped towards the school. Emmie must be inside with a teacher. They weren't allowed outside the school gates. But then why hadn't they phoned Celine? And where had Celine been?

Despite the warning from the hospital today he was in desperate need of a cigarette, but he was in Celine's car and it was unlikely that she would have any. She smoked very rarely but nonetheless he fumbled in the glove compartment and found not only a packet of cigarettes but a box of matches too. The cigarettes were not a brand he ever remembered Celine smoking but Claude wasn't feeling fussy. Pulling a cigarette from the packet he reached over for the matches and noted with surprise that they came from the Hotel de Paris.

The school gates were firmly shut. There was no sign of either a teacher or his young daughter. He ran down the lane shouting Emmie's name but there was no response.

Should he call the police? Too late he remembered that his phone was in his jacket which was in the bedroom. Throwing himself into the car he slammed the door shut and sped out into the lane. The chateau was nearer than the house, he would ring from there.

He tore into the driveway of the chateau seconds after a bright red sports car. It skidded to a halt in the front courtyard. The roof was down, music was blaring and there in the passenger side sat Emmie. Her hair had blown everywhere and the golden curls framed her face like a halo. She had ice cream in her hands and an awful lot of it on her face. Claude was astounded.

Stephanie and Rosa came running out of the house. Emmie leapt out of the car.

'I got me an ice cream.'

'You certainly did,' Stephanie said, surveying the mess.

'She wouldn't stop to eat it, she was desperate to get back here to put up a banner.' The young man came over to greet them as Claude leapt from his car.

'What the hell is going on?' Claude demanded.

The young man raised his eyebrows and nodded in the direction of Emmie.

'Emmie, run along with Rosa and get cleared up,' Stephanie said before Claude had time to interrupt. 'Henri's waiting to do the banner and then you need to get into your party dress.' As soon as they had left she turned to Claude. 'Claude, you remember Michel, don't you? He is Luc's best friend.'

The young man stepped forward and Claude nodded vaguely. His heart was hammering at an alarming rate.

'What happened, Michel?' Stephanie asked. 'Why on earth is Emmie with you?'

'She was sitting on the pavement all alone. The school gates were locked.' He looked over at Claude. 'It was hot, she was crying and she'd had no lunch.'

'On the pavement?' Claude looked bewildered. 'Why wasn't she in the playground?'

'I have no idea,' Michel said shortly. 'She said she was waiting for Maman. She said she had been waiting a long time, she was worried about being late for Philippe.'

'Anyone could have come along, anyone could have picked her up.' Stephanie was furious.

'She didn't really remember who I was, I haven't seen her since Luc went away,' Michel said. 'I was desperate not to scare her. I scanned the road several times to check no one was coming.'

'Thank you very much, Michel,' Claude said rather stiffly. 'We are very much in your debt.'

'I'm just glad I happened to be there at the right time,' Michel replied.

Emmie was standing next to Henri with the little piglet as always by her side. They were proudly surveying her banner.

'Looks good, ma petite.' Henri smiled down at her. 'Uncle Philly and Luc will be delighted.'

Emmie beamed with delight.

Minutes later her parents drove into the driveway and Emmie waved hesitantly.

They got out of the car and walked towards her with big smiles on their faces. Emmie sensed immediately that something was wrong.

'Emmie.' Celine bent down to her daughter. Emmie backed away and Celine overbalanced in her high heels and lurched forward, pushing Emmie backwards. The little girl and her piglet both squealed in fright.

Claude rushed forward to help Celine, and Henri pulled the scared girl close to him. He could feel the genuine shiver of fear course through her and was concerned. No child should be that frightened of their mother, it wasn't natural.

'Nothing to worry about,' Claude said as Stephanie came running into the courtyard. 'Celine tripped up and it scared Emmie.' He laughed too loudly. 'Come on, Emmie, no need for tears. Maman and I just wanted to say sorry that you had to wait outside the school on your own. I thought Maman was collecting you and she thought I was.' He turned to the others. 'Celine was delayed, she left me a message but I never got it.'

Claude had been uncharacteristically angry with Celine. Not because she had been delayed, he had seen Celine's message and knew that she hadn't forgotten Emmie, but because Emmie had been waiting outside the school gates and Claude knew that she would never have done so if she had not been encouraged.

'You must have told her to wait there,' he said as they drove towards the chateau. 'She wouldn't do that of her own accord.'

'Oh, Claude, you know what she's like,' Celine said quickly. 'I probably said something once about it being easier not going in. She obviously picked up on it.' She reapplied her lipstick in the mirror. 'Who knows what goes on in her head?' She was relieved that Emmie had been found but was very anxious to make sure the girl didn't breathe a word about waiting outside the gates.

Claude was not convinced by her explanation, but they had arrived at the driveway so he let the matter rest. 'Please say sorry to her,' he said unexpectedly.

'Of course I will say sorry to her,' she snapped. 'I'm not a complete monster, Claude.'

Celine was back on her feet, hugely embarrassed and furious with her daughter for making such a fuss.

Emmie had seen the look of anger on her mother's face and was trembling like a leaf.

Stephanie looked at Celine and took a deep breath before speaking.

'Well luckily no harm was done so let's not spoil the party. Did you manage to pick up the gateau whilst you were in town this morning, Celine?'

Celine put her hand to her mouth. She had completely forgotten the gateau. This damned day went from bad to worse. 'I was, um, I was barely in town this morning,' she stammered. 'I had thought I would go back there after picking up Emmaline but obviously I was delayed.' That was why Madame Granet had been trying to attract her attention.

Stephanie raised her eyebrows but said nothing. She had seen Celine going into the hair salon and the patisserie was two doors away. Stephanie had been tempted to pick it up herself but Celine so rarely volunteered to do anything that she hadn't wanted to interfere.

'I'll go,' Claude said. 'They will still be open.'

'Let me go, Claude.' Michel stepped forward. 'You stay here and form the welcome party.' He grinned. 'I'll be back just as you are opening the champagne.'

'Michel to the rescue again,' Stephanie said. She turned to Celine. 'I'm not sure if you remember Luc's friend Michel. He was Emmie's knight in shining armour.'

Michel turned to greet Celine and was momentarily lost for words. He knew Claude but had only met Celine on a couple of occasions and only then very briefly. But he recognised her right now.

He had seen her in the Hotel de Paris at lunchtime. His girlfriend, or soon-to-be girlfriend, on reception had murmured something about her being the manager's latest squeeze.

'Michel, thank you so much.' She held out her hand. He was relieved that she hadn't recognised him from the Hotel de Paris. 'How lucky that you came along. I hope you thanked him properly, Emmie.' She turned to her daughter who merely nodded, unable to utter a word.

'My pleasure, we had a great time, didn't we, Emmie? We had the roof down and the music blaring out.' He winked at Emmie. 'But I'm astonished that the school let her out of the playground. It doesn't seem particularly responsible behaviour.'

There was a short pause after this. Something didn't ring true but no one could put their finger on it. During the silence Stephanie's phone bleeped. She looked at the screen and smiled. 'They're nearly here.' She was grinning from ear to ear. 'Emmie, shall we go to the top of the driveway and welcome them in.'

'He's only been away for a week.' Celine spoke without thinking.

'Philippe may have only been away for a week but Luc has been away for five months,' Stephanie said quietly.

Michel stepped into the slightly awkward moment. 'I'll nip into town to collect the gateau,' he said. 'I won't be long.'

Stephanie beckoned to Emmie. 'Come on, cheri, I'll race you and Sausage to the end of the driveway.'

Giving her mother a wide berth, Emmie ran after her aunt and the piglet ran after his mistress.

'Silly creature,' Celine said, and the others were unclear whether she meant her daughter or the piglet.

Claude chose to believe the latter. 'I actually think he is rather sweet.'

Henri and Rosa exchanged glances.

'Maybe the worm is turning,' Rosa muttered under her breath as they walked back into the house.

CHAPTER TWENTY-SIX

Philippe got out of the car and held out his arms to Emmie who was bounding down the driveway. She flung herself into his embrace, clinging on to him like a limpet. The emotions of the day caught up with her and she hung on to him as if she never wanted to let him go.

Tuned to her every mood, Philippe sensed her distress and tightened his arms around her. He could not bear to think of her being unhappy and was desperate to know why but now was not the time to ask.

'Look who else is here, Emmie.' He gently untangled her arms and beckoned Luc over.

Emmie knew Luc, of course, but it had been a long time since she had seen him and he had grown a beard in the intervening months. She was overcome with sudden shyness and hid behind Philippe's legs, leaving Luc staring down at Sausage.

'Mon Dieu!' he cried. 'What has happened? Emmaline has been turned into a pig. What wicked witch has cast this spell?' He winked at Philippe. 'I have to reverse this curse with a little verse.' He paused for a moment to think and then waving his arms around started singing.

'Witches of France, hear my plea

A piglet is not what I want to see.

Bring back a girl, her name's Emmaline

She is the prettiest little fairy queen.'

Giggling, Emmie ran from behind Philippe's legs and straight in the arms of Luc.

'Emmie is here,' she cried, kissing him and then tugging his shaggy beard.

'Don't you like it?' He stroked it ruefully.

She shook her head.

'OK, then I'll shave it straight off in the morning.' He grinned at her. 'I can't have young girls hiding from me in fear.' He ruffled her hair. 'I've missed you, ma petite. Now I need to know, is young Daniel still your boyfriend?' She squealed with protest, putting her hands over her ears. 'No?' He laughed. 'I'm pleased to hear that because I've found someone for you. A young Californian lad, well not that young, in fact he may be a bit old for you, well quite a lot old for you, but his parents are very wealthy and we have to think about my future.'

Everyone was laughing, including Emmie, and watching the interplay it slowly dawned on Claude that no one else treated her any differently. It didn't seem to matter to them that she was slow or clumsy or had difficulty talking. In fact, with them she didn't actually appear to have any difficulty talking. When she was alone with him and Celine she was tongue-tied and awkward, stammering so badly at times that she could hardly get a sentence out. Celine had no patience with her and if he were honest he wasn't much better. Watching her now looking so relaxed and happy he suddenly felt incredibly sad. He loved Emmaline, she was his daughter, but he didn't really know her. He had watched her grow up, they occupied the same space, he clothed and fed her but he had no relationship with her.

He had always known that there was an incredible bond between her and Philippe. It hadn't worried him, in fact he encouraged it. He knew that Emmie was happier in the chateau and he knew that Celine was happier if Emmie was not in the house, and keeping his wife happy was one of Claude's main targets in life. He had dedicated the last twelve years to doing exactly that.

He still found it hard to believe that Celine had chosen him. She was a beauty, she could have had her pick of anyone, but miraculously she had picked him. He was under no illusions about himself, he had not inherited the tall athletic build that most Fontaine men had. He took after his mother, he was slightly built, short-sighted, and these days alarmingly short of hair. It remained a mystery why Celine had wanted him, but she had and he was determined to do everything in his power for it to remain that way.

But however much he tried it never seemed to be quite enough. He was aware of the restlessness within her and had hoped that the birth of their first child would bring her more contentment but she had loathed being pregnant. She'd had a terrible time giving birth and when she had been told that Emmie had suffered as a consequence had virtually turned her back on her tiny daughter.

He had been baffled both by her behaviour and by the baby and had been only too happy for Philippe and his family to step in. Now, however, something stirred deep within him and watching his daughter laughing with Luc and Philippe he began to suspect that he might have missed out on something very special those last nine years.

He felt empty. He sensed the laughter and love flowing around him but felt as if he were in an eddy, swirling in circles, near but never actually in the current. He looked over to his wife who was also standing on the edge. He had known for a long time that she was unhappy but for the very first time he acknowledged that maybe he was too.

'Claude?' Rosa was beside him. 'This is a celebration, not a funeral,' she chided gently.

'I'm so sorry, Rosa, I've a lot of things on my mind.'

'Can I help you?'

He shook his head sadly. Rosa was almost like a mother to him but even so he couldn't unburden himself.

'Then go and join the party.' She smiled.

Nailing a smile to his face, Claude followed instructions. He accepted a glass of champagne, greeted Luc and Philippe and watched his young daughter dance around giddy with joy. He was relieved that her ordeal seemed to have had no lasting effect. He turned to Michel. 'Thank you once again for rescuing Emmie.'

'My pleasure,' the young man said, taking a packet of cigarettes from his pocket. 'She's absolutely gorgeous, you must be very proud of her.' He offered Claude a cigarette.

'Thank you, yes.' Claude took the cigarette without making it clear whether he was responding to Michel's statement or his offer. Michel took out a box of matches and with a jolt Claude saw that they were from the Hotel de Paris.

Was there a connection between him and Celine? If so, what the hell was it? Or was it mere coincidence? Before he could continue this train of thought a squeal from Emmie interrupted him.

'Uncle Philly, look what Luc made.' She held up a small brown circular tube which had been tied at intervals and now resembled a string of small chipolatas. 'A collar what is for Sausage.'

'No.' Stephanie laughed. 'Isn't that a bit too cruel?'

'I imagine he will remain a Sausage in name only, so I think it is safe for him to wear.' Luc hugged his mother. 'I have a gift for you too.'

'I hope it's more tasteful than that.'

'I have presents from Bea for everyone,' Philippe announced just as Celine was walking over to greet him. 'Let's go inside.'

Celine stopped in her tracks. How did this happen? Even when Beatrice wasn't here she managed to ruin her moment. Perhaps it was true, perhaps the bloody woman really was a witch.

'Everything alright, Celine?' Philippe stopped to give her a quick kiss. 'You look as if you've seen a ghost.'

I have, she thought, a ghost that has haunted me half of my life, only this particular ghost is alive and kicking.

CHAPTER TWENTY-SEVEN

Philippe sat gazing at his special little girl. Emmie was fast asleep and snoring gently. As usual her arms were flung out above her head and her tousled curls lay spread on the pillow. They had forgotten to braid her hair the night before and it would be a tangle of knots when she woke up. Long lashes rested on her chubby cheeks and her tongue stuck out from her open mouth.

He remembered a precious night nine years ago. The night he had fallen in love with Emmaline. Celine was still recovering from the birth, it had been long and difficult and the recuperation period was taking weeks. The rest of the household, barring himself and a teenage Luc, had succumbed to a particularly virulent flu that was spreading around the town like wildfire.

He had heard Emmie's cries echoing around the chateau until finally, unable to bear it any longer, and mindful of those trying to sleep, he'd got out of bed and gone to see what was happening. A white-faced Claude was clumsily pacing the kitchen, jogging and jolting the little baby with every heavy step. He looked like death. Philippe had immediately reached out for the screaming child and ordered Claude to bed.

Settled gently into the crook of his arm, Emmie's screams subsided immediately. Stammering vague instructions about her bottle, a relieved Claude had relinquished all responsibility and staggered off upstairs.

Philippe had fed her and changed her, he had sung to her and waltzed with her in his arms. Careless of hygiene, he had placed her next to Belle and the big dog had gently snuffled and sniffed her and Emmie had lain entranced.

He had finally fallen asleep in the big wicker chair by the fireplace with Belle at his side and little Emmie in his arms. He woke to see her huge blue eyes staring up at him. He smiled at her and she blew a raspberry. Their mutual love affair had begun.

She opened her eyes sleepily and then sat up with joy on seeing him. She flung open her arms and he got up to hug her.

'Morning, fairy queen.'

'Morning, fairy king.' She giggled.

'So I hear you had an adventure yesterday, Emmie?' He stroked her matted hair.

She looked puzzled.

'A lift back in the sports car with Michel,' he said winking at her. 'I bet everyone at school was jealous when they saw that, Emmie.'

Incapable of telling a lie, she hesitated before replying, 'Nobody didn't see me, Uncle Philly.'

'Why didn't they see you? Where were you, cheri?' He was being slightly cruel pretending he didn't know, but he wanted to hear the reason from her.

She didn't immediately reply, torn between desire to tell her uncle and terror that her mother would find out.

'It's OK, Emmie, you can tell me.' He tightened his arms around her.

'Emmie was outside,' she said softly.

'Why was that, Emmie?'

'Easier.' She chewed furiously on her lip.

'Easier for who, cheri? Easier for Maman?'

She nodded miserably. Philippe's blood was boiling but he managed to keep calm.

'So Maman asks you to go outside, does she? I expect it's quicker for her than going into the playground.'

181

She nodded again, relieved that he seemed to understand.

'And do you slip out every day?'

'Sometimes.'

'Emmaline, can you promise me something?' Philippe took both her hands. 'Will you promise me never to leave the playground by yourself again?'

The little girl looked confused. She was imagining her mother's reaction. She hated not to do what her uncle wanted but she knew Celine would be furious if she found out she had told Uncle Philly what Celine referred to as 'their little secret'.

Rightly interpreting her fear, Philippe hastened to reassure her. 'Maman won't know you've ever said anything. We'll tell her that the teachers are being extra strict.' He smiled at her. 'I don't think she realised quite what the rules were. She wouldn't want you to disobey your teachers.'

Emmie was not really convinced but smiled up at him.

'So do we have a bargain, cheri? You promise me you will stay inside the gates?'

'Promise,' she whispered.

He kissed the top of her head. 'I've missed you, Emmie.'

'Missed you too.' She buried herself in his arms, breathing in his familiar scent.

'I smell Rosa's hot chocolate, do you?' He put his nose in the air and bayed like a bloodhound.

Emmie looked up and copied him.

'Race you to the kitchen.' Philippe stood up. 'But a slow race, I can only walk, no running now.'

Giggling they marched side by side down the corridor. Just as they reached the kitchen door the phone rang.

'OK, we'll have to call it a draw,' Philippe said breathlessly.

'You sound like you've been running.' Beatrice laughed down the phone.

'I've been having a quick walking race with Emmie,' Philippe replied, dropping his stick to the floor and sinking gratefully onto the huge leather armchair.

So Emmie had stayed at the chateau again last night, thought Beatrice. This was getting too regular to be normal. What on earth was going on?

'Did you tell them our ideas?' She was eager to hear what the family had thought of their plans.

'No,' Philippe answered slowly. 'It wasn't quite the right moment.'

'Really?' Beatrice was surprised.

'There was a strange sort of atmosphere, a few things were out of kilter,' he said quietly.

'What things?' She reached for a cigarette, instantly intrigued.

'I'm in the hallway, Bea,' he said, seeing Emmie's face appear in the kitchen doorway.

'OK.' She understood immediately. The hallway was vast and it echoed. Everywhere. Not the place for a private conversation.

'I'll tell them over breakfast and then I will call you back.'

'Before you go, I've had another idea.' She paused for a moment. 'Sky should come over to the chateau.'

'Why?' Philippe said, standing up immediately. 'What on earth for? Why do you want Sky to come over?'

'I'll tell you if you give me a chance.' She was amused at his reaction. 'She is hugely talented, Philippe.'

'So?'

'Cheri, don't bite my head off, just listen to me.'

He sank back into the chair.

'She has done the most wonderful paintings for me. Small pictures of the riad. She has captured everyday life here. She has drawn Bushara cooking in the kitchen, Ibrahim sweeping the hallway, the tortoise eating a lettuce leaf, bougainvillea flowers floating at the edge of the pool, she has caught the very essence of the riad. I'm going to have them made into cards and I think she should do the same for you.' She paused to inhale the cigarette. 'The pictures are bewitching.'

'She certainly seems to have cast a spell on you.' Philippe was amused.

'They are very unique. I'll e-mail them to you so that you can see.' She changed the subject. 'Go and have breakfast, is it a Rosa special?'

'I'm not sure, but we do have a Rosa Basque chicken for lunch.' Philippe licked his lips in anticipation.

'Mon Dieu, I'm getting on a plane now.' She laughed. 'A bientôt, cheri, I love you.'

'I love you too, Bea, I love you very much indeed.'

At the other end of the line Beatrice raised her eyebrows, as did Stephanie, passing by with her arms full of freshly baked baguettes. Was something going on between her ex-sister-in-law and her brother that she was not aware of?

She looked at Philippe curiously but he was giving nothing away.

'So what do you think?' he asked them all a short while later as they were finishing breakfast. 'How do you think that sounds?' He had been outlining the plans for the wine tasting weekend to them.

'Sounds as if you had one hell of a week.' Luc grinned.

'It certainly wasn't dull.' Philippe reached for the coffee.

'It's interesting,' Stephanie said hesitantly.

'Maman it's more than interesting.' Luc leapt up. 'It's exactly what we need, it's an amazing opportunity.' He paced around the table. 'To have the opportunity to showcase our wines to some of London's top restaurants is beyond our wildest dreams.'

Philippe smiled to himself as Luc launched into a speech about the magic of the Californian marketing machine. He remembered Bea and himself doing exactly the same to his father. They had been spilling over with ideas and suggestions which had all been met with a polite smile and a nod of the head. His father's lack of enthusiasm had dampened theirs and Philippe remembered his desperate disappointment when he realised that his father was frightened of change. He had seemed unusually tired and blinkered. In hindsight Philippe guessed it must have been the start of the cancer which had eventually carried him off, but at the time it had been immensely frustrating.

Suddenly determined that he must never be like that, he interrupted as Luc was speaking about the importance of image.

'You are right, Luc, you are absolutely right. We need to do something to make us stand out.'

His nephew looked delighted.

Philippe continued, 'We have a wonderful product which is not getting the attention it deserves.' He paused before adding, 'Maybe it is time for new labels, in fact Bea, always one step ahead, has someone in mind to help us. Her name is Sky, she was staying in the riad and she is a very talented artist.'

'She must be if Beatrice recommends her,' Stephanie said. 'Beatrice has very exacting standards.'

'Bea is going to e-mail me some of the pictures Sky has done of the riad, and she also has a website.'

His sister however was looking far from convinced. 'We have had the label from the start. It is part of our heritage, people recognise it.'

'But it is like a hundred other labels, Maman,' Luc replied. 'A picture of a chateau, it is hardly original or eye-catching.'

'It is classy, classic and symbolises our wine,' his mother retorted. 'We don't need some shiny bright label. It cheapens the wine. I see them in the supermarket and shudder.'

Philippe butted in before Luc could respond. 'All we are doing is throwing ideas around right now.' He smiled gently.' Let's all try and keep an open mind.'

'But we are definitely going with the chefs' invitations?' Luc demanded.

'We are definitely going with it,' Philippe agreed. 'We can't afford to miss a chance like that.'

He looked around the room. 'We have to be more proactive, otherwise we will stagnate and then…'

He didn't finish the sentence but his Gallic shrug said it all.

There was silence. Philippe looked at their faces. Luc's full of enthusiasm and energy, Stephanie's anxious yet thoughtful whereas Henri was his usual implacable self.

He stood up and reached for his stick. 'It's exciting, we just need to think positive and keep pushing forward.' He smiled reassuringly. 'Luc, Henri, let's take a walk through the vines.' He walked towards the door and yelled, 'Emmie, get your boots on we're going for a wander.'

At the door he suddenly turned around. 'Oh, one more thing, we have someone coming to help for a few months.' He was talking quickly. 'Beatrice rang the agency she uses for her hotel in Paris. He'll be arriving some time next week. I can't really pull my weight at the moment so it seemed only fair.' He had expected some murmurs of dissent but no one disagreed, in fact no one seemed remotely surprised by his statement.

He must have been worse than he thought. Bemused, he started to turn around and out of the corner of his eye caught his sister and Rosa exchange a smile. He realised he had been duped.

'You knew about this, didn't you?' He glared at them. 'You asked Bea to persuade me to hire someone?' Stephanie simply smiled and Rosa avoided looking him in the eye. He wheeled around to face Henri, who said nothing but his blue eyes were twinkling.

CHAPTER TWENTY-EIGHT

I was pacing around the flat waiting for Miles to come and collect his things. I could have taken the coward's way and gone out for the afternoon but he'd said he wanted to talk to me and I'd realised that I couldn't hide away for ever.

My relationship with Nick was still tenuous and fragile. After the initial euphoria of discovering him alive we were back to skating on thin ice. I knew we had a strong bond and I knew the relationship had to change, but I hadn't a clue how to move it forward. I still felt as if I were treading water. Only a few weeks ago I had had a husband and a best friend and life was good. Now all that had been taken away from me, my once ordered life lay in tangles and I could see only dense fog ahead.

The doorbell rang, I jumped nervously and glanced in the mirror. I'd taken care with my appearance, I'd chosen a new top from Marrakech that complimented my light tan, I'd put make-up on and sprayed some new perfume. I wasn't really sure why I'd bothered. I doubted he was going to launch himself back into my arms.

Taking a deep breath I went to open it and stared at him.

Ye gods, what in the world was he wearing? He looked bloody awful. He had on a hideous green baggy jumper that I'd never seen before, jeans and an old pair of trainers. He looked gaunt and pale. Dark shadows circled his eyes and he clearly hadn't been near a razor in days. And this was the man who used to spend more time getting ready than me. What was he playing at? I'd never seen him look so rough.

'You look lovely,' he said, looking me up and down.

'You look like shite.'

I opened the door to let him in, wondering if his strange appearance was a deliberate attempt to elicit my sympathy and felt a rush of annoyance. I was the victim here, he had no right whatsoever to try and make me feel sorry for him. It was a ploy that was unworthy of him.

'Would you like some tea?' I offered. Christ, how bloody British, our lives were falling apart and I offered tea.

'Not really.' He opened his bag. 'I brought some wine.'

He'd brought a bottle of my favourite Rioja. I couldn't think why, this was hardly a celebration.

He opened it swiftly and silently poured and handed me a glass. There was a long pause.

'I'm pleased that you and Nick are talking.'

'Barely.'

'It's a start, Sky. It will take time.' He paused again. 'It won't be easy for you but you are soul mates and no one can tear you apart.'

'You certainly gave it a go.' I took a large gulp.

'Sky, you know it's not all about Nick.' He picked at a thread in his ghastly jumper. I wished the whole damn thing would unravel, much like our relationship. He continued hesitantly. 'He may have been the catalyst but deep down I think we both knew we weren't really meant for each other.'

I was stunned. I couldn't believe what I was hearing. What the hell was going on? Did he really think that was true?

'I loved you,' I said. 'I wanted to get married and unlike you I wanted to stay married. I actually believed what I said on our wedding day.'

'You may have believed what you said, Sky, but did you ever really feel it?'

'Don't you dare try and tell me how I felt,' I screeched. 'Don't try and make out I didn't love you just to make it easier on yourself. Please don't give me any more crap about the final piece of the jigsaw or finding the one who made you whole. It only makes it worse.'

'I'm sorry.' Miles threw back his wine. 'You're right. I'm so sorry, Sky, I'm just trying to be honest, I'm just trying to let you know how I feel but I'm making a very poor job of it.'

'You're the one who walked out on me, Miles.' I was spitting with rage. 'Don't lay the blame on me, have the courage to take responsibility.'

'Maybe I should just go and grab a few things, I'll come back another time for the rest.'

I watched him walk away. I was very angry but also very confused. What was this obsession everyone seemed to have about me not loving Miles? Including Miles, it would seem.

Maybe I should have paid more attention to Nonna but I'd been too cross and upset at the time. And talking of Nonna, I was aware that I still hadn't told her or my father the news. They still thought that Miles and I had been having the time of our lives in Marrakech.

I'd have to ring them soon, they'd be wondering why I hadn't called them, but I was dreading it. What the hell could I say? Bad enough telling them that Miles had swapped his sexual preferences, but how would they feel when they heard that his new love was none other than their beloved Nick.

'Sky?' Miles stood in the doorway with a full bag slung over his shoulder. He looked awkward but I wasn't prepared to help him. He cleared his throat. 'I'm not sure what you want to do, where you want to stay? Have you made any plans?'

Once again I stared at him in disbelief. 'Of course I've not made any plans,' I said slowly. 'Are you trying to kick me out? I'm aware that you pay most of the mortgage but I would be grateful if you could give me a little more time to make arrangements.'

'I was just going to say that if you wanted to stay here then I would be happy to continue to pay my share.'

I looked around the flat that I had so lovingly decorated, taking in the gentle greys and greens which I'd believed were cool and calming. After the vibrancy of Marrakech, they now looked dull and uninspiring.

Similarly, the white walls and stainless steel equipment in the kitchen appeared cold and clinical. I thought back to Bushara's kitchen. Her glowing terracotta tagines, the deep blue and gold crockery, the copper pans, bright baskets of fruit and overflowing pots of sharp green herbs.

'I don't want to stay here.' I knew that with sudden clarity. 'I've no idea where I want to go but I don't want to stay here.'

'OK.' He paused. 'I'll come back another time.'

'Wear something decent.'

He had the grace to look abashed. 'I wanted you to know I was suffering.'

'It didn't work.'

'I can see that.'

When he left I poured myself a large glass of wine and waited for the despair to hit and the tears to flow, but instead I felt completely numb. Everything felt surreal, as if it were happening to someone else, as if I were watching myself from the wings.

The telephone shattered the silence. I was disorientated, the number wasn't one I recognised, probably a sales call, nonetheless I picked it up.

'Yes.' I was brusque.

''Allo? Sky?'

I immediately recognised the rich tones of Philippe and was completely thrown. How had he got this number?

'Sky?' He spoke into the pause. 'It is Philippe here. Philippe Fontaine.'

I smiled to myself. As if it needed qualifying? How many other French Philippes did he think I knew?

'Is this a bad time?'

I realised that I still hadn't spoken. Pulling myself together I said, 'No, not at all, it's just a surprise, that's all.' I tried to put a smile into my voice. 'Lovely to hear from you.'

I could tell he wasn't convinced. He remained silent. Our conversations never seemed to be straightforward.

'Philippe?'

'Yes I'm still here.' He paused again and I waited. 'Listen, I have a proposition for you, well actually Bea suggested it.' Once again he hesitated and I was intrigued.

'I'm listening, Philippe, tell me more.'

'Bea showed me your paintings of the riad, they are absolutely stunning. I wondered if you'd like to come here and do some of the chateau?'

I gasped, this was the last thing I'd expected.

'Bea thought that the chefs and wine buffs who are coming out might be interested in buying them.'

I was still in shock.

'I mean, only if it appeals to you, maybe you have something lined up. Bea seemed to think you didn't have anything for a while but maybe she was wrong?'

I smiled to myself. This was typical of Beatrice, trying to control everyone even after they had left the riad. But I didn't mind, quite the contrary, I was overwhelmed that Beatrice had thought so much of my paintings that she was recommending me to Philippe. It was all too much to take in. I was aware that Philippe was still speaking.

'Obviously we would pay for your airfare and you would be welcome to stay in the chateau, and we, um, well, we would come to some sort of, um, financial arrangement...' He trailed off lamely. I was about to respond but before I could reply he quickly said, 'Anyway, there is no need to give me an answer now.' He sounded as if he were wishing he'd never asked me and I leapt in quickly.

'Philippe, I think it sounds wonderful.'

'Really?' He sounded surprised.

'I'm so sorry, I'm a bit all over the place right now.' I grinned. 'I know you think that's how I always am.'

'Not at all.' He began half-heartedly to protest.

'And probably with good reason,' I cut him off again. 'It's just that Miles, my husband, my ex-husband, well not yet but soon to be, has been to see me and I'm feeling a little fragile.' I was aware that my voice was breaking and desperately tried to control myself. God, he must have thought I was a total fruitcake.

'Sky, I'm so sorry. This must be such a difficult time for you. 'I was amazed to hear such warmth in his voice. 'I cannot imagine what you are going through. Listen, I'm sorry to disturb you, I'll ring another time.'

'Philippe, I think coming to France is probably exactly what I need right now,' I said, suddenly realising that this was true. 'But I need to get a few things straightened out first. Is that OK?'

'Sky, of course that is OK. Just ring when you know when.' He hesitated for a moment. 'You are strong, Sky, you can cope. Au revoir.'

I stood staring at the receiver. I was astonished. What had prompted him to say that? I walked to the window. It was dull outside, a dismal, murky day. I watched the people walking down the street, hunched over themselves, scurrying along like lab rats. I'd never actually seen any lab rats but I imagined this was what they must look like. Grey, miserable and expressionless.

After Morocco everything looked dreary, as if I was seeing the world in black and white. I suddenly couldn't bear it another moment.

I made a decision. I'd drive to Scotland tonight, I'd talk to my dad and Nonna. It was unfair to keep them in the dark any longer. I had a sudden longing to be in the big kitchen with the dogs at my feet and the donkeys braying outside.

Then I would come home and take up Philippe's offer and go to France. The thought sent a shiver of anticipation down my spine. I glanced at my watch, I wanted to ring Gail. It was weird how close I felt to her after such a short time together.

CHAPTER TWENTY-NINE

'Gail, it's Sky.'

'Sky! How lovely to hear from you.'

'How are you? How were your last few days?'

'Hectic, magical and rather scary.'

I laughed. 'How did Sonny take the news?'

'Oh, Sky, it was incredible, I've never seen him so happy, he was lit up from within.'

'How wonderful. So what happens next?'

'Tariq wants us to move to Marrakech. He owns the house next door which he will convert for us. I can help him with his business and Sonny can go to the International School.' She paused. 'He has it all worked out.'

'Are you OK with all that?'

'It's all I've ever dreamed of and yet I do feel rather terrified.'

'Of course you do. It's a huge change, Gail, but a very exciting one.'

'He says if I don't go there he will come here.'

'He would follow you to the ends of the earth,' I said, but Gail remained silent. 'You are going to go, aren't you?'

'Well, it doesn't seem fair to ask him to swap a thriving business and a close-knit family for a three-bed semi in Chigwell and a sister-in-law who hates him.'

I laughed. 'Talking of which, have you spoken to Dawn?'

'Not yet, she's coming over tomorrow and I am dreading it.'

'Gail, I'm so sorry, but I guess you need to clear the air.' That was an understatement, I thought to myself.

'Yes, things need saying that should have been said a long while ago.' She paused. 'Enough about me. How are things with you?'

'I had an awkward meeting with Miles this morning. We didn't resolve anything really, it was a bit of a nightmare, and then…' I hesitated. 'Then Philippe rang.'

'Philippe?' She sounded amazed. 'What did he want?'

'Well, actually he wants me to go to France.' I heard her gasp. 'Beatrice showed him the paintings I did of the riad and he wants me to do some for the chateau.'

'Sky, how fabulous!' There was a pause. 'You said yes, right?'

'I said I was certainly interested, but we didn't make definite plans.'

'What's stopping you?'

'I've only just got back here; I really need to go to Scotland and enlighten my father and grandmother who think I've been having the holiday of a lifetime with Miles; I need to sort out where I'm going to live. You know, there are lots of things happening.' I felt a bit defensive.

'All that's happening is procrastination, Sky,' Gail said firmly. 'If you go to Scotland you will end up spending a week there, why don't you ring them instead? They will want you to go to France, I'm sure, and you don't need to sort out where to live right now. I doubt Miles is throwing you out on the street.' She paused. 'You need to strike while the iron is hot, Sky. Philippe is clearly keen. It's a great opportunity; you can't let it slip by.'

'My God, you can be very strict.' I smiled.

'Go and pour yourself a glass of wine, ring Scotland and then call Philippe back and say you would love to come at the earliest opportunity.' She giggled. 'That is an order.'

Gail was right, if I went to Scotland I would spend a week there, maybe more, lulled by the comfort and security of being back at home. I would ring them now and tell them everything, and if they sounded distraught then I would drive up there tomorrow.

They were not distraught. They were shocked but there were no histrionics or apportioning of blame. They listened together on speaker phone without interrupting and I left nothing out, ending with Philippe's job offer.

'When do you go, Sky?' my father asked.

'When do I go where?'

'To France, to the chateau.'

'I'm not sure.' I hadn't expected the question. 'We haven't spoken dates yet, I mean I didn't know if you would want me to come up.'

'Why would we be wanting you to come up, cara?' Nonna asked in her forthright manner. 'You coming up won't be solving anything but you going to France might be.' I wasn't clear what she meant but that was normal with Nonna. 'If you don't say yes now, cara, then your Frenchman may be changing his mind, he may be finding someone else.'

'Nonna is right,' my father replied in his gentle manner. 'Come and see us when you get back, and we can talk over everything then and you can tell us about France.' I could hear him puffing at his pipe. 'Good luck, my darling, we are only a phone call away.'

They really were incredible, I thought, draining the last of the Rioja into my glass. There weren't many families who would take that sort of news so stoically. Well, it looked like I had no option but to go to France. It was daunting but also quite exciting. I looked at my watch. France were an hour ahead so I decided to leave the call to Philippe until the morning. I was tired and I had drunk nearly a whole bottle of wine. I didn't want to give him any excuse to rethink the whole thing. I'd get up early and check out flights and appear organised and in control, which would be a novelty.

I nestled under the duvet on the sofa where I had been sleeping since my return. I couldn't bear to sleep in the bedroom, it felt wrong and it felt lonely. I turned the light off and the telly on.

I woke with a stiff neck and the telly still blaring. My throat was sore and my mouth was parched. I thought back to the Chateau Fontaine wine with its blissful absence of after-effects.

An hour later, after strong coffee and a blast in the shower, I had compiled a list of flight options for Philippe. I poured myself another coffee and glanced at the clock. It would be just after nine o'clock in France. Was that too early? Did that reek of desperation or merely come across as enthusiastic? I decided to opt for the latter.

'Oui, bonjour.' His deep voice sounded even deeper on the phone.

'Philippe, it's Sky.'

'Hello, hello, Sky.'

Was it my imagination or did he sound a little wary?

'I've been looking at flights to Bordeaux.'

'Ah. OK.'

It definitely wasn't my imagination, he sounded distinctly uneasy, but I ploughed on regardless.

'Well I was thinking about your offer yesterday and I would love to take you up on it. I thought I should come out sooner rather than later so that you can have pictures ready for the wine weekend, in fact…' I paused for a moment and gulped my coffee. 'In fact, I wondered if you might like me to help design the invitations?'

'How funny. Nick had the same idea.'

'Nick?' My heart started hammering. What the hell had Nick got to do with this? Why was he involved?

'The thing is, Sky, Nick rang last night.' Philippe paused but I said nothing. 'He wanted to come over to get a feel for the place before the wine weekend, look at my kitchen, source local supplies and so on.' He paused but once again I remained quiet. 'He's desperate for it to be a huge success. So am I, of course.' I could hear him inhale his cigarette, no wonder he had sounded uncomfortable.

'Well, I guess that makes sense,' I said over-brightly, although my heart had plummeted. I was desperately disappointed. I hadn't realised how much I wanted to go until there was a possibility I couldn't. Bloody Nick, how had he managed to ruin things yet again? 'I'm sure there will be another time, no worries.' My voice had risen and tears were threatening, I was keen to end the conversation as quickly as possible.

'No, Sky, wait.' Philippe stopped me from putting the phone down. 'I'd still really like you to come over. I just didn't know how things were between you, I didn't want to assume anything, I wasn't sure, you know, what had happened after Marrakech?'

'You want us both to be there?' I wanted to make sure I understood.

'Well, it would make sense, but I don't want to put you in an awkward position.'

Poor Philippe, we were the ones putting *him* in an awkward position. It wasn't fair for him to be caught up in our drama. It had nothing to do with him, he was simply trying to run his business. I made up my mind quickly. 'I'm happy to come out, Philippe, I can't speak for Nick but I can't imagine there will be a problem.'

'Oh, that is great, Sky.' He sounded very relieved. 'As long as you are sure.'

'Of course I'm sure,' I sounded sharper than intended. 'We can all be adult and professional about this.' I wasn't at all sure that was true but was determined not to let Philippe think otherwise. 'I'll ring Nick and one of us will be in touch re flights. I imagine that it will be more convenient if we arrive together.'

I poured myself yet another mug of coffee and then decided against it. I couldn't bear the silence of the flat anymore. I needed noise and bustle. Grabbing my bag and jacket I made my way to a café we seldom frequented. It was dark and shabby but it suited my mood right now. Despite the slight chill I chose an outdoor table. I needed the air. Pulling my mobile out of my bag I noticed I had a missed call from Gail. I'd give her a quick buzz before phoning Nick.

'Hello?'

She sounded strained. 'Gail, is this a bad time to ring?'

'Sky, hello, no I'm just waiting for Dawn to arrive.'

'Ah, no wonder you sound tense.' I felt so sorry for her. 'I saw I had a missed call from you.'

'I just wanted to know if you had followed my orders and how you got on with Scotland and France.'

'Scotland were incredible, France is slightly more complicated.'

'In what way?'

'Nick is going.'

'Nick? Really?'

'Really.' I grimaced. 'Apparently he rang Philippe last night wanting to go and suss out the place before the wine weekend.'

'Well, that is understandable – but where does it leave you?'

'It leaves me being adult and professional.' I laughed. 'At least that's what I told Philippe, I'm about to phone Nick right now.'

'Well done you. Sky, I've got to go, I can hear Dawn's car.'

'Good luck,' I yelled down the phone.

CHAPTER THIRTY

'It was just one or two friends.' Dawn was looking mutinous. She'd marched in with a face like thunder, barely stopping to give her nephew a hug before he scuttled over to play next door.

'Dawn, please don't lie to me, Margaret said there was a whole group of you.'

'Interfering bloody cow.'

'Dawn, just listen to yourself. This is Margaret you're talking about, Margaret who has been so kind and generous to us both over the years and who, I might add, cleaned the whole house after you left it looking like a tip.'

'If you hadn't thrown us out then we'd have tidied up and you'd never have known.'

Gail stared at her sister in astonishment. 'I'd never have known? Six of your mates came into my house while I was away, drank my wine, slept in my room, raided my cupboards for food and you think it would have been OK not to have told me?'

'You're my sister, for Christ's sake,' Dawn retaliated. 'It's hardly like breaking and entering is it?'

'Well, as my sister, wouldn't you think of asking beforehand?' Gail demanded. 'Your friends have always been made welcome here. So why suddenly all the secrecy? Why on earth couldn't you have asked me instead of skulking behind my back?'

Dawn shrugged. 'It was a spur of the moment thing, seemed like a good idea, I didn't realise bloody World War Three would break out.'

'You just don't get it, do you, Dawn? You honestly believe you have nothing to apologise about,' Gail fumed. 'You're one of life's takers, you take everything and give nothing back in return.'

'Look, if you're going to hurl insults at me then I'm out of here.'

'No you don't.' Gail stood firmly by the door. She looked her sister straight in the eye. The sister she had given up everything for. The sister she had devoted most of her life to. 'We've a few things to sort out, Dawn, not least of which is why you stole five years of my life?' Tears sprang into her eyes. 'Why, Dawn? Why did you tell such lies? You knew how much I loved Tariq so why would you not want me to be happy?'

Dawn remained silent.

'Please, Dawn, I need to know. I don't understand why you would do such a terrible thing.'

'Jesus, Gail, there's no need to be so bloody dramatic.' Dawn scowled at her sister. 'You had a good life here, Simon was a nice guy, he had a huge house, he was rich, why would you want to throw all that away on some greasy Arab?'

Gail stared open-mouthed. Dawn continued. 'Besides, what would have happened to me?' She forced a tremble into her voice. 'I'd already lost a mother, I didn't want to lose a sister too.' She felt rather pleased with that tack. That should shut Gail up. It usually worked.

But this time the ploy didn't have the desired effect.

'Don't play that card, Dawn.' Gail's voice was icy. 'I lost my mother too. At the age of twenty-one I lost my mother. I gave up university to look after you. I gave up everything. I have looked after you all your life and you have never wanted for a thing.'

Dawn opened her mouth to speak but the floodgates had opened and Gail was in no mood for stopping the tide. 'At the age of twenty-one I suddenly had a child to look after and a mortgage and bills to pay. At a time when I should have been studying, partying and getting drunk I was working in the bank you are so keen to mock. I worked my way up in the bank through hard graft and determination and I am proud of it. Whereas you hop carelessly from one job to the next no, Dawn, you just hear me out,' she yelled as her sister once more tried to stem the flow.

'These are things I need to say and things you need to hear. First it was a florist, grand ideas of society weddings, I found you a job in the local florist where you lasted about four months. Next it was catering, again images of elite private dinners for the wealthy, so I enrolled you in a college, I can't remember how long you lasted there, and now you're a personal shopper but how long will that last? The list is endless, Dawn, you have never stuck at anything in your life.'

Dawn was stunned into silence, amazed by the ferocity and intensity of her sister's speech.

'All I wanted was for Mum to be proud of the way I'd brought you up, I only ever wanted the best for you, but Mum wouldn't be proud, she'd be horrified.' Once again the tears started to flow. 'It's my fault, I'm to blame, I've spoilt you. I have made you the selfish, shallow woman you are today.'

Dawn stood up. She was shaking with rage. 'How dare you speak to me like that, how dare you?'

'I dare, Dawn, because it's true. I sacrificed so much for you, I sacrificed it willingly because I love you. But how do you repay me? You lied to me, you lied to Tariq and you nearly denied Sonny the chance to know his father. I'll find it very hard to forgive you for that.' She paused and took a deep breath. 'I'm not sure you even realise what you have done wrong.' She looked at her sister as if seeing her for the first time. 'You haven't apologised and you show no remorse.'

There was a short silence as Gail struggled to find the next words and Dawn remained mutinously quiet. 'I'll never stop loving you, Dawn,' Gail said very softly. 'You are my sister and I very much hope that one day we can be friends, but for now it's time for us to make our own ways in the world.'

In stony silence Dawn spun on her heel and marching out of the house slammed the front door. Gail sank onto the sofa and putting her head into her hands wept as if her heart would break. She wept for her mother, she wept for her sister and she wept for the years lost to her and Tariq.

She was vaguely aware of footsteps, was aware of someone sitting beside her and then felt herself pulled into a comforting embrace.

'Let it all out, sweetheart.' Margaret held her tight. 'Let it all out.'

'Sonny…?'

'Is busy in the garden with Jeff.'

'I said such terrible things to her.'

'And not before time, sweetheart.' Margaret stroked her hair. 'She's had everything handed to her on a plate, it's time she stood on her own two feet.'

'Mum would be heartbroken,' Gail sobbed. 'I've made such a mess of bringing her up.'

'Far from it, your mum would have been so very proud. If you were my daughter, Gail, then I would be immensely proud of you.'

'But Dawn…'

'Is smart and bright,' Margaret interrupted, she could have added a few more adjectives but wisely decided that now was not the time. 'You can only do so much, Gail, then they have to take responsibility for their own lives.' She continued to rock Gail gently in her arms until she gradually felt the sobs begin to subside. 'It's your turn now, it's your turn to live.' She handed Gail a tissue. 'You have to let your own life take shape now, sweetheart.'

'I've a feeling it will be shaped like Morocco,' Gail sniffed.

'That's an interesting shape.' Margaret smiled.

CHAPTER THIRTY-ONE

'Hello, I'm Philippe.'

'Hello, I'm short.'

Philippe stared at the small lad in front of him. 'How can I help you?'

'There's nothing you can do, it's a permanent condition.' The young man burst into laughter and Philippe found himself joining in.

'That usually breaks the ice.' The young man held out his hand. 'I'm Rudolph.'

'Like Rudolph the reindeer?' Emmie asked, standing beside her uncle.

'Like Rudolph Valentino,' he replied. 'But with the body of Toulouse-Lautrec.' He turned to Philippe. 'Do you want me to leave?'

'You've only just arrived.'

'But I'm not what you were expecting.'

'I wasn't really expecting anything.'

'Oh good, then maybe you won't be too disappointed.'

'I guess not.' Philippe was absolutely baffled. What was going on? Who the hell was he?

'I thought you might think I was too short.'

'Perhaps when you is all growed up you will be taller?' Emmie instinctively liked this stranger and wanted to make him feel better.

'I is all growed up.'

'Oh.' She hesitated and then smiled as another thought came to her. 'Maybe you is an elf?'

'Do you like elves?'

'Yes.' She nodded vigorously. 'Mostly.'

'Well then I don't mind being an elf.' Rudolph grinned at her. 'Mostly.'

He turned back to Philippe. 'Well, boss, what do you think? Am I too small?'

'Too small for what?' Philippe felt as if he was in some sort of parallel universe.

'Too small to work in the vines?'

'You is the same size as me and I works in the vines.' Emmie took hold of Rudolph's hand, squeezing it reassuringly.

'Well maybe I'll be OK then?' He looked at Philippe, his face creased with anxiety.

Understanding was gradually dawning on Philippe. 'Did the agency send you?'

Rudolph nodded. 'They should have warned you, I tell them to warn people, saves a lot of embarrassment.'

Philippe didn't say anything.

'I'm very strong.' Rudolph let go of Emmie's hand and flexed his muscles. She smiled at him encouragingly.

'What do you think, boss? Am I too short?'

'You are the same height as the vines, which I guess is just about perfect.' Philippe grinned down at him. This lad was something else. 'We may lose you though.'

'I'll put a bell around my neck.'

'I'll find you,' Emmie said earnestly. 'I knows all the vines.'

'Is it a deal, boss?' Rudolph couldn't quite hide his desperation.

'It's a deal.' Philippe nodded his head and held out his hand. 'But call me Philippe.'

'OK, boss, and I'll answer to Elf, I never liked the name Rudolph.' He shook Philippe's hand. 'You won't regret it.'

Emmie clapped her hands with delight. 'Come and meet Sausage.'

She smiled at him. 'He's my piglet, a piglet what mustn't be eaten,' she added quickly lest there be any confusion.

'How old are you, Elf?' Philippe stopped him before he went off.

'Nineteen,' he replied quickly, a little too quickly, Philippe thought, but he let it go.

'Slow down, Philippe.' Beatrice laughed down the telephone a few days later. 'You're going far too fast, tell me again what Sky said?'

'Well, I can't remember the exact words but something about her and Nick not wanting to stand in each other's way, putting professions before their personal life and not wanting to let me down.'

'I can understand Nick wanting to do his homework. He'll be cooking for some top chefs, there's a lot at stake. And I'm over the moon that Sky has decided to come, but how brave of them to come together.'

Philippe remained silent.

'What on earth have you got against her?' Beatrice was half amused, half exasperated. 'She is a very lovely girl, with a lot of talent, going through a very bad time and yet you seem totally unsympathetic.'

'I'm not unsympathetic,' Philippe said shortly and then changing the subject quickly said. 'The young man from the agency has arrived.'

'And how is he?'

'Extraordinary,' Philippe chuckled.

'Extraordinary in what way?' Beatrice reached for her cigarettes.

'Well, for starters he's about a metre high.'

'What?'

'He has a maze of crazy curls and fiery eyes in a freckled face. He looks about twelve but claims he's nineteen.'

'Mon Dieu.' Beatrice drew deeply on her cigarette. 'What an odd choice for the agency, I told them it could be hard manual labour.'

'Seemed bizarre to me too. But he's very keen.'

'Will he be OK, do you think?'

'He certainly has guts and gumption and he tells me he's very strong.' Philippe paused for a moment to light his cigarette. 'But behind the bravado his self-esteem is as low as his stature, I don't think life has treated him kindly. Frankly I don't think I'd have the heart to tell him to go.'

'You can't employ him because you feel sorry for him, he's there to help you.' She tipped back on her chair. 'What's his name?'

Philippe laughed suddenly. 'He wants us to call him Elf.'

'You can't call him Elf!' Beatrice nearly fell off her chair.

'That's what he wants. Emmie asked if he was one and he clearly liked the thought. He has her completely captivated, Rosa too, she's even given him permission to sleep in the old gypsy caravan.'

'He must be quite something, she doesn't give permission to just anyone.'

'He's an intriguing fellow, right now he's trying to teach Emmie to ride his unicycle.' Philippe looked out onto the lawn where the two of them lay in fits of giggles.

'A unicycle?' Beatrice stood up in amazement trying to picture the scene. 'An elf riding a unicycle?'

'I told you he was intriguing.'

'Now this I have to see for myself.'

'I know.' He chuckled.

'I'm serious.'

'I know.'

'Nick and Sky are enough to tempt me but an elf on a unicycle makes it a must.'

'I know.'

'Stop repeating yourself, Philippe, you sound like a parrot.'

Philippe said nothing.

'When do Sky and Nick arrive?' she asked impatiently.

'The day after you.'

'I beg your pardon?'

'It's booked, Bea.'

'What are you talking about?' She ground her cigarette out.

'I knew you wouldn't want to miss all this. I cleared it with Bushara.' He paused for dramatic effect. 'Your flights are already booked.'

There was a sharp intake of breath before her husky laugh floated down the phone. 'Mon Dieu, after all these years you still have the power to surprise me.'

'I surprise myself.'

'I love you, cheri.'

'And I you.'

CHAPTER THIRTY-TWO

We had landed at Bordeaux airport. It was hot. I felt the heat as soon as we stepped off the plane and I welcomed it. Our journey had been uneventful. Nick and I had been reserved but polite with each other and we had both pretended to sleep on the plane. Our bags arrived without delay and we made our way through customs.

Almost as soon as we had set foot outside the arrivals hall a young man bounded up to us.

'You must be Nick and Sky, I recognised you immediately from the photos.' He extended his hand. 'I'm Luc. I'm Philippe's nephew.'

They looked very similar; he wasn't quite as tall as Philippe but he had the same olive complexion, the same hazel eyes, the same slightly aquiline nose and the same effortless sense of elegance. He was dressed simply in jeans and a shirt but even so managed to look stylish and chic.

How did French men achieve that, I wondered? I looked at the casual scarf slung across his shoulders, the sunglasses perched on top of long dark hair, sleeves rolled up to show just the right amount of bare tanned flesh, a silver bracelet, a necklace and a ring all worn without a hint of embarrassment or self-consciousness. You could dress a British man in exactly the same clothes but he would never look the same, never have that understated confidence and flair that came so naturally to the French.

'Philippe is so sorry not to have come himself.' Luc smiled at me and took my bag, leading us outside into the bright Bordeaux sunshine. 'Something unexpected came up and unfortunately he has to deal with it now.' His accent was charming and laced with more than a hint of American. 'He sends apologies to you both and hopes you will not find him too rude.'

To be honest I was relieved. I found Philippe unnerving, although I couldn't really pinpoint why, and I'd been anxious about meeting him again. I knew that Gail had found him easy company, Nick had struck up an instant rapport and Sonny thought he was wonderful but I felt unsettled in his company. I found him judgemental and unsympathetic. We'd never really managed to have a decent conversation without one of us saying something to offend the other, and to be honest I'd resolved to keep out of his way as much as possible without appearing rude.

'Are you the "flying winemaker"?' Nick asked and Luc nodded in agreement. 'I want to hear all about it. I want to hear every single detail.' I could see that Nick was absolutely delighted.

'That is a dangerous request.' Luc laughed. 'I can bore you to death.'

'Exactly, bore me to death, please, I couldn't be happier.'

'And what about you, Sky?' Luc turned to me. 'Are you interested in wine?'

'I'm interested in drinking it,' I said. 'Does that count?'

'Of course that counts, that is the most important factor!' He grinned down at me. 'I will talk to you all about wine but you have to tell me when to shut up.' He threw an arm carelessly around my shoulders. 'I will probably ignore you but you must try.'

He was charm personified, I thought, a very different kettle of fish to his uncle.

'I tell you what!' He stopped suddenly and grinned at us both in excitement. 'I have a plan, we will call and see my good friend at a nearby chateau on our way back. His wine is superb, we'll spend some time there. You will enjoy it. Is that OK?' His enthusiasm was contagious and Nick clapped him on the back.

'Very OK with me, frankly I couldn't think of anything I'd rather do.'

'Sounds lovely.' I smiled but glanced surreptitiously at my watch.

Luc saw my gesture and laughed. 'You are in France now, Sky, it is never too early for a drink.'

'My sort of place,' Nick said, throwing out his arms as if to embrace the countryside.

I couldn't do anything but nod my agreement and, besides, why not? It would be nice to visit this chateau. I felt rather light-headed and carefree, not a feeling I had experienced for a while.

Luc led us to the car. It was a battered old green Renault and I was slightly taken aback. I'm not sure what I'd been expecting, I hadn't given it much thought, but certainly something of a better class than this.

'That will also give Philippe time to conclude his meeting,' Luc said to us while wrenching the dented door open.

Philippe was not looking forward to his meeting. He had been shocked but not altogether surprised at Beatrice's revelation about Elf the night before. He'd had a feeling for a few days that he was not being given the whole picture.

Nonetheless he was disappointed, he was very disappointed. He didn't like being lied to and he hated the idea that someone was taking him for a fool.

'Do you want me to stay, cheri?' Beatrice asked.

'No, that may look too intimidating.'

She blew him a kiss and left the study. She was halfway down the corridor when she heard him call after her.

'No, on second thoughts, Bea, come back, I may need your help.'

Elf knew exactly why Philippe wanted to see him. He had known that it was only a matter of time before he was found out and he knew that he should have been straight with Philippe from the start.

To be fair he'd had every intention of telling him the truth, but from the moment he'd stepped inside the chateau he'd known this was where he wanted to be, so rather than risk being sent away he had held his tongue and risked instead losing the trust of Philippe. A decision he now regretted very much.

He didn't want to leave the chateau, he didn't want to leave its inhabitants. He had never felt this sense of belonging anywhere else before and wished with all his heart that he'd had the time to make himself indispensable before being dismissed. With a very heavy heart he knocked on the study door. With an equally heavy heart Philippe went to open it.

Elf squared his shoulders and marched straight in. Beatrice gently motioned for him to sit down and Philippe closed the door behind. Elf felt as if he was stuck in a pincer movement.

Philippe moved behind the desk and they all stared at each other for a moment. Elf looked down at the floor. There were a thousand things he wanted to say but the power of speech had momentarily deserted him.

'Beatrice rang the agency before she arrived here.' Philippe could hardly bear to look at the small figure perched disconsolately on the edge of the leather chair. 'They had never heard of a Rudolph Baudin.'

Elf still remained silent. Philippe glanced over to Beatrice. She walked over to the chair and as she would with a little child she crouched down in front of it.

'They said they had sent a young man called Bertrand Royen. Do you know him, Elf?'

The power of speech suddenly returned to Elf and he couldn't get his words out quick enough. 'I did you a favour really, he was stupid, he would never have fitted in, I know I should have told you and I meant to, but I loved it here and then I met Emmie, but still I should have told you and then I saw the gypsy caravan and it all seemed like fate, I wanted you to see how hard I could work, I wanted you to see beyond my height and realise that it was no limitation, but I should have known it couldn't last, I should have repaid your trust with honesty and for that I can never forgive myself, but Bertrand was a bad man, I spared you that at least, and I want you to know that my short time here has been the happiest in my life and you have to buy Emmie a unicycle because she is exactly the right age to learn.'

Sliding off the leather chair he made a quaint bow to Philippe. 'Signing off now, boss, with heartfelt apologies.' He turned to Beatrice. 'Madame, I wish I had been able to get to know you better, I instinctively know that you are an extraordinary woman.' He looked at them both. 'You make a good team.' Tears were streaming down his cheeks as he headed towards the door.

Philippe, who had been listening in utter bewilderment to this mad flow of words, suddenly came to life. Springing up from behind the desk he rushed towards the door, but Beatrice was there before him.

'Elf, you are not going anywhere until we hear the full story.' She put her hands on his shoulders and gently spun him around to face Philippe.

'Come and sit back down, Elf, start at the beginning, slowly and one step at a time.' Philippe went to the old cabinet and took out the pastis bottle whilst Beatrice reached for the cigarettes and lit two.

'OK, Elf, fire away.' He handed him a pastis. Elf had never had a pastis before but now seemed as good a time as any to start.

'I had been around a fair few chateaux looking for work but I had no joy.' He sipped tentatively at the cloudy mixture. 'I admit I was feeling very dispirited. I'd been walking around for days. Mostly they were politely dismissive but the last one, an enormous chateau halfway up a hill with a ludicrously long driveway, I can't recall the name, well, they had been particularly insulting.' Elf paused, he could of course remember the name of the chateau, indeed he would never forget it or the arrogant young lad who had laughed in his face, nor the jeers and taunts that had followed him down the driveway. But the owner might have been Philippe's great friend, it was a small world and Elf didn't want to risk upsetting him again.

Beatrice and Philippe merely exchanged glances. They knew exactly which chateau Elf was talking about.

'I walked into a bar. Bertrand was there, although obviously I didn't know he was Bertrand then. He was slumped in front of a beer, clearly not his first of the day, a hulk of a man, built like a tank with a brain that never reached full throttle. I took an instant dislike but we got chatting and I bought him another drink.' He took another sip of his pastis and licked his lips appreciatively. He could get used to pastis. 'He told me that he was going to work for a chateau, your chateau. He said he'd worked in a chateau before, somewhere in southern France, said it was piss easy, that he'd spent most of his time drinking, smoking spliffs and shagging the boss's daughter. I guess I saw red. Here was someone who could walk straight into a job simply because of his build. He didn't deserve to work, he wouldn't work as hard or as conscientiously as me, but no one would give me a bloody chance because in their eyes I'm a freak.'

He downed the rest of the pastis in one single gulp and held his glass out for a refill. Philippe took it without comment.

'I'm afraid what I did next was below the belt but I don't regret it.' Elf took the refilled glass and waited for Philippe to sit back down. 'I told him that I'd already been to your chateau and that you weren't looking for anyone. You had changed your mind. I may even have hinted that you may not be the best boss to work under.' He looked a little shamefaced.

'What exactly did you tell him, Elf?' Beatrice took a long drag on her cigarette.

'I said that the owner was a real tyrant, he never allowed his employees to consume alcohol on the premises, smoking was likewise forbidden and the food was utter merde.' Elf shrugged. 'I was angry and I was on a mission. I told him the word on the street was that no one wanted to work at Chateau Fontaine. It had a terrible reputation and paid peanuts.' He smiled ruefully. 'I told him to try the last chateau I had been to. I told him they were looking for people but they wanted a big chap like him, not a dwarf like me. I told him how friendly they were. It didn't take long to persuade him, he's not the brightest match in the box and he was pretty drunk. When he staggered to the loo I stole the paperwork from his jacket, noted the name of the agency and your address, made my way here and the rest you know.'

There was silence.

'I'm sorry, boss, I just wanted a chance. Just one chance to prove myself.' Philippe said nothing. 'Shall I go?' Elf once more slid down the leather chair.

Beatrice looked at Philippe. He gave her the merest hint of a smile. 'Yes, Elf,' he replied. 'I'd like you to go.'

Elf nodded and headed once again towards the door.

'I'd like you to go to the cellar and bring up a couple of bottles of champagne, and give them to Rosa to put in the fridge.' Elf spun around. 'We can celebrate the arrival of Nick and Sky along with the arrival of our latest employee.' Elf stared wide-eyed and Philippe grinned at him. 'Welcome to Chateau Fontaine, Elf. I'm giving you that chance you wanted, the chance to prove yourself under a tyrant of a boss.'

Elf sank back onto the chair. The tears sprang up in his eyes again. 'You won't regret it, boss.' His voice was thick with emotion. 'You will never ever, ever, have cause to regret it.'

'No,' Philippe said. 'I don't think I will.' He smiled at the young lad. 'You've already saved us from that bruiser Bertrand, and if it's the same chateau that I'm thinking then he will have the same treatment that you described for him here which, I guess, is a kind of rough justice. God knows where he got the idea that the work is "piss easy" – working in the vineyard is notoriously back-breaking, which is where you hold the trump card, Elf: no bending down for you.' He grinned at the young lad and then a thought occurred to him. 'Elf, how old are you really? I want the truth now.'

'Two weeks shy of seventeen, boss.'

'Mon Dieu.' Beatrice laughed softly.

'Do we need to let anyone know you are here?' Philippe reached for another cigarette. 'Your parents, for example?'

'I'll drop them a quick line,' Elf replied quickly. 'We tend not to concern ourselves too much with each other, it's an arrangement that suits us best.' It was said lightly but his eyes were dead and something about the tone of his voice struck a chord deep within Philippe.

'I'll need their address, Elf, I need to know who your next of kin are.'

Elf just nodded.

'How long have you been on the road, Elf?' Beatrice asked gently.

'Long enough to know I want to get off it.'

Beatrice said nothing but raised her eyebrows.

'Two years,' Elf finally conceded. Once again Philippe and Beatrice exchanged glances. The young lad had been on the streets for over two years. What sort of life had he had?

'Go and get the champagne before they all arrive.' Philippe's eyes were a touch misty. Elf saluted him and marched joyfully down the corridor.

Beatrice raised the pastis glass to him. 'Good decision, cheri.'

'The only decision,' he replied.

CHAPTER THIRTY-THREE

I was entranced by the journey from the airport. Luc deliberately chose a back route which enabled us to see more of the countryside.

'It's longer but much more picturesque and we are in no hurry.' He was a delightful tour guide, pointing out the landmarks, the famous chateaux, the not-so-famous chateaux, chatting about the wine, the grape variety, the soil and the climate. We were both fascinated.

'I don't really know what I was expecting,' I said, looking out of the car window. 'But certainly not these neat rows of vines. My Italian grandmother used to have vines and my memory of them is of wild untamed plants growing all over the place. I guess I imagined that was what most vineyards looked like. These regimented rows are a total surprise.'

Luc grinned. 'How funny, that is exactly what Philippe calls them. He refers to them as his army of soldiers.' He pulled over to the side of the road. 'See the big church on top of the hill over there? That is Saint-Émilion. We'll go there another day, you need full concentration. It is a paradise, for artists, for wine lovers, for food lovers, for just about anyone really.'

'It's so beautiful here.' I gazed around. 'A thousand different colours all gently blending into one another. It's magical.'

'Wait until we stop at Michel's chateau, that will take your breath away.'

Michel's chateau was indeed magnificent. Situated on top of a hill, it was very imposing and very formal. The grounds were large and exquisitely maintained. I imagined that he must have a small army of people working for him. There was a large swimming pool alongside a BBQ area and outdoor kitchen, there were two tennis courts, a boules pitch and even a small church.

We sat drinking rosé wine on a huge stone terrace overlooking the beautiful Bordeaux countryside. Michel was a fun guy with a great sense of humour, he and Luc were the best of mates. The time passed very quickly and frankly I was reluctant to leave but when we pulled through the pillared gates of Chateau Fontaine my heart simply soared.

The cobbled driveway was lined with small round hedges, several fruit trees were dotted around the front lawn and a large and rather incongruous sculpture of an iron bird stood in the centre. A young girl was practising cartwheels on the lawn, watched proudly by a huge dog and a piglet.

Two fairy tale turrets flanked the sides of the beautiful creeper-clad chateau. Silvery slate roof tiles glistened in the soft morning sunshine and fragrant wisteria framed the arched entrance. Pale grey shutters with their paint slightly peeling surrounded large gracious windows. It was full of charm and character and I very much preferred the slight shabbiness and understated elegance to the grandeur of Michel's chateau.

I clambered out of the car and stood gazing around, breathing in the unfamiliar scents. A slight breeze lifted my hair and with it some of the heartache and hurt from the past few weeks.

The young girl scampered over to us at the same time as Philippe emerged from the chateau. Nick walked over to meet him but I stood still looking around me.

'I've started as I mean to go on, Philippe,' I heard Nick announce. 'I've already sampled the most delicious wine, not a patch on yours but not too shabby.'

'I'd like to have seen Michel's face as you described his grand cru as "not too shabby".' Philippe was laughing.

'Well, those weren't the exact words I used,' Nick chuckled. 'It's good to see you.'

'And you, Nick.' Philippe turned to me. 'Welcome to Chateau Fontaine, Sky. I'm afraid it doesn't quite match the splendour of Michel's chateau.' He came over to kiss me.

'Oh, Philippe you are so wrong, this is absolutely gorgeous.' I couldn't help it, I threw my arms around him. 'This is enchanting, this is magical, nothing could be more perfect.'

'Thank you so much, Sky.' He looked taken aback and I instantly regretted my exuberance.

Luc however dropped a light kiss on my head. 'What a very lovely thing to say, Sky.' He smiled at me.

'I is Emmie.' The little girl with the blonde curls stepped forward, her light blue eyes staring straight into mine.

'Of course you are, and this must be Belle and this must be Sausage.' I bent down to say hello. 'I've been so looking forward to meeting you.'

'Sausage is a pig what is not got to be eaten.' It was clearly important to Emmie that the rules be made clear.

'Gosh, no, he's a Sausage to be treasured and loved.' I tickled the adorable piglet.

'Hi, Emmie, I'm Nick.' He stepped forward. 'I'd like to meet Henri's cat, I believe we have something in common.' He patted his ginger hair.

Emmie giggled. 'Nearly. Cat is brighter.'

'Is she talking hair or intelligence, Nick?' I said without really thinking, lapsing automatically into our old mode of teasing.

I sensed rather than saw Philippe's amazement that I was able to joke and I realised how terrible my behaviour must have been in Marrakech. I must try and make up for it out here, I thought.

'Leave your bags for now and come on through. We've a surprise for you.' Philippe led us inside. We walked down a glorious corridor which ran the length of the house: huge high ceilings, tiled floors and pale grey walls completely covered with paintings. Large doors off either side offered an intriguing glimpse into the rest of the chateau and I couldn't wait to explore but Philippe marched us straight past an enormous curved stone staircase and into a large, colourful room with French windows opening onto a sun-drenched inner courtyard.

I could just make out the river glinting in the background and in the foreground orderly rows of vines stretched down to its banks. Glorious sandstone barns flanked the courtyard and behind some rusty wrought iron gates I could glimpse the bright blue of a swimming pool. Wild flowers were growing up between the paving stones and the stone fountain was covered in the same creeper that covered the house.

Hens roamed around the garden, ignoring the squeals of the piglet, and in a far corner stood an old gypsy caravan. I couldn't tear my eyes away. There was something extraordinarily special about this place, I couldn't define it but within minutes it had crept into my soul. It was with great reluctance that I turned back to the room when Philippe called my name.

'Sky, Nick, I'd like you to meet my sister, Stephanie.' I smiled at her shyly but Nick bounded over to kiss her.

'I'm being very French and kissing absolutely everyone. It's probably not the done thing but I'm past caring.'

Stephanie was a female version of Philippe, not exactly beautiful but very striking with gleaming dark hair cut into a shoulder-length bob. She was tall and exuded physical strength. She had the same deep hazel eyes and generous smile as her brother.

'And this is Rosa who manages us all, or so she likes to think.' Philippe had his arms around a lady who had come in carrying large plates of charcuterie and strong-smelling cheeses. Her jet black hair was peppered with white but her beauty was undiminished and her dark eyes sparkled with vivacity and humour. I warmed to her immediately.

'You will meet Henri at lunch,' Philippe continued. 'But in the meantime there is one other person who needs no introduction.' The door opened and in walked Beatrice.

I exclaimed with joy and Nick turned to me. 'Did you know Beatrice was coming?'

'No, but you know somehow I'm not surprised.' I clapped my hands. 'It feels absolutely right.' I danced over to greet her. 'Oh, Beatrice, how lovely to see you, thank you for inviting me here,' I said.

'Cheri, it was not me, it was Philippe.' She hugged me.

'I know.' I realised I'd been rude. I could feel Philippe's eyes on me. 'But I know that you instigated it all.'

'Who rides this?' Nick was looking with interest at a unicycle propped against the wall.

'Elf rides,' Emmie replied. 'I is learning too.'

'Elf?' Nick looked at her in amazement. 'You have an elf?'

'Of course they have an elf.' I laughed. 'This is an enchanted castle, there are bound to be elves and fairies, witches and wizards. I wouldn't be surprised to find a unicorn amongst the vines and a fire-breathing dragon in the underground cellar.' I held out my arms to the little girl. 'Am I right, Emmie?'

Philippe looked stunned and once again I realised that this was not how I had behaved in Marrakech. He must have thought I had some sort of split personality disorder. He handed me a glass of champagne and I smiled at him reassuringly but there was a wariness in his eyes.

'And when do we get to meet Celine?' I asked, trying to break the tension. It didn't work. He stared at me in astonishment.

'Celine?' He shook his head. 'Why do you want to meet Celine?'

'I thought, well I thought, isn't she, well, isn't she Emmie's mother?' I was puzzled. What the hell had I said wrong now? Wasn't it natural that we would want to meet his partner?

'Yes she is.' But he still looked mystified. 'Are Claude and Celine coming for lunch?' He turned to Stephanie.

'As far as I know,' she replied, looking as bemused as her brother.

'Who is Claude?' Nick asked.

'Claude is our cousin.'

'And is Claude married?' I asked. There seemed to be a lot of them and I was keen to establish all the relationships.

There was a moment's silence. Everyone looked at each other in bewilderment. I'd obviously committed some terrible faux-pas but I had no idea what. Sensing my anxiety, Emmie slipped her hand into mine. 'Claude and Celine is married,' she said quietly.

'Celine and Claude?' I was completely baffled and turned to Philippe. 'But I thought Celine and you... I mean you said in Morocco... so I assumed...'

'You thought Celine and Philippe were together?' Beatrice threw back her head and laughed.

'Why on earth would you think that?' Philippe stared at me openmouthed.

I didn't know what to say. I felt myself turning red. I felt desperately embarrassed. Maybe Celine was his mistress, they were keen on mistresses on the continent, maybe Emmie was his love child, if so it was very much out in the open. I couldn't think of what to say but luckily Nick came to my rescue.

'To be fair, so did I.'

'You thought what?' Philippe stared at him.

'I thought that you were with Celine,' he replied and at that moment I could have hugged him.

'But why?' Philippe demanded.

'Something about Emmie being like your own child, knowing Celine for many years…'

'Merde, I remember now!' Beatrice giggled. 'I remember thinking that you had got the wrong end of the stick but I can't remember why I didn't correct you.'

'So if you're not with Celine, who are you with?' I wanted to get the facts right.

'I'm not with anybody, Sky.' Philippe knocked back his champagne. 'Certainly not Celine.'

'It wouldn't be a match made in heaven, Sky,' Stephanie whispered softly.

I wondered what on earth was wrong with Celine.

'Elf is coming,' Emmie shouted.

I turned to the window and saw a lean, weather-beaten man wearing a battered straw hat making his way into the courtyard. On his shoulder was a ginger cat and bouncing by his side was a very short young man with a mad mop of unruly curls. He was chattering non-stop, taking three steps to every one long stride of his companion. I assumed they must be Elf, Henri and the infamous ginger cat. Emmie went running out to meet them.

I turned to the room quickly. 'I do hope that I've not caused any offence by my mistake.' I gulped at my champagne before turning to Philippe. 'I'm so sorry, it was a genuine mistake, I hope I haven't upset Emmie.'

'No offence taken at all,' Philippe reassured me. 'I was just a bit surprised, that's all.' He grinned. 'Of all the people you could have picked for me to be having a relationship with, Celine is certainly the most unlikely.'

'What the hell is the matter with Celine?' Nick echoed my thoughts. But before anyone could reply Emmie came running through the French windows dragging Elf behind her.

'This be Elf,' she proudly announced, pushing him forward.

'Hello, Elf.' I was a little uncomfortable calling him Elf although clearly he was happy with the name. I smiled gently at the young lad who was standing awkwardly in the middle of the room. 'I'm Sky, I hope you speak English because my French is rather rusty.'

'Your French is very good, Sky,' Stephanie said.

'Which is why you are all talking to me in English,' I laughed.

'Elf, I understand that this is your bike.' Nick gestured towards the unicycle. Elf nodded. 'Will you teach me? I've always wanted to ride one.' This was news to me but it was typical of Nick to try and put Elf at his ease and he succeeded. Elf was delighted, he was on safe territory here and he promptly began an in depth explanation into the finer points of mastering the unicycle.

Philippe turned to Henri. 'Well, how was he?' Elf stopped mid-sentence and looked around. His smile faded and anxiety crept into his eyes. I wondered what had happened to make him so vulnerable.

'He'll do,' Henri replied laconically. 'But I may have to gag him, he never shuts up.'

'I'm just asking questions.' Elf was clearly keen to justify himself. 'Just to make sure I understand everything and get it right. I never ask the same question twice. You never have to explain anything twice.'

Henri turned to Philippe. 'See what I mean.' But I could see that his blue eyes were laughing.

'Henri, I have been longing to meet both you and Rosa ever since Philippe told us your story.' I crossed the room to greet him.

'It gets more exaggerated every time he tells it.' Henri shook his head.

'But you can sing, can't you?' I asked. 'Philippe said that when you started to sing the world stopped to listen. I'd like to have the chance to listen to you sing.' I smiled at them. 'In fact I have a present for you and Rosa.' I hesitated but it was too late to backtrack so I rushed on. 'I adored the story so much that I drew it. I hope you don't mind, it's in the car, I'll go and fetch it.' And without waiting for an answer I ran out.

'Here.' I held out a large package to Rosa and Henri. 'This is your story, I really hope you like it.' I was suddenly very nervous and wished I had opted for a less public showing. What if they hated it? I was behaving in a most peculiar fashion today.

Rosa gently opened the paper and withdrew the painting. She and Henri stared at it. My heart was hammering. Oh my God, suppose they really did hate it?

They were silent for what seemed like ages. Finally Rosa looked up, tears were falling unchecked down her cheeks and I felt my eyes prickle too.

'Sky, it is beautiful, it is hauntingly beautiful.' She held out her arms to me and I went to embrace her.

Henri was still staring at the painting. 'It is magical,' he said finally. 'You have given us a gift from the heart and we will treasure it for ever.'

The others seemed stunned by the painting, even Nick who was so familiar with my work looked impressed.

I had painted a montage of all the elements of the story Philippe had told us. There was a young Henri playing his guitar, straw hat pushed back on his head and blue eyes twinkling at a teenage Rosa as she sat entranced at his feet. Her long dark hair flowed down her back and she was surrounded by all the creatures of the forest. In one corner an angry gypsy family rained down curses whilst a sullen young prince glowered in the background, and in another a weeping mother was holding a ginger cat, knowing that she would never see her daughter again. It was all there in one fairy-tale illustration.

'Sky, it's breathtaking.' Nick sounded very proud and I smiled modestly but, in truth, I was delighted with the picture. The images had been playing in my mind since first hearing the story. Back in London and unable to sleep, I'd started it at midnight and had not stopped until it was complete ten hours later. I'd then gone back to bed and slept solidly.

'You have a huge talent, Sky,' Stephanie said and I blushed.

'She is a very clever young lady.' Beatrice put her arms around my shoulders. 'And a very brave one,' she added in a quiet aside. I knew exactly to what she was referring and glowed. Praise from Beatrice was hard earned.

'It's very good, Sky,' Philippe stated. Then he smiled. 'Sorry, that was inadequate. I meant…' But before he could finish Luc leapt in.

'It's much more than very good, it's marvellous.' Luc's smile was wide and I couldn't help but respond. 'Genius and beauty, it's a lethal combination.' He looked at me and I could sense his admiration but I was also aware of Philippe frowning and I had no idea why.

There was the sound of a car in the driveway.

'That will be Claude and Celine,' Stephanie said.

Rosa gathered the picture to her. 'Let's go and sit for lunch.'

Everyone started to move to the dining room. The arrival of Claude and Celine seemed to have put paid to the party atmosphere, and I also noted that Emmie remained firmly by Philippe's side, making no effort to go and greet her parents.

CHAPTER THIRTY-FOUR

The following morning I stretched luxuriously in the large bed and looked around me. It was a lovely room, the pale blue wallpaper was slightly faded but all the nicer for it and two huge windows overlooked the back courtyard. I'd been too tired to wrestle with the shutters the night before and the sunlight was streaming in.

A massive oak wardrobe stood in one corner, it matched the bed with the same intricate carved rose in the woodwork. I was no expert but would hazard a guess at the nineteen thirties. Along one wall hung a series of pen and ink sketches of a dog. They were rather good and I clambered out of the bed to take a further look. The dog was similar to Belle, they must have been related.

Pulling on my old kimono which travelled everywhere with me I flung open the window, causing several pigeons to take flight. The cool morning air was fresh and invigorating.

The river sparkled in the distance and the dew hung over the vines like a silver cobweb. I drank it all in. I was itching to get my paints out but I wanted to explore first and discover all the hidden corners of the chateau. I'd ask Emmie to show me around, the little girl clearly knew every inch of the house and gardens.

I wondered, what the story was there? Emmie hadn't wanted to go home the night before. I'd seen the pleading look she'd given her uncle but her parents had seemed insistent. I blushed when I recalled my mistake about Celine. The knowledge that Philippe was single was disturbing, I felt disquieted and once again the earth tilted ever so slightly on its axis.

'She seems light-hearted, almost carefree.' Nick was on the phone to Miles. 'I was going to say like the Sky of old but actually I'm not sure I've ever really seen her like this.'

Miles was surprised, he would have thought that Nick of all people had seen Sky in pretty much every mood. A thought occurred to him. 'She's not taking anything, is she?'

'You mean happy pills?' Nick thought about it for a second. 'I guess that would explain the good mood but no, I don't really think so, it seems natural, she doesn't have the look of someone on medication.'

'Well maybe, just maybe, she is simply coming to terms with the situation.'

'She's certainly creating quite a stir here.' Nick smiled. 'She unveiled an amazing painting, it took my breath away, well it took everyone's breath away, Philippe's nephew Luc seemed particularly impressed.' He chuckled. 'He couldn't take his eyes off her for the rest of the day.'

'Did she respond?' Miles was curious and slightly jealous. He knew he had no right to be but felt the pang nonetheless.

'I think she was flattered, there was a degree of coquettishness about her.'

'That doesn't really sound like Sky.'

'I don't think the master of the house was too impressed either.' Nick chuckled as he recalled Philippe's darkening brow and his frequent references to Luc's age. He had exchanged a few covert looks with Beatrice and knew they were on the same wavelength.

'You sound very upbeat, Nick,' Miles said quietly and Nick was instantly contrite but before he could say anything Miles continued. 'I'm desperate for you to make things work but it's not bloody easy being the one left behind. I'm listening to tales of you all drinking wine under a blue sky in the grounds of a chateau whilst I sit alone in a dismal hotel room barely daring to venture out for Nando's chicken and wondering just what the fuck I've done with my life. I miss you and I miss Sky.' He paused. 'Sorry, I sound like a sullen schoolboy. I just feel raw and inadequate.'

'I'll make it work, Miles, I promise,' Nick said.

'Good,' said Miles. 'In the meantime send photos so that I can start thinking about a website for this chateau and the wine. I could do with a distraction.'

'I love you.'

'And back.'

Philippe was thrashing up and down the pool trying to clear his head. He had slept badly but had no real idea why he was feeling so out of sorts. It had been lovely to see Nick again and Sky had been a revelation. But he had felt out of control of things, he hadn't been able to relax and was scared that he had come across as stuffy and formal, two things he really wasn't.

In contrast to Luc's exuberance and vitality he had felt old, and if he were totally honest a little jealous. He had watched with increasing bad humour the banter between Luc and Sky. He had felt pushed aside and unable to join in.

Clambering out of the pool he shook himself mentally and physically. He adored his nephew, loved him as if he were his own. How on earth could he feel jealous of him? He was in danger of turning into some sour middle-aged man. He mustn't ever let that happen.

Maybe he should drink less? Maybe he should drink more? Maybe he should leave them on their own? That left an unpleasant taste in his mouth but nonetheless he determined to behave in an adult fashion.

Beatrice could have told Philippe what was the matter. She had lain awake most of the night thinking about him and had come to the conclusion that he had to work things out for himself. She loved him dearly but she had meddled enough, it was time for her to take a back seat. Not something that came naturally to her but she needed to try.

She shook her hair loose from the tight braid she slept in and brushed it until it fell in gleaming waves onto her shoulders. Then throwing a cashmere jumper over soft cotton trousers she made her way downstairs, where she knew that Rosa would have her favourite coffee brewing.

She was not the only one to have lain awake all night. Back in his house, Claude had barely got a wink of sleep. In the early hours he finally gave up the attempt altogether and made his way to the kitchen. Without Celine to object he grabbed a stale croissant, sliced it in half and piling it high with cheese and ham placed it under the grill. Bad for his waistline but necessary for his sanity.

He felt certain that Celine was having an affair, but with whom and for how long? He couldn't shake off the feeling that the box of matches from Hotel de Paris was significant. First he had found them in her car, the very same evening he had seen Michel using them and then yesterday Luc had produced a box. When Claude had questioned him Luc had shrugged and said casually that he must have picked them up from Michel.

It couldn't be a coincidence, could it? But surely it wasn't Michel? Celine couldn't be having an affair with Michel? She was old enough to be his mother.

The thoughts were tumbling about his head, producing a headache of epic proportions. He knocked back some painkillers along with his mug of hot chocolate.

He was tempted to cancel his golf today but knew that Celine would be furious. She adored having lunch at the prestigious club. There were usually five or six couples dining, all fairly wealthy, the husbands sporting the same designer labels and all the wives manicured and made up in the same salon with the same sleek haircuts and the same style of clothes. In fact Claude often had trouble telling them apart. Celine was without doubt the most attractive of them all, a fact that she was well aware of. The other women were envious of her and the men were envious of him. If only they knew, he thought, if only they realised how hard it was to keep her happy. And no matter how hard he tried it was never enough.

I met Beatrice on the stone stairs.

'Can you smell the coffee too?' Beatrice laughed.

'I certainly can.' I sniffed. 'It smells absolutely gorgeous.'

'You have me to thank for that.' Beatrice grinned. 'Rosa knows it's my favourite but for some reason I only ever have it here. It just doesn't seem to taste the same anywhere else.'

'Coffee is just one of many things I have you to thank for, Beatrice.' I looked her up and down. 'How come you always manage to look so glamorous? Share the secret.'

Her hair was gleaming, she had a soft cashmere jumper over Capri pants and wedged espadrilles. My hair lay in long, dishevelled coils and my kimono was very faded and very old and I was wearing flip-flops.

She laughed. 'I don't know what mirror you look in, Sky, you seem to have no idea how stunning you are.'

'You're right, Beatrice, this is amazing coffee.' I took another sip and closed my eyes, savouring the sensation. 'Where do you buy it, Rosa?'

'I buy a mixture of beans in the market and grind them here.' Rosa smiled.

'It is a market ritual.' Beatrice laughed. 'Gilou has coffee and a florentine waiting for her. They spend thirty minutes putting the world to rights, Gilou knows everything and everyone, he can talk about the latest scandal to rock the States in as much lurid detail as he can tell you about the sex lives of our local politicians.' She winked at Rosa. 'It is Rosa's weekly fix.'

'What is Rosa's weekly fix?' Philippe came in through the door. His wet hair was dripping, his shirt was half undone and I caught a glimpse of a tanned, muscular chest. 'Are we talking about Gilou or has she developed a drug habit?' He grabbed a mug and helped himself from the huge cafetière. 'I warn you Sky, this is powerful stuff, more addictive than heroin.'

'That I can believe.' I held out my cup for a refill. 'Tomorrow I will follow your example and have an early morning swim, if that's OK?'

'Be my guest.' He smiled. 'It isn't heated though.'

'I'm used to sub-zero Scottish lochs, Philippe, in comparison to those your pool will feel positively tropical.'

'I'll second that.' Nick entered the kitchen. 'There is nothing quite as cold as a Scottish loch, my voice is several octaves higher for days after.'

'Then why do you do it?' Beatrice laughed.

'A question I ask myself every time I leap in.' Nick shook his head. 'It beguiles you, sparkling blue water surrounded by stunning scenery, you ask yourself what could be better? You take the plunge and the answer hits you immediately. Better would have been to have stayed on dry land.'

'But think of the self-satisfaction you would miss.' Luc entered the kitchen hot and sweaty after a morning run. It was beginning to feel like Piccadilly Circus. 'Think of how good you feel after.'

'Are you feeling good right now?' Nick laughed.

'I feel virtuous and ready for breakfast.' Luc grinned. 'But I prefer running in company. My uncle usually runs with me but right now he is confined to the pool until his knee heals.'

'You make me sound like some decrepit old man,' Philippe

scowled. 'You wait, it won't be long before you're running to catch up with me.'

Luc shook his head before turning to me. 'What about you, Sky? Do you run?'

'Not if I can help it.' I loathed running. The only exercise I really enjoyed was swimming. My father would occasionally march us all up the hills and had once rashly suggested attempting Ben Nevis. After seeing our faces he admitted defeat and even the excruciating hill climbs became a thing of the past.

'Nick?' Luc was obviously keen to find someone.

'It doesn't suit me, pal,' Nick replied. 'My hair gets more ginger and my face turns into a tomato. Doesn't fade for hours… no it's absolutely true,' he said as Luc started to laugh. 'People think I'm having some kind of seizure, but I'm more than happy to oblige with a brisk walk.' He turned to Philippe. 'And talking of brisk walks, can you point me in the direction of the market you were talking about?'

'You can borrow the car,' Philippe told him. 'You are bound to buy things, you could never walk back with them all.'

'Luc, go and shower, the rest of you come to the table,' Rosa commanded.

Philippe obediently led the way to the kitchen. 'We don't stand on ceremony for breakfast here, sit down and grab what you want, first come first served.'

'This smells divine.' I breathed in the scent of newly baked baguettes and fresh croissants. 'Who has been to fetch all these?'

'We have an accommodating boulanger.' Philippe smiled. 'He drives past our gate every morning. We exchange eggs and Rosa's homemade confiture for baguettes and croissants.' He grinned. 'He also secretly fancies my sister, which helps, he stands no chance but we tell her to keep encouraging him.'

'Stop spreading vicious rumours about me.' Stephanie walked into the kitchen. 'You should treat me with a little more respect.' She glared with good humour at her brother. 'What a beautiful kimono, Sky.'

'Thank you.' I paused. 'It belonged to my mother, it's a firm favourite.'

'She never leaves home without it,' Nick added softly.

'Quite right too.' Stephanie smiled. 'What are your plans today?'

'I thought I might explore a little, if that's OK?' I turned to Philippe. 'I wondered if Emmie might like to show me around? Could I ask Celine and Claude if that would be alright?'

'She'll be here any minute.' Philippe looked at his watch. 'Claude plays golf on a Sunday and Celine joins him for lunch. Emmie hates the golf club, it's too boring for her so she comes here.'

I wondered why they always went to the golf club if Emmie hated it so much but it wasn't my place to enquire. I'd already made a fool of myself about Celine.

As if reading my thoughts, Beatrice shrugged. 'Their loss is our gain,' she said, completely ignoring Philippe's frown. 'In fact that is probably her.'

I heard the crunch of car wheels on the gravel and the slamming of a car door.

I heard Luc shout a greeting followed by the sound of her laughter. Minutes later Emmie ran into the kitchen. Claude and Luc brought up the rear.

'Time for a coffee, Claude?' Rosa asked. 'Or some breakfast?'

'No, it's an early tee-off today, here's her school bag.' He ruffled Emmie's hair. 'Bye, cheri, be good.'

'Where's Elf?' Emmie demanded as soon as her papa had left.

'He's with Henri,' Rosa said. 'He thought he heard something last night and went to investigate.' She turned to Philippe. 'There were *sanglier* tracks, wild boar.'

'What the hell was he doing investigating on his own?' Philippe slammed his coffee mug down with force. 'Mon Dieu, anything could have happened, they're not exactly known for their sweet temperament.'

'Perhaps he didn't know it was a wild boar,' Rosa reasoned.

'Here he is, you can ask him yourself.' Stephanie pointed at the two of them strolling up the garden.

'What the hell were you doing on your own in the middle of the night?' Philippe demanded as soon as Elf walked in the door. Concern was making him angry and I was touched by it.

'Never fear, boss, I had my bongos. I made enough noise to frighten whatever it was away.'

'Bongos?' We all turned to stare at Elf.

'They are percussion instruments…'

'I know what they are,' Philippe interrupted him. 'What the hell were you doing with them?'

'I was banging them very hard.'

'Don't joke, Elf, this is serious, you could have been hurt.'

'I'm not joking, boss, the bongos make a lot of noise.'

'He's not joking, he played them for us.' Rosa smiled. 'I'm amazed we slept through them.'

'First a unicycle, then the bongos, what else have you got in your box of tricks?'

'The complete works of Shakespeare.'

Philippe widened his eyes in astonishment and then threw back his head and laughed. He had a great laugh, deep and rich, and I realised that I'd like to hear it more often.

'Never a dull moment with you, Elf.' Philippe shook his head. 'But promise me you'll come and get me next time you hear anything,' he demanded. 'No more bongo playing for the sanglier.'

'Hand on heart, boss.'

'Were they near the vines?' Philippe turned to Henri. Henri nodded.

235

'Will they damage the vines?' Nick was interested and so was I.

'Not now,' Philippe replied. 'But when the grapes are ripe they can create havoc. They adore the grapes so we certainly don't want them making it a regular track.'

'I'm going to Michel's today, I'll ask him if he too had visitors last night,' Luc said, wandering back into the kitchen fresh from his shower. 'Anyone fancy coming along for the ride?' He glanced casually around the room before his gaze fell on me.

I was sorely tempted, yesterday had been such fun and Luc was easy company but out of the corner of my eye I could see Philippe frowning. I shook my head. 'I'm here to work, Luc.' And actually I realised that I couldn't wait to get started. 'I'm exploring today and I'm hoping Emmie will show me around.'

She was overjoyed. 'Emmie knows everywhere.'

'I'll come too,' Philippe said suddenly.

'Are you sure?' I asked. 'I mean, I don't want to disturb you if you're busy.' Memories of the Majorelle garden visit weren't that far away.

'I've a vested interest in making sure you see all the most beautiful places.'

'Yes, yes of course.' He sounded sharp and I was taken aback. Well that put me firmly in my place, I thought. Mental note to self, this is a working trip not a holiday.

Philippe looked embarrassed, maybe he'd meant that as a joke but it certainly hadn't come out that way.

'Ask Michel to lunch.' Stephanie swiftly covered the awkward moment. 'Tell him it's a Rosa special.'

Nick's eyes lit up. 'Do you need anything from the market, Rosa?' he asked hopefully.

'What he really means is, can he come into the kitchen and watch you cook?' Beatrice grinned at him.

CHAPTER THIRTY-FIVE

Once outside I felt the same exhilarating lightness of spirit that I'd felt since arriving in France. The whole atmosphere of the chateau acted like some sort of drug on me, I could feel some of my old energy and vitality returning.

'Come on, Emmie.' I laughed. 'Last to the bottom is a loser.'

We raced down the slopes of the vineyard, ending up weak and giggling in a tangle of limbs at the bottom. Philippe walked down behind us.

'It was a draw,' I protested as Emmie stood victorious over me. 'I just fell over at the end, Sausage got in the way.' The little piglet looked back at me indignantly. 'Philippe, tell her it was a draw.'

'Surely you can't be encouraging me to lie to Emmie,' he laughed. 'But it was close.'

Emmie giggled and ran off to the river with Sausage.

'Can you swim in there?' I asked Philippe as I watched Emmie trying to encourage the piglet into the water without any success.

'We used to when we were kids,' Philippe answered. 'And we fish, we have a small boat.' He pointed to a little motor boat moored to a jetty. 'Actually I haven't been out since the accident, we could go if you'd like.'

'Now?'

'Well, not now, we haven't got the equipment with us, but later in the week if you would like.'

'I'd like.' I smiled at him. 'But only after I've done some work,' I quickly added, remembering his comment from before.

We made our way up through the rows of vines and again I marvelled at how ordered they were.

'They don't look very impressive right now,' Philippe commented and I nodded. 'It's hard to believe that they will produce such amazing fruit but if you look closely you will see the buds just starting to grow.'

He squatted down and beckoned me to join him. 'We train the vines to control the canopy.' I nodded. 'You see, we need to find the right balance of ensuring enough foliage to aid photosynthesis but without shading the grapes too much.'

'I see,' I said, not really seeing at all but loving his passion.

'Sorry.' He smiled. 'Do tell me to shut up.'

'Not at all,' I was quick to reassure him. 'It is fascinating, I know absolutely nothing about winemaking.'

'If you like, one morning I can talk you through the whole process.' He paused. 'We'll finish with a grand tasting.'

'Sounds like a plan.'

We walked up through the vines, down a beautiful avenue of poplars, past the remains of an old stone church and around to the huge derelict sandstone barns.

'Oh my God, these are stunning.' I stood gazing at the two barns. 'Can we go inside?'

The inside was beautifully cool and even more impressive, with a glorious vaulted ceiling and mammoth dark oak beams.

'This is enormous, this has so much potential, you could do so much with this, Philippe.' I was overawed.

'I could, and indeed I should, but I'm afraid that time and money have been the obstacles.'

But I wasn't really listening to him. I was pacing around visualising how it could be. 'The light is fantastic, it would make a great studio, you have that amazing mezzanine level, you have room for several bedrooms, people would pay good money to come and paint here.' I ran to one end of the building. 'You could have a massive picture window here, with these fantastic views down to the river, and another at the other end looking up the chateau.' I was in full throttle. 'You could have a terrace outside under those trees, it's just beautiful, Philippe, it is simply beautiful.'

He looked around as if for the first time. 'You're right, it's a lovely building, but sadly there has always been something higher on the list of priorities.'

'Nick would have this mapped out as a restaurant in a heartbeat.' I smiled. 'Don't show it to him unless you're prepared to build some sort of brasserie in your grounds.'

'You two are getting on much better, aren't you?'

I shrugged. 'Sometimes.' I didn't meant to be evasive, it was simply that I didn't know myself what was happening. One moment I thought I was able to forgive him but the next I was filled with fury again and I hadn't spoken to Miles since his last disastrous visit.

I could sense Philippe watching me and prayed he wouldn't try and probe. He didn't, he carried on with the conversation we were having before.

'Luc would love to convert it into some sort of shop and wine tasting area.' He grinned. 'Perhaps we could combine all three. And talking of Luc, he thinks we should redesign our wine labels.' He smiled ruefully. 'Apparently we are woefully behind the times. His spell in California has him all fired up.'

'He is full of enthusiasm,' I agreed.

'He is.' Philippe stated with feeling. He lit a cigarette and gazed down at the long rows of vines. He seemed lost in a world of his own and I didn't want to disturb him.

Emmie was playing with Sausage and Belle was lying at her master's feet. Philippe was leaning against the door with his weight on his right leg, stretching out his bad knee. It was clear that he was in some pain but despite the walking stick he still managed to exude elegance and grace.

As I watched the sun highlighting the silver strands in his hair it occurred to me that he was as much a part of the landscape as his beloved vines. He belonged here, he'd been born with wine in his blood as had his father and grandfather before him. His hazel eyes matched the wood of the door, his hair was a shade darker, and the smoke from his cigarette curled gently into the air exactly as it must have done with his ancestors before him.

I had no idea how long his family had been here but how incredible it must have been to have such a history, how incredible to have such a future. I thought of my own uncertain future and momentarily the sun lost a little of its sparkle.

Philippe turned suddenly and I was embarrassed to have been caught staring at him.

'I've been guilty of not seeing what is in front of me,' he said abruptly. 'We need a new image, we produce fabulous wines and they deserve to be recognised.' His eyes blazed with passion. 'Sorry, that sounds very conceited.'

'Not conceited,' I replied. 'Realistic, I'd say.'

'I was hoping you might be able to help us with some new labels.' He looked at me. 'As I said, I'm happy to talk you through the wines so you understand a bit more about us. Luc and Stephanie can help too. What do you think, Sky? Do you think that would be possible?'

'It's not what I'm used to but I'll certainly give it my best shot.' His enthusiasm was contagious. 'But first I think I ought to get some ideas for the invite, I imagine you're keen to send them to the chefs as soon as possible.' I called over to Emmie. 'Emmie, maybe you and I can sit this afternoon and do some pen and ink sketches of the chateau? Would you like that?' Emmie's shining face said it all and I was glad I had suggested it. I thought she was absolutely adorable, full of fun and imagination. Her speech was a little slow at times and she struggled with sentences but apart from that I didn't think she was particularly behind.

'Thank you, Sky.' Philippe turned to me.

I wasn't sure what he meant. 'You haven't seen anything yet.' I smiled. 'They may be rubbish.'

'That wasn't really what I was thanking you for,' he said, looking at Emmie.

I was captivated by the chateau and the grounds. Everything was just as it should be. Nothing jarred or seemed out of place. The sandstone buildings gleamed in the soft sun, a purple mist hung over the river and the sky was already turning into a deep blue with barely a cloud in sight. All was harmonious and unbelievably I felt an incredible sense of peace.

I was seeing a different side to Philippe too. In Marrakech he had seemed arrogant and superior and I knew that he had thought me uptight and emotional, probably with good reason. We had rubbed each other up the wrong way and even now it was still slightly awkward. But here I was discovering a man passionate about his wine, devoted to his family and ambitious for the future. I could sense his anxiety but loved his new vision. He didn't want to stagnate, he wanted to push the boundaries, explore new territories, and I had no doubt he would succeed.

CHAPTER THIRTY-SIX

As always, Nick was in his element in the market. He had forgotten to ask Rosa for any bags so had bought an enormous basket on wheels which was getting heavier by the minute. He cut quite a figure with his shoulder-length copper curls and wide boyish grin.

He'd bought numerous different cheeses, some stupidly expensive foie gras, a variety of plump olives and spicy tapenade. On top of the basket lay bunches of multi-coloured tulips coupled with dark green ferns and a large chilli plant.

He now stood in front of the oyster stall deliberating how many to buy. He had no idea what Rosa was cooking but oysters went with everything. He decided to buy a whole crate, nothing worse than skimping on the oysters, and he would nip into the wine shop on his way home and buy some Cremant de Bordeaux.

Delighted with his purchases, he was dragging his basket back towards the car when he spotted a stall he hadn't clocked on the way through. It was a hat stall, beautiful, bright coloured hats of every texture and shape imaginable. Pastel straw boaters, floppy velvet hats, cute felt caps and berets. Sky adored hats and Nick simply couldn't resist buying her one. She may not appreciate it at the moment but he would take the risk and before he could change his mind he chose a dusky pink straw boater which would protect her in the sun and a dark blue velvet cap for the winter. At the last moment he spotted a cute cloth hat adorned with roses and ribbons which he grabbed for Emmie.

Once in the car he completely lost his bearings, took the wrong turn and found himself driving around the outskirts of the town without a clue in which direction he should be heading.

Fifteen minutes later not only was he still circling around but had somehow managed to cross the river twice. The countryside was gorgeous but now was not the time for a long tour. He was looking for a place to pull in and phone back to the chateau for instructions when he spotted a sign saying Hotel de Paris, where the terrace looked inviting and he could ask them for directions.

'Can I help you?' The young waitress appeared by his side.

'I'll have a small beer, please,' he replied and then immediately contradicted himself. 'No I won't, I'll have a glass of red wine, just the house wine, and a glass of water. Thank you.' He smiled at her and she blushed.

Once inside the young girl scurried to the counter. She had no idea where or what the house wine was but she spotted an open bottle without a label and assuming it must be the house wine grabbed it and quickly poured a generous quantity into a large glass. She knew she shouldn't be serving but no one else was around and she was desperate to prove to her Uncle Arnaud that she was capable of working here. It would be a fantastic weekend job, she was almost sixteen, nearly old enough to work, and she really needed the money. She rushed outside and, nearly tripping up in her haste, plonked it down in front of him, spilling some out of the glass.

'Mon Dieu, I'm so sorry.' She wiped at it with her sleeve. Nick was amused, maybe this was her first shift.

'Have you worked here for long?' he enquired, gently mopping up the wine with a tissue.

'Yes, well, no, not really, but I will be working soon, I hope. My uncle owns it.'

That explained it, Nick thought. She rushed away and he took a sip of his wine and then he took another.

This was bloody delicious and strangely familiar. He must have been getting used to the taste of Bordeaux wines. He wished his house wine was half as good. He would have to ask Philippe's advice and then it suddenly hit him.

Sitting up straight he gargled some water. Then he took another, longer taste of the wine, closing his eyes, rolling it around his mouth and letting it slide down his throat. He repeated the procedure and by the end he was positive he was right.

This was Philippe's wine, one of his superior wines. The Hotel de Paris must have been one hell of a classy establishment to serve this as a house wine. He was impressed.

It was beautiful sitting out on the terrace. Nick lit a cigarette and let his imagination take over. He pictured a small chateau with a cheerful bar and brasserie at the front and a stunning restaurant to the rear. He envisioned a candlelit terrace with sweeping views over the vineyard. A gleaming kitchen with the same tranquil atmosphere he had experienced at Maad's restaurant in Marrakech. He could see himself walking down the steps to the cellar, he could almost breath the earthy smell and imagined running his eyes along the rows of dusty bottles.

'Can I get you another?' The young wee lass was back at his side, breaking his thoughts. He was tempted but looking at his watch decided he had better get back.

'No, but that was delicious.' He drained his glass. 'Was it Chateau Fontaine?' He saw the hesitation on her face and grinned. 'Don't worry it's not important.' The poor girl clearly had no idea. 'But you can give me directions back there if you can. I took the wrong turn from Libourne and am now completely lost.'

She was bringing the glass in when her uncle spotted her. His brow darkened, as she had known it would and she hastened to reassure him.

'It was just one glass, there was nobody around.' She gazed at him from under her fringe, she was usually able to win him over. 'I couldn't leave him sitting on his own.' She smiled sweetly.

'Well where the hell is everyone?' Arnaud was angry. 'What the fuck do they think I'm paying them for?' He quickly smiled at his niece. 'Apologies for the language.' She smiled beguilingly back. 'What did he order?'

'Just a glass of house red, he seemed very impressed, he was English I think.'

'Of course he was impressed, they don't know the first thing about wine.' He stopped at the bar. 'What did you pour him?' he demanded, suddenly looking around. She pointed to the open bottle. He swore under his breath. 'Anaïs, that isn't the damn house wine.' He grabbed the bottle and glared at her. She bit her lip and widened her eyes. Sensing tears he quickly said, 'Never mind, no harm done, you were only trying to help.' He ruffled her hair and silently thanked the Lord that the customer had been foreign.

Nick was unpacking his basket and spreading the contents over the kitchen table. Rosa looked astonished, as indeed did everyone. I could have told them that actually he had been quite restrained this time but I still found it hard to talk about our past relationship.

'Oysters, how wonderful.' Luc licked his lips.

'I couldn't resist them.' Nick smiled. 'I know Sky is squeamish but I hope everyone else likes them.'

'I'm not squeamish,' I said sharply. 'I just don't like them.'

'Ah, but you've never had oysters from Arcachon.' Luc picked one up. 'Famed throughout France for its oyster farms.' He draped an arm around my shoulder. 'We'll convert you yet, Sky.'

245

I was unconvinced.

'What else is in the basket?' Rosa asked, peering in.

Nick hesitated.

'Come on.' Rosa laughed. 'Let's see the worst.'

Nick looked uncertain then reached inside for a bag. 'Beautiful hats for beautiful ladies.' He handed me a package and plonked the cute cap over Emmie's curls. She giggled in delight.

I felt desperately uncomfortable. I could feel everyone's eyes on me.

'Thank you, they're nice,' I said, barely glancing inside the package. I knew I should sound more grateful but I didn't really know how else to respond. Why was he always putting me in these uncomfortable situations? We were getting on better and I knew he was trying to be nice but I just wasn't ready for nice. It annoyed me. I mumbled something incoherent about going to change my clothes and virtually ran from the room.

Flinging the hats and myself on the bed I lay there trying to marshal my thoughts. One moment I was OK and the next moment – wham – it hit me all over again. The more he tried to recapture our past the more I realised how much I was going to miss it. And he was responsible for that, he and Miles together had shattered my whole bloody life. I wanted to rebuild it but really did not know how. This sort of scenario belonged in the movies, it didn't belong in real life.

There was a tentative knock and the door and Emmie poked her head in. I sat up and beckoned her.

'Is you angry?' Her little face was full of concern as she came towards me.

'I am, sweetheart, but certainly not with you.'

She nodded and then picking up the straw hat said, 'Is you wearing this?'

'Well I'm not sure it's really suitable for lunch, darling.'

'We is lunching outside.' She stared at me earnestly. 'I is wearing mine.' She patted her head as if to make sure the cap was still there. 'It will make everybody pleased.' She looked pleadingly at me and I marvelled at this little girl. Through no fault of her own she had been set apart from others of her own age, her parents were seemingly disinterested in her and yet she still loved the world and sought only to make people happy. I could learn a lot from her.

I got off the bed and went to the wardrobe. Picking out a floaty vintage cheesecloth dress bought in Greenwich Market I held it against me and turned to her. She smiled her approval and clapped her hands. Discarding my jeans and shirt I slipped it on and pirouetted around for her. She laughed and then determinedly held out my hat. I took it from her, hesitating for a moment before turning to the mirror. Tying my hair into a loose ponytail I put it on. It suited me, as I had known it would. Nick had been buying me hats for years.

'Pretty,' Emmie said. 'You is very pretty.' She held out her hand.

The kitchen was a hive of activity. Luc and Michel were shucking the oysters, Nick was prowling around watching Rosa, Stephanie was arranging the olives and tapenade, Beatrice and Philippe were organising the champagne and outside I could see Henri and Elf setting up the table. They looked up when we arrived and I felt horribly self-conscious. Emmie kept a firm grip on my hand as if she realised I might turn tail at any minute.

'You look beautiful, Sky.' Beatrice smiled at me and I could sense her approval. Nick didn't say anything but his face said it all. Luc gave a low wolf whistle. I smiled at him but turned to Philippe.

'I thought the hat a wise move.' I grinned. 'I don't fancy a repeat of the sun burn in Marrakech.'

'A wise move indeed,' he agreed and I knew that we had forgiven each other for that little episode. 'It suits you.' He nodded in appreciation and I blushed.

I saw Nick and Beatrice exchanged a quick glance and wondered why. But before I could say anything Nick said, 'I stopped at Hotel de Paris on my way back home from the market.'

The others looked surprised.

'On your way back?' Luc raised his eyebrows.

'Well, I got lost,' Nick explained.

'Badly lost.' Luc laughed.

'I went to ask for directions, which as it turned out were useless, but I sat and had a glass of wine on the terrace.' He turned to Philippe. 'Do you sell to them? I'm sure they gave me a Chateau Fontaine.'

'Unlikely,' Philippe replied. 'The manager and I don't exactly see eye to eye.'

'Celine certainly does, in fact she sees more than his eye,' I overheard Michel murmur to Beatrice and Luc.

'How on earth do you know?' Beatrice was instantly curious, as indeed was I.

'I have my sources.'

'The source being the sexy receptionist.' Luc grinned.

'You know, I could swear that wine was Chateau Fontaine,' Nick continued. 'I'd lay money on it, I really would.'

'Really?' Beatrice looked thoughtful. 'We'll go tomorrow, Nick, just you and I.' She turned to Luc and Michel. 'You'd be recognised, but I've never been and I'll certainly know if the wine is Chateau Fontaine.'

'Good plan, one problem.' Nick grinned. 'I'll need instructions, I've no idea how to get back there.'

'I do,' Elf said.

I looked around surprised, I hadn't even realised he'd come into the kitchen.

'I asked about work there,' he explained.

'Was there anywhere you didn't ask for work, Elf?' Beatrice asked him gently.

'No,' he replied shortly.

'But they'll certainly recognise you, Elf,' Nick said.

'I won't go in, I'll simply sniff around outside like a bloodhound.' He chuckled. 'You'd be amazed how invisible you are when you are small.' He winked at me and I flushed.

Luc laughed. 'Elf, you are certainly a character, it was a lucky day for us when you arrived.'

'I'll second that,' Philippe said.

Elf smiled and he suddenly looked ten feet tall.

CHAPTER THIRTY-SEVEN

Arnaud watched them walk into the bar of the Hotel de Paris. She was an absolute knockout, effortlessly chic in a simple silk dress with her blonde hair swept up in a chignon. Diamond studs glinted in her ears but her neck remained bare. Her companion was equally impressive in a cream linen suit just the right side of crumpled. They looked business-like, elegant and wealthy, which was exactly the look Beatrice was aiming for.

Nick hadn't been sure as to why Beatrice had insisted on him borrowing a suit from Philippe.

'I have a pair of decent jeans, Beatrice, they'll be fine.'

'They won't be fine, we need to play a part. I'll explain it in the car.'

Arnaud stopped the waitress from going over and went to serve them himself.

'Madame, monsieur, welcome to Hotel de Paris. How can I help you today?'

Beatrice turned towards him. He was very handsome in an obvious sort of way and it was clear why Celine would fancy him, but he had an oily charm that immediately made her flesh creep.

'Good morning, what a charming hotel,' she said, flashing him a vivid smile. 'My colleague came yesterday and persuaded me to visit today. I'm glad he did, he's right, it is exactly what we are looking for.'

She knew that would pique his curiosity, as indeed it did. He recognised her Parisian accent and she went up even higher in his estimation. He was desperate to know who they were. He glanced over to Nick lounging in the chair, he hadn't seen him yesterday and he would have been hard to miss with his gleaming red curls.

'Monsieur, would it be possible speak to the proprietor or the manager?' Beatrice continued.

'You are speaking to him, madame.' He held out his hand. 'Arnaud Olivier at your service.'

Nick smiled to himself, there was more than a hint of Uriah Heep about the Frenchman's manner.

'Beatrice Pignal, and my companion Nick McPherson.' Beatrice stood up and held out her hand. Nick followed suit. 'Delighted to meet you.'

'Can I get you a drink?' Arnaud was burning to know what their business was.

'You can indeed.' Beatrice had held his hand slightly longer than necessary. She now sank back gracefully onto her seat. 'Nick has been enthusing about your wine since yesterday.'

Arnaud looked enquiringly at Nick.

'I was seated on the terrace,' he said. 'Your young niece served me.'

'Ah, the Englishman, I remember her telling me.'

'Scottish, not English.' Nick grinned. 'There is a big difference.'

'Yes indeed, forgive me.' Arnaud smiled without having a clue as to why he was apologising. Scotland was in England, wasn't it?

'She served me a glass of your house red. I have to say it was simply delicious.'

'Ah, well, I'm afraid young Anaïs made a slight mistake, monsieur.' Arnaud flushed. 'It was not house wine she served you but my Bordeaux superior.'

'I did wonder.' Nick smiled. 'Nonetheless we would like the same today, please.'

'Monsieur Olivier, I wonder if we might steal a few minutes of your time?' Beatrice gazed up at him, her smile was radiant and he was like a rabbit caught in the headlights. 'I realise how busy you are but we would be most grateful.' She touched his arm lightly. 'Please, don't worry, I can assure you we are not here to sell you anything. We are not here to interest you in new bar stools or a cocktail shaker.' She held his gaze. 'I am a hotelier myself.' She produced a glossy brochure from her briefcase. 'My young companion is a Michelin-starred chef, he has already made a name for himself in London and I'm hoping to persuade him to come to Paris.'

Nick shrugged in what he hoped was a nonchalant but slightly arrogant manner.

'I am looking for new opportunities and would welcome the chance to talk to you.' Her voice was like a soft caress and Arnaud went weak at the knees. When Beatrice decided to bewitch you there was no escaping, and like so many men before him he was under her spell.

'Let me, er, let me just see to the drinks and then I'll return at once,' he managed to stammer.

'He's gone to check on you,' Beatrice grinned after he left. 'He's got my brochure and now I bet any money he's looking you up.'

'You are one class act, Beatrice.' Nick was impressed. 'You have me completely fooled and I'm in on the act, and you have Arnaud eating out of your hand.'

'With a man like him it is not hard,' she whispered.

'What is your Paris hotel like?' he asked.

'Full of style, quirky but charmingly elegant.' She laughed. 'That is a quote from a magazine.'

'I imagine it's stunning.'

'Actually it is rather special,' she acknowledged. 'I was very lucky, I inherited the house from my parents who inherited it from my grandparents.'

'Did you live there as a child?'

'Some of the time, but we moved around a lot, my father was a diplomat.'

'That must have been an interesting life.'

'It had its moments,' she said briefly and he sensed a reluctance to talk. He changed the subject.

'Why the move to Marrakech?'

'I like new projects.' She smiled. 'I get bored easily, it used to drive Philippe mad, still does.' She paused. 'What about you, Nick? Will you always stay in London?'

'I'm not sure, yesterday I was fantasising about a restaurant here. Why do you ask?'

'No reason.'

'There is always a reason behind your questions, Beatrice.' He smiled at her but before they could continue Arnaud arrived at their table.

Beatrice had been right, having barked out orders for a carafe of wine and canapés Arnaud had rushed immediately to his office to google Nick McPherson. He was impressed, numerous accolades, some excellent reviews and to cap it all the Michelin star. His heart began to beat a little faster.

His mobile rang, he saw that it was Celine but he didn't have time to talk to her now, he needed to get back to his important visitors.

'Nick was right, this wine is nectar.' Beatrice licked her lips in appreciation and swirled it around her glass. 'What is the name of the chateau?'

Nick leant forward, this should be interesting but Arnaud didn't miss a beat. 'It is blended especially for the hotel. The grape varieties are Cabernet Sauvignon, Cabernet Franc and Merlot but more than that I cannot tell you. It is our secret recipe.' He looked ingratiatingly at Nick. 'I'm sure monsieur understands.'

'Oh, absolutely, I wouldn't dream of prying. I'm just delighted to be drinking it, in fact if I may make so bold I'm going to top myself up and take it to the terrace to enjoy with a cigarette. I will leave you two to talk.' And assuming a carelessness he was far from feeling he got up, stretched and strolled towards the open door.

Once outside, making sure he was out of sight of the window, he pulled a small water bottle from his pocket and poured some wine into it. He slipped it back into his pocket and brought out his cigarettes. After today he was even more convinced that the wine was Philippe's. But how the hell had it got here? He looked around for Elf, but the lad was doing as he had promised and keeping well out of sight.

Beatrice leant forward and Arnaud could smell her perfume. He would hazard a guess at Guerlain.

'I will get straight to the point, Monsieur Olivier.' She smiled at him. 'I have a meeting after this so I don't have too much time. As I said, I own a hotel in Paris, I also have a riad in Marrakech but it is the Parisian hotel I am really here to talk about.'

'I'm intrigued, madame.'

'For some time now I have been toying with the idea of a sister hotel.' She paused to let that sink in. 'As you will be aware, the new TGV will soon take just over two hours from Paris to Bordeaux.'

Arnaud's eyes were gleaming and Beatrice began to reel him in.

'I like the idea of dual tailor-made holidays, sightseeing in Paris followed by wine tasting in Bordeaux or vice-versa.' She was warming to her subject.

'Gourmet meals in Paris, gourmet wine tours in south-west France.' Arnaud was excited. 'The new Cité du Vins has just opened in Bordeaux and we also have Saint-Émilion on our doorstep.' He took a sip of his wine. This could be just the break he had been looking for. A collaboration with a celebrated chef, a top Parisian hotel and an extremely sexy owner.

Beatrice could see his mind racing. He was ambitious and he was bright. He was too smarmy for her taste but she understood why Celine was attracted to him. He was the polar opposite of Claude.

'I am of course meeting with other hotels, but I like what I see here.' It was true, she did. There was a lot of potential. It was classy and intimate. It was clear that Arnaud knew what he was doing and his next words confirmed it.

'If you could spare the time then I would be delighted to see you again, madame.' He smiled. 'I will give it some serious thought and outline some suggestions.' He paused. 'I have a few ideas that I think will interest you, it is something that I too have been thinking about.' But not wishing to appear too pushy he stood up and held out his hand. 'I don't wish to hold you up now.'

'I think that went rather well, don't you?' Beatrice asked as she and Nick sped away from the hotel.

'I think he fell for it hook, line and sinker, I almost feel sorry for the man.' Nick grinned and Elf chuckled.

'Actually a sister hotel is not a bad idea.' Beatrice expertly lit her cigarette while simultaneously flinging the car around a steep bend. Nick reached for his seat belt and Elf in the back seat closed his eyes. 'I've had the idea before but I've been too busy in Marrakech. Maybe now is the right time.' She opened the window to let the smoke out.

'And did you think the wine was Philippe's?' Nick asked, also lighting up. Elf surreptitiously opened the back window.

'Without a shadow of doubt,' she replied. 'Did you manage to decant some?'

Nick reached into his pocket and waved the water bottle at her.

'We make a good team.' She grinned. 'We should set up in business, we'd never be short of work.'

'Is there a lot of wine-swindling going on?'

'Mon Dieu, yes, sadly not everyone is as straight as our Philippe.'

'So how did it get there?' Nick was intrigued. 'And how long has it been there?'

'How indeed?' Beatrice had some ideas but it was too early to share them yet. 'Did you see anything, Elf?'

'I saw some bottles without labels in one of the outhouses but there were a couple of staff hanging around smoking. I couldn't really get too close.'

'Interesting,' Beatrice said before turning back to Nick. 'How are things with you and Sky?'

He was taken aback by the change of subject. 'OK, I think.' He ran his hands through his hair. 'She seems different out here, I'm not sure how to describe it, more relaxed, more at peace, I can't quite put my finger on it.'

'It does seem to suit her.'

'It's still hard to get close.'

'Well of course it is, you've got to build a new relationship and that won't happen overnight.' She swung the car around another steep bend and flung the cigarette out of the window.

Nick merely nodded.

'How is Miles?' Beatrice pursued the subject.

'And I thought we were investigating Hotel de Paris.' Unlike Beatrice, Nick carefully stubbed out his cigarette in the ashtray.

Beatrice laughed. 'Stop being so British and throw it out of the window, Stephanie will kill me if she thinks we've been smoking in her car.' She glanced over at him. 'I'm sorry, Nick, you're right, I'm prying when really it's none of my business.' She shook her head. 'It's not like me, you can ask Philippe, I don't normally meddle, unless it's to do with him.'

'I love the relationship you two have.'

'It will be the same for you and Sky, trust me.' She turned to smile at him.

'I'd trust you more if you kept your eyes on the road.' Nick was gripping the side of his seat whilst his brake foot slammed into the floor. Elf had given up trying to be brave and was lying down on the back seat.

'Does my driving scare you?' She was amused.

'No, it doesn't scare me,' he replied. 'It fucking terrifies me! What is it about Continental women? Sky's Italian grandmother is exactly the same, she's the terror of the Scottish Borders.'

Beatrice threw back her head and laughed, but she did slow down and Nick began to breathe once again.

'I guess it is your business, Beatrice,' Nick said after a while. 'We made it your business when we came to your riad.' He paused. 'And actually it's good to be able to talk about it, there isn't really anyone else I can talk to.'

She nodded.

'Miles isn't great, things didn't go particularly well with him and Sky on their last meeting, his fault, he played it badly. I'd sort of thought of bringing him here, he's had some good ideas about a website, but when I heard that Sky was coming we knocked it on the head. Now he's holed up in some bleak hotel in Bayswater.'

'He'll come over here at some point,' Beatrice said firmly. 'Once Sky has forgiven you both.'

'If she does.'

'Oh, I think she's much closer than you may imagine.'

Nick turned to look at her but she merely smiled enigmatically.

CHAPTER THIRTY-EIGHT

I finished the pen and ink drawings of the chateau that Emmie and I had started yesterday. I'd been impressed with Emmie. She had a bold, simplistic style all of her own. She drew with confidence. I spread my drawings out on the table and felt relatively pleased with the result. They looked simple but classy and would make an elegant invitation.

I stood up to stretch my legs and wandered to the French windows. God, I loved this view, I could spend hours simply staring out, absorbing the variety of colours, the constantly changing light, the vineyards and the sparkling river beyond.

The kitchen door opened and I watched as Sausage came trotting out with Belle at his heels. The old dog was content to lie in the sunshine but the piglet went to chase the hens. I suddenly thought of Sonny and I got out my phone to take some photos to send to him. I hadn't spoken to Gail since I'd been here, I'd give her a call now.

Sonny answered. 'Yes,' he said uncertainly.

'Hello, sweetheart, it's Sky here, I'm just going to send you some photos of a piglet and some hens.'

'Wow!'

'I'm in France at the chateau Philippe was telling us about. Do you remember?'

'You are lucky!'

I chuckled. 'Is Mummy there, sweetheart?'

'She's on the sofa, she can't walk,' he replied.

'What?' I stopped in my tracks. 'Is she OK? Pass the phone to her, Sonny.'

'Hello?' Gail sounded tired.

'Gail, it's Sky, what on earth is wrong?'

'Oh, Sky, how lovely, I was going to ring you today, how is France?'

'More to the point, how are you? Why can't you walk?'

'I can walk.' Gail laughed. 'I just have a very swollen and bruised ankle right now.'

'Oh, Gail, how?'

'Playing football with Sonny, a dirty tackle, I showed him the red card.'

'Is he upset?'

'At the red card or my ankle?'

'Both, I guess.' I giggled.

'Furious at the red card and desperately upset at my ankle, poor lad.' She laughed. 'He keeps bringing me flowers from the garden and bars of chocolate.'

'Oh, God, you poor thing.'

'Oh, I'm fine, it's just a bit inconvenient.'

'Have you got help?'

'Yes, my next-door neighbour is being marvellous and Holly, a friend of Dawn's, is coming over later.'

'And Dawn?'

'Won't be coming over. We haven't spoken since the last argument.'

'Oh, Gail, I'm so sorry.'

'No, it's for the best, Sky.' But I could hear the sadness in her voice. 'We're both so angry and hurt, we need time apart.'

'What about Tariq? Is he coming over?'

'Yes, that's the plan.' She paused. 'I think it means decision time.'

'I think the decision is already made.'

'I guess, it's just, oh, I don't know, it's just all a bit terrifying.'

'You've done the terrifying bit, Gail, now is the fun part.'

'Yes, you're right. Anyway how is France?' She clearly didn't want to talk anymore about Tariq. 'I'm longing to hear all about it.'

'It's magical, Gail.' I glanced around. 'There is a soft mist hanging over the vines, the river is glinting in the distance, the chateau is enchanted, there is a piglet chasing the hens and an elf and a man with a ginger cat on his shoulder.'

'Have you been smoking something, Sky?' Gail asked. 'Or maybe you've hit the booze, I know they start early over there.'

'Nothing like that.' I giggled. 'I'm telling you the exact truth, I wish you were here.'

'Trust me, so do I,' Gail said with feeling. 'I'd like to see all that for myself. How is Philippe?'

'Philippe…' I paused. 'Philippe is at home.'

'That much I knew,' Gail replied drily.

'No, I mean he's an integral part of the landscape, he belongs here.' Gail was silent. 'I'm not explaining this very well.' I tried again. 'Put it this way, he's not the arrogant man we met in Marrakech.'

I knew that Gail had found Philippe charming but she kept quiet.

'He's friendly, mostly, he's passionate, he's knowledgeable, he's totally devoted to his family, who are all gorgeous by the way, including his nephew who is flirting with me.'

'Really?' Gail was intrigued. 'How old is he?'

'Oh, far too young, about twenty-five, but it's kind of flattering.'

'And how is Nick?' Gail asked gently.

'OK.' I hesitated. 'Well, sort of OK.' I sighed. 'He's trying so hard and I so want to forgive him but I also want to make him pay. Does that sound awful?' It sounded pretty awful even to me. 'I mean, I'm desperate to get back to how we once were but then I just get so angry when I think how he threw it all away.'

'Of course you're still angry, Sky,' Gail replied in her soft, measured tones. 'He didn't deliberately throw it away, though, he had no choice, you know that.'

If anyone else had said that I would have flared up but Gail was so gentle and understanding that I couldn't be angry with her. She was also quite right.

'Well, I guess we're making progress but we still have a way to go. At the moment he's out with Beatrice uncovering some wine scam.'

'Beatrice?' Gail squeaked. 'Beatrice is out there?'

'God, yes, sorry, I forgot that bit.' I laughed. 'She was here as a surprise when we arrived.'

'Oh no, this is most unfair. I'm lying here with an ankle the size of a football while you're staying in a fairy tale chateau surrounded by misty vines protected by elves and piglets and Beatrice the grand high witch of the world.'

She made me laugh. 'I'll ask the high witch to wave a magic wand and bring you over.'

'Please do, and get the Lotto numbers while you're at it.' She chuckled. 'Seriously, Sky you do sound happier, it's lovely to hear.'

'I don't know if happy is exactly the right word, but you're right, there is something about this place that seeps into your soul, it soothes you.'

'Send some of it over here. And send my love to everyone. How is young Emmie?' she added as an afterthought.

'She is an angel.' I closed my eyes to picture her. 'A chubby, spirited, short-sighted, beautiful angel.'

'Oh, Sky these are excellent.' Philippe was looking at my pen and ink sketches. 'This one in particular I like.' He held up one of the back of the chateau with the crumbling stone fountain in the foreground. 'But they're all lovely, I've no idea which to choose.'

'Well we'll show them to Nick and Beatrice, see what they think, and then get them copied and sent off to the culinary big guns as soon as possible.' I was delighted with his reaction and felt bold enough to put forward my next suggestion. 'I know Nick is going to contact some foodie magazines back at home but I wondered if you could get anyone here to write an article? I mean, it's not every day you host a party for some top London chefs, it would be good publicity.'

'Yes, it had crossed my mind too. I think we need to spread the word, get the place buzzing.' He smiled at me. 'Thank you for being so enthusiastic, Sky.' We held each other's gaze for a moment before he suddenly said, 'You like it here, don't you?'

I was startled. 'What's not to like?' I replied flippantly and the moment was broken. I was cross with myself. Why couldn't I have answered honestly? Why hadn't I admitted that I loved it here, that the beauty and magic of the chateau had cast a spell over me, that I adored his family, adored his animals and that I was dreading my inevitable departure? I shook my head and stood up and stretched.

'I wondered if Emmie could come here after school?' I flexed my arms above my head and arched my back. It eased the tension after painting but I was suddenly aware of Philippe's eyes on me and stopped abruptly. 'I thought I would make a start on the wine labels and I promised she could help.'

'Yes, she's coming here,' he replied, still staring at me, it unnerved me. He suddenly seemed to collect himself and turned away. 'Claude is driving Celine to her parents, her father was taken ill during the night, so Emmie will stay here tonight.'

'Oh, I'm sorry to hear that. I hope it's not too serious.'

'Claude didn't say too much, but he has been ill for quite a while now.'

'When did your father die, Philippe?' I hoped I hadn't gone too far but he turned around and smiled.

'About twenty years ago now.' He shrugged his shoulders in a gesture that was fast becoming familiar to me. 'And I still expect him to come walking through the door.'

'Were you very close?'

'He was stubborn, proud and self-opinionated.' That sounds familiar, I thought to myself and stifled a smile.

'He had a huge heart and a huge laugh.' Philippe laughed. 'We used to argue late into the night, we disagreed more than we agreed, we drove each other mad but I miss him very much, very much indeed.' He smiled. 'He also taught me how to drink pastis.'

'Not that you needed much teaching,' Beatrice laughed her low husky laugh. She had walked up and overheard the last part of the conversation.

I gawped at her in admiration. She always looked good but in this outfit she was sensational. 'Beatrice, you look a million dollars.'

Philippe meanwhile was staring at Nick in astonishment. 'Is that my suit you are wearing?'

I turned to look at Nick and nodded in appreciation. 'Wow, you should buy it off him, Nicky, it looks great.'

'What the hell have you been up to?' Philippe turned from one to the other. 'You are looking both shifty and smug, it's a combination I've learnt to be wary of.'

'Pour us a drink and let's sit down,' Beatrice commanded. 'Where are Henri and Luc? We need them here too.'

'So what do you think?' Beatrice asked looking at Philippe, Henri and Luc a short while later. They had all tasted the wine that Nick had decanted from his glass. Luc knew what was going on but Philippe and Henri were totally bemused. 'Philippe, which wine is it?'

'It's 2009, Bea.'

'Where from?'

'What do you mean where from?' Philippe was starting to get annoyed. 'It's Chateau Fontaine.'

'Henri?' Beatrice turned to him.

'Of course.' He was equally puzzled. 'What are you trying to prove, cheri?'

Luc rolled the wine around and sipped it. 'She is trying to prove that the Hotel de Paris is selling your wine.'

'We don't sell to the Hotel de Paris.' Philippe was perplexed. 'I told Nick that yesterday.'

'Well they're getting it from somewhere,' Beatrice replied.

'Start from the beginning, how did you get this wine? Tell us what you know.' Philippe stood up and leant his long frame against the window. Too much sitting was bad for his knee. 'Before you start we had best get Stephanie and Rosa.'

They all listened in silence as Beatrice and Nick recounted the morning.

'You should have seen her,' Nick said, looking at Beatrice with admiration. 'She was quite superb, Arnaud was putty in her hands, he is a man obsessed, totally smitten. I've never seen anything like it.'

'When Bea decides to reel you in there's nothing you can do about it.' Philippe grinned as he blew her a kiss.

I felt a sudden and unexpected flash of jealousy.

'It wasn't hard,' Beatrice replied. 'He's somewhat self-centred, hungry for admiration and very susceptible to flattery.'

'A real charmer.' Stephanie raised her eyebrows.

'Nick played his part well, a lethal combination of nonchalance and arrogance.' Beatrice winked at him.

'But how the hell has he got our wine?' Philippe paced the room.

Beatrice glanced over at Luc and nodded. Luc cleared his throat. 'Michel has been spending quite a lot of time at the Hotel de Paris, he's, er, well he's rather taken with the receptionist.' He paused.

'And your point is, Luc?' I could see that Philippe was fast becoming impatient. He obviously sensed there was something that he wasn't being told and I imagined that he wasn't a man who liked to be kept in the dark.

'My point is that Celine has also been seen there a lot.'

'Celine?' Philippe stared at him. But before he could carry on Elf stepped in.

'Boss, the manager and Celine are having an affair,' he said bluntly. 'It's an open secret at the hotel that the manager has an amoureuse and that the amoureuse is Celine.'

'Jesus, did you all know about this?' he demanded. 'Am I the last to know?'

'No, I suspect Claude will be the last to know,' Beatrice said drily. 'But it does answer the question as to how they are getting our wine.'

'You think Celine is cheating us?' Philippe looked genuinely shocked. 'But she is family, why would she cheat on her family?' No one answered him. 'What has she to gain by cheating on us?' he repeated. 'She's married to Claude.'

'I doubt it is the first time she has cheated on *him*, cheri,' Beatrice said gently.

'Well why the hell did she ever marry him?'

Again the room was silent.

I found his dogged belief and faith in Celine rather touching. I'd only met her once and hadn't been massively impressed, I'd thought her rather cold and distant and frankly I wasn't at all surprised to hear about the affair; neither would it seem was anyone else. But I could tell that Philippe seemed genuinely hurt and upset and I suddenly had an overwhelming urge to put my arms around him, which was weird given that I didn't really like him that much.

'Perhaps we should have a chat with Claude,' Stephanie said.

'You don't think he's in on the wine scam, do you?' Philippe stared at his sister in astonishment.

She shook her head. 'No I don't, but he may be able to shed some light, he may have heard something.'

'Where is Claude?' Beatrice asked.

'He's gone to Celine's parents, her father was taken ill in the night.' Philippe grabbed the pastis bottle and poured himself a hefty slug. 'When he comes back I'll have a quiet word with him.' He offered the bottle around the room. 'I can't believe he knows anything, if he'd suspected anything surely he would have told us.'

'He'll be protecting Celine,' Luc said.

'We don't know she's done anything yet,' Philippe said sharply. 'Let's not jump to conclusions until we know the facts.' He swirled the pastis around his glass. 'While we are all here I'd like you to see Sky's paintings,' he said in an abrupt change of subject. 'They are wonderful, she has captured the charm of our chateau quite beautifully.'

I was over the moon with such high praise from Philippe, especially since I sensed it was not easily given. Once again I was aware of his intense scrutiny and I blushed, wishing for the millionth time that I didn't have such fair skin.

There was a good deal of exclamation over the paintings. No one could decide which they preferred. It boiled down to a choice of two, the one Philippe had liked of the back of the chateau with the stone fountain and a more formal one of the front. Everyone had been very complimentary but I could sense that spirits were low. They were all concerned about Claude and Celine. No one liked to think of a traitor in their midst.

'Could I have a word?' I stopped Philippe and Beatrice.

'As long as the word is outside or in my study.' Philippe smiled. 'I'd like a cigarette.' He paused. 'And maybe another small pastis.'

'You don't know how to pour a small pastis.' Beatrice laughed.

'I'll grab another if I may.' Nick held out his glass. 'I could get used to this.'

'You are getting used to it,' Beatrice responded.

'Sorry, do you want to talk in private?' Nick hesitated as we headed outside. 'Am I interrupting?' We were both treading on eggshells and I suddenly felt intensely weary of it all.

'No, of course not,' I replied.

'We really must give up this filthy habit,' Beatrice said, lighting her cigarette.

'We tried.' Philippe smiled at her ruefully. 'I can't remember how many times we tried.' He turned to me. 'Have you ever smoked, Sky?'

I glanced over to Nick and we couldn't help laughing. 'Once, when I was about fourteen, my sister, Nick and I stole my father's fags. They were very strong, some strange Italian make. We smoked them one after the other for about an hour. Iona and I were sick as dogs.' I grimaced at the memory, still so clear even after all the years. 'God, we were ill. We took days to recover and never smoked again. My father was so distraught at the thought that he was indirectly to blame that he gave up immediately.' I grinned at Nick. 'Sadly, Nick here took to it like a duck to water and hasn't looked back since. He's an addict.'

'I wish to God that had happened to me,' Philippe said.

'It did, you are,' Beatrice said with her husky laugh.

'Not the addict part,' he said, shaking his head in despair. 'Sky, what did you want?'

'I spoke to Gail today.'

'How is she?' Beatrice enquired.

'Well, not that great actually,' I replied. 'She was lying on the sofa with a bad ankle.'

'How did that happen?' Nick asked.

'Dirty tackle from Sonny during a football game.' I smiled. 'He's devastated apparently. Keeps bringing her flowers and chocolate.' I hesitated. 'I just wondered, I mean, she just seems a bit low, she had a huge row with her sister…'

'About bloody time,' Nick interrupted.

'So I thought, well, maybe...' I floundered. It suddenly seemed terribly presumptuous of me to ask if Gail could come over, especially in light of recent events.

'Is Tariq there?' Beatrice asked.

'No, but he's going over soon.' I looked across at Philippe. 'I sort of thought it would be interesting to hear what he thinks about your barn.' Philippe looked at me blankly. He was not getting the drift of this conversation at all and I wished I had never brought it up.

'I think it would be a wonderful idea,' Beatrice said, getting the drift immediately.

'She knows you're here,' I turned to her gratefully. 'She sounded very envious that we were all here. I mean, I'm sure she would be happy to contribute something and so would I, I mean it's my idea, I don't want you out of pocket or anything.' God, I was making a pig's ear of this. I started again. 'I don't mean to impose, I, um, well I haven't said anything to her yet of course so if you think there is too much going on...' I trailed off, worried that I may have been rather tactless.

'Why the hell is everyone talking in riddles today?' Philippe was lost. 'What are you talking about?'

'Sky was thinking that it might be a nice idea to invite Gail and Sonny over, and Tariq of course.' Beatrice shook her head at him. 'You're really not on the ball today, Philippe.'

'Thank you for that vote of confidence, cheri.'

'Sky is right, it really would be interesting to get his take on the barn,' Beatrice continued. 'He's a very clever man and it's about time we did something useful with it.'

'Bea, "*we*" are not really in a position to do much with it.' Philippe turned to me and Nick. 'Sometimes she forgets she doesn't live here.'

Beatrice was not remotely offended. 'Getting ideas doesn't cost money.' She reached up and kissed him. 'Shall I go and ask Stephanie and Rosa?'

'Do I have a choice?'

'It will be fun.' Beatrice smiled at him. 'Emmie will adore Sonny and I'm serious about Tariq looking at the barn. I think we are really missing a trick here.'

He shook his head in despair. 'Go and ask Rosa and Stephanie, I have to go and fetch Emmie.'

'I'll go if you want,' Nick offered.

'Do you want me to drive you?' Beatrice stopped in the doorway.

'Christ, no.' Nick looked horrified at the thought. 'I escaped with my life earlier, I certainly don't want to risk it again.'

'There is nothing wrong with my driving!' Beatrice was indignant.

'There is so much wrong with your driving,' Nick replied, 'I don't know where to start, it is wrong on every level.'

Philippe was chuckling. 'Take my car, Nick.' He threw him the keys.

'I'll come with you,' I said suddenly, surprising myself as much as Nick.

CHAPTER THIRTY-NINE

'Do you really think it's Celine?' I asked Nick.

'Well, everything points that way,' Nick replied, slowing down at a crossroads. 'Did Philippe say right or left here?'

'Straight over.' I shook my head in despair. Nick was hopeless with directions. It had always been me who had guided them, come to think of it Miles was the same. God knows how the two of them would ever get anywhere. I smiled at the thought and then suddenly gasped, realising what I'd just done. I'd actually thought of them both as couple, but not only that, I'd thought of them without rancour, without anger. I'd thought of them as if they were supposed to be together.

'I mean, who else could it be? Well perhaps Claude, but Philippe seemed fairly certain that it wasn't.' Nick was carrying on with the conversation. I tried to concentrate. I'd think about what had just happened later on. I couldn't cope with the implications right now.

'Will she be making a lot of profit?' I asked.

'Depends on how much she sold the wine for and how much mark-up there is?' He thought for a minute. 'Maybe the Hotel de Paris isn't the only place this is happening, maybe that's just the tip of the iceberg – in fact I'd lay money on it.'

'I just don't understand why.' I shook my head. 'Why does she want to rob her own family?'

'God only knows,' Nick replied. 'I didn't really take to her, she doesn't seem to fit in, seems like a cold fish.'

'Poor Philippe.' I sighed. 'He works so hard, he loves his wine and he loves his family.'

'Why the change of heart?' Nick grinned at me. 'I didn't think he was your favourite person.'

'He seems different out here.' I paused. 'More approachable somehow.'

We drew up at the school gates but before turning in Nick suddenly pulled into the side. 'You know I love you very much, don't you, Skylark?' He was staring straight ahead as if afraid to look at my face.

I paused before speaking. I wasn't sure I was ready to have a heart-to-heart. 'I love you too, Nicky,' I said slowly. 'But you've broken my trust and I'm not sure how to get over that.'

'If I'd had an inkling that I was going to hurt you, that I might fall in love with Miles, then I would have moved to the other side of the world and never set eyes on you again.' He ran his fingers through his hair. 'But even then I would have broken your heart because you would never have known the reason why I'd left you.'

I was silent.

'You and Miles would have split up eventually, Sky.'

'That just makes you feel better,' I snapped.

'No, it's true.'

'Why? Why do you say that?'

'Eventually you would have found the person you really loved. Miles was never the love of your life.'

'Why does everyone seem to think that?' I slapped the dashboard in frustration.

'Everyone?' Nick looked puzzled but I ignored his question.

'Do you honestly believe that, Nicky?' I was struggling.

'I really do, and not just because it makes me feel better.'

'In the hospital you started to say I needed someone more passionate, "someone like…", but you never finished the sentence. Who were you talking about?'

'No idea,' he lied and then changed the subject quickly. 'I spoke to Miles today.'

I didn't respond.

'He's not coping very well.'

'Really,' I said coldly. If he expected sympathy he was going to be disappointed. Frankly if he *had* been coping than I would have been furious.

'Sky, he hates that we've hurt you so much. I hate that we've hurt you so much, I don't know how we can expect you to forgive us when we can't forgive each other.

I'd had enough talking for now. 'Let's just take things day by day, Nick.'

Emmie was over the moon to see us both. I let her sit in the front beside Nick, the two of them were chatting non-stop and I was more than content to sit in the back and mull over my thoughts.

I mentally prodded the most recent revelation and found once again that although I still felt betrayed and hurt the agonising pain was no longer there. In fact, I could go one step further and acknowledge that Miles and Nick were well suited. Forcing myself to probe further I thought about their relationship. They had always got on well. They complemented each other, it was an easy relationship.

I had loved the laissez-faire attitude that Miles had but, if I were honest, his laid-back nature had occasionally driven me insane. Sometimes I'd longed for him to take the initiative, to be more decisive, whereas Nick was more than happy to take the lead himself and Miles more than happy to let him. It had always been easier when we were doing things as a threesome.

With a start I realised what I had just admitted, and if I were honest I realised how true it was. Sudden flashes of memory came back to me. I remembered a conversation during a holiday in Greece and I could still hear the sadness in Miles' voice. *'You seem so angry and impatient with me, Sky, and I have no idea why, maybe we should take separate holidays in future.'*

At the time that comment had only made me more angry. I was furious with him for not understanding but looking back, I could see it from Miles' point of view: he actually hadn't done anything wrong, he was just being himself, but clearly that hadn't been good enough for me.

Had I driven him to Nick? Was it my fault? They would make a good team, I could see that. Nick would always be the dominant partner but he needed Miles's gentle sensitivity and understanding. He needed someone to bring him down to earth sometimes and Miles would fulfil that. I had never been able to do that for Nick, we were too alike.

I lay back on the seat and closed my eyes. Was everyone right? Had Miles and I been incompatible? Had I just wasted five years of my life? Tears sprung into my eyes and I gazed out of the window, willing them to stop. I forced myself to focus on the countryside. I couldn't cry in front of Emmie, it wouldn't be fair.

It was beautiful countryside, vineyards stretching as far as the eye could see, gentle rolling hills with the silhouettes of chateau perched on the top. Mellow greens and soft purples contrasted with the bright blue of the sky and the occasional burst of yellow sunflowers. It was soothing and enervating at the same time and I gradually felt myself breathing easier.

I must have dozed off because the next thing I knew Nick was parking the car in front of a small café and Emmie was talking to me.

'What is your favourite, Sky?'

'Sorry, darling, favourite what?'

'Favourite flavour.' She wriggled around to look at me.

'Sky doesn't like ice cream,' Nick said and then laughed at the look of astonishment on Emmie's face. 'I know, weird isn't it?' He winked at her.

'It's not weird, I just prefer chocolate.' Emmie looked marginally relieved to hear that I wasn't a total freak but still didn't look totally convinced.

'I'm sorry to hear that your grandpa is ill.' I took her hand as we left the car.

'Is he?' She looked surprised. Damn, I had put my foot in it, obviously no one had told her. 'I don't think it is anything to worry about, sweetheart.' I was quick to reassure her.

She was silent for a moment before looking up at me. 'Grandpa is not a man what likes me very much.' She said it without rancour or bitterness. Her eyes were wide and guileless behind her glasses, I wanted to scoop her into my arms and never let go.

CHAPTER FORTY

Beatrice walked into the kitchen as Henri was walking out. He stopped and touched her shoulder.

'You were right, cheri,' he said, his blue eyes were clouded with sadness. 'You and Rosa were right.'

'What has got into him?' Beatrice stared after him.

'He's upset about Celine.' Rosa handed her a mug of coffee. 'He feels he has let Philippe down.'

'He wasn't to know.'

'He says that in hindsight certain things were clear.'

'Well, everything is clear in hindsight.' Beatrice sipped her coffee.

'We said that Celine was not to be trusted, he thinks he should have listened more closely.'

'Everyone should have listened more closely,' Beatrice remarked. 'Rosa, do you know what Philippe asked me today?' She looked at her old friend. 'He asked me why Celine had married Claude.'

'And did you tell him?'

'He'd never believe me.'

'No, you're probably right.'

'Rosa, we have a few more people arriving. Is that alright with you?'

Rosa nodded, the more the merrier in her opinion.

'Where is Stephanie?' Beatrice asked. 'I need to clear it with her but I think it is a good idea.'

'If you think it's a good idea then so will she.' Rosa smiled at Beatrice. She adored her. It had been obvious that she and Philippe would never last but it had been equally obvious that she would always remain a part of their lives.

Henri was angry with himself. He had promised Philippe's father that he would look after his son. He felt he had let him down. He should have kept a careful eye on things. He should have checked what was going out and where. He should never have trusted Celine. How could he have let this happen?

He sat down on his favourite stone bench and looked out at the river. There was another reason for feeling so disconsolate. Another reason that was sitting on his chest and weighing him down.

He knew that old Ginger was not going to last much longer. He could see it in his eyes, the old cat had looked at him tenderly this morning as if begging to be allowed to die and Henri knew that it was time to let go. Tears rained down his cheeks and he put his head in his hands.

Moments later a caress as soft as a breeze ruffled his hair. An arm slipped through his and a soft kiss brushed his cheek.

'Don't grieve, mon coeur.' Her voice was like the low murmur of the river. 'He has been loved and he has been cherished, he's been a faithful friend and we'll never forget him, but he's tired now.'

She leant against him and they sat in silence for a while, each drawing comfort in the other.

'We'll go tomorrow to get a new Ginger,' Henri finally said, turning to kiss his wife. 'We'll take Emmie and Elf and go and fetch our new charm.' He gazed into her dark eyes so full of love and compassion. 'Do you know how much I love you, my gypsy princess?'

'I never tire of hearing it.'

'Why the hell haven't you answered my calls?' Celine hissed into her mobile.

'I have been busy, Celine,' Arnaud replied, annoyed at her tone. 'I have been entertaining a hotelier and a top chef from Paris and I think…'

'I can't make this afternoon,' Celine interrupted him.

'Ah, well, er, not to worry, maybe tomorrow?' Arnaud was caught out. He had completely forgotten their rendezvous for this afternoon. He had been daydreaming about expanding his empire, about trips to Paris, a sister hotel and a rather gorgeous proprietor. His meeting with Celine had completely slipped his mind and if he was honest he was more than a little relieved that she couldn't come.

'Don't you want to know why?' Celine was not impressed with his casual acceptance.

'I assume there must be a good reason,' Arnaud replied coolly. Did the woman think he had nothing else on his mind?

'Papa is ill,' she snapped. 'I'm at my parents' house.'

'I'm so sorry, Celine, is it bad?'

'He'll be out of hospital tomorrow or the day after, I'll come home then.'

'I'm pleased to hear that,' Arnaud lied. 'Phone me when you get home. I've got to go now, cheri, someone is calling me.' He hung up quickly, aware that she would not be happy.

She was becoming a bit intense. Maybe it was time to ease off. Celine was very beautiful and without doubt she had been very useful. He enjoyed his time with her, she was very intelligent and she was an absolute tiger in bed, his loins tightened at the thought. But there were other beautiful women and into his mind floated an image of Beatrice. If all went according to his dreams he would be very busy in the forthcoming months.

Celine was not best pleased. Without knowing why she felt that she no longer had the upper hand in the relationship with Arnaud and that annoyed her very much. She liked to be the one calling the shots. He had seemed keen enough the other day, what had suddenly changed? What was all this about a hotelier from Paris? She didn't understand why but vague alarm bells began to ring.

She rubbed her eyes, she was tired that was all. She'd ring him again later and suggest the plan that she'd thought of. Her idea was for him to come and pick her up, she knew of a cosy auberge on the way back. They could stop there for the afternoon, maybe they could stop there for the night, and she shivered in anticipation. She'd been delighted when Claude had suggested driving her, it had seemed that fate was playing into her hands. She hadn't quite worked out her excuse for him not picking her up but she'd come up with something.

Claude was enjoying the drive back home. It was a beautiful day and as always he was relieved to escape his in-laws' house. It was like leaving a prison.

Celine's mother disliked him intensely and made no attempt to disguise the fact. He knew that she thought Celine had married beneath her. She put him down at every opportunity and not once had Celine stood up for him. She merely laughed when he tried to talk to her, telling him he was making a mountain out of a molehill and to be more thick-skinned.

Conversations with his father-in-law were equally stilted. They usually ran out of things to say after a few minutes. Claude hated their snobbery, hated the formal house stuffed with precious antiques and expensive paintings. It was all show, a public parade of their wealth. They didn't particularly enjoy them or indeed know the origin or background of half the objects. They only knew what they had cost, which was usually a considerable sum.

Emmie hated the house just as much as Claude. As with Claude, her grandparents made no effort to disguise their dislike of her. Her stutter and stammer always became more pronounced when she was with them and they made absolutely no effort with her. She became withdrawn and silent.

Claude and Emmie usually showed their faces once a year and to be honest he never really knew why they even did that. He had driven Celine this morning out of a sense of duty, not because he was concerned about her father. She had barely slept all night and she had actually seemed grateful when he suggested driving her. It had pleased Claude to be needed. It happened so rarely. He had even wondered if they might stop for a nice coffee en route, have a chat about things. But once in the car Celine had put the car seat back and slept for the whole two-hour journey. He didn't think she would have appreciated being woken up.

He rang Philippe.

'Ah, Claude how is he?'

'They are keeping him in for observation but he'll be out tomorrow. Bit of a false alarm, he was certainly not at death's door. I think Nadine panicked. Celine is staying the night.'

'Come over for supper when you get back,' Philippe said, feeling slightly queasy. He was aware that with Celine away now was the perfect time to ask Claude some probing questions but it was not something he was looking forward to.

'Is Emmie OK?' Claude asked.

'Yes, she's designing wine labels with Sky. But Claude, that reminds me, she needs some form for a school trip. She says she gave it to Celine, she's worrying about it, she needs it by tomorrow. Can you try and find it?'

'Of course.'

Philippe sounded rather strained, Claude thought. Maybe his knee was bothering him. He rarely complained about it but they all knew it gave him considerable pain.

'It all looks very industrious here,' Philippe said, walking into the salon where Emmie and I were painting. 'Can I take a look?'

'No you can't.' I covered my drawings with my hands rather like a schoolgirl and Emmie copied me. 'They're not quite ready yet.' I smiled at Emmie. 'You can't rush genius, can you, sweetheart?'

Emmie's little face lit up and her eyes shone behind her glasses. 'Sky done lots, Uncle Philly, I just done one.'

'It's quality not quantity that counts, ma poulette,' Philippe replied.

'That's put me in my place.' I smiled.

'Rosa wants to know if you will help her collect the eggs.'

Emmie slid from her chair immediately.

'Not so fast, cheri. Don't you need to help Sky clear things up?'

'No, don't worry,' I reassured her. 'I'll put everything into my big folder and we can finish them tomorrow.'

'Thank you for letting her help,' Philippe said after she had scampered out of the room.

'She was the one helping me.' I grinned. 'She knows a lot about wine.'

'She's been in the vineyards with me since she could toddle,' Philippe said. 'She used to ride on Belle's back until she got too heavy. She has a good nose and an excellent sense of smell.' He chuckled. 'You should see her tasting the wine, she takes it very seriously, screws her face up, closes her eyes and rolls it around her mouth before spitting it out and giving her judgement, which more often than not is very accurate.'

'She's obviously had a good teacher.' I smiled. He didn't reply and there was a slightly awkward pause.

'I hope these are the sort of thing you're looking for,' I said finally, glancing at my sketches. 'I've tried to remember everything you told me.'

I had spent a fascinating couple of hours with Philippe, listening as he explained the different wines of Chateau Fontaine to me. There was a smooth, easy drinking rosé, a superior oak-aged Bordeaux, the very one which the Hotel de Paris was serving, another red made from his oldest vines and a delicious sweet white wine.

I had sniffed, swirled and sampled the different grape varieties. He had explained everything in great detail, from picking the fruit to the final blending. I learnt about the terroir, what the ideal weather was, what conditions made a good year. I heard how they used natural methods to keep the vines healthy. They didn't believe in spraying them with pesticides.

It was a complete revelation to me, I'd no idea how complex the whole process was and I was absolutely hooked. I'd vowed that never again would I simply neck wine without giving it a second thought. Philippe had laughed but I could tell he was pleased with my enthusiasm.

I was desperate to create labels that would showcase his wine. They were beautiful wines and deserved something rather special. I was also intending to speak to Henri, Luc and Stephanie and hear their views on what they wanted. They were a team and I wanted everyone to be happy.

As I had told Philippe, Emmie had actually been really helpful too. Her knowledge of wine was impressive and her explanations of each were straightforward. She didn't waste time with flowery language but described them in simple and direct terms which I found easy to understand.

I began to gather the things up and Philippe sat down with a heavy sigh. I looked over at him. He was frowning. 'Are you in pain, Philippe?'

'I am in pain, yes, but it is mental anguish rather than physical.'

'I'm so sorry.' I meant it. He worked so hard and he was so passionate about his wine. I hated to think of someone abusing his trust. Especially since that someone was supposed to be family. 'What are you going to do?'

'I don't know, really, try and establish the facts, I suppose. I mean… it may not be Celine.'

'It is unlikely to be anyone else,' Beatrice said, marching into the room and catching the last remark. 'It's not Henri or Luc, is it?' She turned to me. 'Cheri, Stephanie and I are going into town, do you want to come along? You could have a look at the Maison de Vin, cast your eye over the wine labels?'

'Yes, I'd love to.' It would be a good idea to have a look at the competition, see if my labels were up to their standard. It was beyond my usual remit so I was feeling a little anxious.

'Philippe?' Beatrice turned to him.

'No, cheri, I will stay here.' He frowned. 'I need to think things through. I have to talk to Claude tonight.' He pushed his hair back off his forehead. 'How the hell do you tell your cousin that you suspect his wife of theft?'

'You do it very gently,' Beatrice answered 'You don't make waves, it's like tickling a trout.'

Philippe looked at her in exasperation. 'Like tickling a trout? How the hell is that supposed to help me?'

'You feel your way, you tickle the underbelly softly.'

'In Scotland we call it guddling,' I added rather unhelpfully.

Philippe stared at us in disbelief and I giggled.

'It is good advice but you don't have to take it.' Beatrice was unperturbed.

'If I understood it, Bea, then I would take it.'

'I've spoken to Tariq,' Beatrice said, changing the subject completely. 'He would love to come but he wants to surprise Gail so don't say anything.'

'That's wonderful.' I hesitated. 'I feel a bit guilty, though, it was my idea and now you have three extra guests at a time when you may not really want to.'

'I'm very much looking forward to seeing them.' Philippe smiled. 'They may be the distraction we need right now.'

CHAPTER FORTY-ONE

Claude searched in the kitchen for Emmie's form but couldn't find it pinned to the notice board where her school stuff would normally be. He tried ringing Celine but only got her voicemail.

It must be in her office. He rarely went in there, it was her inner sanctum and she didn't welcome visitors, but Emmie needed the form for tomorrow so he had no choice.

It was pristine and ordered, very different from his own chaotic study. He smiled when he saw the pile of papers secured by the marble paperweight he'd bought her in Italy. She had spotted it in an exclusive and hugely expensive antique shop down a tiny side street. It weighed a ton and it had cost a fortune but he was ridiculously pleased to see it still used.

The form was on the top and with relief he grabbed it, glancing casually at the bank statement beneath. He was halfway down the corridor when he stopped abruptly. He turned around and returned to her office. Picking up the marble weight he studied the bank statement. It was in her maiden name and there was a very healthy balance.

He'd had no idea that she even had a separate account, let alone one with this sum of money. Feeling slightly sick he picked it up. His hands were shaking. He didn't know what to make of it. Should he confront her or pretend that he hadn't seen it? No, he couldn't do that, he had seen it and he needed to know what it was all about.

Maybe her father had given her the money? Claude knew that he handed out substantial cheques from time to time, it annoyed him and it hurt his pride but Celine merely laughed and told him not to be so ungrateful. But if it was money from her father then why would she keep it secret? Why put it in an account under her maiden name? It didn't make any sense.

Making up his mind he swiftly folded the statement and putting it in his pocket reached over for a pen to sign Emmie's form. He grabbed the first one that came to hand. Celine adored pens, expensive pens, and Claude was surprised to find a cheap biro on her desk. Turning it around he saw that it had a logo on it and his heart beat a little faster when he read *Hotel de Paris*.

Emmie greeted him when he arrived at the chateau.

'Did you got the form, Papa?' Her eyes were creased in anxiety. Her teacher had been most insistent that she bring it or she would not be allowed on the trip to see the nearby prehistoric cave drawings. She had loved the lesson from her beloved Madame Martinez and was desperate to see the paintings.

'Yes, Emmie.' Claude handed it to her. 'Go and put it in your school bag now, cheri.'

She treated him to a huge, heartfelt smile and then, clutching the paper, raced back into the chateau. Claude smiled, he didn't see that smile on his little girl's face very often. At home she seemed to be always tense and anxious. Her big eyes behind the thick glasses permanently round with worry.

He felt as if a huge weight had settled on his chest. He had failed her and he had clearly failed Celine.

Philippe was uneasy throughout dinner. He was dreading the conversation with Claude and the fact that Claude looked as if he had the weight of the world upon his shoulders already didn't help. How the hell was he going to broach the subject? He could have done with some advice other than tickling the underbelly of a bloody trout.

As if reading his mind Beatrice turned and winked at him. She raised her glass in a silent gesture of solidarity and despite himself he instantly felt better. There must be some mistake, surely Celine would never deceive them. There must be some explanation.

At the end of the meal, just as Philippe was about to ask Claude to come into his study, Henri stood up to announce that the new ginger kitten would be arriving tomorrow.

There was excitement, but there was sorrow as they all realised the implications. Emmie's eyes immediately filled with tears.

'No crying, Emmie,' Henri commanded, conveniently forgetting his earlier tears. 'Old Ginger is ready to go, he's tired, you know that.' She nodded but her lip still trembled. 'I thought you and Elf might like to come with me to collect him.'

Emmie was delighted and Elf looked stunned. 'Why me?' He asked.

'Why not you?' Henri smiled gently.

'Well, I don't know really.' Elf looked around the table as if expecting someone to tell him why not, but all he saw were smiles of encouragement. He suddenly felt embarrassingly close to tears. At best he was used to being ignored and at worst taunted or bullied. He had developed a thick hide although the odd sharp missile sometimes pierced his skin – or, as in this case, a kind word.

Not trusting himself to speak he merely nodded. Emmie grinned across the table at him.

Nick turned to Philippe and whispered, 'So the story really is true?'

Philippe nodded. 'Didn't you believe me?'

'I thought there may be a grain of truth in it but imagined you had embellished it for us all.'

'A few embellishments, but the facts remain the same.' He drained his glass. 'Henri and Rosa take the curse very seriously and therefore so do we.'

'Wouldn't do to meddle with gypsy magic.'

'Wouldn't do at all,' Philippe agreed and then in a quiet aside said, 'I could do with some gypsy magic for my conversation with Claude.'

'I wish I could wave a wand,' Nick sympathised, then quickly added, 'No fairy jokes please.'

Philippe laughed. 'Nick, you may be gay, but anyone who looks less like a fairy would be hard to find.'

'I'm pleased to hear it.' He grinned. 'In the absence of a wand, would more wine be appreciated?'

Philippe pushed his glass towards his guest.

Handing Claude a large armagnac, Philippe leant against his desk. Ignoring the gentle underbelly approach he plunged straight in.

'Claude, what do you know of the Hotel de Paris?'

'Only that its damned name keeps cropping up everywhere.' Claude felt suddenly very apprehensive. 'Why?' he demanded. 'What's going on?'

'I'm not sure exactly, it's rather delicate.' He paused. 'Luc was talking to Michel the other day...'

'No, it can't be true!' Claude leapt up. 'I suspected something but never believed it.'

'Ah, so you do know.' Philippe was surprised.

'How could she do this?'

'Well, I was asking myself the same question.' Philippe paused. 'What first alerted you?'

'The matches,' Claude replied.

'The matches?' Philippe was bewildered.

'But he's young, he's Luc's age, he's far too young for her, it's obscene.'

Philippe stared at him. 'Claude, what the hell are you talking about?'

286

'Celine and Michel.'

'What?'

'I saw the Hotel de Paris matches in her car, Michel had an identical box, I saw him light a cigarette with them and then…' He got no further.

'Claude, don't be so damn ridiculous.' Philippe was astonished. 'Michel and Celine aren't having an affair. You honestly cannot have believed that?'

Claude sat back down. 'She's having an affair with someone.'

'Not with Michel, you idiot, he's pursuing the young receptionist.'

'Then who?'

'I suspect it's the owner,' Philippe said quietly. 'He has also been selling our wine.'

In a few succinct sentences Philippe explained what had happened. Claude sat clutching the crystal glass, drawing comfort from its familiar solidity whilst his world disintegrated.

'I had no idea, Philippe,' he said at the end. 'No idea at all.' He looked up at his cousin, his childhood friend and close companion. 'You believe me, don't you?'

'Of course I believe you.'

CHAPTER FORTY-TWO

Celine was not having a great evening. She was desperately worried about the sudden coldness from Arnaud. She had rung him and put forward her suggestion, but instead of leaping at the chance to spend more time together he had hesitated and made some excuse about wanting to be around for a possible business meeting with this Parisian lady. It could be very useful for him, it was very important he told her, it could be the chance he had been looking for to put his hotel on the map.

She hadn't really listened, she'd been too angry. She wasn't used to being rejected. It had happened only once before and the memory of that was still excruciatingly painful. She had sworn never to put herself in that humiliating position again.

She was angry and frustrated, there was no reason for her to be here. Her father was not in any danger and was coming home tomorrow. She was now trapped here without transport, with no means of escape and an evening alone with her mother. It was not a pleasant prospect.

Her mother had never forgiven her for marrying Claude when she knew Celine could have had the choice of anyone. She had been led to believe that Philippe Fontaine was the man who would be waltzing down the aisle with her daughter, indeed had hinted to more than one acquaintance that an alliance with the Fontaine family would soon be formed. When Celine had announced her engagement to Claude, the poor relation, the younger cousin, Nadine had been incandescent with rage.

In public she'd put on a brave face but deep down she burned with humiliation. She had never understood the reason Claude had been chosen over Philippe, Celine had never explained and the relationship between mother and daughter had never recovered.

Celine resisted the temptation to ring Arnaud again. She didn't want him to think she was chasing him. He had made it quite clear that tomorrow was out of the question. She tried to remember exactly what he had said. Something was nagging at her, something was making her feel uneasy but she couldn't figure out what.

'So your friend is unable to collect you tomorrow?' Nadine and Celine were picking at some bread and cheese, neither of them were very hungry. Nadine stressed the word 'friend' and looked at her daughter knowingly.

'He's a business partner,' Celine was quick to correct. Her mother was sharp and she didn't want to give her any reason to suspect anything. Not that her mother would care, in fact she would probably encourage it, but Celine needed to be careful.

'What line of business is your business partner in?' Again the same slightly sarcastic stress on the word 'partner'.

'The hotel business,' Celine said briefly, unwilling to say too much. Why was her mother suddenly so bloody interested?

Nadine was enjoying watching Celine squirm a little. Her daughter was normally so controlled and composed, never giving anything away. Clearly this business partner, whoever he was, had got under her skin. She would probe a little further.

'A shame I won't meet him tomorrow. What is preventing him from coming?'

Celine was taken aback. 'A meeting, he has a meeting with a hotelier from Paris, apparently she is in the area with her chef and they…' She stopped mid-sentence. The colour drained from her face.

Christ, how could she have been so blind? How many Parisian

hoteliers were in the area? She desperately tried to remember exactly what Arnaud had said? She should have paid more attention. She was sure he had mentioned a chef, yes, he had definitely mentioned a chef. Mon Dieu, it had to be Beatrice and Nick, it was too much of a coincidence otherwise.

What the hell was Beatrice doing sniffing around the Hotel de Paris? Surely she couldn't suspect anything? What the hell did she want with Arnaud? What was all this about a business meeting? Unconsciously her grip tightened on the wine glass.

That woman had ruined her life once, she wasn't going to let her do it again. Celine felt the familiar tightening in her chest as the rage coursed through her. How she hated her. The hatred had grown over the years until at times she felt it would stifle her. She forced herself to breathe. Her heart was pounding. She had to warn Arnaud. Beatrice was dangerous, very dangerous, and she could spell trouble.

'Maman, excuse me, I need to make a phone call.' She walked out of the room quickly, leaving Nadine more intrigued than ever.

She had never seen Celine so emotional. Her daughter was verging on hysteria. She had observed her white knuckles clutching the wine glass, indeed had worried that it might shatter. She'd heard her quickening breath and watched the blood flush her normally pale face. Whatever it was, it was something very important. It certainly wasn't concern for her father, Nadine knew that neither parent would cause this reaction in their daughter.

Arnaud was not answering his phone. Celine left a message but she knew that it was garbled and confused. She really needed to speak to him.

She had to get home, she had to get to the bottom of exactly what was happening. She would ring Claude, make up some forgotten meeting and demand he come and pick her up. But there was no answer at home. Where the hell was he? No doubt he was staying at the damned chateau. She tried his mobile but got no joy from that either.

Thrusting her phone back into her bag she stormed into the kitchen. Her mother was busy putting the food away.

'Maman, I need your car tonight, it's urgent.'

Nadine slowly turned to face her daughter. There was a look of contempt in her eyes that Celine had never seen before. 'Out of the question, Celine,' she said quietly. 'In case you had forgotten we are collecting your father from the hospital tomorrow.' She paused for a moment to study her daughter. 'May I remind you, Celine, that your father has been very generous to you over the years, very generous indeed, and I think you would be wise to remember that.' She poured herself a glass of water. 'I'm going to bed now, Celine, it has been a long day and I'm rather tired.' Without even stopping to kiss her daughter goodnight she left the room.

Celine poured herself a large glass of wine. She sat down at the table. Things were really not going her way, her plans had been thwarted. She felt powerless and for the very first time in her life rather scared.

Arnaud listened to Celine's message with growing annoyance. What the hell was she talking about? It made no sense to him at all. What was all this nonsense about people not seeming to be who they were? She sounded faintly hysterical, maybe this business with her father had upset her more than he realised. He glanced at his watch. It was getting late, he would ring in the morning. He certainly didn't feel like talking to her right now.

Arnaud was buzzing with various plans for Beatrice. He had laid out a business plan, he'd done a lot of research and outlined various proposals. Everything was sitting in a smart folder ready for her perusal. He was an ambitious man and he felt excited at the prospect of furthering his career. He was good, he knew he was, he had a quick mind, he was sharp and he was business-savvy. He was very much looking forward to seeing her again and he didn't want anything or anyone to get in the way.

Claude had no intention of speaking to Celine either. He was, as she had rightly surmised, staying at the chateau in their old comfortable room. The room to where he had first brought his young bride, he remembered, thinking he was the luckiest man in the world. He was now thinking the exact opposite.

His mind was in turmoil. He hadn't mentioned the bank statement to Philippe. He needed to confront her with it, he needed to hear her explanation. It was clear that that she had been deceiving him for quite some time, had been deceiving them all, and he felt a sudden surge of anger.

She could make a fool out of him but how dare she make fools out of his family. The family who had brought him up, who had given him everything, who had been so generous to them both. How could she have cheated them? What was she planning to do with all the money?

He wondered how long the affair had been going on. How many affairs there had been before that? How long after their marriage had they started? How could he have been so blind? How could he have been so naïve as to think that she could be content with him?

The anger suddenly left him and he felt numb, devoid of all emotion. His wife didn't love him and his daughter was almost a stranger. He felt a total failure.

CHAPTER FORTY-THREE

I was having trouble sleeping. I'd come to bed early after dinner but my mind refused to shut down. My thoughts were skidding all over the place. I was re-running the conversation I'd had with Nick and speculating about his opinion that Miles was not for me. I was confused as to my sudden acceptance of them as a couple even though I still felt hurt and betrayed. Added to which was the unfolding wine scam, and last but not least I was thinking about my next lot of paintings.

I was chuffed with my work so far. I'd enjoyed the challenge of designing the wine labels and it had been fun working with Emmie, she had great imagination and, as I'd said to Philippe, an outstanding knowledge of wine for one so young. I needed to perfect the rough ideas but there was a lot of potential there. I was absurdly pleased at Philippe's reaction to my paintings so far. I wasn't sure why I craved his approbation so much, but then again he was paying for me to be here so maybe it was only natural.

I glanced at my watch and wondered if it was too late to ring Gail. I suddenly felt in need of a friendly voice. I wondered if Tariq had mentioned the idea of coming here, it would be so lovely to see them again. Beatrice had said he was planning it as a surprise.

Deciding to risk it I dialled her number.

'Gail, it's Sky, have I woken you?'

'Oh, God, Sky you're telepathic, I was just debating whether to ring you.'

'How is everything? How are the injuries? Are you still on the subs' bench?'

'Sadly very much so,' Gail replied. 'I ache everywhere, I'm miserable and irritable. I've made Sonny cry and I've upset Tariq. I need someone to lift my spirits.'

'What happened with Sonny?'

'He was misbehaving, I shouted at him, I lost my temper. Poor Sonny, he's had so much thrown at him, he's every right to be confused and frightened. I should have reassured, instead I just yelled, I feel like the worst mother ever.'

'Gail, you are a wonderful mother.' She sounded so upset, I was desperate to calm her down. 'You can't be perfect all the time, there are bound to be tricky moments, a lot has happened.' I paused. 'When is Tariq coming over?' I was longing to know if he'd said anything about France.

'Tomorrow.' Gail paused. 'He said he had a surprise for us. He was so happy and I completely ruined it by being so foul.' I could tell that she was close to tears. 'Poor Tariq, he sounded so hurt, I just don't know what's the matter with me.'

'Gail, you've been through quite an emotional time.' I leant back on my pillows. 'Your whole life is about to change, you've got a thousand and one decisions to make, of course you're feeling anxious and worried.'

'I just seem to be getting everything wrong.' She was sobbing now. 'I feel out of control, everything is happening so fast, I feel so afraid, I know it's pathetic but I can't seem to help it.'

'Hush now, Gail, deep breaths, calm down.' I hated hearing her like this. 'You're tired and you are in pain. You can't think straight, you need some sleep.'

'I'm so sorry, Sky, this is probably the last thing you wanted to hear.'

'Oh, Gail, don't be daft, you don't have to apologise,' I laughed. 'Now go and ring Tariq back and tell him you can't wait to see him and that you are in suspense about the surprise. Then take Sonny into your bed and fall asleep with your arms around him. That's *my* order.'

'Sky, thank you.' She managed a shaky laugh. 'I'm so glad we met.'

'So am I, Gail.'

I really meant it. I felt remarkably close to Gail, we'd shared so much together in such a short time that it felt like I'd known her for years. I did have plenty of female friends but not one particular best friend. I'd always had my sister and Nick. But right now Iona was on the other side of the world and Nick and I still had some way to go.

I hoped Tariq would persuade Gail to come over here, if only for a couple of nights before we all went our separate ways once again. I was absolutely dreading the thought of returning to London. In fact I couldn't bear to think about it, so I clambered out of bed. I'd concentrate on my work for a few more hours. It was clear that sleep was not going to be an early visitor tonight. My folder was in the kitchen so I threw on my kimono and headed downstairs.

Claude was boiling some milk for a hot chocolate when I walked in.

'A guilty pleasure of mine.' He smiled at me slightly sheepishly. 'It was a toss-up between this or another armagnac, the hot chocolate won.'

'When we were kids my father used to put brandy in our hot milk. Brandy and cinnamon, we never knew about the brandy of course and I remember thinking in later life that it was a shame hot milk never seemed to taste the same as when we were children.' I smiled. 'He'd be hauled into the police station these days for such irresponsible behaviour.'

'Sounds very responsible to me.' Claude indicated the armagnac bottle. 'Want to try some?'

'Hot chocolate and armagnac, how very decadent, yes please.' I nodded. 'So can't you sleep either?'

'I'm usually out like a light but sadly not tonight.' He sounded very weary.

'A lot on your mind?' I sympathised.

'You could say that.' He handed me a mug. 'Amongst many other things I think my wife is having an affair,' he said bluntly.

'Oh, Claude, I'm so sorry.' I was surprised he was being so open.

'I feel rather stupid,' he said. 'Stupid and sad.'

'I know exactly what you mean,' I replied with feeling. 'You wonder if you were the last to know. You wonder why you didn't see the signs. You wonder what the hell you did wrong.'

Claude looked at me, astonished. 'Sky, I cannot believe anyone cheated on you?'

'Believe it,' I said drily.

'But look at you, you're beautiful, young and extremely talented.' He was shaking his head in disbelief. 'Your husband must be blind.'

'No, just gay.'

Claude's jaw dropped to the floor and I actually giggled at the sight of his face. 'Did Philippe not tell you?' He shook his head. 'My husband is having an affair with my best friend. My best friend is Nick.'

'Mon Dieu.' Claude was astounded. 'No, Philippe never breathed a word, well not to me anyway.'

'Well that was kind of him, or maybe it would have been kinder to warn you?'

'Maybe. Sky, I have to admit I like Nick, I wish I didn't now, but I do.'

'Everyone loves Nick,' I said. 'Including me, and that is what makes it so damned hard.'

'And do you still love your husband?'

'Claude, I've no idea what I feel towards him.' I shook my head. 'Some people think that I never really loved Miles.' I paused. 'I was furious at first but I'm starting to think that maybe they were right.' I looked at him. 'Does Celine know you know?'

'Not yet,' Claude said. 'It's not a conversation I'm looking forward to.' There was a short silence as we both concentrated on our chocolate.

'You have a wonderful daughter,' I said after a few minutes. 'She's just gorgeous, you must be so proud.'

'Probably not as proud as I should be, Sky,' he said slowly.

'She showed me around, she loves it here, she knows every inch, every nook and cranny.' I smiled.

'Yes she does love it here, loves it far more than her home.'

'I'm sorry, I didn't mean...' I was confused, had I been tactless?

'It's alright, Sky, she's right, I love it here too.' He looked around the kitchen and I did too.

It was a beautiful room with buttermilk walls and pale oak cupboards. A huge wrought iron pot rack stood in one corner next to a basket full of sweet-smelling straw for the eggs. Pots of herbs lined the windowsill, strings of saucisson hung beside pink garlic plaits. The wild flowers that Emmie collected were crammed into jam jars and bright rugs lent warmth to the uneven stone floor. We were seated on a wooden bench at the side of a long table that had apparently come from a monastery. Belle lay snoring in a chewed wicker basket by the fireplace with Sausage stretched out beside her.

'It's gorgeous, isn't it?' I broke the silence once more. 'I love this room.'

'Our house has been furnished for show, not for comfort, which is ironic as we have very few guests,' Claude said sadly. 'This chateau is full of love, full of character. There is no character stamped on our house, maybe we don't have the right personalities?' He smiled wistfully.

'I think you and Emmie have wonderful personalities,' I replied quickly. 'Of course I don't really know Celine.'

'Neither do I, Sky, neither do I.'

CHAPTER FORTY-FOUR

'How did it go last night with Claude?' Beatrice strolled outside with her coffee to join Philippe. He was seated at his favourite rickety wooden table underneath the old olive tree. The olive tree was purported to be well over a hundred years old and Philippe adored it. Its gnarled old boughs had heard over a thousand secrets. It had witnessed laughter and sorrow. Children had hidden their priceless treasures in the cracks and crevices within the twisted trunk.

The sky was already a deep blue and the beautiful silver green leaves gleamed in the sunshine. It promised to be a fantastic day.

Beatrice sat down and reached over for Philippe's cigarettes. 'Well?'

'The affair didn't seem to come as a huge surprise, but he had no idea about the wine.'

'Poor Claude, he has spent the last few years pursuing what he can never have and not realising what he has already.'

Philippe looked at her through narrowed eyes. 'I'm in no mood for riddles this morning, cheri.'

'And talking of riddles, here he comes,' Beatrice waved at Claude.

He came striding over towards them, looking tired but otherwise remarkably calm and composed.

'Morning.'

'Morning, Claude, how are you?' Beatrice stood up to kiss him.

'I've felt better.' He too reached over for Philippe's cigarettes. 'Have you seen Sky this morning?'

'She's probably still in bed.' Philippe was surprised at the question.

'No, she told me she wanted to get up early to capture the mist.'

'She did?' Philippe raised his eyebrows. 'When did she say that?'

298

'We had a heart-to-heart last night,' Claude replied. 'Bared our souls to each other and I wanted to thank her.'

Beatrice and Philippe stared at him in astonishment. They had never known Claude to bare anything, let alone his soul, and certainly not to a relative stranger.

'She's a rather special girl, she helped me a lot. It was good to talk.' He looked at his watch. 'I'll take Emmie to school and then I've got some things to sort out at the house.' He smiled at them briefly. 'I'll see you later, I'll let you know when, er, well, I'll let you know when I've, when I've got to the bottom of everything.' He strode off, leaving Beatrice and Philippe open-mouthed.

I had been studying both of them for a while, sketching them from a distance, hidden behind the fountain. I always liked observing people unseen, Nick called it stalking. I wasn't sure that Philippe or Beatrice would like what I'd drawn but it had amused me. I made my over to towards them.

'You look amazing, Sky,' Beatrice said to me as I got nearer.

'Really?' I was surprised. 'I guess it's the shawl.' Over my faded silk kimono I wore a multi-coloured woollen shawl. 'Nonna knitted it years ago. It's incredibly light and incredibly warm, some rare Italian sheep's wool.'

'I think it's the whole ensemble.' Beatrice laughed. 'You've got a smear of green paint across your forehead, you look like a tribal princess.'

'I'm not sure that tribal princesses wear wellington boots.' I laughed, looking down at my feet. 'Certainly not ones several sizes too big.' I glanced at Philippe. He was staring at me with a strange expression. Surely he wasn't upset that I was wearing his boots. 'I'm sorry if they're yours, it was very dewy first thing this morning, I just grabbed the first pair.'

'Claude was just looking for you,' he said abruptly. 'Wanted to thank you for last night.'

Was it my imagination or did he not sound best pleased? 'We had a lovely heart-to-heart, shared a few secrets, helped by hot chocolate and armagnac.' I smiled at them hesitantly. Had I done something wrong?

'How long have you been up, Sky?' Beatrice asked.

'Oh, I've no idea, I got up with the sun, well to be honest it doesn't really feel like I've been asleep but I've had the most wonderful few hours, I hope you like the results.' I glanced uneasily at Philippe.

'I can't wait to see them,' he replied shortly.

'I'll try and get them finished today.'

'You work hard, Sky.' Beatrice smiled.

'Well, that's why I'm here.' It came out sharper than I intended. 'I mean, you don't want me hanging around here for ever.' I smiled but felt an unaccountable tightening in my chest at those words.

'Sit down, cheri, and I will get you some coffee.' Beatrice stood up.

'I can get coffee, you don't have to go in.' To be honest I didn't really want to be left on my own with Philippe.

'I need some cigarettes. Sit, cheri.' She turned and walked back to the chateau.

There was an awkward pause after she left.

'I bet this old beauty could tell us a few stories,' I said finally, stroking the rough bark of the old olive tree. 'I wonder what she's heard over the years.'

'Yes, I often wonder that.' He smiled and I was relieved.

'If there's anything...' I leant forward to speak at the same time as Philippe.

'Do you need...' He laughed. 'You go first.'

'Is there anything you would particularly like me to paint?' I asked.

'I don't think so, I'll leave it up to you. You're the one with the artistic eye.' He shrugged. 'Though maybe this old tree should feature.'

I grinned and opening my sketch pad held it out for him to see.

He gasped. 'When did you do that?' He looked absolutely amazed and I was delighted.

'I was lurking behind the fountain watching you. It's a bad habit, I know.' I giggled.

It was a wicked cartoon. I'd depicted them both as cigarettes with their faces in the middle. Philippe with his sunglasses and Bea with her cloud of hair. Every branch of the olive tree had a cigarette, the leaves curled around them like hands and plumes of smoke curled upwards.

Philippe took the sketch pad from my hand. He looked at me and grinned and I loved the way his eyes crinkled with laughter. 'I love it, Sky, I absolutely love it. This one is for me, I'm buying it, but you may have to sketch another for Beatrice.'

I laughed and suddenly I wanted to throw my arms around him.

Beatrice smiled to herself when she heard the sudden laughter from the garden. She hummed while making the coffee.

'I know that face,' Rosa said as she came into the kitchen. 'It's a face that spells mischief. What are you plotting, Beatrice?'

Beatrice winked at her. 'I love it when a plan starts to come together.'

'You are a witch, Beatrice.'

'Takes one to know one, Rosa.' Beatrice laughed and kissed her cheek before walking outside with the coffee.

'I may go to Hotel de Paris again today,' Beatrice announced, handing me a mug.

'Why?' Philippe looked puzzled.

'Well I may be able to discover something else, and I have to admit the idea of a sister hotel is quite interesting. The more I think about it the more I like it.'

'You're not serious?'

'I am, Philippe, and why not?' She raised her eyebrows. 'It's actually a very good idea.'

'But not with him?' I was as surprised as Philippe.

'Why not?'

'He slept with Celine.'

'Who hasn't?'

I gasped.

Beatrice laughed. 'Well, maybe that was a bit cruel, but no, seriously, Arnaud has a beautiful hotel, he runs a tight ship and I suspect he is a canny businessman.'

'He's a crook.' I couldn't believe she was serious.

'He won't try it on with me.'

'How do you know?' I persisted.

'This is Beatrice's world, Sky.' Philippe laughed. 'We merely inhabit it.'

CHAPTER FORTY-FIVE

Claude could not face going to pick up Celine. He could not face the two-hour journey back with her. He had some things he needed to look at first, some facts and figures he wanted to check before confronting her.

She had always helped him with the accounts, helping him with the odd thing at first but over the years gradually doing more and more. It had made sense, she was involved in the marketing, she was quick with figures, she'd been eager to learn and he had been delighted that she had shown such an interest. He had been more than willing to teach her all she wanted to know about the wine business. He had loved the idea of working with her, of being her mentor and had failed to realise when she had overtaken him.

He no longer felt foolish, that had been replaced by a cold anger, anger at her betrayal of not just him but of his family. He guessed the warning signs had been there for a long while but he had neglected to read them, clinging desperately to the hope that their marriage would survive. He realised now that he had been living in a fantasy world. If Celine had ever loved him it was all too evident that those feelings had long ceased to exist.

He dialled her number to tell her she would have to get the train, and as expected she was livid.

'I need to come home as soon as possible, Claude. Leave now and then you will be here when we return from the hospital with Papa. We can leave straight away.'

But for once Claude stood firm. He remained adamant and there was nothing that Celine could do. She was seething and Nadine, who had overheard most of the conversation, was amused. Things really did not seem to be going well for her daughter. She had been spurned by her lover and now it seemed that her normally biddable husband was taking a stand. Nadine was looking forward to the next instalment.

Beatrice drove slowly into the driveway of the Hotel de Paris. First impressions were important and these impressions did not disappoint. Since pretending to be interested in a sister hotel the thought had been niggling away in the back of her mind. With the new TGV reducing the time from Paris to Bordeaux to just over two hours it would seem the perfect time to expand the business.

She didn't particularly like Arnaud but then you didn't need to like your business partner as long as you trusted him and, as she had said to Sky, she had no fear of Arnaud ever trying to cheat her. Once she had made it known that she was aware of his deceit he would be bending over backwards to gain her trust.

Arnaud had been watching out for her. She hadn't actually said that she would come but he had been hopeful. He had dressed with care, he had made sure that the bar and restaurant gleamed and had personally overseen the huge vase of fresh flowers in the foyer.

Arnaud wanted this badly. He had studied her hotel online the night before and he had been impressed. He was determined that she should be equally impressed with his. He had ignored the numerous calls from Celine, refusing to let anything ruin his focus. He had no idea what her garbled message the night before meant but he had neither the time nor the inclination to go into it right now.

Beatrice leant back in her chair and studied the proposals Arnaud had given her. He had met her on arrival and escorted her to a quiet table in the corner overlooking the garden. A young waitress had brought coffee and a gorgeous selection of viennoiserie.

Arnaud had toyed with the idea of champagne but on reflection had decided that may be a bit presumptuous. He had instead offered a small armagnac which to his joy Beatrice had accepted.

She looked up at him. 'You have some interesting ideas.' She wasn't giving too much away but actually she was impressed. She had been right, Arnaud had an eye for detail and a good sense of business. She thought that they could work together.

Celine would be spitting if she formed an alliance with Arnaud. That alone was enough to tempt Beatrice. She was under no illusions about Celine, had always known that they harboured a viper in the nest. Philippe had accused her of being dramatic but Beatrice knew what Celine was capable of. What was that saying, '*hell hath no fury like a woman scorned*'?

She was pleased that it was all out in the open, that everyone now knew exactly what she was like. It would be interesting to see what would happen. She doubted that Celine would be able to wriggle out of this mess and very much hoped that Claude would finally find the strength to stand up to her.

She would let Philippe deal with Arnaud, she imagined that he would be willing to pay back any amount of money, especially now there was the prospect of working with her. Unlike Celine, she suspected, he would have a way of extricating himself from this.

Arnaud was talking to her and she forced herself to focus. He was talking about a forthcoming trip to Paris he had planned. She doubted very much that he had any such trip planned but admired his determination to make this work.

They parted after an hour, both pleased with what they had achieved.

Arnaud watched Beatrice drive away feeling very satisfied with the way the meeting had gone. He had enjoyed himself. She was a smart lady, astute and perceptive, and he knew she had liked his suggestions. She was also very sexy.

Celine was sexy but in a very different way. Celine was glacial whereas Beatrice was the sun. Rather pleased with this analogy, he turned to go in and as he did so his phone rang. He knew without looking that it would be Celine. It was and she was angry and agitated. She launched straight into a torrent of words that made no sense to him.

'Celine, for Christ's sake calm down, I have no idea what you are talking about.'

'I'm talking about bloody Beatrice, don't be fooled by her and for God's sake don't see her again.'

'Don't tell me who I can or cannot see, Celine.' Arnaud was not impressed. 'As a matter of fact I have just had a very interesting meeting with her.'

'With Beatrice?' Celine was dry-mouthed.

'Yes, with Beatrice.' What the hell was Celine playing at? How did she know Beatrice?

'Arnaud, she is not who she says she is.'

'She says she owns a hotel in Paris. I have seen the details, she does indeed own a hotel in Paris, there can be no doubt that she is who she says she is.' He was growing impatient. 'What is this all about, Celine? Do I detect a hint of jealousy?'

He could have had no idea of the effect that this would have on Celine. He was unaware of her deep-rooted hatred towards Beatrice. She had kept a tight lid on it for so long but now it threatened to explode.

'Arnaud, you fool,' she hissed and he was shocked to hear the venom in her voice. 'She is Philippe's ex-wife.'

'Philippe who?'

'Philippe Fontaine, of course.' She spat out the name. 'Tell me you have not been so bloody stupid as to have given her the wine.'

Arnaud was becoming increasingly angry. He did not appreciate being called a fool or labelled as stupid. 'Would it matter if I had?'

'Of course it would matter, she will know it's Philippe's, she knows his wine, they'll soon realise your scam.' She was screeching down the phone now.

His brain kicked quickly into action. 'Whose scam, cheri?' he said very slowly. 'As far as I'm concerned I paid exactly the price you were asking for the wine.'

'You know that's not how it happened.'

'But they don't.' He lit a cigarette. 'In fact, I would be more than happy to pay the correct price for it. I will declare that I'm mortified if there has been any mistake, if I have paid less for such an excellent wine.'

'How dare you!' She couldn't believe what she was hearing.

'Celine, stop being so hysterical.' He was bored now. She had completely ruined the enjoyment of his meeting with Beatrice. 'You always tell me how much power you have, tell them it was a special promotion, pretend it was human error, we're not exactly talking the swindle of the century here.'

There was a very long pause and suddenly the penny dropped. 'Oh, Celine, what have you done?' Arnaud asked softly. 'It's not just me, is it?' There was no answer, he didn't expect one. 'Mon Dieu, this has been going on for years, hasn't it? A little bit here, a little bit there and a little bit more each time. Nothing could go wrong, but now it seems it has.' He shook his head in disbelief. 'Well, who is the fool now, Celine?'

Celine put the phone down with shaking hands. How could everything have spun out of control so quickly? She instinctively knew that Beatrice would have found out about the wine. It would be too much to hope that she hadn't. Once more she was filled with cold hatred and fury, only this time there was an element of fear too. Cold beads of sweat were running down her back and she felt slightly sick. God, how she hated that woman, why must she always ruin everything? For the millionth time she cursed her. If Philippe had never gone to Paris, if he had never met her, then Celine's life might have been so very different.

She must keep calm. There would be a way out. She could manage Claude. She'd always been able to manage Claude. He would have to help her, she would somehow convince him that she had done it for them. He would cover for her. She had come so far, there was no way she was going to throw it all away.

Beatrice passed Nick walking up the road weighted down with a heavy rucksack. Screeching to a halt and giving him the fright of his life she wound down the window. 'Do you want a lift?'

'Nothing would induce me to get into a car with you again, Beatrice.' He grinned at her. 'But you can take the rucksack.' He shrugged it off his back.

'Not another market, Nick?' She laughed.

'A tiny one, stumbled on it by chance, just a few stalls mainly selling ducks, so I bought mainly ducks.'

Beatrice laughed again. 'Are you sure about the lift? You've still a fair way to walk.'

'Very sure, Beatrice.'

'Your loss,' she said, opening the door and reaching for the bag.

'That is exactly what I would be afraid of,' he chuckled.

CHAPTER FORTY-SIX

I'd replaced my kimono with a pair of paint-spattered denim dungarees, which always made me feel like a kids' TV presenter from the early eighties, and espadrilles had taken the place of the wellies. I realised it was an eclectic mix but it was comfortable and practical. I grabbed my bag and my easel and stealing an apple from the kitchen went outside. I was eager to get started again, the early morning hours had been magical and now I wanted to capture the images in a different light.

I had several ideas of what I wanted to paint. The old stone fountain was a must, as was the gypsy caravan, but right now I headed towards the chai which to my mind was one of the most important places. It was the place where the lifeblood of the chateau flowed. I wanted to capture the rows of barrels, the soft wood contrasting with the shine of the huge metal vats.

I was fascinated with a small ante-room that Philippe had shown me. The room where the wine was blended. It was a magical room strewn with test tubes, measuring jugs, bottles and notepads. A room where the alchemy took place, where wines were perfected, a room where science and philosophy combined

I wondered how long Philippe thought I ought to stay. The ticket he had booked me was open-ended, I needed time to do my work properly, but at the same time I didn't want to overstay my welcome. Nick was going home after the weekend, maybe I should go back with him, that should give me enough time.

My heart sank at the prospect and my eyes unexpectedly filled with tears. What the hell was I going to do back in London? What was going to happen with my life? Here, time seemed suspended, I could almost pretend that everything was alright. I had fallen in love with the area, the countryside, the chateau and all its inhabitants. I never wanted to leave. I couldn't bear the thought of going home. I wasn't even sure if I knew where home was anymore. Certainly not the flat in London.

Shaking myself, I made my way to the chai. Henri was there. He looked up and smiled.

'Where is old Ginger?' I asked. I had never seen him without the cat and I was suddenly worried.

'He is sleeping,' he said gently. 'He is very tired, it won't be long before he leaves us.'

'Henri, I am so sorry.'

'He has had a good life, cheri, it's time to let him go.'

'Do you mind if I sit and paint?' I asked him, heading towards the huge leather armchair that Philippe had told me had been brought in for his father when he was ill. It was shabby and worn and extremely comfortable.

We sat in companionable silence. I worked quickly, trying to capture the intense concentration on Henri's face, the way he gazed into the distance, lost in thought, and the way he drummed his fingers on the table. He had an expressive face, a face that had spent most of its time outdoors, a kind face with eyes the colour of the sky outside. He was as passionate about the wine as Philippe and Luc and again I thought how heartbreaking it was that someone was betraying them.

'Do you think Celine is behind the wine scam?' I asked, voicing my thoughts.

'Well it's not me or Luc,' he replied.

'That's what Beatrice said.' I hesitated. 'I get the impression that she is not that fond of Celine.'

'She isn't, she warned us about her from the start.' He sighed. 'We should have listened.'

310

'I just don't understand why she would do this.' I was really puzzled. 'I mean, why does she want to steal from her family? What has prompted her to be so vindictive?'

'Celine is not a happy lady, Sky.' Henri got up and walked towards the window. 'Life has not given her what she wanted and she wants retribution.'

'From where I'm sitting she has everything.' I certainly couldn't summon much sympathy for Celine. 'She has a gorgeous daughter, a husband who dotes on her, a huge house, a fantastic family. She has a life most people would envy.'

'Sometimes other people's lives are not what they seem, Sky.'

'Yes, you're right, I guess I should know that,' I said with feeling and Henri smiled in sympathy.

I put my sketch pad down on my lap and lay back in the chair. The sun was streaming through the window, creating rainbows on the glass bottles. I could hear the birdsong outside. It was hot and very still. My eyes felt heavy and tucking my knees under me I began to doze off.

Then Henri began to sing. His voice was soft and pure. He filled the chai and my heart with his music. The notes seemed to hang in the air like living things. I felt a sense of peace and tranquility such as I had never ever felt before. Henri was weaving a magical web and like a fly I was caught in the middle, but unlike the fly I never wanted to leave.

Sometime later I opened my eyes. Henri was nowhere to be seen. I felt happy and content, as if a spell had been cast over me. I didn't want to break the magic. I wanted to stay in this chair for ever. I closed my eyes once again, desperately trying to will myself back to sleep.

'You look as if you and that chair are one.'

I opened my eyes at Philippe's voice. He was leaning against the doorway grinning at me.

'I feel as if I have melted into the fabric, we have swapped atoms, I am now half leather chair.' I smiled back. 'I must have dozed off, what time is it?'

'Coming up to midday.'

'What?' I sat bolt upright. 'It can't be, that means I've slept for nearly two hours.' I was shocked and a little embarrassed to be caught sleeping on the job, so to speak.

'Henri didn't want to wake you.'

'It was his fault, he sang to me, he put me in a trance, the most beautiful trance.'

'Ah, yes, that tends to happen.'

'I'm so sorry.' I flexed my feet, I'd expected to feel stiff but my limbs felt weightless.

'Sky, what are you apologising for?' Philippe looked perplexed. 'You obviously needed it.'

'I should have been working,' I mumbled.

'You got up at dawn to work, Sky.' Philippe laughed. 'You don't have to work around the clock.' He stooped to pick up my sketch pad which had fallen to the floor. 'May I?' he asked, starting to open it. I nodded my assent. He turned the pages slowly and I held my breath. 'These are exquisite, Sky, truly exquisite.' He looked at me with admiration, I felt a warmth flow through my veins and a large smile spread across my face.

'They're just preliminary drawings.' I paused. 'Actually, though, sometimes they are the best, I often prefer the lightning sketches to the full-blown paintings.'

'Well, do nothing more to this one of Henri, you have captured him quite perfectly.'

'Thank you, Philippe,' I said softly.

'No need to thank me, it should be the other way around.'

'No, I mean thank you for inviting me here, for giving me this chance, for allowing me to experience the beauty.' I paused. 'I can't tell you how much it has meant to me.' It must have sounded a bit over the top but I meant every word. I felt so alive here, and despite everything that was going on I felt so happy.

'It's a pleasure to have you here, Sky.' It sounded formal but I could see that he was genuine and I glowed.

We looked at each other for a few seconds before Philippe broke the silence.

'We are all going out for lunch, Nick and several ducks have taken over the kitchen.' He laughed. 'Rosa has thrown in the towel so I've booked a table at the little auberge around the corner.'

'Well, maybe I should get on with some more...' But he interrupted me.

'Don't be silly, Sky, you need to eat. You'll love the auberge, everyone does, run by three generations of the same family, four if you include the latest arrival.'

'Sounds perfect.' I got up and stretched, I was aware of him watching me. 'I need to get changed.'

'You look fine to me,' he said briefly before adding. 'Some are going in the car, it's about a fifteen-minute walk.' He hesitated. 'Would you like to walk with me?'

I nodded, suddenly feeling absurdly nervous.

CHAPTER FORTY-SEVEN

Gail was standing at arrivals in Stansted Airport with Sonny by her side. She had arrived far too early and during the long wait had become increasingly nervous. She spotted the tall figure of Tariq walking into the arrivals hall but she stood rooted to the spot, overcome with apprehension. Sonny had no such inhibitions and flew across the airport and into his arms. Tariq hugged him tight, his eyes searching for Gail who seemed completely unable to move. He walked slowly towards her. Her heart began to pound and her breathing was ragged. She felt tongue-tied and tense. She managed a tight smile and stumbled awkwardly into his embrace.

'The car is miles away, I'm afraid, which is a bind especially as my ankle still hurts, the parking is ridiculous here, it used to be much better but then they changed it and now it's a complete mess.' She knew she was speaking too fast and talking nonsense. Why would he care about the parking for heaven's sake? She was making an idiot of herself.

Tariq smiled gently at her.

Sonny talked non-stop on the way home and Gail was relieved that she had made the decision to take him out of school for the morning. Without his constant chatter it would have been a rather uneasy journey home.

'I don't know if you remember the house?' Gail said as they parked in the driveway. 'I mean it's not changed or anything, obviously it's nothing compared to your wonderful home of course.' She was babbling again but seemed powerless to stop herself.

Tariq covered her hand with his. 'Gail, relax,' he said softly.

And as she gazed into his warm eyes she felt her anxiety subside. She smiled back at him and he leant forward to give her a gentle kiss.

Sonny was already out of the car and at the front door. He was impatient to show his new father everything. He was overflowing with happiness.

Never having had a father he'd never missed one. His mother had been his whole world and he adored her but now his whole word had suddenly exploded and expanded. Without really understanding why he felt instinctively that things would never be the same again. He had loved Morocco, there had been nothing there that he hadn't liked and he hadn't wanted to come home.

Grabbing Tariq's hand he led him into the house. 'We not got animals like you, we only got a fish.' He felt slightly worried about the lack of animals but to his relief Tariq smiled.

'What do you call it?' he asked.

'We just call him Fish.' Sonny shrugged apologetically.

'Good a name as any.' Tariq dumped his bag onto the floor. 'Now then, I'm sure there were a few presents in here for you.'

Sonny squealed with excitement as Tariq pulled five leather camels of varying sizes from his bag.

'These are from Pappy Amir and this is from your Aunt Jasmina.' He handed Sonny a photo album. 'Photographs of just about every animal in Marrakech we could find.' Sonny's eyes were round as saucers and his face when he turned to his mother made her want to cry.

'And this is for you.' Tariq handed Gail a stunning silk pashmina.

'Oh my God, it's exquisite.' Gail wrapped the luxuriant material around her shoulders, marvelling at the softness and quality.

'It suits you,' Tariq said. 'Jasmina said they were your colours and she was right.' He stood back to admire the amber and russet tones that complimented her hair and complexion.

'This is way too generous of them.' Gail was overawed.

Tariq smiled to himself, thinking of what else his bag held, but that was for much later on. In the meantime there was one other thing. 'I've not finished yet, there is one more surprise for you both.'

Sonny immediately turned from his camels. He couldn't think what else could possibly be better than what he already had but he was all ears. Gail turned to look at him and Tariq paused for dramatic effect before speaking.

'How do you fancy going to France?' He looked at them both and they both stared back.

'France?' Gail was astounded.

'France.' Tariq nodded. 'To be more specific, south-west France.'

'Do you mean to Philippe's?'

'I most certainly do.' He grinned at them. 'Beatrice rang me the other day. As you know, Sky and Nick are already there.'

Gail gasped. 'Are you serious?'

'Just for three nights, I thought it would be fun.'

'Are we going to France?' Sonny wasn't sure he had got this right.

'If Mummy says yes.' Tariq looked questioningly at Gail. 'Well, do you say yes?'

She stood open-mouthed for a moment before flinging her arms around him. 'Of course I say yes.'

The day was hectic. Sonny wanted to show Tariq everything, his favourite walk, the go-cart track, his football club, his judo club, the park with the enormous climbing frame and of course his school, although much to his amusement Gail made him duck down in the car as they drove slowly past it.

'You are supposed to be ill in bed, Sonny.' She laughed sheepishly.

'This is the cinema we go to and then we have pizza.' He tugged at Tariq's arm. 'You can draw on the tablecloths. They have crayons.' He turned eagerly to his mother. 'Can we go, Mummy? Can we go for lunch?'

'Well, I bought some lovely food to have at home, sweetheart.' She turned to Tariq. 'Or we can go to a nice pub?'

'Pizza sounds fine to me.' He squeezed Sonny's hand.

'He's finally asleep.' Tariq laughed as he walked into the kitchen later that evening. 'He wanted to know the names of all the animals in the photographs and he's arranged the leather camels in a line on his table so they're the first thing he sees in the morning.' He grinned. 'He's something else, isn't he, Gail?'

'He certainly is,' she agreed.

'You've done a wonderful job. It can't have been easy.'

'We've had our moments.'

'Thank you, Gail.' He looked at her. 'Thank you for giving our son such a good start in life.'

She blushed but before she could say anything more he continued. 'I mean it, I think you are extraordinary, I've no idea how you've found the time for so many activities, he's such a happy boy and it is all credit to you.'

'Be warned,' she laughed, 'he's not all sweetness and light. He can be a little monster, he has a strong stubborn streak.'

'That must come from your side of the family,' Tariq joked, knowing full well where it came from.

'I only wish I'd done as well with Dawn.' Gail hesitated. 'Tariq, I'm so sorry, I know I've said it before but I cannot believe what she did. I simply don't understand how she could be so heartless.'

'It's not your fault, Gail,' he replied firmly. 'You've maybe spoilt her, overcompensated for her not having a mother, but you haven't got a bad bone in your body, you are full of warmth and tenderness. Dawn certainly doesn't take after you.'

Gail didn't really trust herself to speak. Her eyes were misty and tears threatened.

Tariq gazed at her for a moment before walking over to the fridge to take out the bottle of champagne he'd put in earlier. Gail noted with surprise that his hands were shaking. Silently she handed him the glasses and with what seemed like unnecessary deliberation he opened the bottle and began to pour.

The atmosphere had suddenly changed and she could feel the electricity in the room. Her mouth was dry and her legs started to tremble. Abruptly she sat down. He handed her a glass.

'Gail...' he began, but his voice was no more than a hoarse whisper. Clearing his throat he took a deep breath and reached into his pocket. He started again. 'Gail, this ring belonged to my mother.' He held it out to her. 'I would be very honoured if you now felt able to wear it.'

She stared at him, not entirely sure she understood what he was saying. There was a long pause.

'What's your answer?' He could barely get the words out.

'What's your question?'

He stared at her in astonishment. 'Damn it, Gail, I'm asking you to marry me.'

'Then damn it, Tariq, yes. Yes with all my heart.'

CHAPTER FORTY-EIGHT

'Good day at school, Emmie?' Henri asked as she settled into the car next to Elf. They were off to pick up the new ginger kitten. 'What is the drawing?' He indicated the large sheet of paper she was clutching.

'It's a tree what's got family on it.'

'A family tree,' Henri corrected gently. Emmie shrugged, to be honest the instructions had been a bit hazy so she'd just drawn a huge tree with pictures of her family and the animals. Madame Martinez had seemed very happy with it and that was good enough for Emmie.

'This is you, Henri.' She pointed to a huge smiley face hanging off a branch. 'And here's Old Ginger and here's a space what's for New Ginger.' She turned to Elf. 'You is here next to Sausage.'

Elf was delighted. 'You've put me on the family tree?'

'Next to Sausage,' she repeated.

'I'm honoured.' His smile spread from ear to ear.

'What about your family, Elf?' Henri asked. Elf never talked about his past and they were all curious. 'Do you have a large family?'

'Or are they small like me?'

Henri couldn't help but laugh, the lad was incorrigible. 'You know what I mean.'

'No,' he replied shortly. 'No idea who my father is and my mother and I rarely see each other.'

'Why is that?' Henri asked gently.

'She doesn't much like me.' He tried to sound flippant but Henri could hear the hurt and wondered what sort of woman could abandon her child like that.

Emmie slipped her small hand into Elf's. 'No does mine,' she

319

whispered confidentially, unwittingly answering Henri's unspoken question.

'He's all yours, Henri.' Jean placed a scrap of spitting, hissing, orange fluff into the basket Henri was holding out. 'He's small but he's scared of nothing.'

'Old Ginger will soon teach him some manners.' Henri smiled at his old friend. 'Thanks, Jean.'

'You don't want two, do you?' Jean asked hopefully.

'We don't,' Henri replied, firmly ignoring Emmie's excited gasp.

'Or a rabbit?' Jean sensed an ally in Emmie. His wife had told him in no uncertain terms that it was time to get rid of these animals which he'd managed to accumulate. She'd had enough of opening the door to find someone holding out a stray cat or dog for Monsieur Jean to look after and the enormous rabbit deposited a few days ago had been the last straw.

Glaring at Jean, Henri marched Emmie back to the car but Elf hung back. 'A rabbit?' he asked.

'Glorious creature.' Jean smiled at Elf. 'Docile as anything, clearly must have been someone's pet. I've made enquiries but no-one's come forward, must have been abandoned.'

'I'll be back, don't let it go,' Elf whispered before running to the car.

He had a certain fondness for rabbits. He'd collapsed in a field when sleeping rough about a year ago. For two days he'd lain there, sick with fever and weary to the bone. Luckily it had been summer otherwise he would almost certainly have died. He'd finally come to at dawn to find himself surrounded by rabbits nibbling away beside him, they had formed a circle around him and he'd felt protected and privileged. If this rabbit needed help then he felt duty bound to offer it.

Rosa was waiting impatiently when they got home.

'He's got a temper,' Henri warned as she went to open the basket. 'He'll scratch you.'

'I'd like to see him try,' Rosa said grimly. But nonetheless she rolled her sleeves down. She lifted the tiny, hissing creature up by the scruff of his neck and, putting her face close to his, hissed back. The kitten gazed back astonished and then almost as if relieved to give up the fight began to purr. He had recognised the voice of authority. Henri would have his heart and Rosa his respect.

'What are we going to call him?' Rosa asked.

They all gazed at him for a moment.

'Flame,' Emmie said, tentatively reaching out to stroke him.

'Flame is perfect.' Henri smiled at the little girl.

'Claude was here earlier looking for Emmie,' Rosa said.

'I'll take her up to the house,' said Henri.

Emmie's face fell but she put her coat on without a word and followed Henri to the car.

'She hates that house,' Elf said.

'We all do,' Rosa replied.

CHAPTER FORTY-NINE

Claude hadn't actually wanted Emmie to come home, in fact he'd been going to ask if she could stay another night, but when Henri's car drew up he didn't feel that he could ask them to turn around. Maybe it was no bad thing, maybe Emmie would prove a distraction when Celine first came home.

He was dreading the forthcoming conversation. He was uneasy and nervous.

Dinner was a strained affair. Celine couldn't gauge Claude's mood at all. He was polite to her and apologetic about not picking her up but there was something different about him. He was distant, he hadn't rushed to kiss her as he normally would, desperate to establish physical contact. Usually irritated by his attentions, she now found the lack of them disturbing.

She poured herself more wine, aware that she was drinking far more than usual. She was longing to drive to Arnaud and sort out the mess between them but she realised that would have to wait until tomorrow. How could everything have gone wrong so quickly? And once again her thoughts turned towards Beatrice. That woman was her nemesis, and she knocked back her wine in one gulp as the familiar feeling of loathing coursed through her veins. She realised that Claude was talking to her.

'Have you had enough?' He was reaching for her plate. She had barely touched her food but pushed it towards him. Emmie had barely touched hers either. She sensed the odd atmosphere and for some reason it scared her.

'Can I get down, Papa?'

'Yes, it's nearly bedtime, Emmie.'

It wasn't, but neither of them cared really. Emmie was pleased to escape to her room and Claude didn't want to prolong the moment any longer. He needed to talk to Celine. He watched as she poured yet another glass of wine. That was normally his trick but tonight he'd hardly had a drop.

'I think I might turn in too,' Celine said, watching Emmie scarper to her room.

'I would like to talk to you first, Celine.'

'Well it will have to wait until morning. I am tired, it has been a very long few days.' She got up to leave. 'And not helped by that damn train journey,' she added unwisely.

It was that last sentence that was the final nail in the coffin for Claude. He felt his blood turn ice cold. His nerves vanished and he felt suddenly very calm and detached. No longer facing the strain of pretending that all was OK, he was more than ready to face the truth.

'It won't wait until morning, Celine,' he said in a cool voice. 'Please take a seat.'

His demeanour unnerved her. Something indefinable had taken place, their world had shifted slightly and they were both aware of it.

'I heard some disturbing news from Philippe last night,' he stated. 'I wondered if you could shed some light on it.'

Celine swallowed hard but said nothing.

'It seems that we have been selling wine, our superior wine, to the Hotel de Paris.' He paused. 'Neither Philippe nor I were aware of that.'

She shrugged, attempting nonchalance. 'Where did you hear that?'

'It doesn't matter where we heard it from, Celine,' he replied. 'Is it true?'

'Oh, Claude, I give promotional bottles to many people. It's called marketing. It's my job.'

He looked at her with grudging admiration. She was good and

under normal circumstances he would have been happy to believe her. 'It appears to be much more than a promotional bottle, Celine.'

She still managed to look unconcerned but inside her heart was racing. Bloody Arnaud, why had he not returned her calls? This could all have been avoided. 'I'll look into it in the morning,' she smiled, sipping at her wine. 'I'm sure there will be an explanation.'

'I'll come with you, we'll talk to Arnaud together.'

She was taken aback, as he had intended, and her hand shook slightly as she lifted her glass once more to her lips. 'I didn't know you knew each other.'

'I didn't know you did either.' He was suddenly sick of playing games. This was getting them nowhere. 'How long has the affair been going on, Celine?' he asked in a quiet voice.

'Claude, I have no idea what you are talking about.' She feigned huge indignation.

'How long have you been supplying under-priced wine?' he continued.

'I'm not prepared to sit here listening to you hurl accusations at me.' She stood up, swaying slightly. 'You haven't one thread of evidence. I'm surprised that you listen to malicious rumours.'

'I have more than a thread of evidence, Celine.' He looked at her sadly. 'Show me the courtesy at least of being honest with me.'

'You are talking rubbish, Claude,' she snapped. 'I have no idea what Beatrice has been saying to you.' She'd made a mistake and knew it, but added, 'Or anyone else for that matter.'

'I've never mentioned Beatrice.'

'Who else can it be?' She was desperately trying to think on her feet. Why had she drunk so much? Her normally razor-sharp brain was muddled and fuzzy. 'She's always at the centre of things, always creating trouble.' It was feeble and she knew it.

'Well if you won't talk to me about Arnaud then perhaps you will talk to me about this?' He produced her bank statement and had the dubious pleasure of seeing the colour drain from her face.

'How dare you go through my private things!' She was suddenly very scared. Her hands felt cold and clammy and her voice was unsteady.

'I didn't deliberately go through your private things,' Claude said calmly. 'I was looking for Emmie's consent form for her field trip next week. It wasn't in the normal place.' He looked at the statement and raised his eyebrows. 'Are you saving for something special?'

'You know perfectly well that Papa gives me the occasional cheque.'

'Celine, I may not be as bright as some but please credit me with some sense.' He reached in his pocket for his glasses. 'This is much more than the occasional cheque.' He pointed at the amount. 'You know the really sad thing? I was so happy when you showed an interest in my work, I genuinely thought you were interested in the business. I enjoyed teaching you everything. I was delighted to give you more and more responsibility.' He sighed heavily. 'I imagined you wanted to help the family, but all you wanted was to help yourself.' He turned around to look at her. 'Why, Celine? What have we ever done to you?'

'I took what you are owed, Claude.'

He stared at her in astonishment. 'You stole, Celine.'

'Do you want to be the poor relation all your life?' She sneered.

'I am the poor relation,' he replied. 'Don't forget, Celine, that my father nearly ruined the Fontaine business, he drank most of it away and what he didn't drink he gambled, yet despite all that they took me in when he died. I owe *them*, Celine, not the other way around.' He shook his head. 'This is a family business, if you steal from them you steal from us.'

'A family business that Philippe runs,' she said with scorn. 'A lowly accountant comes way down the pecking order, Claude, it's about time you realised that.' She looked at him with utter contempt.

'Why did you marry me, Celine?' He ran his fingers through his thinning hair. 'You, who are so ambitious, why did you marry a *lowly accountant*?'

'My ambitions were thwarted,' she snapped. 'I made do.'

He stared back at her, comprehension slowly beginning to dawn.

She watched his mind working. Had he really never guessed? Did he really think she had married him for love? She had only loved one person in her life and only ever would. Celine couldn't remember a time when she hadn't loved Philippe. She had never envisaged a future without him. The fact that he had done absolutely nothing to encourage her was immaterial, she had always got what she wanted. As far as she was concerned her future had been mapped out and her future was definitely Philippe Fontaine.

Then Philippe arrived back from Paris, and with him came Beatrice. A beautiful girl with a curtain of bright blonde hair, a ready laugh and sparkling eyes. The whole countryside buzzed with the news, they were captivated by the romance. She remembered meeting her, remembered Philippe calling her over.

'Celine, come and meet my bride.' The absolute adoration in his eyes was more than she could bear. She'd turned to Beatrice, seen the pity in her eyes and knew that she had seen, knew that she knew and hated her with every fibre of her being.

There was only one thing Celine could do. She married Claude; if not the wife then maybe she could be the mistress. She was reasonably content for a while, she bided her time, she could see the cracks begin to appear in their marriage and when she judged the time to be right she made her move.

The humiliation of that evening was as raw today as it had been at the time. She could hardly bear to think about it. He had at first laughed at her in disbelief, and then when he began to realise she was serious she saw the look of compassion mingled with disgust.

Sickened to her soul, she'd tried to laugh then, pretend that it was all a joke, pretend that it was the wine talking.

He had been kind, he had been an absolute gentleman, he'd said he was flattered but she could tell he was horrified. They had both put it down to a moment of madness and the subject had never been referred to again. Celine knew him well enough to know that he would never tell anyone and she was certainly never going to reveal her degradation to a single soul.

Claude was watching her. Like a jigsaw puzzle, the pieces were slowly slotting into place and he began to see the whole picture. But strangely he felt no anger, just sadness and pity, the one emotion he knew she couldn't bear.

'You will have to pay this back, Celine,' he said, looking at the bank statement. 'You will need to pay this all back plus interest.' His voice was devoid of all emotion.

She looked at him, she had to act fast, she could see everything she had worked so hard for slipping away.

'Claude, it's not too late,' she said quickly. 'We can make a new life, cheri, we can put all this behind us.'

He couldn't quite believe what he was hearing.

She carried on, barely pausing for breath. 'We can go far away, far away where no one knows us.' Her voice was rising. 'We could go to Canada, Australia, New Zealand, the world is our oyster, Claude. We're still young, we can start again.'

Emmie stood outside listening. She had come for a glass of water but had stopped in her tracks on hearing Celine's words. She put her hand over her mouth to stop herself from screaming. She felt her little world crumbling around her. She turned and ran back down the corridor. She had to get away, she had to run to safety before they took her with them to these faraway places.

She opened the back door with shaking fingers. She was trying to keep as quite as possible but she needn't have worried, the voices coming from the salon were loud and angry. No one would be able to hear her. Her coat was on the back door but she couldn't find her boots, she didn't want to risk the light so she stumbled out in her slippers. It was pitch black outside, Emmie hated the dark but at no point did she hesitate, her fear of being taken away was far greater than the fear of the night.

She headed on down through the vines, she knew every inch in the daytime but the blackness was intense and she became confused. She could hear the river but couldn't tell how far away it was.

She left the vines and plunged into woodland, disturbing a night owl which rose above her with a deafening screech. Screaming with fright she turned to run, caught her foot in a bramble and fell heavily to the ground, shattering her glasses.

At some point during the heated argument which followed, Claude became aware of a distant banging and a cold draught blew through the salon. Without really knowing why he was filled with anxiety. Cutting Celine off in mid-sentence he shouted at her to be silent. The banging was loud and continuous.

With his heart hammering he ran down the long corridor to Emmie's room. The door was open and the room was empty. Yelling her name, he raced to the source of the banging and found the back door swinging wide open in the wind. He knew instinctively what had happened. He knew what she must have overheard, his heart went out to his little girl and for the first time ever he realised how very much he loved her.

CHAPTER FIFTY

'So there you have them, four very different wine labels, four very different wines.' I lined them up along the dining room table and everyone crowded around to see.

Inspired by Philippe's description of the various wines, I'd tried to produce four different styles that reflected the differences. The first was a modern take on the traditional picture of the chateau with clear lines and a bold outline, the second depicted the letters C & F intertwined with vines, the third was a sketch of a wine glass, a sun lounger and a sparkling pool and the fourth, and in my opinion the most striking, was a box with three vertical lines in dark purple drawn on top of three horizontal lines in blue, yellow and brown. It was bright and eye-catching and it demanded your attention.

I stood back and chewed my lip as they examined and exclaimed. I'd taken a risk with them, I knew, but I'd listened carefully to Philippe and Luc and was pleased with the end result. I very much hoped I'd managed to incorporate something for everyone.

Beatrice looked over at me and smiled. 'You're a clever girl, Sky, a very clever girl.'

'Each wine has a different personality,' Luc said. 'Each label has a different personality, they are perfect.' He smiled at me in frank admiration.

I smiled back but held my breath, waiting to hear the verdict that mattered to me the most.

'I admit I wasn't keen on the idea of new labels,' Stephanie said. 'But you may just have changed my mind.'

Finally, after what seemed like ages, Philippe turned to me. 'Sky,

I'm in awe. I didn't really know what I wanted, but I know now that *this* is exactly what I wanted.'

I smiled and once I'd started smiling I couldn't stop. I was so relieved. I'd put so much effort into them, trying to envisage the bottles on the supermarket shelves, picturing them on the tables in restaurants. I let out a long breath then walked over to the table. 'But which is your favourite?'

'I'm not sure I have a favourite,' Philippe said. 'But I guess for me the one that stands out the most is this one.' He said, indicating the horizontal and vertical stripes.

'I love that one too.' Luc nodded in agreement. 'It's bold, it's primary and…'

'And it's Emmie's,' I interrupted.

I was thrilled and I laughed in delight at the surprise on their faces. 'It's wonderful, isn't it?' I clapped my hands. 'It only took her about five minutes, I couldn't believe it. She just said that was how she saw it. The purple vines, the sun, the sky and the earth. I shook my head. 'I train for years and she achieves this in an instant.'

'You didn't help her at all?' Stephanie was gazing at the picture.

'Not one bit,' I replied. 'I mean, I re-drew it and tidied it up a bit but the idea was pure Emmie.'

'Where did you train, Sky?' Philippe asked.

'Glasgow School of Art,' I replied.

'One of the top students, commissions before she'd even left,' Nick added, looking at me with pride.

Philippe opened his mouth to speak but before he could say anything the phone rang. He answered it and for some reason we all fell silent. He uttered a loud exclamation and turned ashen.

'Emmie's missing,' he said in a shaky voice. 'She's not in her room and the back door is wide open, Claude thinks she's coming here.'

'Of course she is coming here, where else would she be going?'

Beatrice said. 'Stephanie, come with me up the road.' She grabbed her car keys. 'The rest of you take the vines and the river, take torches, spread out. She can't have gone far.'

I prayed she was right.

'We'll take Belle and Sausage with us.' Philippe called for them.

'Rosa, stay at the chateau in case she gets here first.' Henri took command. 'Elf and Luc, come with me, Nick and Sky, follow Philippe.'

I raced out of the room after Philippe, forcing myself not to think of the swollen river or the recent wild boar activity.

Emmie lay trembling and terrified. She had lost her glasses and couldn't see a thing, not that it mattered, it was so dark she couldn't see anything anyway. Warm blood trickled down the side of her head. Somehow her coat had become tangled in the brambles and was trapping her. She tried pulling at it but succeeded only in scratching her hands on the sharp thorns. Tears were streaming down her face but she was trying very hard not to make a noise. She was terrified that she would be found.

The thought of being taken away from everyone she loved was hurting her so badly she could hardly breathe. She felt that she would rather die than live a life without her Uncle Philly.

Perhaps if she stayed very still and prayed very hard she would die. Henri had told her that the angels would come and take old Ginger very soon, maybe they could come to get her at the same time. It would be nice to be with old Ginger, he would keep her company.

She wasn't sure how they would know she was here. She didn't want to call out to them in case Celine heard, but maybe if she closed her eyes they would think she had died. Angels must be able to see in the dark.

Belle was going quickly for a dog her age but Sausage was like a pocket rocket. He hurtled down through the vines with his nose to the ground and we tried our hardest to follow. He was heading towards the river and my heart was thumping not only with the exercise but with a cold fear. I could see the torch lights of Luc, Henri and Elf in the distance and prayed that one of us would find her quickly. In front of me Philippe stumbled and cursed under his breath.

'Be careful of your knee,' I called out to him.

'Sod my knee.'

Sausage suddenly swerved to the left and headed towards some thick scrubland which ran alongside the river. Trying to keep up I lost my balance and fell to the ground, sliding onto the same track Emmie and I had raced down a few days earlier. Philippe was ahead and didn't notice but Nick was by my side in an instant, hauling me up.

'OK?'

I nodded, too breathless to speak. I could hear the piglet whining and we both rushed into the thicket in time to hear Philippe's scream.

Emmie was lying so silent and motionless my blood ran cold and my heart nearly stopped beating. Philippe stood stock still for a second before throwing himself down beside her with a heart-breaking cry. Sausage and Belle leapt upon the prone figure, licking and nuzzling her face.

Pushing them aside, Philippe felt for a pulse and with a yell of relief turned to Nick and me.

'She's breathing, oh, Mon Dieu, she's breathing.' He clasped the little girl close to him. 'Call the others.' Nick went out to yell for them while I bent down beside Philippe. He was cradling Emmie in his arms. 'Oh my angel, my darling angel, you're safe now, Uncle Philly is here, you're safe now my angel girl.'

Emmie felt relief on hearing the word 'angel'. She had been vaguely aware of her name being called in the distance but had not wanted to answer. She'd wanted the angels to think she was dead so she kept her eyes tightly shut. But there was nothing angelic about the two animals licking her face and the arms that rocked her felt familiar. She breathed in the well-known scent of cigarettes and aftershave that belonged to only one person. She opened her eyes and smiled, she was with her uncle and that was better than being with the angels.

She was shivering. I took off my shawl and gently laid it over the little girl. 'Oh, Emmie darling, you gave us such a fright.'

Luc, Henri and Elf came crashing through the undergrowth.

'Is she OK?' Henri's breath was ragged.

'She's OK.' Philippe stood up slowly with Emmie in his arms. 'She's cut her head but she's OK.'

Luc held out his arms but Philippe shook his head. Although I could see that his knee was hurting him he clearly wasn't prepared to relinquish his darling girl. 'Someone needs to ring Claude.'

Emmie let out a startled cry. 'Want to stay, I don't want to go away with them.' She struggled in Philippe's arms.

'Cheri, calm down.' He kissed her. 'You're not going anywhere, you're safe now.'

Claude came racing across the lawn to meet us. 'She's safe, oh, she's safe.' He was deathly pale. 'Oh, Emmie, I'm so sorry.'

She looked at him with large eyes. 'Don't want to go.'

'You're not going anywhere, cheri.'

'Yes she is.' Rosa had arrived followed by Beatrice and Stephanie. 'She is coming with me.' She held out her arms to her. 'Come on, ma poulette, we'll fix that head and then a hot bath and hot chocolate and bed.'

Philippe surrendered her to Rosa then bent over to rub his knee. I could see he was in a great deal of pain. He turned to Claude with a face like thunder. They'd both had a huge shock, now was certainly not the time for blame and accusations and so I stepped forward quickly.

'Philippe, let's go inside, you need to sit down.' He hesitated for a moment but I gently took his arm and moved towards the chateau.

CHAPTER FIFTY-ONE

We all gathered in the kitchen. Stephanie made coffee and Luc produced the armagnac bottle.

'Lucky we didn't finish it last night.' I smiled over at Claude. The poor man looked haunted, it had obviously not been an easy conversation with Celine. I glanced around the room but she was nowhere to be seen.

'Where is Celine?' Beatrice was thinking along the same lines as me.

'On the way to an airport, probably,' Claude said. Everyone looked astounded. 'That's why Emmie ran off, she overheard Celine talking about moving away.'

'Claude, start at the beginning.' Philippe sat down, massaging his leg. He looked around the table and then realised someone was missing. 'Where's Elf?' he said, getting up again almost immediately.

'I'm here, boss.' Elf walked in followed by Sausage and Belle. He was clutching his hat in his hands. It obviously had something in it.

'Claude, you need to thank Sausage and Belle, they found Emmie, well actually it was more down to Sausage, he was a piglet on a mission.' Philippe patted the little pig.

'That wasn't the only thing he found,' Elf muttered mysteriously. I glanced over at him.

'Let's hear about that later,' Beatrice said. 'Claude, tell us what the hell is going on?'

I wasn't sure whether I should be here during the family conference. I looked over at Nick but he was obviously suffering no such apprehension and was leaning forward as eager as everyone else to hear the news. I looked around at Philippe but it was Beatrice who caught my eye and smiled reassuringly and I wondered yet again how the hell she seemed to read my mind.

Claude told us what had happened. His voice was flat and emotionless, which was maybe how he was feeling. He said that he couldn't quite believe that Celine hadn't followed him out of the door when he realised that Emmie had gone. He'd raced into the salon to tell her what had happened, grabbed the phone to ring Philippe and rushed outside. It had never occurred to him that she would not be right by his side. He said that proved how little he actually knew his wife, or indeed how little he wanted to know his wife. He looked so utterly wretched and my heart went out to him.

He turned to Philippe and Stephanie and in a voice heavy with emotion said, 'I'm so sorry, so very sorry, somehow I will make sure she pays this back. I'll make it up to you, I promise I'll make it up to you.'

'I'm not worried about the money, Claude. I'm worried about you.' Philippe poured himself another hefty armagnac. 'I mean she must come back, what about Emmie? She can't have left for good?'

'I fear that is exactly what she has done,' Claude replied.

'In that case you are better off without her,' I said unexpectedly. Everyone looked around in surprise. 'She doesn't deserve you and she doesn't deserve Emmie.'

It was unlike me to interfere but I couldn't believe a mother could behave as Celine had done. My mother had died when I had been younger than Emmie. I could remember how hard she had fought for her life and I remembered the cold, dark day when she had lost that fight. I was filled with fury against Celine. There was a short silence after my outburst. Nick got up and came to stand behind me.

'I think that maybe you are right, Sky,' Claude nodded.

'But I just don't understand…' Philippe was dazed.

'There are a few things you don't know about Celine,' Claude said.

I saw Beatrice quickly frown at him and I wondered what it was she didn't want him saying.

Claude hesitated for a moment as if tempted to say more but in the end merely said, 'I'll go and see Emmie and then I'll head off to the house.'

'Stay here, Claude.' Philippe looked anxious.

'No, I need to sort things out.' Claude sounded remarkably calm. 'Celine may have left a message. Goodnight, everyone, and thank you, thank you all so much.'

We watched him leave the room, a broken man but somehow still managing to maintain a quiet air of dignity.

'How could she do this?' Philippe sounded close to tears. 'How could she leave her family?'

I thought it was rather lovely that he was more concerned with that than the money.

'She's never really regarded any of you as family,' Beatrice remarked.

'From what Claude says this has been going on for ages.' Luc was certainly concerned about the financial side. 'What have we done to make her hate us so much?'

No one spoke and once again I had the feeling that something was not being said.

Elf spoke into the silence that followed.

'Ladies and gentlemen, if I could have your attention for a moment.' He knelt on a chair and placed his hat carefully on the table. He beckoned us around. 'Take it, sniff it and pass it around.' For once it seemed he was enjoying taking centre stage.

I was next to him and I dutifully took the hat, peering into the damp soil inside and sniffing but frankly I was none the wiser. I could tell Beatrice had no idea either but when it came to Nick his eyes lit up and he stared into the little hat with reverence.

'Bloody hell,' he whispered. 'If this is what I think it is then you have found the crock of gold at the end of the rainbow.'

Elf looked delighted that someone had finally understood what he was showing them. Philippe was next and his smile went from ear to ear. He passed it to Henri who adopted the same evangelical look as Nick.

What was I missing?

'Rosa, come here,' Henri called to his wife.

Rosa reached in and dug out a handful of earth. She sniffed and closed her eyes briefly as if offering up a prayer.

'I can't stand the suspense!' Beatrice was exasperated and so was I. 'Have we found the elixir of youth?'

'Close, Beatrice.' Henri smiled. 'We have found truffles.'

Elf coughed slightly.

'Sorry, Elf, you have found truffles.'

'Sausage found them.' Elf would not take credit away from the piglet.

Philippe grabbed the hat and sniffed once again.

'Aren't they terribly expensive?' I asked.

'Like gold, Sky.' Nick nodded at me. 'Edible gold.'

'How did you know, Elf?' Philippe handed the hat back.

'I grew up in the truffle trade, boss, it was how my maman made a living.' He paused. 'Not legal, of course, but...'

'We used to have truffles here, didn't we?' Rosa turned to Henri.

'Very many years ago.'

'Well, now they have returned.' Elf grinned. 'Keep quiet about it though or the wild boars won't be the only unwanted visitors.'

'You guys sure know how to lay on the entertainment.' Nick laughed. 'We've had wine scams, missing children and now truffles. What will tomorrow bring?'

'Tomorrow brings Gail and Tariq,' Beatrice replied.

'And I have promised to cook.' Nick grinned at Rosa. 'Can I

borrow a car in the morning?' He looked around. 'I thought I'd try another market, Rosa tells me there is a wonderful one on the way to Bergerac, and then I could carry on and pick up Gail and Tariq.'

'You can take mine,' Philippe said.

'Thanks.' Nick glanced across at me I saw him hesitate but he didn't say anything.

'Yes, I'll come with you, Nicky,' I replied to his unspoken question.

His face lit up with joy. He looked as if he were about to say more but I'd had more than enough for one night.

'Bed for me,' I said. 'I'm exhausted.'

'Thanks for everything, Sky,' Philippe said. 'Not just the art but, well, everything.'

I didn't really know how to reply and blowing them all a kiss I quickly backed out of the door.

'Philippe, you should go and get a hot bath.' Beatrice could see the pain on his face. 'Have you done much damage?'

'I've probably set myself back a couple of weeks, nothing permanent.' But he grimaced as he stood up. 'Yes a hot bath is a damned good idea.' He limped slowly out of the door.

'Cigarette?' Nick proffered the packet to Beatrice. She nodded and the two of them went outside.

'I think you may have turned a corner with Sky,' she said.

'Oh, Beatrice, I bloody hope so.' He lit up.

They stood in companionable silence for a few moments then Nick spoke.

'Changing tack slightly, how do you think other matters are progressing?'

She turned to look at him sharply.

He grinned. 'You're not the only one with eyes, Beatrice. Don't pretend you don't know what I'm talking about.'

She laughed her low, husky laugh. 'Well then I think they are progressing rather well, what do you think?'

'I think they are heading in the right direction.' He nodded.

'Is that OK with you?'

'Absolutely.' He smiled. 'You?'

'It is written in the stars.'

CHAPTER FIFTY-TWO

Nick was pacing his room thinking about his conversation with Beatrice. He was finding it hard to believe yet it made perfect sense. It was absolutely the right thing to happen but it was incredible. God, life was weird at times.

He glanced at his watch. Miles would still be up – they were an hour earlier over in the UK. He would give him a quick ring. He felt guilty about Miles, he was aware that he had by far the better deal here at Chateau Fontaine while poor Miles was on his own in a tacky hotel in Bayswater. He had sounded utterly wretched last time they spoke. He understood why Miles had chosen to stay there, he felt that he ought to be suffering, that it would somehow help. Well, he was certainly suffering but Nick doubted that it was helping much. He'd tell him he needed to get out of there.

'Hello, it's me.'

'Hello you.'

'How are you?'

'Ah, you know, party, party, party, wild times, I'm painting the town red.'

Nick remained silent. He hated hearing Miles like this, it was very unlike him.

'In reality I'm creeping along like a leper speaking to no one.' Miles paused. 'No, that's not strictly true, I spoke to Carlo the other day.'

'You spoke to Carlo?'

'And Nonna.'

'Bloody hell, well done, you, that was brave.' Nick was impressed.

'Not really. I had no choice, they deserved nothing less.'

341

'And how were they?'

'They were incredible. Simply incredible.'

'Yes they are.'

'How is Sky?'

'In turmoil, but we're not the cause this time.'

'What the hell are you talking about?'

But suddenly Nick didn't want to voice what he was thinking, he didn't want to give Miles any false hope. 'Let's just say there is magic at work in south-west France.'

'There's no bloody magic at work in Bayswater,' Miles replied. 'Unless you count the fact that I have actually had hot water the last two days.'

'You need to get out.'

'I was thinking much the same, I may go away for a few days.'

'I'll be home soon, I'll be home in a few days.'

'Well if I'm back, I'll see you, if not then you can come and join me,' Miles replied shortly. 'I'm sorry, Nick, I really don't mean to sound curt, it's just that I feel like I'm treading water here. You're talking in riddles about some sort of magic while I'm staring at a TV screen, drinking way too much beer and wallowing in self-pity and guilt.'

'I'm so sorry, Miles.' Nick felt awful. 'But we will get there, I know we will.'

'So you keep saying. I hope you're right.' He paused. 'In fact, I think that I'll give Sky a ring.'

'Yes, that would be OK.'

'I'm not asking your bloody permission, Nick,' Miles said drily.

'No, I know, sorry that came out wrong.' Nick ran his hand through his hair.

'I'm sorry, Nick.' Miles suddenly laughed. 'I shouldn't take it out on you, it's just that I feel so inadequate and helpless here and I hate it.'

'When I come back for the wine weekend you can come too.'

'We'll see.' Miles was non-committal.

'I love you, I miss you.

'I love you too, Nicky, and I miss you too. I miss both of you.'

I'd slept amazingly well given all the drama of the day before and was about to go and search for coffee when my mobile rang. I was surprised to see Miles' name flash up and contemplated not answering but then thought it must be something urgent for him to be ringing me.

'Hello.'

'Sky, it's me.'

'I know.'

'Don't worry, nothing's wrong,' he reassured me quickly, correctly guessing what was going through my mind.

'Good.'

'I, um, well I just thought I'd ring to see how you are, and to, um, well, to tell you that I rang your father.'

'How was he?' That was courageous of Miles.

'Incredibly understanding, as was Nonna, they are both amazing.'

I was silent but was filled with a reluctant admiration for him.

'I also spoke to my mother.'

'Oh?' Probably not so amazing, I thought to myself.

'I spared her all the gory details.'

'Wise move.'

'She was very sad, she sent you her love.'

I doubted that very much. I was under no illusions as to what Edith thought of me. We'd never hit it off, despite my best efforts. She hated my name and hated my profession. She had earmarked the large lesbian from next door for Miles. Her name was Janet and she had a sensible job in an office. I had been a big disappointment.

'Have you told anyone else?'

'No, Sky, we agreed to wait until you were ready.'

'OK.'

'How are you, Sky?'

'How do you think?'

There was a short pause.

'Nick says it's magical over there.'

'It is.'

'He was full of praise for your paintings.'

I knew I wasn't making it easy, he was trying very hard but I felt so damned awkward. 'I'm happy with them.'

'That's great, Sky, really great.'

There was another short pause.

'OK, well I just wanted to check in with you, and let you know I'd spoken to Scotland.' He'd clearly given up. 'Take care, Sky.'

'Miles?' I spoke quickly before he hung up. 'Thank you for ringing, that was very kind of you.'

He was my husband of five years and yet I felt like I was talking to a stranger. We had always been able to chat for hours on any subject. We never ran out of steam. My sister used to joke that he was as good as one of her girlfriends on the phone. I smiled ruefully. But strangely I didn't feel the usual surge of anger or bitterness, just sadness that we had wasted five years. Or was it a waste? We'd had some great times together. There had been a lot of fun and a lot of laughter and he had always been hugely supportive of my career. Surely it wasn't right to discount all of that.

I really wished that I had my mum to talk to, not just about Nick and Miles but about other strange feelings that were beginning to stir. Feelings that were taking me surprise, feelings that I couldn't quite understand.

CHAPTER FIFTY-THREE

'There they are.' I rushed towards them as they finally came out of arrivals and threw my arms around Gail. I was delighted to see her.

'I can't believe you're here.' I turned to hug Sonny.

'Neither can I!' Gail laughed. 'Tariq didn't say a word about it until he came to the UK.' She smiled at him and I was overwhelmed once again at the love in their faces. 'Have you been waiting for long? I'm so sorry we were delayed.'

'Gail, it's hardly your fault.' I laughed.

'And then there seemed to be only one guy on passport control.' She grinned. 'It's a mad little airport, the luggage carousel doesn't go around, the bags just fall off the end.'

'No worries, it just gave Nick more time to buy everything in the market.' I shook my head. 'It's going to be a real squash in the car. Nick basically bought everything he saw for dinner tonight.'

'What are you cooking?' Tariq asked. 'I can still remember every detail of the last meal.'

'I can't.' I raised my eyebrows and Gail chuckled.

Sonny was tugging at my arm. 'Is Sausage here?'

'He's at the chateau, sweetheart.' I grinned at him. 'You'll love him, he's adorable, and there is a new ginger kitten but you may have to be careful with him, he's a bit feisty, you don't want to get scratched.'

'And the dog?'

'Yes, a huge dog called Belle, and lots of chickens, though no goats or camels, they're reserved for Marrakech.' I smiled shyly at Tariq. We hadn't really got to know each other in Marrakech and I was worried that I may not have made the best impression.

345

'Thank you so much for suggesting we come, Sky.' He smiled warmly. 'Have you been having a lovely time?'

'It has been eventful,' Nick said. 'We've had wine scams, wild boars, a runaway wife and um, well, a fair few other things besides.' He glanced in my direction and I shook my head. I didn't think it was a good idea to mention Emmie running away in front of Sonny.

'Well perhaps we'd better turn back then!' Tariq said.

Sonny gasped and Gail took his hand. 'It's alright, sweetheart, Papa is only joking.'

I marvelled at the easy way she used the word *Papa* and the easy way in which Sonny accepted it. A lot had obviously taken place since Marrakech.

'You look really well, Sky,' Gail said as we followed the men to the car park. Sonny was dancing beside them, overjoyed to see Nick once again.

'Do you mean pink?'

'No, definitely more gold than pink.' Gail smiled. 'France obviously suits you.'

'Oh, Gail, it most certainly does.' She looked surprised. 'There's so much to tell you but first I want to hear all about you, clearly things with Tariq are good.'

She didn't answer but held out her left hand for me to see.

I stared at the beautiful solitaire diamond ring and then stared at her. 'Oh my God!' I threw my arms around her.

'Shush, don't say a word yet, we're going to announce it later but I wanted to tell you first.'

'Gail, I am so happy for you,' I whispered. 'When did it happen, and does Sonny know?'

'He proposed the first night he came and yes, Sonny knows and is over the moon.'

'Will you move to Morocco?'

'I think that is the plan.'

'My God, Gail, it's all so exciting.'

'To think a few months ago I hadn't even decided to go and find him.' She bit her lip. 'It's just all so surreal, I can't really believe it.'

'Marrakech seems like light-years ago,' I said. 'And everything that happened before that seems very remote.'

'How are you, Sky?' Gail asked quickly. 'You look wonderful and you sound happy.'

'I'm a bit topsy-turvy,' I replied, using one of my favourite expressions.'

'It's bound to take time, you, Nick and Miles aren't going to sort yourselves out overnight.'

'Well there is another complication too…'

She looked at me enquiringly but we had arrived at the car and to be honest I was regretting saying anything. I wasn't sure that I was ready talk about things I couldn't really understand myself.

'My God, what have you bought?' Tariq was trying unsuccessfully to fit their bags into the boot of the car.

'I warned you,' I said. 'We'll have to balance things on our laps.'

'It will be worth it,' Nick said.

'How many are you cooking for?' Tariq laughed.

'I wanted to make sure there was something for everyone.' Nick was unrepentant. 'We have huge succulent prawns for starters and some beautiful fresh crab for my signature dish of crab cakes.'

'They're good,' I acknowledged. 'Very good.'

'Then we have a veritable meat feast for a BBQ.'

'Assuming Philippe has a BBQ?' I said.

'Of course he has a BBQ, but if not we'll make one.' He shook his head. 'I'm making Moroccan lamb kofta, sweet and spicy chicken wings, tangy pork ribs, homemade mega burgers, chunky coleslaw and baked potatoes dripping with butter.' He paused for a moment. 'Haven't thought about pudding yet.'

'No one will have any room for pudding,' Gail said.

'I will,' Sonny said quickly.

Gail and Tariq were bowled over by the chateau and Sonny was equally bowled over by Emmie and the animals. There had been a new addition to the menagerie in the shape of a glorious, large, floppy-eared rabbit. He was called Gabriel and he was sitting contentedly on Emmie's lap.

Elf had apparently jogged the four kilometres to Jean's house early in the morning. He said that he had been unable to get the idea of the rabbit out of his head. After last night he felt that Emmie needed special protection and that the rabbit might be the answer. Why he thought the rabbit might be the answer was unclear but Emmie was overjoyed. She was rather pale and a large lump had appeared on her head but otherwise she seemed to have suffered no ill effects.

Jean had driven Elf back to the chateau and they had spent the morning discussing plans for the opening of a small zoo.

'A zoo?' Nick asked in astonishment. 'Here?'

'Certainly not here,' Stephanie replied quickly.

'You already have a zoo here,' Sonny said, looking around, his eyes were round as saucers. He had a point, I thought.

'No, a zoo in Jean's garden,' Elf said, pushing a large notepad towards us. 'People are always bringing him animals, but his wife has had enough so this way he gets to keep them all and make some money. Take a look, I've drawn up some plans.'

'Is there nothing you can't do, Elf?' I asked.

'I can't grow.' He grinned at me.

Champagne was waiting for us in the salon.

'Almost every time I walk into this place I hear a cork popping.' I laughed. 'I'm going to miss it.'

'Better make the most of it while you're here.' Luc smiled, pouring my glass obscenely full.

'Don't go home, Sky.' Emmie looked up at me.

'Well not yet, sweetheart but probably quite soon.' Emmie looked as if she might cry and frankly I felt as if I might join her. There was a slightly awkward moment. Philippe looked as if he was about to say something but Tariq got there first.

'Actually champagne is entirely appropriate.' He looked self-conscious and terribly proud at the same time. I glanced over at Gail, she was staring at him with a face that radiated love and joy. 'We have an announcement.' He held out his hand and she glided over to join him. 'Gail has agreed to be my wife.'

There was a huge outburst of applause and once again I flung my arms around her.

'Oh, Gail, it really is so wonderful.'

'I can't quite believe it,' she said, hugging me back. 'Oh, Sky, I'm so happy.'

'You don't have to tell me!' I laughed. 'It's written all over your face.' I turned to Sonny. 'And how about you, young man?' I bent to give him a kiss. 'Isn't this exciting?'

'We is going to live by Pappy Amir and the parrot.' Sonny's face was shining as much as his mothers. 'And Jasmina,' he added quickly.

'Talking of which, has she had the baby?' I turned to Tariq.

'Not yet, but any minute. I'm hoping she can wait until I return.'

'An upcoming marriage and a baby,' I said. 'What a lot to celebrate.' I smiled at them but there was a wobble in my voice as I realised they would be celebrating the very two things I had lost.

'Ladies and gentlemen.' Nick clapped his hands. 'If I may have your attention for a moment. Phase one of the *Engagement BBQ* will commence in about two hours.' He grinned over at the happy couple. Gail laughed.

'How many phases are there?' Philippe raised his eyebrows.

'How long is a piece of string, Philippe?' Nick grinned. 'You do have a BBQ, don't you?' he added quickly.

I very much hoped so, for Nick's sake.

'We have a large converted pig trough, Nick, and plenty of old vines to burn. Henri will show you, he has it down to a fine art.'

'We'll need a delicate rosé for the starter before moving on to a robust red for the main,' Nick continued and I marvelled at his ability to take control so easily.

'I think that can be organised.' Philippe grinned. 'But let's finish off the bubbles first.'

I allowed myself one more glass before making a move. 'I'll see you all later, I'm going to do some work before the gastronomic BBQ and hard-hitting red.'

'Robust, Sky, not hard-hitting.' Nick shook his head.

'Do you really have to work today, Sky?' Philippe said. 'Gail and Tariq have only just arrived.'

'I honestly won't be long. There are just a couple of things I need to finish.'

The truth was that I needed to be on my own for a while. I was over the moon to see Gail and Tariq so obviously happy but it highlighted my own ghastly situation. Every time I thought about my return I started to panic. I simply couldn't contemplate leaving here but knew I had no choice.

Smiling at everyone and promising to be back soon, I fled to my room, collected my sketch pad and took refuge amongst the vines I had grown to love.

CHAPTER FIFTY-FOUR

The thought of going back was unbearable and I knew with certainty that I could no longer live in London. Maybe I should move back to Scotland? But no sooner had I thought of it than I dismissed it. Marrakech and France had given me a taste for the exotic, they had inspired some of my best paintings and I craved more. Perhaps I should unleash my Italian side, I had relatives over there and my rusty Italian would surely improve with time. My illustration work needn't suffer, I could illustrate books anywhere in the world and I knew that I was in high demand. So yes, maybe Italy could be the next step – or was I merely running away again?

Tears fell unchecked down my cheeks and I made no effort to brush them away. I didn't know what I wanted, I didn't know which way to turn.

No, I had to be honest with myself even if I wasn't honest with anyone else. I did know what I wanted. I didn't know how it had happened or even when it had happened, but I knew exactly what I wanted. I wanted it with my whole heart, my whole being. I'd never felt like this before in my life.

How on earth had these feelings crept up on me, and how on earth had they taken root so deeply and so damned quickly? I was shaking, there was no way I could hold a paintbrush so I simply sat there letting the tears flow for a while longer before taking a deep breath and attempting to control myself.

There was no point in dreaming of a future that would never happen. I had to push it to the back of my mind. I had invited Gail and Tariq here and I needed to be there to help entertain them. I would work for an hour and then call it a day and throw myself wholeheartedly into the BBQ and the party.

I made another decision. Provided I was happy with my paintings, I would go back to the UK with the newly engaged couple. There was no point in prolonging the agony. It would be easier leaving with someone else.

I had hoped to escape into the house unseen, I wanted to wash any traces of the tears away before joining the others, but as I was making my way to the side entrance Claude called out to me.

'Sky, have you got a few moments?'

Reluctantly I stopped and waited for him to catch up with me.

'I wanted to thank you for helping to find Emmie. It was so kind of you and Nick.'

'Well of course I wanted to help search for her, I adore her.'

'The feeling is mutual.' He peered at me closely. 'Are you OK?'

'Must be allergic to something in the vines,' I lied, adding quickly. 'I'm just so relieved that she's OK.'

'When I think of what could have happened my blood runs cold.' He shook his head.

'I'm very sorry about Celine,' I said carefully.

'*Shocked* is probably the word you are searching for,' he said grimly. 'I'm certainly shocked, particularly when I realise how little I actually knew my wife.'

'Have you said anything to Emmie?'

'Not yet, but obviously I will have to at some point.' He paused for a moment. 'There wasn't a lot of love lost between them but nonetheless I don't want Emmie to think Celine has abandoned her, which of course is exactly what she has done.'

'Do you really think she won't come back?' I simply couldn't understand her behaviour. It was beyond my comprehension that someone could do something like this.

'She won't come back, Sky,' Claude said emphatically. 'Everyone knows what she has done, she'll never come back and face the music.'

'I'm so sorry, Claude,' I repeated inadequately.

'I'm not, Sky,' he replied. 'I don't think I ever want to see her again.' He sighed. 'I'm sorry for the waste though, the waste of all those years.'

'Don't think like that, Claude,' I said. 'I've been thinking along those lines too but you have to remember the good times, the fun and the laughter before it all went wrong.'

'I'm not sure there was any fun and laughter.' He looked incredibly sad and my heart went out to him.

'There must have been, Claude, when you first got married, when you were both in love.'

'Sky, to be honest I'm not really sure I was in love with Celine. I worshipped her but I'm not sure I ever really loved her and she certainly never loved me.'

'She must have done when you got married.' I was struggling. 'I mean, why else did you get married?'

'I was flattered, she was beautiful, she was bright, she was a real catch and I couldn't believe my luck that she'd chosen me.' He shrugged. 'I must have been blind, how could I ever have thought she loved me?'

'But then why did she marry you?'

He turned to look at me, frowning as if weighing up what to say. He was silent for a moment and then said slowly, 'Celine married me, Sky, because she loved Philippe.'

'What?' I was really shocked.

'It's true, she couldn't have Philippe so she settled for second best.'

'I just don't understand.'

'If not the wife then maybe the mistress.'

'And was she the mistress?' I questioned quietly. Please let that

353

not be the case, oh God please let that not be true. My heart was pounding.

'Mon Dieu, no,' Claude laughed bitterly.

I nearly fell over with relief. 'So what happened?'

'I'm not sure. I suspect she made a fool of herself and Celine hates to be made to look like a fool.' He ran his hands through his hair. 'I only found this out the other day, Sky, I'm still trying to come to terms with it all.'

'Did Philippe never say anything?'

'No, he wouldn't want to hurt me.' He paused for a moment. 'He probably saw it as a moment of madness on her behalf, he's probably forgotten it ever happened.'

I doubted that but said nothing.

'I don't really care about me but I do care very much that she has cheated the others.'

'So all of this because Philippe turned her down?' Celine was turning more monstrous by the minute.

'Love, hate and anger, they are all powerful emotions, Sky. They can destroy reason.'

'What will she do?'

'I've no idea.' He shook his head. 'She's won, she has all the money, there's nothing I can do.'

'She hasn't won, Claude,' I said. 'She may have the money but she hasn't won.'

He looked at me.

'She will have to start a new life, a life based on nothing but lies, it will never be a real life and she will always be terrified of someone finding out. She will always be looking over her shoulder.' I reached out to touch his arm briefly. 'You have your family here, Claude, you have Emmie. You are the one who has won. I almost pity Celine.'

'Pity is not my overriding emotion right now,' he replied gruffly and then in an abrupt change of tack asked, 'How are you, Sky? How are things with you?'

'Complicated,' I replied shortly. And luckily before he could ask anymore we heard voices in the background.

'I'd better go and get ready,' I said, quickly heading towards the door.

Once in my room I had a swift shower and splashed cold water on my face. My eyes were still a touch red and very puffy. I always looked bloody awful after crying, my sister always managed to look sad and rather glamorous at the same time whereas I looked like my face had been rubbed with a bunch of nettles.

I put on some bright lipstick and grabbed large sunglasses to hide my eyes. I chose the kaftan that Gail had bought me in Marrakech, it was made of fine cheesecloth and was very cool. Piling up my hair I reached for the floppy straw hat that Nick had given me. I certainly didn't want to risk another neck-burning incident.

I stood still for a few moments before leaving the room. Taking some deep breaths I gave myself a stern talking to. I would have a great afternoon, I would throw myself into everything that was organised and I would try my hardest to keep these new and heart-stopping emotions in check.

As I walked across the lawn Emmie came running over to greet me.

'We is playing a boules competition what Elf is organised.' She grabbed my hand. 'You is playing with Luc.'

'Poor Luc.' I smiled. 'I have never played boules before.'

'I is playing with Elf,' she chatted on. 'Uncle Philly be with Nick, Henri with Aunt Stephanie, Tariq and Sonny and Gail with Papa.'

'What about Rosa?' I asked. 'Is she not playing? Or Beatrice?'

'Rosa has many talents but sadly boules is not one of them.' Philippe laughed as we came within earshot. 'She has a habit of flinging the boules high in the air, our lives have been in danger on many occasions, it's best she stays well away. And as you know, Beatrice has a pathological hatred of any sport.'

'OK, first round, Emmie and me versus Tariq and Sonny.' Elf was reading from his piece of paper. 'Followed by Luc and Sky against Philippe and Nick.' He smiled at us all. 'Then Henri and Stephanie against Gail and Claude.' Elf was clearly in his element.

I watched Emmie scamper over to him and was struck by their similarity. They were the same height with the same curly hair. I smiled as Elf took her hand.

'They are firm friends.' Philippe followed my gaze.

'I was just thinking they could be brother and sister.' I grinned. 'I think it fair to say that Elf has finally found his true family.' I looked up at Philippe. 'I think he's here to stay.'

'I very much hope so. Emmie would kill me if he ever left.' He laughed. 'Are you and your sister alike?'

'Not really, she has my father's olive skin and my mother's fair hair, I inherited the opposite, my father's dark hair and my mother's pale complexion.' I laughed. 'It's totally the wrong way around.'

'And is she artistic like you?'

'Not at all, she followed my dad into the teaching profession.'

'Did you always want to be an artist?'

'No, for a long while I wanted to be a marine biologist.' I chuckled. 'You've probably never heard of it but one of my favourite films was called *Local Hero*, and…'

'I know it,' he butted in. 'One of my mother's favourites too. I must have watched it a dozen times.'

'Really?' I was absurdly pleased that we had this in common. 'Well then, you know the Jenny Seagrove character, I wanted to be just like her, I had a real crush on her.'

'Who didn't?' He grinned.

'Nick for one, he had a crush on the landlord, and my dad fancied his wife.'

'What changed your mind about marine biology?'

'I realised that it wasn't all about swimming.'

Boules was great fun and I showed a remarkable aptitude.

Luc was delighted. 'We'll make a Frenchwoman of you yet, Sky,' he teased, as yet again my boule landed nearest the jack.

It was so close to what I had been dreaming of myself that I had to turn away, anxious not to reveal my thoughts. But I didn't turn quick enough for Beatrice. She said nothing but silently handed me a glass. Could she actually see into my mind, I wondered? I bloody hoped not. I almost downed the glass in one, it wasn't my first glass but I still felt incredibly sober and I wished I didn't. I wished the drink would block out my feelings.

I caught Gail looking at me quizzically and I gave her a thumbs-up. I would have loved to talk to her about everything but it wouldn't have been fair to offload my madness onto her right now. I turned my attention back to the match, and much to Philippe's indignation Luc and I thrashed him and Nick.

As ever Nick's food was sublime, although he had, of course, massively over-catered. The outside table looked gorgeous, Emmie and Sonny had decorated it in style with leaves, flowers, grasses and ivy. There was barely room for the plates and I prayed that nobody suffered from hay fever.

We took our time savouring each morsel of food and enjoying the unique flavour of Chateau Fontaine wine. Family meals seemed to be such an integral part of life in France and I really loved it. The late afternoon stole into the evening. Rosa lit the candles and the whole image was so romantic it brought a lump to my throat.

I got up to take a picture on my phone. However painful it became, I was desperate to capture every single minute of my last few days, but to be honest I knew that I didn't really need a photo to remind me. I would carry the memory in my head for ever.

'Thank you for suggesting we came over, Sky.' Gail came over to where I was standing. 'I wouldn't have missed this for the world.'

'It's beautiful, isn't it?'

'It certainly is.' She turned to me. 'Are you alright?'

I paused for a fraction of a second before replying. 'I'm fine, Gail, just a bit tired.'

She looked at me intently but said nothing. Instead she gently squeezed my shoulders before wandering back to the table, instinctively knowing that I needed to be alone.

I looked around, the light was fading and there was a reddish glow in the sky, any second now the bats would come out and soar above the pool. I couldn't say I'd ever been a fan of bats but here I loved to glimpse them dipping into the water and then disappearing into the blackness beyond. They were as much a part of the chateau as the swifts, the pigeons, which Philippe hated, the buzzards, which he loved, the tiny field mice I adored and the darting lizards.

CHAPTER FIFTY-FIVE

My mind had been in turmoil last night and going to bed I had been convinced that I wouldn't get any sleep, however I was proved wrong. The hard-hitting red wine had done its job and I slept like a baby, waking, as usual, extremely early.

However despite the deep sleep I didn't feel particularly refreshed. My mind was still whirring and a black mist of depression hung over me. Dragging my thoughts away from the one theme they kept returning to, I decided to go and paint the purple mist over the river one last time. I knew I could paint it every morning for a year and in every painting it would be different.

Wrapping myself in Nonna's shawl and borrowing my usual pair of wellies from by the back door I crept out of the house and made my way down to the river bank. As I approached I caught my breath in amazement as there on a rock jutting out of the river stood a magnificent heron. He was incredibly beautiful and I cursed myself for not bringing either my phone or camera to capture the image. I sat down as quietly as possible and quickly began to sketch. He stood there motionless for about ten minutes before turning to gaze at me as if to say *'your time is up now'*. Then, opening his impressive wings he took off and flew gracefully into the distance.

I stayed there for another hour or so before the early morning chill began to seep through my shawl and the caffeine craving kicked in. I was fairly pleased with the result although wasn't sure I had done justice to the glorious bird.

I gathered my things and wandered up to the chateau. Never had it seemed so beautiful as it did this morning, the moon was still high in the sky and the gentle early morning mist was swirling around the turrets. The thought of leaving all this behind created such a physical pain in my chest that I was forced to stop and bend over.

'Sky, are you alright?' I was amazed to see Stephanie hurrying down the lawn towards me.

'Fine, just a bit of a stitch,' I lied, hastily brushing away the tears which had once again started to flow. My eyes seemed to be like bubbling streams these days. 'You're up incredibly early.'

'So are you.' She smiled. 'Can I take a peek?' She indicated my sketch pad.

'I was just trying to capture the morning mist for the last time and look who joined me.' I showed her my painting but she wasn't paying attention.

'The last time?' She frowned. 'Sky, you're not leaving us are you?' She looked genuinely upset at the thought which, I had to admit, was gratifying.

'Well, I can't stay for ever.' I tried to smile. 'My agent has been e-mailing me, and, er, well, I think that over the next couple of days I should be able to finish everything, I mean providing Philippe is happy.'

'He won't be happy that you're going,' she said and my heart soared. What did she know that I didn't?

'None of us will,' she added and my heart plummeted back down as I realised that she hadn't meant anything by that last remark. 'When are you thinking of going?'

'The day after tomorrow,' I replied. 'I thought I'd travel back with Nick, Gail and Tariq.'

'In that case we must make sure that tomorrow is party time.'

'Every day is party time here.' Once again I tried to smile and once again I failed. 'Why are you up so early?'

'I'm going to collect some of Emmie's things from the house, I thought I'd do it before she gets up, we're giving her a few days off school for obvious reasons but she needs to go back soon.' She paused. 'Do you want to be nosy and come with me to see the "monstrosity", as we call it.'

'Oh, I'd love to be nosy but can I grab a coffee first?'

'Of course, I was just making it before I saw you doubled over.'

'Well it's certainly not warm or welcoming but my God there are some exquisite pieces,' I said, examining a slim glass vase that I was almost sure was Murano.

'Her parents are wealthy, they were always giving her presents.'

'Jesus Christ, this is Lalique,' I exclaimed, picking up a stunning figurine of a dancing girl. 'Stephanie, this is worth a tidy sum.' I looked around. 'In fact, I should imagine that a lot of them are.'

'Walk around, Sky, see what else you can spot,' Stephanie said. 'I must admit that I've never looked too closely. To be honest I hardly ever come here, really, none of us do.'

I wandered around the large room. There was some serious stuff here. I didn't know how much she had creamed off the family over the years but I imagined that this would go some way to recompensing them. I was surprised that she had left it but then I guess she had been in a rush. She was clearly desperate to escape while she had the chance and once again I was filled with rage at a mother who could abandon her little girl.

Christ, she didn't even know if Emmie had been found safe. What kind of monster would do that? How come the powers that be allowed her to be a mother and yet had taken my much-wanted unborn baby away from me? Not for the first time I thought we lived in a very unjust world. I hoped that I'd never see her again, I would find it hard not to throttle her and I suspected I wouldn't be first in the queue.

What was I thinking? Of course I wouldn't see her again, I was leaving the day after tomorrow and once again I was poleaxed by the thought.

'OK, I think that is enough for now.' Stephanie came in with a suitcase. 'I'll just check the fridge and make sure there is nothing that will go off.' I followed her into the kitchen which, like the rest of the house, lacked any personality or character. There were expensive knives, a state of the art cooker which looked like it had barely been used and a vast American-style fridge. Stephanie opened it and shook her head in disgust.

'This absolutely typifies Celine.' She beckoned me over. There was a stack of cheap budget pizzas obviously meant for Emmie, a jar of expensive foie gras, some Roquefort cheese, a ready-made meal of boeuf bourguignon, an enormous bottle of Diet Pepsi and several bottles of serious-looking white wine.

'I don't think she has cooked anything in her life,' Stephanie said as she took out the bourguignon, wine and cheese. 'The pizzas and Pepsi can go straight in the bin.' She shook her head. 'Emmie doesn't even like Pepsi.' She turned to me. 'Did you see anything of interest?'

'Well I'm no expert, Stephanie, but I think there are some fairly valuable pieces here.' I shrugged. 'I know this isn't exactly a crime hot spot but I wouldn't leave them here in an empty house.'

She nodded. 'Come and have a look outside before we go back for breakfast.'

I grinned. 'My God, is it only breakfast? I feel like I've been up for hours.'

'You have.' She laughed.

We wandered outside, the house was modern and soulless but it did actually have potential. Even though you couldn't quite see the river from there the views were magnificent.

'You know, if you painted the shutters a lovely soft green, grew some plants up the wall, put some hanging baskets up then that alone would make a huge difference.' I turned to Stephanie. 'It just needs some personal touches, it lacks… oh my God!' I stopped mid-sentence. 'Well, it certainly doesn't lack a pool.' I stared at the infinity pool carved out of the gentle hillside. It was glorious and it must have cost an absolute fortune.

'Celine's father gave them the money,' Stephanie said, reading my thoughts. 'The irony is that hardly anyone uses it. Celine only goes in if it's like a very warm bath, the same applies to Claude and Emmie is only allowed in under supervision, but as there is rarely anyone to supervise her that hardly ever happens.'

'God, what a waste.' I was appalled. 'What will happen to the house?'

'I imagine Claude will sell it,' Stephanie said.

'He shouldn't sell it,' I said slowly. 'You should rent it out, you'd get a lot for something like this in high season.' I was gathering momentum. 'Trust me, I've stayed in loads of villas over the years, this could be a gold mine for you, people would love it and they'd love being near the vineyard, they'd buy your wine by the bucketload.'

'That is not such a bad idea, Sky.' Stephanie smiled at me. 'I wish you weren't going home.'

'Oh, so do I!' I exclaimed without thinking and Stephanie stared, startled by my cry from the heart. I tried to justify it. 'I mean, it's been so lovely here, it's so beautiful and everyone is so gorgeous and compared to London this is paradise.'

She looked at me quizzically. 'I'm going to drive back, Sky, but you should walk. You can cut through the vineyards but if I were you I'd go down the lane, around the first corner there is a wonderful view of the chateau. I think you'd enjoy that.'

After breakfast Luc took Nick, Tariq and Gail to Michel's chateau, Elf took Sonny and Emmie for a unicycle lesson and I took the opportunity to tell Philippe that I would be leaving soon.

He was sitting in his study, the door was wide open but I knocked nonetheless. 'Can I have a quick word?'

'Of course, Sky, please come on in.'

'This is a fantastic room,' I said, looking around. It was an old-fashioned room. It was a room that held history, I could almost feel the presence of his predecessors sitting on the leather chairs watching us. Philippe's desk dominated the room; made from oak, it was huge and sturdy and completely covered with papers. I raised my eyebrows.

'There is a semblance of order,' he pleaded, looking at my face. 'But it's only apparent to me.'

'That's all that matters then.' I laughed as I walked over to get a closer look at some drawings on the wall.

'There are some like that in my bedroom,' I said. 'Are they related to Belle?'

'Yes they're her ancestors.' He smiled. 'My father drew them.'

'He was very talented.'

'Only when it came to dogs.' Philippe chuckled. 'He tried drawing Stephanie and me several times but he always managed to give us some canine feature, it was really rather unnerving.'

I smiled and took a deep breath. 'Philippe, I think I may go home soon.'

He stared at me. 'Really?'

'Well, I don't want to outstay my welcome, and, um, well, there are things I should get back to, I guess.'

'I see.'

He sounded cross. Did he think I should stay longer? Did he not think I'd done enough?

'Providing you like what I've done, obviously,' I said. 'I mean if you're not happy then obviously I'll stay longer.'

'Of course I like what you've done,' he said curtly. 'It's excellent.' He stood up and, lighting a cigarette, went and stood by the open window. 'Of course, you have things to do at home, I quite understand.' His voice sounded strained. 'We can't keep you captive here.'

If only, I thought to myself, if he only knew how much I wanted to be kept captive.

'When were you thinking of going?'

'Probably with the others,' I replied. 'If that's OK?'

'Of course it's OK, Sky.' He paused. 'It's just that...' He stopped abruptly.

'Just that what?' I asked quietly.

'Nothing, nothing, just that it came as a bit of a shock.' He looked at me and gave the briefest of smiles. 'We must make sure that tomorrow is a celebration.'

A celebration was not exactly what I was feeling like but I nodded mutely and then mumbling something about going to finish the work I hurried out of the room and ran straight into Beatrice.

'Slow down, Sky.' She smiled. 'Did I just hear you say you were leaving?'

'My God, you really do have magical powers, Beatrice.' I shook my head. 'Nothing escapes you, does it?'

'Not a lot, but this time it has less to do with magic and more to do with open doors.' She grinned. 'I have no idea why but voices tend to carry in this chateau.'

I merely nodded, keen to get away but not wanting to appear rude.

'Do you have to go home, Sky?'

'Well yes, I mean no, it's not urgent, but... I can't stay here for ever, can I?'

She looked at me and as ever I felt unnerved by her scrutiny.

'Don't rush into things, cheri.'

CHAPTER FIFTY-SIX

I made my way to the pool, I needed to collect myself before the others came home and I always found swimming therapeutic. Emmie came bounding across the lawn to me.

'Sky, is you going swimming? Can we come?'

'Of course, cheri, but finish your lesson with Elf first, you want to be able to impress your friends with the unicycle.' It was her dream to take the unicycle to school and show them she could ride it.

I grabbed my costume from the changing room, I hadn't hung it up properly and it was still damp from yesterday, but a soggy swimsuit was the least of my worries right now.

I dived in, it was cool and refreshing. It would have been my absolute dream to have a swimming pool of my own and I thought of the fabulous infinity one not being used up the road. A sudden thought occurred to me. Maybe I could rent the house and paint there?

Oh, stop being so bloody stupid, Sky, I chided myself, choking on a mouthful of water. That would be absolute torture and besides, where the hell would I get the money from? I'd already told Stephanie that they could get a fortune from renting it out.

And talking of money, I'd have to seriously sort out my finances now that I was on my own. I should maybe have an exhibition, see if I couldn't flog some stuff. Perhaps I'd have to be less picky with what I chose to illustrate. Turning down books like *Colin the Clever Carrot* may not have been an option any more. Perhaps I should consider teaching, I'd been approached several times by various schools and colleges but had never really fancied the commitment. I'd taught the odd private student and had done a few courses which I had loved. A sudden vision of a class in Philippe's old sandstone barns floated into my head. With the greatest difficulty I pushed it away and concentrated on my front crawl.

'Sky, we is finished the lesson.'

Emmie stood at the end of the pool in her costume with Sonny by her side. Elf was hovering at the back.

'Come on in, then,' I shouted. They both plunged fearlessly into the water.

'Come in, Elf,' Emmie yelled at him.

'I've not got any swimming things.' He turned to walk away.

'I've got some more.' Sonny scrambled out of the pool.

'He can swim in his shorts,' I said quickly. Elf may have been short but he was fully developed and my mind boggled at the thought of him in Sonny's swimming trunks. I smiled up at him. 'They'll dry in no time, come on and we can have a relay race.'

He shook his head nervously and it suddenly dawned on me.

'Elf, you can't swim, can you?'

'I probably can, I just choose not to,' he said with dignity.

'Well that is not a choice anymore,' I said firmly. 'Get in, I'll teach you.' He still looked hesitant so I played my trump card. 'Elf, you cannot possibly live in a house by a river with a pool and not know how to swim. What if Emmie fell in? How would you help her?'

Emmie immediately started to thrash around as if in danger and Sonny joined in.

Elf scowled at me. 'OK, you win.'

Thirty minutes later he was able to swim a width unaided. It wasn't exactly a recognisable stroke but it was progress and he was delighted with himself and so was I. It had also helped occupy my mind.

'Boss, come and watch me,' Elf yelled to Philippe who was walking across the lawn with the others. 'Sky's taught me to swim.'

'We helped,' protested Sonny.

'You never said you couldn't swim,' Philippe said.

'You never asked,' Elf responded.

'Sky looks blue with cold,' Gail said, and I realised that I was indeed shivering.

'Lesson over, Elf.' I smiled at him. 'But well done, you're a quick learner.'

'Give me a few more lessons, please, Sky,' Elf pleaded. 'I'll teach you the unicycle in return.'

'I think I'd rather learn the bongos.' I laughed. 'Less likely to hurt myself.'

'OK, the bongos then, is it a deal?' He held out his hand. 'Shall we start tomorrow?'

'Well, the thing is...' I hesitated and glanced quickly over to Philippe. 'The thing is, Elf, I'm going home soon.'

'Home?' Elf repeated as if I'd just said I was flying to the moon. He stared at me horrified.

'No, Sky, don't go.' Emmie burst into noisy tears and I wished that I could join her.

'Emmie, don't cry, sweetheart.' I tried to gather her into my arms but she wasn't having any of it.

'Why is Sky going, Uncle Philly?' She rushed out of the pool and threw her wet arms around his legs. He winced as she hit his bad knee.

'Cheri, Sky has to go home,' he said, bending down with difficulty to untangle her. 'Sky has work to do.'

'She can work here,' Emmie sobbed.

'She's finished her work here, Emmie,' he said shortly.

The words cut me to the quick. I guess that told me all I needed to know. Clambering quickly out of the pool I grabbed the nearest towel, not really caring if it was mine or not. I wrapped it around me. 'I'll go and get a hot shower.' I went over to caress Emmie's hair. 'I thought

I'd show Uncle Philippe all my paintings later, darling, do you want to show him what you've done too.'

She turned her tear-stained face to me. 'Don't go.' She looked so sad and I felt heartbroken.

'I'm so sorry,' I whispered.

'I've booked a lunch in Saint-Émilion tomorrow,' Philippe said suddenly. 'As it's everyone's last day.'

I remained silent, not trusting myself to speak.

'Oh, that sounds wonderful.' Gail stepped in. 'Sky, go and get changed, you look freezing.' I looked at her gratefully and headed off towards the chateau.

I was halfway across the lawn when Philippe called after me.

'Sky.'

I turned around.

'I'm going to show Tariq the barns if you wanted to join us.'

I nodded, although it was the last thing I felt like doing. I had no inclination to discuss plans about barns that in all likelihood I would never see again. It would be sheer agony. Out of the corner of my eye I caught Nick looking at me strangely. Was that a look of pity on his face? I bloody hoped not. I quickly shouted back at Philippe, 'OK, I'll just get changed and come and find you.'

I had a quick shower, threw on some clothes and plaited my wet hair. I was about to rush out of the door when on a sudden impulse I picked up my mobile from the bedside table. Before I could change my mind I dialled Miles.

'Sky?' He sounded anxious.

'Nothing to worry about,' I reassured him quickly. 'I just wanted to say that everything is fine, well actually no, everything is far from fine, but it's sort of OK between us.'

There was a pause. 'What are you saying Sky?'

'Just that things have changed, everything is a bit up in the air and

I'm totally confused but I'm not angry anymore, well I am still angry, but not as much, and I understand that you had no choice. Bye.'

I hung up, aware that I hadn't really made much sense but hopefully he would have got the drift. It seemed important to let him know that I was ready to move forward, ready to forgive. I knew now that whatever I'd felt for him had not been true love.

I was wandering around the barns with Nick, Tariq and Philippe when Nick's phone rang. He answered it immediately and I guessed at once that it must be Miles. He was no doubt ringing to find out what the hell I had been gabbling on about. Nick glanced quickly in my direction, confirming my suspicions.

He wandered outside and I felt suddenly very lonely. I wasn't at all sure I could face another day of smiling and pretending to everyone. I wondered if there was any way of getting out of lunch in Saint-Émilion tomorrow, perhaps I could feign a sudden illness. Actually I may not have had to pretend, I really didn't feel great, my heart felt heavy and my limbs felt like lead. A black fog had descended and it was weighing upon my shoulders. I was suddenly aware of silence and realised that Philippe and Tariq were staring at me.

'Sorry,' I mumbled. 'Miles away, did you ask me something?'

'I was just telling Tariq about some of your ideas for the barn.' He sounded irritable and once again I wondered if I had done something to piss him off. Maybe he wasn't happy with my work, although he had seemed genuinely impressed. I was aware that they were talking and forced myself to pay attention.

'As far as I can see the structure is fairly sound,' Tariq was saying. 'It really has a huge amount of potential, Philippe, there are so many things you could do with it.'

'One of them is to build a restaurant,' Nick said, walking in from outside.

'What did I tell you?' I smiled at Philippe. 'I say art studio and he says restaurant.'

'To be honest, there's room for both.' Tariq was pacing around much as I had done earlier in the week. 'You even have the second smaller outbuilding which could be converted.'

'Luc can have his tasting room and shop.'

'Now that is a seriously good idea,' Nick said. 'Cheese and wine tasting evenings, Henri could play his guitar.'

'Sounds like something the Conservative Party used to do back home.' I grimaced. 'Minus Henri of course.'

'The views are stunning and the stonework is beautiful.' It was clear that Tariq had taken a shine to the buildings. 'You would need to install some big picture windows, we could recycle the sandstone from those.' He looked around. 'You have so many resources at your fingertips here, we need use only natural products.' His eyes were shining. 'This place could really be very special and it needn't cost a fortune.'

I could see why Beatrice rated him so highly. He was enthusiastic and quick-thinking. I loved his appreciation and immediate understanding of the old building. I had seen too many old buildings completely ruined by plasterboard covering everything that was not neat and even. Tariq was someone who would let the character of the barn speak for itself.

I was about to follow them to the other outbuilding but Nick stopped me.

'Miles just rang me.'

'Yes, I guessed that.'

'He said you rang him.'

I nodded.

'He couldn't make much sense of the conversation but thought that perhaps there was light at the end of the tunnel?'

Again I merely nodded.

Nick looked at me closely. 'You can talk to me about anything Skylark, you know that don't you?'

I looked at the friend with whom I had shared everything and I was tempted. I was sorely tempted to unburden myself as I had so many times in the past. It would be a relief to talk, to see what he thought, to see if he could shed any light.

I opened my mouth to speak but no words came. I wasn't ready to express the powerful emotions that were swallowing me up. I couldn't begin to explain them to anyone else. I was too scared to put into words the feelings that were surging through me.

CHAPTER FIFTY-SEVEN

As normal I woke early but unusually I rolled over in bed. I simply couldn't bear to see the mist hanging over the river this morning knowing that it was my last day. I actually wanted the memories of this magical place to start to fade, I wanted to be able to push them to the back of my mind where they couldn't hurt me.

Like a kid I pulled the duvet over my head in an attempt to shut out the world. It wasn't a good idea, I became hot, I dozed fitfully for an hour and woke up feeling like shit.

I dragged myself out of bed and into the bathroom. Glancing in the mirror my spirits plummeted further. My eyes were swollen and puffy and my tan seemed to have faded overnight. I looked bloody awful. I knew that I should really go for a swim but my limbs seemed heavy and lifeless. I doubted I could even float. Stepping into the shower, I blasted myself with freezing water. It refreshed my body but not my mind. However I knew I had to put on a good act. Philippe had booked a table for us all in Saint-Émilion and I was determined not to spoil it by being miserable.

I had promised Emmie yesterday that I would come back, I wasn't sure if it was a promise I would be able to keep but nothing else would satisfy her. I'd also promised that she could choose my dress and do my hair for lunch. I very much hoped that she was a little more restrained with hair than table decorations. Glancing at my watch I saw that it was still reasonably early but I knew that the coffee would be on. I gathered the big cardboard folder from the desk and tied it with a red ribbon. There were half a dozen finished paintings inside and several pen and ink drawings as well as the wine labels. I was working on a couple more which I would complete at home and my sketch pad was full of images if more were needed.

The bloody pigeons were making a racket on my windowsill and I clapped my hands to get rid of them.

'Go and shag somewhere else,' I yelled through the open window. 'I don't want to hear you.'

I met Philippe at the bottom of the stairs. He had a towel slung over his shoulder and his dark hair was damp from the pool.

'You put me to shame.' I smiled. 'I should have gone swimming.'

'I thought you'd be at the river,' he replied.

'Well I thought about it, perhaps I should have gone, maybe I missed the heron.'

'You didn't. I went for a walk before swimming.'

'Gosh, you've been quite the action man this morning,' I said and then watching him frown wished I hadn't. What a stupid bloody thing to say. It sounded so patronising.

'I'm not always so incapacitated, Sky,' Philippe said brusquely. 'I hardly think a gentle stroll and a quick swim qualify me as action man.'

'No, of course not, I'm sorry.' Why did I always manage to rub him up the wrong way? 'I've got the paintings here.' I indicated the large folder under my arm. 'Shall I leave them in your office?'

'Yes please.' He hesitated. 'Sorry to snap, Sky, totally unacceptable, I've got out of bed the wrong side, I've shouted at Belle for lying in a doorway, I've shouted at Sausage for running between my legs and I yelled at Elf for leaving the unicycle propped against the back door where I nearly fell over it.' He shook his head ruefully. 'I should come with a danger sign on my forehead today.'

I laughed, I liked his honesty. 'Something like "keep away, unexploded bomb."'

'Exactly that.' He grinned at me and my heart flipped over.

Emmie came into my room later that morning bearing a basket overflowing with flowers and feathers. My heart sank, Minnehaha was not the look I'd had in mind. Emmie, however, placed the basket confidently on the table and marched up to the wardrobe. She pulled out a blue kaftan and held it up.

'Bit too see-through, darling,' I said quickly. 'More for wafting around the pool.'

She discarded it on the bed.

'How about the cheesecloth dress?' I went over to the wardrobe. 'You liked it last time.'

She shook her head. 'They've seen that.' I was sure 'they' wouldn't mind seeing it again but I kept quiet.

She pulled out a long, flowing pink batik dress that I had bought many years ago in Greece. 'This is pretty.'

'Are you sure it's smart enough?' I was hesitant. It was one of my favourites but it was also ancient. 'Wouldn't this be better?' I pulled out my new long linen shift dress.

'Green, yuck,' she grimaced, dismissing without hesitation the most expensive dress in the wardrobe.

She won, of course, and we settled on the faded pink batik. It had a low neckline and I was anxious that I may be showing off more than necessary. I reached for a scarf but Emmie shook her head. 'Put up your hair, Sky, I is going to decorate it.' She picked up the basket and studied it intently.

I laughed at her serious face. Oh, what the hell? No one knew me in Saint-Émilion and I would probably never go there again. 'OK, cheri, do your worst, but I'm not that keen on feathers, they make me sneeze, and save some flowers for your own hair.'

The others were waiting in the kitchen. There was a general intake of breath as we walked in and I felt myself blush.

'You both look incredible.' Nick clapped and the rest joined in.

'Is it a bit too much?' I glanced quickly in the mirror, there was nothing subtle about the colourful circlet of flowers and the sparkly clips that Emmie had insisted on.

'It's fabulous, Sky,' Beatrice laughed. 'You look like something from a storybook.'

'It's true, you look like one of your own illustrations.' Nick laughed and I glared at him.

'You both look like princesses,' Philippe said quietly, staring straight at me. 'Saint-Émilion will think royalty has arrived.'

Saint-Émilion was breathtakingly beautiful. Steep cobbled streets and enchanting medieval squares. Flowers tumbling out of hanging baskets, it was a world heritage site for a reason, a town full of history and romance.

'You fit right in, Sky.' Luc laughed. 'You look as if you have arrived from a different century.' I curtseyed to him.

We had champagne in the cloisters of a ruined church and tied the corks onto the branches of a tree growing in the middle.

'You have to make a wish, Sky,' Beatrice said, handing me the last cork. I took it from her and slowly tied it on. Closing my eyes I wished like I'd never wished before, I wished with all my heart and when I opened my eyes she was smiling at me.

The restaurant was fun and quirky. A huge bar stood in the middle, the floor tiles were metallic and glittery and the tables had been made from leftover wine boxes. The owner directed us to a round table situated by the window. It was clearly the best table and yet another bottle of champagne was chilling in the middle. The place was packed and buzzing with conversation and laughter.

Philippe insisted that we had the special 'gourmet meal' and lunch lasted for hours. I lost count of how many courses were served, but they were all perfectly balanced, perfectly sized portions and simply delicious. Nick of course was in seventh heaven.

Despite the emotions swirling around in my head I threw myself into the party atmosphere with a desperation that almost bordered on hysteria. Taking a leaf from my heroine Scarlett O'Hara I kept telling myself 'tomorrow is another day', and besides, I had made my wish on the cork tree. Surely if you wished on a champagne cork in an old church in a medieval town you stood a healthy chance of it coming true? Well, I was clinging to that hope anyway.

Philippe had declared at the start that he wanted it to be a party we would all remember and looking around the happy faces I thought he had probably succeeded.

He himself had been behaving very strangely, one moment he was the life and soul of the party and the next quiet and morose. Several times I was aware that he was staring at me and I saw Beatrice and Nick exchange glances. I wondered what the hell was going on. What was I not getting?

Nick had inevitably wandered off to the kitchen after the meal and was now engaged in conversation with the chef. Frederick, the owner and one of Philippe's closest friends, had joined us at the table where he was busy entertaining us with his speciality card tricks. He was good, the others had seen it all before but I was captivated, I'd always loved tricks.

'No!' I shrieked, leaping up. My hair had come loose and wilted flowers fell onto the table. 'How could you possibly know it was the five of clubs? It's impossible.'

'It's magic.' Frederick laughed and immediately topped my glass up. He glanced over at Philippe and winked. 'How come you have all the pretty ladies at your house?' He laughed. 'Rosa, Stephanie, Beatrice and now Sky, you should share them out Philippe.'

'If you'd been less keen on sharing, Frederick, then maybe one of your pretty wives might had stayed.' Beatrice laughed.

He didn't seem to take offence but smiling reached for yet another bottle. Clearly the lunch was not yet over.

CHAPTER FIFTY-EIGHT

I hurled my things haphazardly into the suitcase the following morning and with huge difficulty zipped it up. I'd slept fitfully and had woken with a pounding headache and tears that seemed to flow non-stop.

The bright sunny day did nothing to lift my spirits, in fact it only served to deepen my depression. Slowly I closed the door to the bedroom and went downstairs. I could hear voices and I could smell the coffee but not even my craving for caffeine could make me go into the kitchen. I simply couldn't face seeing everyone and instead turned into the salon and headed out of the French windows into the garden.

I stood in the middle of the lawn breathing in the intoxicating smell that I'd grown to love. A scent unlike any other, a heady blend of lavender, spicy herbs and sweet flowers. I gazed around, committing to memory every single detail although I knew that I would never forget this place. My heart had been stolen in France and part of it would always remain here.

I tried hard to analyse my feelings. I'd never ever felt like this before. I recalled Gail telling me how she felt about Tariq, how he brought colour into her world, how she loved him more with every heartbeat. At the time I'd no real comprehension of what she was talking about, but my God I did now.

Now I knew exactly what she meant. Once again my world had been turned completely upside down.

Philippe grabbed a cup of coffee from the kitchen table and mumbling an excuse headed straight into his study. He perched on the desk and lit a cigarette. Belle followed him, troubled by his misery, and so did Beatrice.

'It's sad to see them go.' She spoke softly. He merely grunted in reply.

'It will be quiet without them.'

He said nothing but the misery etched on his face said it all.

Beatrice realised that the time for subtlety had gone, some straight talking was needed. 'Not everyone has to go, Philippe.'

He looked at her in bewilderment.

'There is one person who would very much like to stay.' She lit a cigarette and looked at him. Mon Dieu, but he was being dense, clearly she would have to spell it out. 'Someone who is standing not very far away.'

He frowned at her. 'Bea, you can stay as long as you like, you know that, cheri.'

'Not me, you imbecile.' She was exasperated. 'Look outside.'

He turned to face the window and saw Sky standing on the lawn, her back to them. He turned back to Beatrice.

'Oh, Philippe, it is so obvious.' She stamped her foot in frustration. 'You don't want her to leave, it's clear that you hate the thought of her going, I've never seen you in such a state.'

He stared at her.

'And Sky certainly doesn't want to go,' Beatrice continued, determined to drum the message home. 'Philippe, you must be the only person who doesn't realise that.' She watched as, finally, comprehension slowly began to dawn.

'She is much younger than me,' he whispered finally, voicing a fear which until that moment he hadn't really been aware he'd had.

'She's getting older by the moment.' Beatrice smiled at him. 'As are you.' She kissed him gently. 'Go, cheri, what are you waiting for?'

But still he hesitated as if hardly daring to believe what was happening.

'Philippe.' She threw her hands up in frustration. 'Philippe, think about how you feel.'

She watched as an inner glow seemed to light up his face. It was as if a light bulb had been switched on.

'Mon Dieu, I love her,' he gasped. 'Bea, I love her, I love Sky, I really love her.'

'It's not me that needs to hear this, Philippe.' She grinned as she ushered him out of the door.

Nick joined Beatrice in the study.

'Well?'

'He was being particularly dim but the message finally sank in.'

Nick watched Philippe walk across the lawn. 'I feel like a voyeur,' he said.

'I feel exhausted,' she responded.

I heard footsteps behind me and I knew that it was Philippe. He stopped and I remained motionless.

'Sky?' His voice sounded low and uncertain. My heart rate was dangerously high.

'Sky…' he began again and then stopped. My mouth was dry and a trillion butterflies fluttered around in my stomach.

'I, um, well, the thing is… Sky, do you have to go?'

I couldn't move a muscle. I could barely breathe.

'Would you be able to stay, Sky?'

'Why do you want me to stay, Philippe?' My voice was cracked and softer than a whisper. I licked my lips and tried again. 'Tell me why you want me to stay.'

The silence seemed endless and I closed my eyes to stop the world from spinning out of control. Still he said nothing and I couldn't bear the tension any longer.

'Why, Philippe?' I asked again 'Why do you want me to stay?' I wheeled around to face him and realised that he was talking at the same time.

We both stopped at once. I opened my mouth to speak but he silenced me, putting his finger to his lips.

'I love you, Sky.' His voice was hoarse and raw with emotion but I'd never heard anything more beautiful in my life. 'I've fallen in love with you.' His eyes were full of tears. 'I love you, Sky, I love you, I love you, and I don't want you to go home.'

'Oh, Philippe.' I stood on tiptoe and, wrapping my arms tight around his neck, whispered, 'I am home.'

Drawing deeply on their cigarettes, Nick and Beatrice watched misty-eyed from the study window.

Running out into the garden with her animals Emmie stopped short at the sight of the embrace and, as she watched them kiss, she thought her little heart would burst with joy.

Somewhere, high above, a skylark soared, and as Philippe's lips met mine I felt a lightness of being and a joy such as I had never experienced before.

The earth had finally stopped wobbling. The world was a happy place.

THE END

ACKNOWLEDGEMENTS

Firstly I'd like to toast my fabulous agent David Headley – thank you for your belief and trust, your good humour and your friendship.

Then a big cheers to The Dome Press and my inspirational editor Rebecca Lloyd who is such fun to work with and whose advice I value and respect enormously.

Bottoms up to my very early readers Chris and Bernie, your continued support and enthusiasm means so much.

To the medical team at both the Bergonie Hospital in Bordeaux and Robert Boulin hospital in Libourne where a lot of this book was actually written – you are all simply incredible and I thank you from the bottom of my heart.

A further toast to Mark Hoddy for giving me an insight into the wine business.

To our wonderful writers who come regularly to Chez Castillon – you all know who you are – thank you for the laughter and encouragement.

A hug to our hound Rory and his side-kick Charlie for making me giggle every single day.

And finally I want to raise the biggest glass to my husband Mike – none of this would be possible without you. I love you – '*we are here and it is now*'.